JUNGLE UP

NICK PIROG

JUNGLE UP

**BLACK
STONE**

Copyright © 2021 by Nick Pirog
Published in 2021 by Blackstone Publishing
Cover and book design by Zena Kanes

Printed in the United States of America

First edition: 2021
ISBN 978-1-9826-7389-5
Fiction / Thrillers / Suspense

1 3 5 7 9 10 8 6 4 2

CIP data for this book is available
from the Library of Congress

Blackstone Publishing
31 Mistletoe Rd.
Ashland, OR 97520

www.BlackstonePublishing.com

"The tropical rainforest is the greatest expression of life on earth."—Thomas Lovejoy

"I hate the jungle."—Thomas Prescott

1

"I was walking down the road and I saw a donkey, Hee Haw!" I read from the popular children's book *The Wonky Donkey*. "He only had three legs, one eye, he liked to listen to country music, he was quite tall and slim . . . and he smelt really, really bad."

Clark had his little arm extended and was moving his finger over the donkey on the page. At sixteen months old, he could say a handful of words, among them: *Ma-ma* (Lacy), *Da-da* (Caleb), *Un-kee* (me), *boo-ger* (taught by me), and *don-key*.

"Don-KEY Don-KEY!" Clark exclaimed.

"Yeah, that's a donkey," I told him. Currently, he was sitting on my lap on the couch. He was a porker, weighing close to twenty-six pounds. He had my sister's and my gray-blue eyes, but he had inherited his father's dark-brown, nearly black hair, which cascaded sideways on his forehead and lipped out over his ears.

I continued reading: "He was a stinky-dinky lanky honky-tonky winky wonky donkey."

Clark's body bounced with each word, and he emitted a low rumbling cackle that started me laughing as well.

"You think that's funny?" I asked. "That he's stinky?"

At the word *stinky*, he erupted into laughter.

I squeezed his fat little thigh, and his laughter went up another octave. That's when I "smelt" it.

I scrunched my eyes and leaned back a couple of inches. "Oh, man. It's not just the donkey." I let out a few light coughs.

I set the book down on the coffee table and lifted up the still-giggling twenty-six-pound Porta-Potty.

After babysitting Clark nearly every Saturday for over a year—it was the busiest day of the week at the art gallery my sister and her husband owned—I still dreaded changing the little guy's diaper.

Sometimes it wasn't all that bad, but sometimes it was a crime scene. And I'd seen my fair share of crime scenes in my tenure as a homicide detective and a consultant with the FBI's Violent Crimes Unit. I had no doubt that what was awaiting me in the Huggies Little Mover was what we in the business like to call "a real bloodbath."

I carried Clark to the counter and hefted up the diaper bag. After a couple of long deep breaths, I unclasped the diaper, revealing the carnage. I said, "Dude, what has your mom been feeding you?"

My best guess was cabbage—and lots of it.

After some light gagging, a bit of moaning, and four "You've got to be kidding me's," I had Clark cleaned up and in a fresh diaper. I picked him up off the counter and set him on the floor, where he waddled off.

After double-bagging the diaper, I made my way to the sliding glass door of the two-bedroom flat. Nice, pronounced "niece," is a coastal city in the southeasternmost of France, sitting on the pebbly shores of the Mediterranean Sea. From Lacy and Caleb's sixth-floor balcony there was a perfect view of glimmering cobalt water. The boardwalk running the length of the shore was packed with locals and tourists strolling the open-air markets and riding bicycles.

It was a much better view than the one from my small rented flat a quarter mile away. I'd lived at Lacy and Caleb's for the first few months after moving to France, but after the baby came, it was just too much—the crying, that is—so I rented a place not far away. It came fully furnished, and there was an amazing café just a hundred feet away. But in the French Riviera, I suppose there is an amazing café every one hundred feet.

Anyhow, it was a nice day—a few lazy clouds in the sky—and if I hadn't been on diaper-duty, I would most likely have been on the boardwalk myself, engaging in my new favorite activity.

Rollerblading.

Yeah, I know, the once mighty Thomas Prescott—detective extraordinaire, fearless defender of justice, and according to one post by the fourteen-member Facebook group Prescott Posse, "unconventional sex symbol"—had been reduced to a rollerblading nanny.

And sure, if Old Thomas could see what New Thomas had become, he would most likely stake out New Thomas's house; wait for him to put on his kneepads, wrist guards, and helmet; strap on his "blades"; and put in his earbuds. Then when New Thomas was least expecting it—riding that blader's high, hands beating to Michael Jackson's greatest hits—Old Thomas would gun the engine and *Mad Max* New Thomas into oblivion.

Or Old Thomas would just be really sad.

One of the two.

There was a diaper pail in the far corner of the balcony, and I walked over and deposited the diaper. I had nearly replaced the lid when I noticed something small and gray among the rolled-up balls of white. Shaking my head, I reached down and extracted my sister's pug, Baxter.

As was often the case with narcoleptics, Baxter was fast asleep.

I shook him, his beady eyes finally opening, and I said, "Of all the places to take a nap."

He panted in reply.

I set him down, and he scurried in through the door where he promptly began chasing Clark around the living room. I watched the two play for a few minutes until Baxter's body went limp and he somersaulted a few times before coming to rest against a book-shelf. I took a little off for the landing, but it was still a solid 9.2.

I checked the time on my watch—it was nearly noon—and said, "I think it's time for someone else's nap."

Clark fought me for his requisite twenty minutes, but by 12:15 p.m. he was down and out.

I grabbed the baby monitor and made my way to the carpet in the living room and began doing my daily rehab.

Two years earlier, I was involved in a crash. Not a car. A hot-air balloon. I counted myself lucky that a sprained knee was my only injury. The other two occupants fared far worse. Wheeler, the small-town veterinarian I was dating at the time, broke her arm in two places, and the third occupant, well, let's just say that he's doing his best Stephen Hawking impression.

I moved to France a month after the crash. At the time, I'd recently gotten back into shape—after gaining nearly forty pounds—and was running five miles a day. But my knee continued to bug me. Finally, at the constant urging of Lacy, I went to get an MRI.

The verdict: a torn meniscus.

I wasn't a stranger to hospitals, having been shot twice, fallen off a cliff into the Atlantic Ocean, been technically dead for seven minutes, collapsed a lung, and most recently, been attacked by a pack of wolves. So I put off surgery for over a year. But it finally got to the point where I could hardly chase after Clark without my knee doubling in size.

I was initially scheduled to go under the knife in early March, but a few weeks before surgery, Lacy had one of her worst MS flare-ups in years. Lacy was diagnosed with multiple sclerosis her junior year in college, and she'd had several bad flare-ups in the following years, the most severe resulting in two months of temporary blindness.

In late February the incurable autoimmune disease once again reared its ugly head; this time attacking Lacy's balance and coordination. She was weak, could barely hold a fork, and couldn't go three feet without the assistance of a walker.

With Caleb pulling double duty at the art gallery, I knew I would need to help my sister look after Clark. And I did, moving back in with them and sharing a room with the then one-year-old. It was during this time that I noticed my first-ever gray hairs—there they were, sprinkled among the cinnamon-brown ones. Was there a direct correlation between this onset of graying and my sharing a bedroom with a crying baby?

Yes.

Yes, there was.

Thankfully, before I went full Ted Danson, Lacy's symptoms waned, and her strength and coordination came back. And a couple of weeks later, I had my knee repaired.

My main rehab for the past few months had been swimming in the warm waters of the Bais des Anges—Angel's Bay—which is what the fishermen had named the Mediterranean waters off the coast of Nice. (And, of course, rollerblading, which I took up after Lacy sent me an article about how much better it was for your knees than running.) But I also had to do a number of grueling exercises and stretches with a resistance band.

I pressed my foot against the purple band and counted out ten leg extensions. After working my knee for another fifteen minutes, I spent the remainder of the hour stretching. At thirty-seven, I had the aches and pains of a baby boomer, and the orthopedist who fixed my knee said that if I wanted to be able to get out of bed in my forties, I should start doing yoga.

I was holding one hell of a Warrior II when I heard Clark stir on the baby monitor.

I fed him some mac and cheese, apple slices, and some green beans, then I crawled around with him on my back—I was *his* donkey—which wasn't the best decision for my knee but well worth it for the amount of giggling and clapping I received for my performance. After a little arts-and-crafts time—basically, Clark throwing crayons while I skillfully finished up two pages in my adult coloring book—the two of us settled in on the couch for some TV time.

Clark was probably too young to understand the complexities of *Veep*, and I couldn't stomach any more *Paw Patrol*, so I selected a Blu-ray from my sister's enormous collection. I'd watched a hundred kids' movies over the past year, my favorite being *How to Train Your Dragon*, with *Frozen*—yes, *Frozen*—a close second. I picked one I hadn't seen before, *The Incredibles*, and popped it in.

Clark started to fidget within a few minutes, but I was committed to the movie—mostly because Mr. Incredible reminded me so much of myself—and I handed Clark my cell phone, which historically would buy me an hour.

He took it with glee, and as always, I reminded him, "Whatever you do, don't erase my *Tetris* score."

He giggled and put the corner of the phone in his mouth.

Elastigirl had just donned her outfit for the first time when I heard a voice come from my phone.

"*. . . interested in our new Xfinity promotion . . . Forty-four ninety-nine a month for both internet and TV . . .*"

Clark had opened my voicemail app.

"I don't think they have Comcast in France," I said with a laugh, then turned my attention back to the superheroes on screen. *Who was the black guy in the blue suit? Where did he come from? Was that Samuel L. Jackson's voice?*

"*Thomas!*"

I whipped my head around and glared at the phone in Clark's lap.

It was a voice I hadn't heard in over a year.

It was Gina.

She was in trouble.

2

Even in the dry season, every tree, vine, and leaf was dripping with condensation. A light mist danced in the small pockets of rising sun that filtered through the thick canopy overhead. A low din of hoots, hollers, calls, and screeches filled Gina Brady's ears as her feet pounded the soft earth.

Gina had been running this trail each morning for the past two years. The trail was an old friend. Ever reliable. Gina knew that six minutes into her run she would pass a line of leaf-cutter ants carrying their prized cargo to their nest; at eight minutes she would hear shouts from the howler monkeys swinging high overhead; and at roughly sixteen minutes she would pass a mottled knot of lianas—woody, climbing vines abundant in the rainforest—that resembled a clenched fist.

The Fist, as Gina had come to think of it, came into view, and Gina checked the watch on her wrist: a little over seventeen minutes. Slower than usual. She thought about picking up the pace but decided against it. In Seattle, at the park across the street from the health clinic where she briefly worked, Gina could knock out four miles in twenty-five minutes. But in the jungle, even with her encyclopedic knowledge of every centimeter of the trail, she would rarely finish the loop in less than half an hour. But whereas the only threat at the park in Seattle was stepping in a pile of dog crap, in the jungle there were a thousand different things that could kill you.

A year earlier, during her morning run, Gina *had* picked up her pace. She was speeding along when she screeched to a halt, kicking up dirt like in a cartoon, seven feet shy of a fer-de-lance. The pit viper was the deadliest snake in South America, responsible for more than a hundred thousand deaths a year. Luckily, the snake only gave her a quick assessment, then slithered into the brush.

It was a healthy reminder that in the jungle you had to be vigilant.

For better or worse, Gina had been conditioned for vigilance at a young age. Her mother had died when Gina was five years old, and she was raised by a single father. A single, *military* father. Throughout her early childhood, Gina followed her father to seven military bases on three different continents. In addition to her daily school load, her core curriculum included combat lessons, threat assessment, and weapons safety.

Finally, after a promotion, William Brady and Gina found a home at Marine Corps Headquarters in Arlington, Virginia. Jumping from military base to military base had made it difficult for Gina to make long-lasting friendships, but within a few weeks, when a young freckled boy moved onto base, Gina made her first real friend.

Paul and Gina were inseparable, and a few years later, on Gina's sixteenth birthday, that friendship blossomed into fiery passion. The two dated throughout high school and undergrad at the University of Virginia. After undergrad, he went to Georgetown to get his MBA in political science; she stayed at UVA and started med school. After a year doing long distance—which wasn't all that long, it was only a two-and-a-half-hour drive— Paul called it quits.

Crushed, Gina put everything into her studies. She graduated from med school, aced the MCAT, and cruised through her first three years of residency. There were flings, of course, but it was always physical. Nothing more. A means to an end. Then, in the last year of her residency, Gina's father died in a car crash. At the funeral, she saw Paul for the first time in years. He had a redhead on his arm, and she was brandishing the engagement ring that, even after their break-up, Gina had always envisioned on *her* finger.

Parentless and broken, at the age of thirty Gina needed a change, and she applied to the World Health Organization (WHO). Her first posting was to Romania, where for two years she bounced around, treating different rural communities. When there was an outbreak of tuberculosis in Bolivia, Gina jumped at the opportunity to move to South America. With her background in infectious disease and four years of college Spanish under her belt, she was a perfect candidate. A week later, she and a team of two other doctors made the exhausting journey into the dense Amazon rainforest and to the remote village of Tibióno.

The "Death Cough," as the villagers called it, stoked fear in the small community of just over eighty. Eleven confirmed cases. Three fatal. Two of those, small children. With the combination of antibiotics and vaccinations, within a few months they had quelled the outbreak. Gina remained in Tibióno for two years, playing host to several other doctors and researchers. Living in a thatched hut among the villagers, Gina came to love the people, the pace of living, even the seclusion. Though most of the villagers spoke Spanish, several of the older residents spoke only their native Tibióno. Gina learned the language, their culture; she was treated as a member of the community. She could have stayed there forever, but then the satellite phone call came. Paul Garret, her ex-lover and now White House press secretary, had tracked her down. And he needed a favor.

That's how she found herself traveling to South Africa. Ultimately, the trip nearly cost Gina her life, but there was one silver lining.

Thomas.

She hadn't planned on falling for him; in fact, she found him quite aggravating at first. But she fell, and she fell hard. She moved to Seattle and found a job at a small health clinic. It was a whirlwind romance, and she was about to move into his house overlooking Puget Sound when the WHO contacted her. There had been another outbreak of tuberculosis in the Tibióno village.

Gina was forced to choose between Thomas and the villagers. In the end, she chose the villagers. That had been two years earlier.

Gina eased into the second half of her run. The trail ran even with the river for half a mile, the waking sun shimmering off the moving water. Ten minutes later Gina passed a large fern she'd decided long ago was her finish line and slowed.

As Tibióno's thatched huts came into view, Gina could tell something was off. There had been several villagers eating breakfast when she left on her run, but now there was no one in sight. In a climate where the heat would rapidly intensify all day long, until at its peak it was nearly unbearable, the temperate hours of the morning were usually the busiest of the day.

Where was Dominga? She was almost always kicking her soccer ball around at this time of day.

As Gina neared the first hut, a man stepped out. He was tall, dark-skinned, wearing military fatigues, and he held an automatic rifle. It was pointed at Gina's chest.

"¿Médica?" he shouted.

Over his shoulder Gina could see the rest of the villagers huddled between two of the huts. Two more men—two more soldiers—had their guns pointed at the group.

Gina nodded lightly. "Sí."

The tall soldier reached forward and grabbed Gina by the shoulder. Gina's hundreds of hours of combat training took over, and she clamped the man's hand and twisted. The man fell to his knees with a loud groan. Gina kept twisting his hand until a loud gunshot echoed through the high canopy.

Gina glanced at a second soldier striding toward her. He was holding a pistol to the left temple of Miguel, a six-year-old boy Gina had been teaching English for the past year. Just a few days earlier, Gina had helped pull out one of Miguel's stubborn front teeth.

"Let him go," the soldier said in stilted English.

Gina released the man's hand. He shook out his arm with a grimace and shouted, "¡*Puta!*" *Whore.*

The second soldier yelled at him to go watch the group of villagers, then he settled his eyes on Gina and said, "You is doctor, yes?"

She locked eyes with Miguel, willing him to be strong. His bottom lip trembled. "It's going to be okay," she said to him in Tibióno.

To the soldier she said, "Yes, I am a doctor."

"You come with us."

"Come where?"

He ignored her. "You come now."

"And if I don't?"

The man pressed the gun hard against the small boy's head.

"Okay," Gina said. "I'll come with you. Just don't hurt anyone."

3

I listened to Gina's voicemail three more times—each time, the muscles in my chest constricting a notch tighter.

"Thomas! I don't have much time! Four days ago, a group of men came to my village and abducted me. They said they needed a doctor. I think they are narcotraff—Oh, shit, here they come! . . . Please find me, Thomas! Please!"

I'd met Dr. Gina Brady three years earlier in South Africa under grim circumstances. But like any good romantic comedy, after the two of us barely survived a thermobaric missile and mass genocide, Gina and I fell in love. She moved to Seattle and found a job working at a health clinic, and life was good—no, life was *amazing*. But then, six months later, and just a week after I asked her to move in with me, Gina got news that the village in Bolivia she used to live in had been struck by another outbreak of tuberculosis. Like me, Gina had lost both her parents, and she'd once confided that the villagers were the closest thing she had left to family.

She asked me to go with her to Tibióno. But even as much as I loved her—and I did, more than I'd ever loved a woman before—I couldn't fathom living in a hut in the Amazon jungle.

Where would I get my pumpkin spice latte?

Anyhow, she left for Bolivia, and, well, as aforementioned, I fell into a fit of depression that ultimately ended with my bingeing *all* of Netflix, developing an adult–coloring book obsession, and packing on forty pounds of extra cushioning. Fast-forward a year: Harold (my grandpa) dies, I inherit his farm in Missouri, piglets, Wheeler, cold case, GMOs, corruption, weight loss, balloon crash, France, Uncle Thomas.

Throughout it all, Gina was never far from my mind. I considered trying to get in touch with her several times—she gave me a satellite phone number on her departure—but I could never get myself to dial the numbers. She left me. She chose a village over me. If she wanted to talk to me, she would call me—I kept my same cell phone number when I moved to France—and a few months after Clark was born, she did.

The tuberculosis scare in Tibióno had been contained, and the World Health Organization, which was bankrolling her operation, was pulling out and taking their satellite phone with them. She was staying behind and wanted to call and say hi while she still had the chance. Our conversation only lasted a few minutes— both of us *not* saying what we really wanted to say, then wishing each other the best of luck.

I played the voicemail one final time, listening to Gina's panicked plea for help, then I took a long, deep breath and flipped a switch in my brain that, much like my sex life, had been collecting dust for going on two years.

I checked my call log. My last two calls were from Lacy, but the third was fourteen digits long. I knew from Gina's previous call that this was a satellite phone number. It came in at 1:03 a.m. on August 10.

Yesterday.

Clark was clawing for my phone back, and I stood and walked a few feet from him. He began crying. I ignored him. I called the satellite phone number back. I had little hope the call would be answered, but like the start of any good investigation, it was a box that needed checking.

The phone rang once, then stopped. No voicemail, no automatic message, just silence. I hung up and redialed. Same thing: one ring, then silence. The phone was either powered off or dead. Next, I scrolled to the saved satellite phone number Gina had used when she called me a year earlier. I paced the small living room as the phone rang two, then seven, then fifteen times. I hung up and redialed. After sixteen rings, I gave up.

I ran to my sister's office and pulled a piece of computer paper out of the printer. I jotted down the new satellite phone number, then the date and time of the call. But the call log was misleading. The call registered in my phone at 1:03 a.m. yesterday, but that was Central European Summer Time. Bolivia was in the same time zone as the eastern United States, which was six hours behind. So Gina *placed* the call at 7:03 p.m. on August 9.

Two days earlier.

I replayed Gina's voicemail.

"*Thomas! I don't have much time! Four days ago, a group of men came to my village and abducted me. They said they needed a doctor. I think they are narcotraff—Oh, shit, here they come! . . . Please find me, Thomas! Please!*"

The men came to her village four days before she placed the phone call to me. Which means Gina was abducted six days earlier: August 5.

I sat down and flipped open my sister's laptop. Gina had often talked about Tibióno, and I knew it was in northern Bolivia— not too far from the Brazilian border. I pulled up a Google map and zoomed in on northern Bolivia. I recognized the name of a town—Riberalta. Gina had said she would travel there every few months for supplies. It would take her nearly an entire day by river to reach the town I remember her calling "the Bolivian capital of the Amazon."

Riberalta sat on the confluence of two major rivers, the Río Madre de Dios and the Beni. The Río Madre started in Peru, then ran west to east through Bolivia, intersected with the smaller Beni in Riberalta, then headed north into Brazil, where it fed into the mighty Amazon.

But Tibióno wasn't located on either of these rivers. According to Gina, the river structure of the Amazon basin was a complex system of interstates, highways, and side streets. And depending on the season, dry or wet, some of those rivers might not exist, or if they did, may not be passable by boat.

Gina once pointed out to me roughly where Tibióno was located on Google Earth, and I clicked the small box in the bottom left corner of the screen marked "Satellite." The map refreshed: blue rivers turning gold, solid lime turning into veiny forest green. Those veins, like hundreds of small capillaries, were rivers.

I recalled the area where Gina had pointed and said, "My little village is somewhere in there." I zoomed in until the sea of green separated into the leafy broccoli heads of the impenetrable jungle canopy.

Gina was somewhere in that thicket of madness.

And I was going to find her.

≈

My next move was to contact the US Embassy in Bolivia, but according to their Google search page they were closed until 8:00 a.m. on Monday, which was almost forty-eight hours away.

I called the number anyway. It went to automatic voicemail.

I found the number for the World Health Organization and

dialed. Gina may no longer work for them, but they would still know the exact location of Tibióno.

Again, no answer.

I did notice that the headquarters for the WHO was in Geneva, which by happenstance, wasn't all that far away. Five and a half hours by car. I was considering the idea of driving there, when I heard a loud crash.

Clark!

I'd left him unattended for going on twenty minutes. I jumped out of the chair and ran into the kitchen. There was dog food all over the floor, and both Clark and Baxter were shoveling it into their mouths.

I scooped Clark up and pulled the remaining pieces of dog food from his mouth. "No," I said. "This isn't for you."

I placed him in his crib, then went back into the kitchen. Baxter was asleep with his mouth full of kibble. I carried him to the sink, turned him upside down, and shook the kibble out. I quickly cleaned up the remaining mess, then went back to check on Clark, who, of course, was MIA. I found him a minute later hiding under the bed in Lacy and Caleb's room and, somehow, diaperless.

I sighed. "Dude, I can't deal with this right now."

I cajoled the naked fugitive out from under the bed, then picked him up. I found my phone and dialed Lacy.

Like anytime I called her at work, she answered, "Is Clark okay?"

"He's fine," I assured her. Then I told her about Gina. Of all my girlfriends, Gina was by far my sister's favorite, and though Lacy was the toughest person I knew, I could hear the strain in her voice as she said, "I'll be home in five minutes."

It took those five minutes to get Clark into a fresh diaper and a T-shirt and to brush his teeth, so his mom wouldn't know I had let him get into the dog food.

Lacy walked into the bathroom and glared at us. With her hands on her hips, she asked, "What did he eat this time?"

"Um, just a little dog food."

Lacy laughed, then took Clark and said, "Did you eat some dog food?"

He nodded and smiled.

She gave him a few kisses, then turned her attention to me. "Now let's figure out how to get you to South America."

≈

I'd been scouring the internet for the last hour, trying to figure out how to get into Bolivia. Lacy was doing the same on her phone. Some countries in South America don't require a travel visa for American citizens, but Bolivia was *not* one of these.

Lacy said, "This company says they can get you a rush visa in three days."

"What company?"

"Swift Passport Services."

"Yeah, I'm on Rush My Travel Visa, and they say the same thing. Three days. But that's business days. And that's for them to process all the paperwork. Then they still have to mail it."

"So you could get it by Thursday?"

"Theoretically. But from what I've read, the earliest most people get their visa is five business days. Then I still have to fly there."

"You could go to the Bolivian Embassy here on Monday morning and try to get someone to help you."

"As an American citizen, I think I would have to fly back to the States and go to the embassy there."

"You're probably right."

"But I can't imagine it still won't take a few days."

"You have to get a yellow fever vaccine too."

"Yeah, I saw that."

In addition to a yellow fever vaccine, I also needed my flight information and hotel bookings for the duration of my stay.

"You could try to sneak in," Lacy offered.

I turned around in the chair and looked at her.

She said, "You don't need a visa to get into Chile. You could get on the next flight to Chile, then sneak into Bolivia."

I'd only had to get a travel visa once before. It was for the ten-day African cruise Lacy and I had taken. A cruise that had been cut short by some pirates and coincidentally enough, eventually lead to my meeting the dark-haired, hazel-eyed WHO doctor I was attempting to rescue this very second.

At any rate, our travel visa for the cruise had covered the various countries where we made stops: Kenya, Tanzania, Mozambique, and South Africa. Not once did we encounter a checkpoint or a border crossing.

I said, "I think you might be confusing me with Jason Bourne."

Lacy forced a chuckle.

After another hour of research and a half dozen more phone calls, it was evident that barring the appearance of a magical visa-dispensing fairy godmother, the earliest I could get into Bolivia would be Friday.

I couldn't shake the nagging feeling that by then Gina would be dead.

4

"What about Paul?" Lacy said, rushing into the office.

Lacy had spent the last half an hour reading to Clark and putting him to bed. Her blond hair was now pulled up into a ponytail. She was holding her transparent pill tray and dumping her nighttime regimen of pills into her hand.

"Who?" I asked.

She had just tossed the pills into her mouth and mumbled, "*Pab Garad.*" She dry-swallowed, squished her eyes shut, then said, "Paul Garret."

Paul Garret was an ex-boyfriend of Gina's. He'd been the one to initially contact Gina three years earlier and coax her into traveling to a village in South Africa to save three small children.

In the last days of the South African debacle, Paul Garret had a meltdown on national television and had resigned as White House press secretary. According to Gina, a few months later he took a job as an executive at US Steel.

Lacy said, "He must still have a bunch of contacts in the government. I'm sure he could help."

Contacting Gina's—and I quote—"first great love" sounded

about as much fun as playing in the sewers of Derry, Maine, but
Lacy was right: he probably could help.

"Okay," I said. "How do we find him?"

My millennial sister rolled her eyes at me, then quickly tracked
him down on Twitter, started following him, and sent him a direct
message. When she was finished, she turned her phone around
and showed me what she'd written. It was clear and concise: *Gina
is in trouble.* Then she listed my phone number.

Nice was six hours ahead of US Eastern Standard, which
would make it 12:30 p.m. in DC. As he was a busy dad of two
young boys, I didn't expect a call from Garret anytime soon.

I did, however, place a call to the most powerful person I
knew personally. Charles Mangrove had been the deputy director
of the FBI when I first crossed paths with him, but about the time
I started playing farmer, he had taken over the top spot.

He didn't answer, so I called again.

And again.

I called thirty-seven times.

"This can't be good," he finally answered on my thirty-eighth
attempt.

It wasn't that Charles Mangrove didn't like me; it's that in his
estimation I was responsible for two of his agents being murdered
a few years back.

"What can I do for you, Mr. Prescott?" he said dryly.

"A friend of mine was abducted in Bolivia, and I need help
getting down there."

He paused for a second, then said, "Bolivia, huh?"

"She was working with the World Health Organization down
there, living in a village. The WHO pulled out last year, but she
stayed. Six days ago, some men came to her village and abducted her."

"I'm sorry to hear that. Who was she?"

I noticed he said *was* and not *is.*

Not a good sign.

"An old girlfriend," I said, though it didn't seem to do Gina justice. But I didn't feel like saying "the one who got away."

"I wish I could help," he said.

"I'm pretty sure that you can."

Sure, the FBI was a domestic agency, but he would still have plenty of contacts who could help secure me a visa to Bolivia. He could make it happen in a manner of hours. He might have to call in a few favors, but there wasn't a shred of doubt in my mind he could do it. *Would he*, was a completely different matter.

"What was it you said the FBI stood for?" he asked. "In that article in *Time* magazine?"

He was referring to an article written about me after I chased down a serial killer in Maine who the FBI—against my protestations—claimed was already dead.

"Umm—"

"I believe you said it stands for Fruitdicks, Backstabbers, and Impersonators."

"That doesn't sound like something I'd say."

It was.

Verbatim.

"Good luck, Mr. Prescott," Mangrove said.

The line went dead.

I couldn't blame him for not wanting to stick his neck out for me. If he did help me get into Bolivia, he would be on the hook for whatever I did down there. At this point I wasn't positive what actions I might need to take to rescue Gina, though I'm fairly certain it was going to take some level of mayhem. Mayhem that Charles Mangrove wanted no part of. So yeah, I couldn't blame him. Just the same, I did make a mental notation in his folder.

Lacy, who had been listening to my side of the conversation, said, "That didn't sound like it went very well."

"It did not."

There was another call I needed to make, and I dialed one of my few remaining contacts at the Philadelphia Police Department.

Mike Gallow.

"Prescott," he answered on the third ring. "I thought you were dead."

"I'm like Jon Snow," I said. "They keep trying, but I keep coming back."

He laughed.

I asked quickly about his wife and son, then I said, "I need a favor."

"Carmen is married now. Two kids." He paused for a half second, then added, "Though, come to think about it, she might be into it."

When I was thirty and working contract cases with the Philly PD, Gallow and I had investigated the murder of a college student during Occupy Wall Street in Philadelphia. During the month-long investigation, I'd had a brief fling with Mike's sister. But she'd been a little too crazy, even for me.

I chuckled and said, "Not exactly the favor I'm looking for."

"All right. What's the ask?"

"Can you track down a satellite phone number for me? I need the owner and last known coordinates, if you can swing it."

"Why?"

I told him about Gina.

When I was finished, Gallow said, "I don't know all that much about satellite phones, but I'll see what I can do. Give me the digits."

I did.

He said it would take him a couple of days—three, tops—then he'd get back to me.

I'd just hung up with him when another call came in. It was a 202 area code. Washington, DC.

I answered.

"This is Paul Garret," the caller said. "You sent me a message on Twitter with this number. What's happened to Gina?"

"This is Thomas Prescott."

"Prescott? Oh, right, from South Africa."

I skipped the pleasantries. "Gina has been abducted."

He went quiet and I told him everything I knew.

"Narcos?" he asked.

"That's what she said in the voicemail."

"Shit."

"Yeah, *no bueno*." It couldn't hurt to start brushing up on my Spanish.

"What can I do?" he asked.

"If I go through traditional channels, the earliest I can get boots on the ground is six days from now. Do you have any contacts left in the government who can expedite the process?"

"I'm not sure. I burned a lot of bridges on my way out of town." He paused, I supposed to come up with names, but then surprised me by saying, "Do you think you going down there is the best course of action? Can't we hire a rescue team to go in there or something?"

Sometimes pronouns are important, and I noticed he had said "we" and not "you." Who knows, maybe he still carried a flame for Gina. Or maybe it was the fact he and Gina had grown up together. It didn't matter to me either way, as long as he was willing to help.

"A rescue team?" I asked.

"Yeah, I heard about some college kid who went missing somewhere down in South America, and the family hired a private search-and-rescue team from Israel to find him."

The idea of not having to go down to Bolivia myself hadn't even crossed my mind. I mean, how narcissistic was I that I thought I was the only one who could find Gina? The only thing I knew about the jungle was what I'd seen on *Naked and Afraid*. Surely there were people far more qualified to find Gina than Thomas Dergen Prescott.

I said, "Okay, so let's hire these Israelis."

"It's going to be expensive."

"How expensive are we talking?"

"Probably a quarter million, maybe more."

A few years earlier, I wouldn't have balked at a quarter million dollars. My parents had left Lacy and me a sizable inheritance when they died just over a decade earlier. Most of that money was now tied up in real estate: the house on Puget Sound, a beach house in San Diego, another house in Maine, Lacy and Caleb's flat in Nice, plus the commercial lease for Lacy's art gallery. Not to mention the rising cost of Lacy's medications, which even with quality insurance was still a few thousand dollars a month.

As for money coming in, Lacy was barely breaking even on the gallery, and any profits she did make went right into improving the space. As for *moi*, my last paycheck had been over four years earlier. Since then, I suppose *freeloading* might be the most accurate term.

The market was good at the moment, and Lacy and I could easily sell any of the four properties for over a million dollars, but that would take time. As for liquid currency, the last time I checked, our joint account was hovering right around two hundred thousand dollars.

"I can do a quarter mil, no problem," I said. I would find the rest of the money somehow.

"Okay," Garret replied. "Let me make some calls. I'll get back to you ASAP."

We hung up.

Lacy brought me a sandwich and a juice box while I waited. Fifteen minutes later, Paul called back.

"Okay, so on the expedited-visa front, I put in a few calls, but I wouldn't hold your breath. The companies on the internet can probably cut through the red tape faster than any government agency will. Plus, no one is looking to do me any personal favors these days. Good news and bad news, as far as the search-and-rescue team goes. Good news is I have a contact who can get the ball rolling on the private Israeli team. He just needs the go-ahead."

"And the bad news?"

"These things don't happen overnight. He said it will take a week to put together. And I was a little low with the estimate. Probably be closer to half a million."

I could scrape together a quarter million, but I wasn't sure about five hundred grand. I let out a groan and asked, "Why does it have to be an Israeli search-and-rescue team? Why don't we hire some Bolivians?" This was code for "Can we get someone cheaper?"

"I talked to my contact about that. It's definitely an option. But he warned me that corruption runs rampant in Bolivia. It's the poorest nation in all of South America. He said there's a fifty-fifty chance whoever we hire will just pocket the money. And on the off chance they do look for her and recover her, they may then try to extort even more money out of you."

"You mean, they'd rescue her from her kidnappers, then kidnap her themselves?"

"He said it happens. He said if it were him, he wouldn't go local."

"What about Chile or Argentina, one of the less corrupt countries? I'm sure they could put together a team and head up to Bolivia."

"Yeah, we can look into that." He paused, then said, "But there might be another option."

"Let's hear it."

"Papagayo."

"What?"

He let out a soft chuckle. "*Papagayo* means *parrot*. He's an old friend of my father's from the Marines. After getting out, Papagayo bounced around South America. My dad said that in the late

'90s and early 2000s, he helped facilitate some shady relationships between the US and some Colombian folks."

"Cartels?"

"My dad never went into the details, but yeah, I think so. The last time my father mentioned him, he'd set up shop in Bolivia."

"Do you think you can get ahold of this guy?"

"My dad might have his contact info in his old Rolodex."

"Where is it?"

"In a box in a storage unit twenty minutes away." He didn't wait for my urging and said, "I'll head out right now."

≈

The sound of my cell phone woke me up. I shook my head groggily and squinted at the screen.

It was Garret.

The time in the corner said it was 12:31 a.m. I'd fallen asleep next to the laptop an hour earlier after doing internet searches for a myriad of topics: *Search and rescue in the Amazon, How to find someone in the Amazon, Narcotrafficking in Bolivia, Flights to Bolivia, Where to get a yellow fever vaccine,* and *How to sneak into a country,* among countless others.

"Hey," I answered.

"Sorry it took so long."

I ignored him, straightening myself up in the chair. "Did you find your dad's Rolodex?"

"Yeah, I did. But he didn't have this guy's contact info."

"Dang," I said, leaning my head back.

"However, I did find a number for a motel in La Paz."

"And . . . ?"

"And, well, I don't speak Spanish, but my wife used to speak it fluently—she even went to Spain in college—"

"Get to the point," I interrupted.

"Oh, right. Anyhow, my wife got on the phone with the owner of the motel, and through some fumbling Spanish, she mentioned Papagayo and the lady on the other end knew who he was. She wouldn't give us his number, but she took down mine. Twenty minutes later, he called me."

"You're kidding."

"No, he did. And better yet, he can help."

"Really?"

"Yeah, he said he can get you into Bolivia on Monday, which I guess, *technically*, for you is tomorrow."

I pumped my fist.

Garret wasn't finished: "And he said he would find a tracker and even put a team together."

For the first time since hearing Gina's plea for help, I felt the slightest bit of encouragement.

"Okay, so how does this work? Is this Parrot going to call me or what?"

"He prefers to go through me. Because of my father."

"Fair enough."

"So the deal is, Papagayo has been helping out one of these jungle expedition teams—greasing the right palms to get permits and licenses—and they are the ones flying into Bolivia on Monday. You can hitch a ride down to La Paz with them, then meet up with Papagayo and go your separate way. But if you don't somehow get on that expedition flight, he probably can't get you in until the following week."

"I'll be on it," I assured him. "How much is this going to cost?"

"Three hundred thousand dollars."

"Done."

He gave me a few instructions on how I would pay, then said, "Now you need to get your ass to Miami."

5

I'd been to Florida once previously when I was contracting with the FBI's Violent Crime Unit. A serial killer had been working his way eastward from Louisiana, through Mississippi, into Alabama, and down into the Florida Gulf Coast, knocking off white-hairs left and right. We nearly nabbed him in Clearwater, then again in Sarasota. It was the middle of winter at the time, and the weather was a pleasant seventy-five degrees, the beaches white sand, and the fresh grouper so delicious it almost made you forget about the three elderly couples who'd been stabbed to death on their sundecks.

Good times.

But Miami in August was anything but pleasant. In fact, it was disgusting. I wiped the beading sweat from my hairline as I jog-walked the nine blocks from my hotel back to Miami International Airport, where I had landed less than twelve hours earlier.

I could have taken an air-conditioned taxi, but traffic headed to the airport was at a standstill, and I was running late.

After getting off the phone with Garret, I booked the next flight to Miami. My Air France flight departed Nice Côte d'Azur Airport at 12:15 p.m., and after a four-hour layover at JFK in New York, I landed in Miami at 10:45 p.m. local time.

Having not slept since my little nap more than twenty-four hours earlier, I walked directly to the nearby Embassy Suites and sacked out for nine solid hours. I woke just in time to catch the tail end of the continental breakfast, cramming down two boxes of Honey Nut Cheerios and a hard-boiled egg.

I again wiped at the sweat openly dripping down my face and adjusted the straps of my newly acquired Osprey Rook 65 pack.

Lacy and I had spent a frantic hour the morning before tracking down all the gear I would need for the trip. Luckily, there was an outdoor sports store, Alticoop, six shops down from Lacy's gallery, and I quickly rang up over two-thousand dollars' worth of gear. The sixty-five-liter teal pack was crammed with everything Lacy and I thought I might need for the "mission": tent, sleeping bag, multiple cans of DEET, sunblock, headlamp, Garmin inReach Explorer (a GPS and satellite communicator), hammock, whistle, first aid kit, compass, lighter, water purification tablets, seven-inch bowie knife, hat, sunglasses, specialty hiking clothes, and a three-liter hydration bladder. I had also bought a pair of hiking boots, which I was now wearing, trying to break them in.

This would be a good time to mention that I have never—not once, not ever—gone backpacking. However, I had gone camping multiple times, and by multiple, I mean twice. Once for one night, once for two nights—both times in Olympic National Park, both times with my father, and both times with a car parked thirty feet away. I think it's safe to say that neither my father nor I particularly enjoyed our time amid nature, and we decided after the second trip that in the future we would much rather do our father-son bonding at Seattle Seahawks games.

So, outdoorsy I was not.

After adjusting the straps of the forty-pound pack, I began jogging the remaining two hundred yards to the airport entrance. I was supposed to meet this expedition team at one of the private-jet terminals on the northern side of the airport at 9:45 a.m. According to Garrett, the plane was leaving at 10:00 a.m. "with or without me."

Unfortunately, I still had an errand to run.

I moved through the sliding glass doors of the airport and into the slightly cooler recirculated air. I checked a large airport directory and found what I was looking for: Bank of America. I hurried my way through the busy airport to the full-scale bank on the fourth floor.

"Thomas?" a fortyish woman asked as I walked through the bank doors.

With my sixteen hours of travel time from Nice to Miami, I had left Lacy the formidable task of securing the $300,000 for Papagayo. I'm not sure exactly how she accomplished the feat, as neither of us had an account with Bank of America—or where she found the extra $100,000 on top of the $200,000 in our bank account—but I woke up to a text on my new burner phone that read "MONEY WILL BE THERE."

As for my old phone, I'd left it with Lacy, just in case Gina was able to call back. Then I bought a cheap burner phone to communicate with Lacy while I was still in the States. The Garmin inReach Explorer I'd purchased would take three days to activate—and technically, it wasn't a phone; it was a satellite communicator. I would be able to send and receive text messages while in the jungle.

At least, in theory.

The woman introduced herself as Cathy and led me to a large wraparound desk. She handed me an envelope and said, "Check that over for me."

I pulled the cashier's check out of the envelope and looked it over. It was for one hundred thousand dollars and made out to Roth Media Inc.

"Looks good to me," I said.

Cathy nodded, then she unlocked a drawer, pulled out a small blue duffel bag, and slid it across the table. Had I gotten the money in hundreds it probably would have come in a large manila envelope, but I'd been instructed to get the $200,000 in fifties.

I opened the bag and counted out the brown-banded $5,000 stacks. There were forty.

"It's all there," I said.

I'm not sure what Cathy was told, if she thought I was paying off a ransom or blackmail or just going to one of the many strip clubs that were literally across the street, but she put her hand over mine and said, "Good luck."

I thanked her, draped the duffel over my left shoulder, and checked my watch.

9:54 a.m.

Then I started running.

≈

I remember seeing an old Hertz rental car commercial when I was a kid. It had O. J. Simpson—young, handsome, pre–murder trial—and he was running through the airport hurdling over banisters and jumping over ropes.

That was me.

"Move!" I yelled, pushing a mother and daughter out of my way, then calling, "Sorry!" over my shoulder.

Both the little girl and the mother flipped me off.

Welcome to Miami.

I sidestepped past a few people on an escalator going down, knocking what appeared to be some fancy coffee drink out of one man's hand, then started down a long, wide corridor.

I checked my watch.

10:03 a.m.

I sprinted—a difficult feat with the large pack and the blue duffel—toward a glass window where a small jet was beginning to taxi toward the runway.

"I need to get on that jet!" I shouted at a young woman behind a desk that read *Elite Charter.*

The woman's eyes opened wide, and she brought a handheld radio to her lips. The plane on the runway continued for several more meters, then stopped.

I slowed down, drew a deep inhale through my nose, and put my hands behind my head.

A minute later, I was walking across the tarmac and up the steps into a compact jet shimmering white under the morning sun. I ducked into the plane and a flight attendant in all black with a white kerchief tied around her neck, said, "Welcome aboard."

Her name tag read Molly.

I unshouldered my pack and handed it to her—she wasn't touching the duffel—then she steered me toward twelve plush seats, six of them occupied.

Sitting in the first row was a man in his early fifties. He had slicked-back gray hair, crow's feet clinging to light-brown eyes, a rakish five o'clock shadow, and teeth that were either a genetic miracle or perfectly polished veneers. It was a face that belonged on a Cialis commercial.

He stood, revealing he was an inch shorter than my six feet and said, "You must be our secret *financier.*"

I stuck out my hand. "Thomas Prescott."

He gripped my hand, firmly, and grinned. "Jonathan Roth." *Roth Media Inc.*

I pulled the check from my back pocket and handed it to him. He took it with a smile, then turned to the other five passengers and said, "This is Thomas. He's catching a ride with us."

Then he nodded at the flight attendant and said, "Now let's get this plane in the air. We have a lost city to find."

6

Andy leaned back in the soft leather chair and took a deep breath. He let the calming instrumental music from his earbuds wash over him and exhaled through his nose.

"You're going to be just fine," he mouthed silently, not wanting any of the other members of the expedition team to hear him. There were twelve seats—six rows of two—on the fancy jet. Jonathan Roth was in the first row, and his production assistant, Libby, sat directly behind him. The newest arrival, Thomas something-or-other, was in the third row. Andy, himself, was in the fourth row; the two-person camera crew (Darnell and Sean, was it?) in the fifth; and Farah Karim in the back row.

"Flying is safe," Andy whispered. His heart thumped against his chest with every word.

He opened his eyes and pulled a blue prescription bottle from his pocket. For all the pills Andy had taken, he'd never tried a Valium. He should have experimented with the pills beforehand. He didn't want to make a fool of himself. What if he was allergic? Or what if it turned him into a slurring drunk? What then?

His current predicament was so ridiculous he couldn't help

but let out a small laugh. *Did he really have anxiety about taking antianxiety medication?*

That was a new one for his therapist.

Andy decided against the pills, sliding them into the pocket of his backpack, then opened a separate compartment and removed a small wooden box. Andy set the box on the shiny table in front of him and, after glancing nonchalantly over each shoulder, flipped it open. He pulled out a white-and-gray-streaked rabbit's foot and gripped it tightly.

The rabbit's foot had been a gift from Brady, a neighborhood kid Andy used to babysit while growing up in Rapid City, South Dakota. The town—the state's second largest, after Sioux Falls—was located right next to the Black Hills National Forest. Andy wasn't much of a hunter himself, but Brady was always running around the forest with his BB gun killing this and that.

One night when Andy was watching Brady—which was mostly the two of them playing video games—the then seven-year-old presented him with the "genuine" rabbit's foot. The following week, Andy flew for the first time in his life—to check out a college in Southern California—the rabbit's foot clutched tightly in his hand, much as it was now.

Andy gave the second of his four good-luck charms—he was *wearing* his first—a few more tight squeezes, his anxiety swept away for the moment as he thought about Brady, now twenty-two years old, and a starting linebacker for the Black Hills State football team. Andy hadn't participated in sports much growing up—he wasn't what most would refer to as coordinated—and he didn't much enjoy watching them either. But for the past three years, he'd absolutely reveled in watching Brady's football games.

Black Hills State was a Division II football school, but they were perennially highly ranked, and Andy had watched their run through the playoffs the past winter and their narrow loss in the championship game. Andy had been decked out in Yellow Jacket gear from head to toe and cheered wildly at the bar across from the University of Chicago campus, where he was an assistant professor of anthropology.

Andy set the rabbit's foot on the table in front of him. Next, he pulled out what would appear to the naked eye as any ordinary rock. It was nearly the same beige as the chair he was currently sitting in, no bigger than a quarter, and pockmarked with little holes.

Three years earlier, Andy had been living in Cusco, Peru, finishing up a yearlong research project for his dissertation. He had been walking around the famed Inca ruins of Machu Picchu, when he was startled by one of the many alpacas that freely roam the area, causing him to trip and fall down one of the steep rocky slopes.

After sliding some thirty feet, Andy came to rest, unable to believe he hadn't broken his neck. In fact, all he had to show for his thirty-foot fall down the incline was a bruised elbow and some scrapes on his legs. A few onlookers couldn't believe it when Andy climbed back up the slope and went right back to his research. It'd been one of Andy's proudest moments when one of his fellow researchers called him "one tough cookie."

Heading home on the bus that evening, admittedly stiff from his fall, Andy felt a small bulge in his jacket pocket. He reached in and found a tan rock that had found its way into his pocket at some point during his slide.

Andy set the rock next to the rabbit's foot and pulled a folded piece of yellow cardstock from the box. It was a menu—Shin's Hollywood. Andy had eaten at the small Chinese diner before landing his one and only acting job. After graduating from the University of South Dakota with an undergrad in anthropology, he'd decided to chase his dreams and moved to LA.

After eight months, he finally landed an audition: Allergy

Sufferer #4 in a Nasonex commercial. He even had a line: "*When my allergies are at their worst, I'm at my worst. [Sneeze!]*"

Andy celebrated his big break with a fifty-dollar bottle of champagne, but over the next year and more than a hundred auditions, Andy failed to land a second gig. He moved back to South Dakota, and three months later, he started toward his master's degree in cultural anthropology.

Andy set the menu down just as the pilot's voice came over the intercom.

"Alrighty, folks. Looks like we got the go-ahead here. Going to be a little bumpy going up through this thick Miami air, but should be smooth sailing from then on. Sit tight for the next few minutes, then feel free to stroll around."

A little bumpy?

Andy watched as the palm trees in the distance began to move across his small window. His stomach lurched, and his vision began to swim. Why had he signed up for this expedition? What was he thinking?

It was supposed to be his mentor, Adrian Heliant—head of the anthropology department at the University of Chicago, and one of the preeminent scholars when it came to Inca history— who was to be the lead anthropologist for the expedition. But the aging Heliant came down with shingles and had recommended Andy—whose class, Ancient Inca Civilization, wasn't offered during the summer quarter—as a last-minute replacement.

The expedition had been hush-hush, and Andy hadn't even known about it until he received a call just three weeks ago. His knees nearly buckled when the person on the other end revealed who he was: famed documentarian Jonathan Roth.

Over the phone, Roth detailed the expedition to find the lost city of Paititi.

Andy was circumspect at first. Hundreds of expeditions had

tried and failed to find the lost city of the Inca Empire. It was widely believed to lie in the dense jungles of Peru, just east of the Andes. But surely after all this time, if the city existed, it would have been found by now.

"Bolivia?" Andy asked when Roth told him where they were headed.

"Yeah, northern Bolivia," Roth replied. He explained that six months earlier, an acquaintance of his—who had assisted with the satellite imagery for Roth's previous documentary—had emailed him a photo. Yewed Global had been hired by an eco-group to take pictures of the rampant deforestation of the Amazon forest. The group wasn't able to come up with the funds to purchase the photos, and ultimately, the group disbanded. The photos were enormous files, and image consultant Jordan Mae was uploading them to an archive cloud folder when he found himself scanning one of them.

In one of the photographs, a dark sliver was visible amid the thick jungle canopy. As Mae zoomed in, he realized that one of the enormous one-hundred-fifty-foot trees had fallen and taken down several other trees with it, leaving a break in the canopy. Mae continued to move in closer, curious if he could see any wildlife in this rare window into the jungle floor. He spotted a few monkeys, but that wasn't what made him bite down on the cheap pen in his mouth so violently that ink spilled onto his lips.

Mae zoomed in until the entire frame of the computer screen was filled by the object. Half buried in the dirt was a golden statue.

A jaguar.

This was the photo Roth received.

Roth hadn't let himself rush to judgment. Of course, Paititi and all that golden treasure of the Incas was the first thing that came to mind, but one lone statue in the jungle could easily prove incidental. For one thing, the statue was in northeastern Bolivia, several hundred miles from the area where Paititi was thought to be located. And, moreover, who knew if the statue was even Incan? There were hundreds of different Indian tribes who had lived in the jungles of the Amazon over the past few centuries.

But it was Incan, at least according to Professor Heliant, who had been studying and teaching ancient Inca history for almost thirty-seven years.

"So," Roth said to Andy over the phone, "I put together a team to do a lidar survey over the surrounding area."

Lidar—light detection and ranging—is a relatively new technology with a vast array of commercial applications; from acting as the eyes for autonomous vehicles to guiding surface-to-air missiles to mapping the surface of Mars. Basically, lidar measures the distance to a target by illuminating it with pulsed laser light and measuring the reflected pulses with a sensor. Differences in laser return times can then be used to create a three-dimensional representation of the target, exposing formations invisible to the naked eye.

This tool was proving revolutionary for climate monitoring, city planning, meteorology, mining, and, of course, archaeology. Just a few years back, lidar had helped unearth one of the greatest archaeological finds in Egypt.

Earlier that May, Roth, his production assistant, and a lidar technician had flown into La Paz. They hired a pilot, and over the course of four days, they flew surveys over a fifty-square-mile area around the site where the statue was located.

"Did anything come up on the scans?" Andy had asked hesitantly, though he knew that if nothing had shown up, he wouldn't be having this conversation.

"Hell yeah, it did!" Roth had exclaimed.

Andy remained skeptical until he opened the email Roth sent him and looked at the scans himself. The thousands of beams of light sneaking through the jungle canopy had revealed a series of large rectangular mounds, pyramids, and enclosures—what must be the ruins of a lost city.

Goosebumps had formed on Andy's arms.

"So are you with us?" Roth asked. "Do you want to be part of the team that finds the biggest archaeological treasure of the twenty-first century?"

Hell yes, he did!

But Andy couldn't help thinking about the many flights it would take to get down there (presumably, each successive plane getting smaller and smaller), not to mention the jungle itself. Andy had lived in Peru for a year and a half—the last time he'd been on a plane—but he'd spent nearly all that time in the Andes. The closest thing to a jungle he'd been to was the Jurassic Park ride at Universal Studios.

As if sensing his trepidation, Roth said, "Farah Karim will be our lead archaeologist."

Dr. Farah Karim was a young Egyptian archaeologist who, three years earlier, at the age of twenty-seven, had led the excavation of an ancient site in the Nile Delta. In addition to having a brilliant mind, Dr. Karim was stunningly attractive. She was something of a celebrity and often posted images of herself at her latest excavation site. At last count, she had more than three million Instagram followers—one of whom was Andy Depree.

"I'm in," Andy told him.

Now, three weeks later, Andy was regretting his decision.

The compact jet accelerated down the runway, and its nose slowly lifted. Andy picked all three of his good-luck charms up off the table and cradled them to his chest.

"Don't freak out, don't freak out, don't freak out," he mouthed.

The plane hit a pocket of turbulence as it rose. Andy fumbled for the prescription bottle in his backpack, slid one of the white pills into his hand, and tossed it into his mouth.

7

"A little bit more turbulence than I anticipated," the pilot said over the intercom, "but it looks like we're in the clear now. Feel free to get up and stretch. Molly will be around with refreshments and snacks here in a bit. Should be about six hours until we touch down in La Paz."

There were six other passengers on board, and I had the third row of seats all to myself. I stood up, stepped past a blond woman in the second row who was preoccupied with a large blue binder, and took the seat next to Jonathan Roth.

Roth had a magazine open on his lap and a red vape pen in his hand.

"Thomas, my man," he said as I sat.

"John, my guy," I replied.

He inhaled on the red pen, then exhaled the vapor, engulfing the both of us in a fine mist. "It's Jonathan."

"My apologies, *Jonathan*."

The sweet vapors from his vape pen—watermelon, I suspect—sent a thrum through my temples.

I squinted against the pain and said, "I just wanted to touch base about what happens when we land."

He ignored me, smacking his hand on the open page of his magazine, and asked, "You ever been to the Maldives?"

"I have not."

"Look at this," he said, lifting the travel magazine to show a picture of turquoise water and white-sand beaches. "Have you ever seen anything so beautiful? Have you ever seen anything so beautiful in your life?"

"It's pretty."

"Pretty? It's gorgeous. What do you say, you and me, Maldives? Beach, snorkel, surf, chase some tail. We'll clean up, you and me."

I would like to point out that I'd known this guy for going on nineteen seconds, and he'd just invited me to go on vacation with him.

There was an emergency door four feet in front of us, and I eyed it. I mean, I wasn't going to pull the door open and jump out just yet, but I was considering my options.

"You keto?" he asked.

"What?"

He leaned over and grabbed my biceps. He squeezed it a few times. "Keto. Are you keto?"

I should mention that I really, really don't like people touching me, but I decided to give this guy a pass. He was doing me a huge favor by letting me catch a ride—a favor he was being paid handsomely for, but a favor nonetheless—so I decided not to cram his vape pen up his nose.

Anyhow, I'd heard of keto in passing, but I didn't know much about it. I said, "No, I'm Eggo."

"What?"

"I'm Eggo. Blueberry, Cinnamon Toast, mostly Chocolate Chip."

He thought I was kidding, and he let out a toothy laugh. Then he said, "I've been keto for six months now. Changed my life."

I tried to steer things back my way. "So when we lan—"

"Sour cream."

"What?"

"Sour cream," he repeated. "I eat it by the tubful."

"That sounds disgusting."

"No, it's great. Blue cheese dressing too. Right out of the bott—"

"Listen," I interrupted. "I just want to know what happens when we land." This came out ruder than I expected, but his vape pen was starting to give me a migraine, and I didn't want to hear any more about his stupid fucking diet.

Roth shrugged, his silver hair bouncing slightly, and said, "I was told to add your passport in with the others, and that everything would be taken care of."

This jibed with what Paul Garret had said, which was that I didn't have to worry about any paperwork—no visa, no vaccine records, no customs form, *nada*. All I had to do was make sure I had $200,000 in cash when I landed.

On that note, Roth seemed pretty nonchalant about aiding and abetting the commission of an international crime. Had he done this before? Was this not as big a deal as I thought it was? Did this stuff happen all the time?

I buried these thoughts for the time being. Who knows how long I could keep this guy on topic. I asked, "Did this Papagayo tell you why I needed to get down here?"

"Something about a missing chick?"

"A missing doctor, actually."

"Right, *doctor*."

I added *misogynist* to Roth's growing list of accolades and asked, "So, how well do you know this Papagayo?"

"Not great. He's what you call a fixer. It's hard to get anything done in these shithole countries, so you need a guy who speaks the language and can grease the right palms."

"What's he like?"

"Straight shooter, from what I could tell. Though rumor has it he's got some serious skeletons in his closet." He slapped me on the arm and said, "But don't we all."

Old Thomas probably would have told him, "If you touch my arm again, the next skeleton in *my* closet is going to be that I once beat someone to death with a travel magazine." But New Thomas—*Uncle Thomas*—bit his bottom lip and nodded.

"Anyhow," Roth continued, "Papagayo got all our permits squared away with the Ministry of Culture and Tourism and nailed down a few other things I was told would take months, if not years, to clear the red tape." He paused a moment, then added, "Or should I say *brown* tape?"

No, you should not say that.

Ever.

"I wouldn't worry much about anything," Roth said. "Bolivia is shit poor. A little green goes a long way down here."

"Good to know," I said.

It was also good to know that in two short minutes, Jonathon Roth had checked all the boxes: narcissist, misogynist, elitist, and racist.

I needed to get away from him before I committed a felony or, at the very least, multiple misdemeanors, so I pulled my passport out of my pocket and offered it to him. He nodded behind him and said, "Give it to Blondie."

"Right. Thanks."

I ducked into the second row and waved for his assistant's attention. It took a moment, but she finally glanced up from the blue binder. Her blond hair was cut short, there were dark circles under her eyes, and she had that slightly annoyed, just-get-through-this look of a mom with three kids at the grocery store.

"I'm Thomas," I said.

"Libby," she said dryly.

I put Libby in her early thirties, and I put the last time Libby had slept at last July.

"I'm supposed to give you this." I handed her my passport.

She took the passport and tossed it into a large manila envelope. She lifted her hands lightly as if to say, "Anything else?"

I gave her a double thumbs-up, then started back to my seat in the third row. It was my first chance to get a good look at the rest of the passengers. In the far back, there was a young woman. She had dark, nearly black hair, large brown eyes, and various colored necklaces around her neck. She was unquestionably attractive and had perfected her don't-even-think-about-coming-to-talk-to-me face.

Duly noted.

In the row in front of her were two guys who looked like a bad wrestling duo. They were both roughly the same age as me; one black, the other white. The black guy had a thin mustache and was wearing an orange and black Cincinnati Bengals hat. The white guy had a bushy brown beard and a full sleeve of tattoos running down his left arm.

That left one last passenger. He had the fourth row of seats to himself. He had curly orange hair that looked as though it had never been styled in its lifetime, and he was donning a lime-green T-shirt. He was lean, maybe five foot seven, and he was wearing what I can only describe as a look of dread.

I slid into the seat beside him, and he pulled two white earbuds from his ears.

"H-h-hey," he muttered. His face was pale and waxen.

"Are you okay?"

"I don't fly well," he said, his Adam's apple bouncing in his throat.

"I'm sure that turbulence didn't help." Our ascent had felt like we were in a dogfight in World War II.

"No," he stammered. "No, it did not."

"I read somewhere that you're more likely to die—"

"I know, I know," he interrupted. "You're more likely to die in your car on the way to the airport than you are on the flight."

I shook my head. "No, I was going to say that I read somewhere you are more likely—" I paused for effect, "—to die in a plane crash than you are to get on *The Bachelor.*"

His eyes—dill-pickle green, and made even more so by his shirt—doubled in size.

"Or maybe it was that you're more likely to die in a plane crash than to get on *Big Brother.*"

He couldn't speak. Maybe it was the phrase "die in a plane crash" that had his tongue tied. Maybe I should stop saying that.

I shook my head. "No, no, that's not it. Now I remember." I gave his hand—which was gripping the armrest so tight his fingers carried a slight tremor—a few light pats and continued: "It's *Survivor.* You are less likely to *survive* a plane crash than you are to get on *Survivor.* That's it."

"Can you, um—" He gulped. "—stop talking about plane crashes?"

If I seriously wanted to mess with him, I would have told him how my parents had died in a plane crash eleven years earlier when my father's company jet, which was similar to this one, had crashed into the Sierra Nevadas.

I let out a light laugh. "Sorry, I was just messing with you."

I have a weird sense of humor. And it gets even weirder when I'm stressed. And flying on a jet to Bolivia to track down the love of my life in the middle of the Amazon jungle had my stress level at Platinum Select.

"What's your name?" I asked.

"Andy Depree."

I introduced myself.

There was a rabbit's foot, a tan rock, and a folded piece of yellow paper on the table in front of Andy and I asked, "What's with the garage sale?"

The corners of his mouth turned up into the faintest of smiles, and he said, "Good-luck charms."

"Ah." I nodded at his lime-green shirt—which on closer examination read I PAUSED MY GAME TO BE HERE—and said, "And let me guess, that's your lucky flying shirt?"

"How'd you know?"

"I don't think anyone would wear a shirt like that voluntarily."

He looked down at his shirt then back up. "It's not that bad."

I let this go and asked, "What makes it lucky?"

"Every time I've flown in it, we haven't crashed."

"Wow. Such sorcery."

He half laughed, then asked, "I'm guessing you don't have many good-luck charms of your own."

After I was attacked by a pack of wolves, one of the rangers sent me a tooth from one of the wolves that had been killed. It was in a box somewhere in Seattle next to the bullet they'd removed from my left shoulder. But I thought of these less as good-luck charms and more as friendly reminders to buy additional life insurance.

"I'm not superstitious," I said, then without planning it, I added a line from *The Office*: "But I am a *little* stitious."

He laughed. "Michael Scott!"

In my fit of depression two years earlier, I'd binged all nine seasons in one week.

"I actually auditioned to be on that show," Andy said.

"No kidding?"

"Yeah, I think it was season three or something. I auditioned to be their IT guy."

"How did you not get the part?" Andy was *all* IT guy.

"I got nervous. Muffed my lines. Wasn't the first time."

"I'm guessing you *aren't* here because you went on to have an illustrious acting career and are now headed to the jungles of Bolivia to research your next part."

"That would be correct." He paused, then said, "I'm a professor of anthropology, specializing in the Inca Empire."

"You look a little young to be a professor." It might have mostly been his stupid shirt, but I'd put him in his mid to late twenties.

"I'm thirty-two. And to be accurate, I'm an *assistant* professor. I'm going into my second year."

I nodded, then asked, "Incas? That's Indians, right?"

"Yes, Amerindians."

"So this expedition you guys are going on, it's to find the lost city of the Incas?"

"Yeah, it's called Paititi. Theoretically, it's the Incas' last refuge after the Spanish nearly wiped them out."

"Do you speak Spanish?"

"I do. Quechua as well."

"What's Quechua?" I asked, pronouncing it as he had: *ketch-wah.*

"It's the language the Incas spoke. A lot of rural Peruvians still speak it. Mostly in the Andean region."

The color had started to come back to Andy's cheeks, and his grip had loosened on the armrests. It must be my calming demeanor. Or more likely, it was whatever was in the pill-bottle-shaped lump in Andy's left pants pocket.

I didn't know how much longer Andy would have his wits about him, and I asked, "So, Roth, he's leading this expedition?"

"Yeah, he's a pretty famous documentarian. It's his rodeo."

I wanted to tell Andy that after my limited interaction with Jonathan Roth, I had slotted him in at #4 on my Most Loathsome People list. He was right behind #3, Stephen Baldwin; #2, Unknown Frenchman who continually puts his yoga mat way,

way too close to mine; and #1, Turd Gregory (RIP). But Andy's eyes shimmered when talking about the guy, and I didn't want to sway his loyalties.

I thumbed over my shoulder. "And who's Princess Jasmine?"

He got a kick out of this, smiling big and goofy. I estimated he had thirty more seconds of consciousness.

"That is, uh, that is Dr. Farah Karim. She's an Egyptian archaeologist."

"She's not bad looking."

"She's *soooooo* hot," he slurred.

I was curious that an Egyptian archaeologist was part of an expedition searching for a lost city in South America, but Andy's eyelids had begun to sag, and I figured I only had time for one more question. "And what about the two guys who look like a wrestling duo called the 'Rustbelters?'"

He mumbled, "Camer-ad cry-you."

Camera crew.

"Gotcha. Okay, buddy, time to go night-night."

I leaned Andy's chair back, and it took his body with him. A minute later, he was softly snoring.

Andy's backpack was on the floor in front of him, and it was partially open, revealing the spine of a book. I felt a little guilty reaching into his backpack, but I had six more hours to kill, and if I left my mind to wander, it was going to start playing tricks on me. And when you've seen the things I've seen, the tricks aren't the pull-a-rabbit-out-of-a-hat kind, they're more along the lines of "Let's saw this body in half . . . and then stab it multiple times . . . and then let's throw it in a dark cellar for a few weeks until it no longer has the will to live."

So whatever book Andy brought along, Inca this or Inca that, or maybe *How to Revitalize Your Acting Career in Your 30s for Dummies*, it would keep Gina and a thousand different grim scenarios at bay.

I pulled out the book. It was titled *Console Wars: Sega, Nintendo, and the Battle That Defined a Generation.* I grinned, thinking back to a Christmas morning nearly thirty years earlier and unwrapping my Nintendo, then playing *Contra* the next two days until I had calluses on half of my fingers.

Now that was a generation.

The Nintendo generation.

My generation.

I cracked open the book and began reading. Molly came by a few minutes later, taking drink and snack orders (club soda and a turkey sandwich for me). I ate lunch; read for two hours, which is about my max; then, after twiddling my thumbs for ten minutes, I leaned my chair back and closed my eyes.

≈

A slight rocking jolted me from a dreamless sleep. I brought my seat back to its full upright position and stretched my arms above my head. After cracking my back on both sides, I turned and glanced at Andy to my right. His chair was still reclined, and his eyes were closed. But on closer examination, his body was rigid, like he was "planking," and his face looked like he had just eaten a lemon wedge. He was either having a Valium- (or Xanax or whatever he'd taken) induced nightmare, or he was wide awake.

The plane shook and a high-pitched moan slipped through Andy's pursed lips.

"It's going to be okay," I told him. "Just normal turbulence."

He shook his head from side to side but said nothing.

We hit a pocket of air, and the plane dropped to the point I got that hollow feeling in my belly. The last time I felt that sensation, I had been plummeting to the ground in a hot-air balloon. If anyone was going to let out a soft wail, it should have been me.

But it was Andy.

I turned and glanced back behind me. Dr. Farah Karim was staring at Andy, trying to bury a smile. Team Rustbelt was staring at him as well, both shaking their heads in disgust.

"Dude, you need to pull it together," I told Andy. "You're embarrassing me."

This was like the time I sat next to Brett Lentz in the high school cafeteria. I was trying to be nice—you know, sit next to the kid who always eats alone. I thought maybe we could be like Zack Morris and Screech, but then Brett took his shirt off and started rubbing his burrito against his nipples before each bite. And next thing you know, Jessica Morris (my #1), Courtney Yonder (my backup), and Heather Richter (my last resort) all "really don't feel like doing the whole homecoming thing this year."

"What's your favorite video game?" I asked.

One of Andy's eyes peeked open. "What?"

"You're wearing that stupid shirt. You're obviously a gamer. So, tell me, What is your favorite video game?"

The plane rocked and both of Andy's eyes instantly snapped shut.

"Come on," I prodded. "*Donkey Kong? Space Invaders? Grand Theft whatever?*"

"*Auto,*" he said, adjusting his seat upright a few clicks. "*Grand Theft Auto.*"

"Right."

"*GTA*'s not bad, but I mostly play *Red Dead Redemption.*"

"What's that?"

He brought his seat fully upright and said, "Oh, it's great." He started telling me all about the game.

A few minutes later, there was a soft thud, and the pilot came over the intercom, "Welcome to La Paz, folks."

8

Exiting the plane, two things were immediately evident: the air was much cooler than it had been in Miami, and there was a lot less oxygen in it.

I knew from my research that La Paz rested on a natural plateau in the Andes Mountains and, at an elevation of almost twelve thousand feet, it was the highest capital city in the entire world. It was located in the far western center of Bolivia, twenty miles from the Peruvian border. Though if you want to get technical, we weren't in La Paz, we were at the El Alto International Airport, eight miles from the Bolivian capital.

La Paz was visible in the distance, a Lego city set against a background of sprawling, white-capped mountains. It was one of the more beautiful views I'd ever seen, but hopefully it wasn't one I would get to enjoy for long.

As I descended the jet's airstairs, I gave the blue duffel bag in my right hand a few small lifts. It felt the same as it had before, though I wouldn't know for certain if Molly snuck out a few bundles while I was asleep until I took the time to count it, which didn't seem like the best idea to do on the tarmac with two airport officials in yellow vests fast approaching.

Roth and Libby, who were the first two off the plane, beelined toward the yellow vests. That we didn't have to go through the official customs line told me we were getting express service. Maybe Roth had paid for it, or maybe the red carpet was rolled out for all charter flights. Regardless, it worked in my favor.

Libby and Roth met the officials fifty yards from the plane and exchanged a few pleasantries, then Libby handed over the manila envelope she'd added my passport to. Both vests had clipboards, and they quickly began pulling the paperwork out of the envelope, flipping open passports, and pulling stamps from some sort of stamp holsters on their belts.

The camera guys and Egyptian Lara Croft huddled in a small group around a pile of bags. Andy stood a few feet from them, by himself. He appeared comfortable in his own bubble, which is something I could admire, though I think he was just happy to be on solid ground.

As for me, I was doing my best to look like a guy who *wasn't* trying to illegally sneak into these people's country. Sadly, this translated into me doing jumping jacks, then arm circles: a ridiculous mash-up of a guy who had taken a long flight and really needed to stretch and a third-grade gym teacher leading calisthenics.

Exchanges in Spanish turned my attention back to Roth, Libby, and the airport officials. It was evident Roth couldn't keep up with whatever the Bolivians were saying, and he barked for Andy to come over.

Andy, who at some point had pulled a blue sweatshirt on over his ridiculous flying shirt, plodded his way to the group and began translating.

I knew there was a problem when, twenty seconds later, all eyes turned toward me.

Uh-oh.

I made my way over to the small group.

Roth cut his eyes at me, then said, "Apparently, your paperwork is missing."

"Well, I gave my paperwork to you," I said with a big smile. "What did you do with it?"

Roth didn't have a chance to respond as one of the officials pointed at my bag and said, "*¿Qué hay en la bolsa?*"

Andy said, "They want to know what's in your duffel bag."

Oh, you mean my blue duffle bag that looked like it was filled with a bunch of cash, which in actuality was a blue duffel bag filled with a bunch of cash.

"Papagayo," I whispered.

Both officials looked at me.

"*¿Qué?*" one of them asked.

I looked at Roth, then back to the officials. "*Papagayo*," I repeated, this time with an accompanying eyebrow raise.

Nothing.

"Parrot."

Nothing.

I started flapping my arms around and bawking my head back and forth.

I'm not sure what I expected—for them to both smile and nod and say, "*Oh, now we get it. Take your big bag of money and enter our country*"?

This did not happen.

What did happen was that one of the officials yanked the duffel bag from my hand and unzipped it, revealing two decades' worth of his salary.

The two officials began barking in Spanish, and Andy translated, "They're going to detain you."

From *Midnight Express*, I knew this was the first chip to fall which would ultimately end with me falling in love with a man in a third world prison.

"Do something!" I said to Roth.

Roth threw up his hands in defeat. He'd already gotten his check, what did he care?

More Spanish was barked, and Andy translated, "If you don't go with them now, they're detaining all of us."

I leaned my head back and took a deep breath. In all honesty, it wasn't a third world prison that scared me—yes, I'm sure their prisons sucked, but I'm sure I would survive—no, I was terrified about Gina's fate.

Regardless of whether they sent me back to the United States or they sent me to prison—who knows what laws of theirs I'd broken by bringing in a bunch of cash—by the time it was all sorted, Gina's trail would be long cold.

I glanced over my shoulder at the rest of the expedition team. They looked on with curiosity, wondering just who this ruggedly handsome mystery passenger they had picked up really was. I thought about running back onto the plane, where the pilot still was, and telling him to take off. I could get him to land in a field somewhere or take me to Chile. Of course, I wouldn't have my passport or any money with me, and I would probably be worse off than I was now.

"Fine," I said, resigned. "I'll go with them."

≈

I was in a small gray-walled room not far from the traditional customs counter. The two men had escorted me there from the tarmac, pushed me down into one of two chairs surrounding a table, and left. There were scuff marks on the table, as well names, Spanish phrases, and drawings—some crude, some not—carved into it. That had been twenty minutes ago.

Another fifteen minutes passed, and then the door opened.

Two men entered. One of the officials from before, plus a man in a suit.

"Mr. Prescott?" the Suit said in slightly accented English. He was older, maybe in his sixties, his Latin features softened by time.

"Yep."

He sat across from me.

"It would appear there is a problem with your entry papers. We do not have any for you."

I considered making up a story about how I lost all the paperwork, but my story would be easy enough to dispute. And I didn't feel like spending another two hours in this room while they tried to pull up my fake hotel reservations and had someone at the US Embassy check their files for a travel visa application that didn't exist.

"You have my money," I said matter-of-factly. "Can't you just take it and let me in?"

A look of disgust flashed across the Suit's face. "Yes, I bet you expect the corrupt Bolivian to take your American dollars, and everything will be fine."

"That's not what I meant."

He shook his head. "Your drug money means nothing to me."

"It's not drug money." Technically, it was bribery money—at least some of it—which didn't sound much better. I was tempted to tell him the real story: that my ex-girlfriend had been abducted, and I was here to rescue her. Surely this would pull at his heartstrings. But before I could continue, he waved in two men. Both men were *policía*.

The officers made me stand up and put my hands behind my back. They clicked handcuffs around my wrists.

Not again.

"*Alto.*"

I turned around.

A fifth person had entered the room. He too was in uniform. But his was military. He had a thick black mustache and hard-parted black hair. He spoke a few words to the Suit, and after a sigh and nod, the Suit instructed the police officers to remove my cuffs. The Suit then said, "I apologize for the misunderstanding, Señor Prescott. Please enjoy your stay in our country."

It was as painful to watch the Suit deliver the words as it must have been for him to deliver them.

Military Mustache led me out of the room to where another man in uniform, who saluted MM, was holding both my pack and the duffel.

"Again, sorry for the misunderstanding," MM said, then stuck out his hand. I shook it, and just as quickly, he turned to leave.

The officer handed me my teal pack and the duffel—which, thankfully, still had a nice heft to it—then waved for me to follow him. I trailed him through the airport and outside to where a line of taxis were waiting. The officer walked to a red Honda, opened the door, and ushered me inside. He gave a curt nod, then closed the door. The taxi—or at least, what I hoped was a taxi—sped away from the busy pickup area and merged onto a road that the signage indicated led to La Paz.

The driver was Bolivian with dark hair and sunglasses. In the rearview mirror, I noticed a few silver-capped teeth.

"Where are you taking me?" I asked, cradling the duffel to my chest.

He nodded and said, "*Sí, sí, sí.*"

I shook my head and conjured up one of the few words I remembered from tenth-grade Spanish, which I should point out I got a C– in because I couldn't roll my r's. "*¿Dónde?*"

"*Aeropuerto,*" he responded.

"Yes, we are leaving the *aeropuerto*, but where are we going?"

"*Sí, sí, sí.*"

For the next few minutes, I watched as the sprawling city of La Paz grew larger. Then the taxi took an off-ramp and headed back away from the city.

I leaned forward, wondering where this guy was taking me and in what fashion he and his pals were going to kill me, when I noticed a chain-link fence in the distance enclosing a bunch of small planes.

He *was* taking me to the airport—just a different airport.

We pulled through an open gate and drove over gravel toward a faded yellow prop plane.

There was a man sitting on a beach chair next to the plane. He was older, well into his late fifties, with a thick gray mustache, and a ruddy complexion. The last third of a cigar was tucked into his cheek and he was wearing a faded maroon hat and a bright yellow, blue, and green Hawaiian shirt, which I have no doubt is where his nickname came from.

Papagayo.

Parrot.

9

The taxi driver sped away before I could even think about tipping him—I assume he'd been paid enough already—the wheels on the old Honda kicking up dust as he left.

"Open the duffel," Papagayo said, pushing himself up from the collapsible beach chair with a grunt. "And count the money."

I unzipped the bag and counted the stacks. There were thirty-four.

"One hundred and seventy thousand," I said.

"Good, good."

The way he said it, I got the impression that in the past he'd had trouble with people taking a bit more than the agreed upon bribe. But evidently, everything that occurred at the airport had gone exactly as intended. This meant MM had been paid $30,000 for his interference. Not a bad day's work.

"Give it here."

I handed him the duffel, and he pulled out two stacks and handed them to me. He had heavily tanned and thick forearms, the kind I've seen on many farmers in Missouri. The kind that have never seen a weight room but can rip a phonebook in three. "Keep these on you," he said. "In case of emergency."

I shoved the ten grand in the front pocket of my pants and

waited for him to elaborate. He did not. He did, however, toss his cigar to the loose gravel, then open a compartment near the back of the plane and push the duffel inside. He waved for my pack. I handed it to him, and he added it to the duffel and another large pack before slamming the compartment shut.

"So what do I call you?" I asked. "Papagayo? Parrot? Mr. Parrot?"

He smiled, revealing a missing left canine. "Vern."

I stuck out my hand and we shook.

"What's the plan, Vern?"

"Right now: get to Riberalta."

I'd done enough reading and stared at a map of Bolivia long enough over the past two days that I had the 424,000 square-mile country (that's twice the size of Texas) memorized both geographically and topographically. I knew the average temperature for each month, average rainfall, who won the last election and by how much. Heck, I even knew the national bird: the Andean condor.

Bolivia was smack-dab in the middle of South America. It was bordered to the west by Peru and Chile, the north and east by Brazil, and to the south by Paraguay and Argentina.

The Amazon basin covers an area of 2.4 million square miles of South America, 2.1 million of those square miles being dense tropical rainforest. More than half of that is located in Brazil, and the rest is spread out over eight other countries: Peru, Colombia, Bolivia, Venezuela, Guyana, Suriname, Ecuador, and French Guiana. Six percent, or 130,000 square miles, of the Amazon rainforest is located in northern Bolivia.

I assumed at some point we would head to Riberalta, which is in the northeastern corner of Bolivia in the Pando Department (Bolivia was separated into seven different "departments") not far from the Brazilian border.

I asked, "What happens after we get to Riberalta?"

"We can chat on the flight," he said, nodding toward the

mountains to the west. "The sun sets early this close to the equator, and I want to get through the mountains while we still have daylight."

Gina had mentioned this once. Unlike the United States—where the amount of daylight varies between fifteen hours during the summer and nine in the winter—near the equator, there are twelve hours of daylight nearly all year long.

I glanced over my shoulder. The sun had disappeared behind the mountains and the cloudless sky had already started to dim.

"You ever fly in one of these?" Vern asked, giving the plane's faded yellow fuselage a few light pats.

"Once." One of the cops I came up with at the Seattle Police Department had his flying license and he took me up in a little Cessna. He was a prankster, so I wasn't surprised when halfway into the flight he acted like we had engine failure. Still, when one is plummeting toward the earth at 150 miles per hour, one can never be entirely certain that it's a prank, and by the time he pulled us out of our dive, yes, I had peed a little. "It was a hoot," I told Vern.

"Don't worry, *Margarita* here is a champ. She should get us there in one piece."

I nodded at this rock-solid assurance of my safety.

"After you," he said, waving for me to get in.

I climbed into the cockpit, taking in the many pieces of duct tape holding the instrument panel together. I had twenty seconds alone with my thoughts, doubts, concerns, and regrets, then Vern clambered into the pilot seat and began flipping switches. The propeller roared to life, and he handed me a pair of headphones, also heavily duct-taped, shouting, "Put these on!"

As I pulled the headphones on, I couldn't help but think about Anthro Andy and what I wouldn't give for his lucky flying shirt.

"Here we go," Vern said, pushing the throttle forward.

The plane lurched, and we taxied a quarter mile to a small runway.

A minute later we were airborne, the plane shaking violently as it gained altitude. Within a few minutes we were closing in on our first hurdle. The altimeter hovered around seventeen thousand feet, but it felt like we weren't nearly high enough to get over the mountain's shark-tooth peak. It quickly became evident we weren't so much going over the Andes as going through them.

For the next ten minutes, Vern piloted the plane through the deep scissoring valleys between the high mountains. Sometimes it felt as though we were barely skimming over the ragged terrain that quickly turned from snow to rocks and finally to unending green foliage.

"You see those cliffs down there?" Vern asked. His voice was reasonably clear through the headphones, but he was still yelling.

I gazed down through the side window at the green rocky cliffs. "Yeah."

"There's a road that cuts through there called the North Yungas. They call it the Road of Death."

I squinted down and was surprised to see a sliver of brown cut into the side of one of the green mountains.

"For a long time, it was the only road connecting La Paz to Coroico. It goes from fifteen thousand feet down to four thousand feet over the course of forty-plus miles. Three hundred drivers used to die on the road each year."

I grimaced.

He continued, "They put in a better road a decade ago, so not many cars these days. Big thing now is cyclists. They come from all over the world to bike it. Killed about twenty of them over the years."

"How many rollerbladers?"

He cut his eyes at me. "Don't tell me—"

"What?" I said. "It's good exercise."

He found this funny and let out a gravelly, smoker's chuckle.

Since I had him talking, I said, "So lay out the plan for me."

"Right." Vern nodded. "I spent three hours this morning at the US Embassy making sure Gina hadn't contacted them. She hadn't. I filled out some missing-persons paperwork, just in case, but there's nothing they're going to do."

"Nothing?"

"They don't have the resources to go looking for a missing woman in the Pando jungle. Maybe if she went missing in Madidi, but not up north."

Madidi National Park is the largest and most popular national park in all Bolivia. When your average tourist wants a taste of the rainforest in Bolivia, Madidi is their destination. Because it's a national park, they presumably have several ranger stations, maintained trails, and access points and can deploy a search-and-rescue team much easier. But from what I'd read on the internet, outside of some small tourism in Riberalta, the rainforest in northern Bolivia was a no-man's-land.

Vern continued: "I checked with the hospital in Riberalta and a few others up north, in case Gina had shown up, but again, she hadn't."

These were all the calls I would have made if I hadn't been stuck on a plane all day. My confidence in Vern was growing by the second. "Did you by chance get in touch with the World Health Organization?"

"I did. They hadn't heard from her since they left a year earlier."

"They offer any assistance?"

"Since she's no longer on their payroll, not a whole lot they can do, and even if she were, they'd probably contact the Bolivian Army and leave it up to them. There's a slim chance they would put together a rescue team themselves, but it would take time."

"And we aren't contacting the Bolivian Army because?"

"Because in my experience they are unreliable and corrupt, and it would be a waste of time."

I considered asking him about Military Mustache but decided against it. I did say, "So what you're saying is that it's up to us?"

"Correct."

He pulled an orange Gatorade from behind his seat and took a drink, then he said, "I've hired a tracker I've worked with before named Diego. He's a jungle guide in Riberalta and knows the Pando jungle as well as anyone. Better yet, he knows the village where Gina was living."

"He's been there?"

"Yeah, a few times."

"That's good to hear."

"Diego is putting together a team and supplies," Vern continued. "Everything should be ready to rock by tomorrow morning. Tibióno is a day by boat up the Río Orthon from Riberalta. If all goes according to plan, we should get there before dusk tomorrow."

That was later than I would have hoped, but I suppose I couldn't just expect to teleport to the middle of the Amazon jungle.

"And then?"

"We track them. Or Diego does."

I'd tracked serial killers across the entire United States, but I didn't know the first thing about tracking in the wilderness.

"And if we do find them?" I asked. "I mean, at this point, we're presuming they're narcos."

"Yeah, Garret played the recording for me."

I had sent a recording of Gina's voicemail to Paul Garret. Evidently, he'd played it for Vern.

"There are a lot of narcos up north," Vern said. "Mostly Colombians. They set up drug labs in the jungle, then move the product across the Brazilian border. Brazil is the largest consumer of coke behind the US, and there's a much smaller chance of seizure than trying to move it up through Mexico."

I thought back to what Paul Garret said about Vern and his involvement in the drug trade. I wondered if he was still connected.

"But they're usually small groups," Vern said. "Four, five guys. We'll be able to handle them. Trust me."

"And by *handle*, you mean?"

"Put a bullet through each of their skulls."

"Good to know we're on the same page."

He nodded.

We had another hour and a half of flight time—plenty of time to go over the mission details—so I switched subjects. "Where did you meet Roger Garret?"

"Vietnam."

I'd put Vern in his late fifties, but to have fought in Vietnam, he had to be in his midsixties. "How old are you?"

"Sixty-five. Enlisted in the Marines at nineteen."

"Where were you living?"

"Carson City, not too far from Reno. I didn't have much going for me. Working a construction job. Drinking most nights. Making bad decisions. I needed structure."

When I was nineteen, I had flunked out of the University of Washington and was taking classes at the local community college and, much like Vern, making plenty of my own bad decisions. Two years later, searching for structure myself, I enrolled in the police academy.

"I can relate to that," I said.

"A year later, and I'm up to my ass in snakes and spiders and black palm. Plus, I have to worry about Charlie jumping out of a hole in the ground and blowing my brains to kingdom come."

"That sounds terrible."

He laughed. "Yeah, it was."

"Was Garret in your platoon?"

"Sure was. He was a riot, funnier than hell, but you could tell he was cut from a different cloth than the rest of us."

"How so?"

"It was a chess game to him, and he was better at it than anybody else. War, I mean. He was just a grunt like the rest of us, but other lieutenants would run their battle plans through him." He paused, then said, "He was the one who busted me."

"Busted you? For what?"

"Hash."

"Smoking it or smuggling it?"

"The latter."

I waited for him to expand.

"Routine patrol," he said. "Three of us stumbled on this hash operation. It'd been firebombed. Everybody was dead, but a lot of the hash survived. Me and another one of the guys were bugging out soon, so we loaded up. A week later, getting on the transport, Garret was on the seat next to me. All our duffels looked the same, and Garret accidentally opened mine. Saw the hash. I can still see the look of disappointment on his face."

"So were you court-martialed?"

"No. The government was taking a lot of heat for still having troops in Vietnam, and the last thing they wanted was the press getting wind of a bunch of soldiers smuggling dope back to the US. Trust me, I wasn't the only one who was caught. I was given a general discharge—which is the worst they can do without court-marshaling you—and told to keep quiet."

"So how did you end up in South America?"

"Spent a few years back in Reno after I got out, but I found myself doing the same shit I did before I left. Had a friend who wanted to backpack through South America. Planned it all out, then he went and flaked at the last second. I went alone. Started in Peru, then ended up in Colombia. Got introduced to some folks, and next thing I know, I'm flying fifty kilos of cocaine to Miami every two weeks."

"Wow."

"Yeah, stupid. Drug smuggling, illegal mining, archaeological looting—you name it, and I was doing it."

"Archaeological looting?"

"Yeah, there are ruins all over South America. People pay big money for artifacts, statues, relics."

"Is that how you ended up being Jonathan Roth's fixer?"

"Don't get me started on that asshole."

"Yeah, my six minutes sitting next to him on the plane was pure torture."

He laughed.

I asked, "How did you get mixed up with him?"

"Fifteen years ago, I met a Bolivian girl living in Colombia. First time I had to think about anybody but myself in my whole life. We moved back to her hometown, La Paz, and I went legit. Had to find a way to make money the old-fashioned way. Didn't plan on becoming what they call a fixer, but because I knew the language and had a good idea of how bureaucracy worked in South America, people—Americans mostly—started coming to me to get things done. Bolivia is the poorest country in all of South America, but if you have money, there's money to be made."

"So when Roth needs a permit to look for Paititi, you're the man for the job."

Roth's eyes twinkled. "You know about Paititi?"

"Just what the anthropologist told me on the plane. Which wasn't a whole lot." I didn't share that our time was pharmaceutically cut short.

"I can't tell you how many of these expeditions I've seen come through here."

"All looking for Paititi?"

"Not Paititi," he said, shaking his head. "Most of those searches have been in the jungles of eastern Peru. But there are tons of undiscovered ruins all over the place. In the jungle, you could be two feet from what could've been a city teaming with thousands of people four centuries ago and not even know it's there."

"Thank God for lidar."

"Now you're just showing off," he said with a laugh.

"According to Andy—he's the expedition anthropologist—it sounds like they have a pretty good lead on something."

"Best lead I've heard of," Vern said. "Might not be Paititi, but there's something there, that's for sure. That's actually how I met Roth. I flew the lidar survey, and let me tell you, four days in an airplane with that asshole is four too many."

"Did he ask you to go to the Maldives with him?"

Vern started laughing so hard I thought he might choke. After his fit, he looked up and said, "You know what? That son of a bitch did ask me to go to the Maldives with him!"

This got me good and I buckled over. When I recovered from my laughter, I asked, "How many miles did you survey?"

"Fifty square miles. But it takes forever because the lidar machine doesn't have a very wide scanning field. So you have to fly a grid back and forth, back and forth, like you're mowing a lawn."

"You've seen the photographs?"

"Actually, they're not photographs, they're three-dimensional *scans*. But yeah, I've seen them. Looks like there are all kinds of man-made formations down there. Pyramids, enclosures, plazas. Could be millions of dollars' worth of artifacts."

"Yeah, but doesn't all that stuff belong to the Bolivian government? Or will all those artifacts get looted and sold?"

He let out a loud laugh and said, "The Bolivian government is the biggest looter of them all."

I glanced out of the plane. We were now flying over dense, dark jungle. It was easy to believe there could be a lost city hidden in there somewhere. Heck, Miami could be cloaked beneath the sea of green, and you wouldn't have any idea.

But honestly, I didn't care about any lost cities or who looted what. All I cared about was finding Gina.

"So, level with me here," I said. "Have you ever dealt with someone being kidnapped in the jungle?"

He nodded. "Just once."

"And did you recover them?"

"Yeah, we did," he said. "In twenty different pieces."

10

There was a giant snake projected on the screen at the front of the room. It was several shades of brown and easily camouflaged among the dried leaves in the photo.

"The fer-de-lance," Mark Holland said in an English accent.

Holland, as he liked to be called, was tall, easily six foot four, muscular, with a light-brown goatee and a shaved head. He wore a white paracord bracelet on one wrist and an enormous black watch on the other. He had spent the previous five minutes recounting his bio: forty-two years old, ex–British Special Forces, advanced trauma medic, skilled survivalist, and senior instructor in jungle warfare. After leaving the military, he started a company called TAFLS, Television and Film Logistics and Safety. He specialized in bringing television and film crews into the most dangerous and inhospitable environments. He'd worked with several TV shows— including *Running Wild with Bear Grylls*, *Survivorman*, *Extreme World*, and *Naked and Afraid*—and on numerous documentaries.

Holland and his partner—Ian Rixby, whom they would meet the following day—would be in charge of Andy and the other expedition team members' safety while in the jungle.

There were eight of them seated around a U-shaped table in

the Republica Conference Room on the fourth floor of the ritzy Hotel Presidente—plus the two cameramen walking around the room shooting footage. In addition to Holland, the fresh faces were Alejándro Cala, head of archaeology for Bolivia; Bernita Capobianco, Bolivian anthropologist; Lieutenant Mauricio Goytia, liaison to the Bolivian Army; and Nathan Buxton, adventure and travel writer for *National Geographic*.

The "orientation," as Jonathan Roth called it, began fifteen minutes earlier. Roth started off the meeting with a rah-rah speech about fate, destiny, and discovery. How over a hundred different expeditions had searched for the lost city of the Incas and none had succeeded. It felt a bit scripted to Andy—no doubt Roth had practiced the speech several times in front of the mirror—and it was certainly as much for the benefit of the cameras on the shoulders of Sean and Darnell as it was for the expedition team. But it was intoxicating nonetheless, and it had Andy buzzing to get into the jungle and get his hands dirty. That is, until Holland stood up and began speaking.

"The fer-de-lance," Holland repeated, "is one of the most poisonous snakes in the world. They hide in the rocks, the trees, the bushes. They come out at night, are attracted to activity, and I can tell you from experience that they are irritable as hell. I can almost guarantee at some point you will encounter one of these arseholes.

"We're going into one of the most isolated areas on earth, where choppers can't fly at night, where weather can change in an instant, and where evacuation might not be possible for days. If you get bit by one of these blokes, you'll lose a limb at best, and that's if you survive. That's why it's important to always wear your Kevlar snake gaiters, especially at night when you get up to piss."

Andy glanced to his left, where Jonathan Roth's production assistant Libby sat. Her head hung slightly—the short blond strands of her pixie cut hanging just above her light-blue eyes—and she looked as though she may vomit at any moment. Andy, who had once locked himself in his room for three days because his dad saw a garter snake in the backyard, whispered, "I'm terrified of snakes too." From Andy's experience, fear loved company.

Libby scrunched her eyebrows and said, "Oh, no, I'm fine with snakes. I'm just not feeling all that well." She bit her bottom lip and took a hard swallow.

"Altitude sickness," Andy said, wondering why it took him so long to notice.

"What?"

"I think you have altitude sickness." At twelve thousand feet, Andy was surprised more of them hadn't been affected.

Andy, of course, had taken precautions, popping a couple of Diamox, a medicine that helped alleviate the symptoms of altitude sickness—pounding headache, nausea, dizziness, and shortness of breath—before they'd boarded the flight in Miami. The Diamox was one of thirty different medicines Andy had packed in what the TSA agent at Chicago O'Hare had dubbed "more pharmacy than suitcase."

Andy had brought two pills with him to take at some point during dinner, and he patted the circular outlines of the small pills in his front pocket. After a moment's hesitation, he slipped them out of his pocket and placed them in front of Libby.

"Take these," he whispered. "They'll make you feel better." He pulled over one of three pitchers of lemon water set out by the hotel and filled a glass. "Drink all of this."

Staying hydrated was the best way to combat altitude sickness. Since landing, Andy had drunk all three thirty-two-ounce bottles of water from the minibar.

Libby didn't question what the pills were, tossing them into her mouth and slugging back the entire glass of water.

"Good, now drink another full gla—"

"Hey!" snapped Holland.

Andy glanced up. A picture of a scorpion was now on the screen, but everyone's eyes were trained on him.

Holland glared at him. "You think I'm doing this for my own amusement? This is bloody serious."

Andy felt his cheeks go flush to the point he thought they might burst. If getting singled out wasn't bad enough, Andy turned and saw both Sean and Darnell had their cameras trained on him, documenting his embarrassment for possibly millions of people on Netflix or Amazon or wherever to someday enjoy.

But possibly worst of all, was Jonathan Roth at the head of the table and Farah Karim directly across from him, both wearing the same look of annoyance.

"Oh, sorry, sir," Andy mumbled. "I, uh, yeah, sorry, please continue."

If teleportation existed, Andy would have gone to the moon.

≈

Holland spent the next twenty minutes briefing them about the different ways the jungle would try to "tap them out" of the expedition.

Andy kept rapt attention, not only to make up for his earlier interruption—which was innocent enough; he was only trying to help out Libby—but because he knew something Holland said here in this conference room could save his life come tomorrow.

Holland put up photos of all the animals that inhabited the lowland Bolivian rainforest and could shred them to pieces: jaguars, caimans (small alligators, usually between six and eight feet long), black caimans (the largest members of the alligator family and, at around fifteen feet long, the largest predators in the Amazon River basin), wild boars, tapirs, and several different types of monkeys. He spoke at length about how it was imperative to remain observant, to keep a watchful eye.

Then came the bugs: mosquitoes, sand flies, chiggers, ticks, kissing bugs. Holland couldn't stress enough how important it was to apply DEET from head to toe several times a day—to spray their clothing with it, to apply it before they went to sleep. Because as if the bugs weren't bad enough, they also carried a plethora of deadly diseases: malaria, dengue, yellow fever—diseases that might not kill them but were so painful that they would wish they were dead.

Andy had gotten his yellow fever vaccine a couple of days after his phone call with Roth three weeks earlier. He'd also started taking malaria pills the previous week, as instructed. But according to Holland, neither the vaccine nor the pills guaranteed they wouldn't contract the diseases. And sadly, there was no prevention for dengue—also known as "breakbone fever"—other than trying not to get bitten by a mosquito that carried the virus.

From bugs and diseases, Holland moved on to plants. Nearly a third of the plants in the Amazon rainforest were poisonous in some way or another. Holland would distribute gloves—the kind scuba divers used—and he recommended wearing them at all times. He urged everyone to be especially careful when going to the restroom, the last thing you wanted was for your privates to brush up against something sinister and swell, burn, and blister. Even with his warning, it was sure to happen to someone.

Don't be that someone.

Holland cautioned how easy it was to get lost. Wandering a mere fifteen feet from the group could lead to disaster. Never detach from the group. Never leave base camp alone. On every trip from base camp, everyone would be required to bring an emergency kit filled with food, water, a flashlight, a knife, matches, DEET, and rain gear.

He took out a box and handed out whistles. He watched as every member of the group, from Roth to each of the cameramen, draped the orange whistles over their heads. "Do not take the whistle off. Not tonight. Not any other night. You are my responsibility," he said, finishing up. "And no one is going to get hurt or bloody dead. Not on my watch."

≈

The restaurant, Café Banais, was three blocks from the hotel. It was 8:30 p.m., and the place was a third full. The expedition team pushed two of the small wooden tables together to make room for the seven of them. Three of the team had opted out of dinner: Lieutenant Goytia, who would be rejoining the expedition on Wednesday with a small group of Bolivian soldiers; Libby, whose altitude sickness had lessened because of Andy's pills, but who said the bathtub and room service were calling her name; and Bernita Capobianco, who wanted to spend the night with her children before heading into the jungle for twelve days.

Andy took his seat next to Nathan Buxton. After shooting some B-roll footage of the restaurant, Sean and Darnell took the two seats across from Andy. Bolivian chief of archaeology Alejándro Cala was seated to Andy's right, at the end of the table, and already in a heated conversation with Sean about *futbol* versus American football. And at the other end of the table sat Jonathan Roth and, to his left, Farah Karim.

Their waiter was a young Bolivian girl in a pressed shirt and tan skirt. She took their drink orders, which for the majority, including Andy, was a Paceña, a beer brewed locally with Andean water.

Drinking alcohol was a surefire way to get altitude sickness, but if it hadn't hit Andy by now, he was probably in the clear. Plus, he didn't want to be the only one *not* imbibing.

The beers came, and the entire table cheered.

"To Paititi!" Roth shouted. "We're coming for you, you son of a bitch."

The whole table erupted in laughter.

"You know what?" Roth said. "Let's do that again. This time on camera." He pointed to Darnell and said, "Would you mind? Just on your phone."

Darnell pulled out his phone, and they recreated the cheers.

"To Paititi! We're coming for you, you son of a bitch." [*Cue laughter.*]

Roth asked to do it, "Just one more time," then the waitress delivered a plate of chips and salsa. If she hadn't, Andy suspected they might have done twenty takes.

"So, you're a professor of anthropology?" Buxton asked from the seat to his left. "At the University of Chicago, correct?"

"That's right," Andy said, choking down a chip loaded with salsa, then following it with a sip of beer. "An assistant professor, actually. I only have the winter and spring quarters under my belt."

"How'd you like it?"

Andy didn't want to tell him how he had been miserable the entire time. How he'd penned his letter of resignation twice but fell short of sending it. How he was dreading the first day of the fall quarter come October.

"It was great," he lied.

"You teach the Incan Empire, correct?"

"I do."

"How'd you fall into that?"

"In undergrad I took an Inca-studies class and loved it. They were so incredibly innovative; their society was so much more complex than what is commonly thought."

"Oh, absolutely."

"And there's so much drama to their demise. Betrayal, heartache, sibling rivalry, pestilence. It's all there." Andy took another chip, then asked, "Do you know much about them?"

"A decent amount. I write an adventure-novel series, and one of my books had an Incan element to it. I did some surface research and it gave my wife and me a chance to go down to Machu Picchu, which, as you know, is simply out of this world."

"*The Cusco Paradox*," Andy said with a smile.

"You've read it?"

"I have." Andy had read most of Buxton's books. "It was pretty good. A few things you got wrong about the Incas, but hey, it's fiction."

"When you're writing fiction and you get something wrong, you just say you took 'creative liberties.'" He gave Andy a light slap on the shoulder. "But yeah, sometime over the next few days, let's chat about what I got wrong. I'm curious."

"I have an email saved in my draft folder if you really want to know."

"Seriously?"

"No, of course not. I'm not one of those people." In actuality, Andy *was* one of those people, and he did have an email in his draft folder listing the many inaccuracies in Buxton's book.

Buxton laughed, then started into a conversation with Alejándro Cala. Andy offered to trade places with the Bolivian so they could talk more easily, which left Andy at the head of the table, opposite Roth.

Andy watched as Roth and Farah chatted, their chairs angled close together and their heads nearly touching. Farah's beer was half empty and her olive skin carried a light glow.

Andy felt a pang of jealousy. He didn't know if he was jealous of Roth or Karim. He surmised it was a little bit of both.

11

The parrot was red, yellow, and blue. And small, which made sense as it was just a baby. The colorful bird was in a cage with six other baby parrots, who I could only assume were his brothers and sisters. Or at the very least, third cousins.

"*Mi amigo*," shouted the booth's owner. "Buy parrot. I give good deal."

Vern and I had been at the outdoor market on the outskirts of Riber Plaza for the past fifteen minutes, picking up last-minute supplies, which, thus far, mostly consisted of snacks.

After a jittery landing at the small Riberalta Airport the previous evening, we'd taken a taxi to the Hotel Jomali. I half expected to find that Vern and I were sharing a room, but apparently the $160,000 I'd forked over secured my own accommodations. The room was two clicks nicer than the Embassy Suites I stayed at in Miami, and it had a kick-ass air conditioner to fight the balmy tropical heat.

Vern called it a night early, stating he wanted to catch as many winks as possible before sleeping in the jungle for who knows how long. He said if I was hungry, there was a good place a few blocks down from the hotel. And since I hadn't eaten since my turkey sandwich on the charter flight, I took his recommendation and walked to Lo Mejor de lo Mejor, which just so happened to be named after my favorite karate movie.

Best of the Best.

After devouring my *silpancho*—beef, rice, diced tomatoes, onions, and potatoes topped with a fried egg—I had a hankering to go break some boards in a garage, but I headed back to the hotel and was asleep by ten.

"*No, gracias,*" I replied to the small Bolivian, who was now holding one of the parrots in each of his hands, squeezing them like they were ketchup bottles and waving them in my face. "*No necesito el papagayo.*"

Speaking of parrots, Vern was two booths away, haggling with the owner over the price of dried plantains. I joined him just as he was wrapping up the transaction. I pulled one of the dried plantains from the three-pound bag he'd purchased, and I popped it in my mouth. It was slightly sweeter than dried banana. After I swallowed it down, I said, "So I never asked, how did you get the name Papagayo?" I nodded down at the shirt he was wearing, which today was lime green, purple, and blue. "Is it the Hawaiian shirts?"

He laughed, his missing canine flashing momentarily, and said, "Actually, it's not."

"What's the story?"

"Back when I first moved to Colombia and I was still learning Spanish, I would repeat a lot of the phrases that the Colombians were saying around me. One of the guys overheard me one day and said in Spanish, 'There goes the parrot again,' and it stuck. From that day forward I was Papagayo." He nodded down at his shirt and said, "And ever since then, all anybody buys me is Hawaiian shirts. I've got a million of these things now."

I chuckled.

After hitting one more booth, Vern was ready to go. He stuck his fingers in his mouth, whistled, and two of the many mopeds filling the small streets zipped to the side of the road. Vern haggled for a ride to "El Madre," and after a quick exchange of money, he and I climbed on the back of our respective mopeds.

My driver was wearing a red sleeveless T-shirt and jean shorts, which appeared to be the dress code for men in their twenties. I held tight to his shoulders as he merged into the honking traffic and zipped through the busy streets. Small houses—some nice, many dilapidated—whizzed by as we drove the mile to the muddy bank of the Río Madre de Dios.

Vern and I hopped off and headed down a steep embankment leading to the river. The "Mother of God" was brown and moving at a nice clip from left to right. The river was a half mile wide, the brown water on the opposite bank giving way to hundreds of miles of dense, impenetrable jungle.

There were twenty boats beached on the muddy banks of the great river, but only one had three Bolivians standing next to it. Like many of the Bolivian men I'd seen thus far, two of the three were trim but muscular, with coffee-brown skin, and shiny black hair. And they were short. Really short. Bolivia had some of the most diminutive people on earth, with the average male standing at five feet three inches, and your average woman just four eight. However, the third Bolivian was an anomaly; he was fairly light-skinned and towered over his two compatriots.

Suffice it to say this was not the elite fighting force I was expecting.

I turned and gave Vern a hard stare.

He said, "Trust me."

"I don't think I have much of a choice."

We drew closer, and two of the men rushed forward and took our packs. They were young—kids really—and I doubted either had seen their twentieth birthday. Like my moped driver, both were clad in T-shirts with cut-off sleeves and jean shorts. They spoke bits and pieces of English. The short Bolivian had a wispy black goatee and introduced himself as Juan Pablo. The other one, the "anomaly"—who in actuality was just a couple of inches taller than me but looked like a giant standing next to his two peers— had a three-inch scar on his neck and said, "I am Carlos."

The third man was older, around thirty-five. He was maybe five foot three, with chubby cheeks and black hair buzzed down to half an inch; his eyes were small and squinty. He stepped forward and said, "Nice to meet you, sir," in B– English. "Boat ready to go."

This was Diego, our tracker.

The boat he was referring to was a canoe. What they call a dugout. It was twelve feet long and faded blue in color; it bobbed in the shallow water at the river's edge. Four equally spaced benches spanned its three-foot width. I was relieved to see a scuffed black outboard motor attached at the back of the boat. I had been worried we'd be paddling for twelve hours.

Juan Pablo and Carlos stowed our packs (Vern's was battered and covered in at least a cubic meter's worth of duct tape) with three large military rucksacks and five gallons of bottled water. Not wanting to deplete my three-liter water bladder quite yet, I asked, "Do you mind if I have a hit of that water?"

The morning humidity already had me parched, and my quick-dry long-sleeve shirt was stuck to my back. Carlos tossed me one of the gallon jugs, and I twisted off the top and drank heartily. I wiped my mouth on my sleeve, then stepped into the boat, my 175 added pounds rocking it slightly. I had just gained my equilibrium when I noticed something crawl out from beneath one of the wooden planks.

I yelped.

All three Bolivians glanced at the creature, then to me, then erupted in laughter. Even Vern was cackling.

Diego patted my shoulder softly and said, "That just Camila. She very friendly."

On cue, Camila *slowly* pulled herself forward, *slowly* wrapped herself around Diego's leg, and *slowly* began pulling herself up. She *slowly* made her way up his body until she was hanging around his neck.

Camila was a sloth.

≈

We'd been on the river for twenty minutes, the slow hum of the motor propelling the boat with the current of the Madre. Juan Pablo was sitting at the back of the boat, playing *motorista*, steering the outboard. Vern and Carlos were on the second bench, and I was on the third. Diego and Camila stood near the helm.

There were several other boats on the water, mostly tourists on boat tours of the jungle, their phones or cameras held tightly in their hands as they snapped thousands of pictures they would soon upload to their Instagram accounts.

When Diego wasn't tasked with tracking down a kidnapped doctor, he was one of these guides, and I'm not sure if instinct took over or if he was hoping for a tip, but he began pointing and explaining this and that—howler monkeys swinging from the branches of the thick jungle canopy; several different birds, one the neon-blue of a Vegas sign; the beady red eyes and long snout of a giant black caiman; the snapping of piranha; this sort of tree, that sort of tree.

After thirty minutes and what I could only assume was three or four miles, we rounded a bend, and Juan Pablo guided the boat toward a tributary feeding into the Madre. From my time on Google Earth, I knew that if we continued east on the Madre, it would take us north into Brazil and eventually feed into the

Amazon River. But now we were headed west, against the current, on the Orthon.

The canoe rumbled through the merging waters, then slipped into the much narrower confines of the Orthon River. The 150-foot-high jungle canopy pressed in from both sides, creating a tunnel effect. Muddy banks were exposed on both sides of the river, which I presume would be underwater when the wet season returned in October.

"How many miles do you think it is?" I asked, interrupting Diego's explanation of another of the zillion birds that lived in the Amazon. "To Tibióno?"

"Miles?" he said, shaking his head. "No miles."

"Sorry, *kilometers*."

"No kilometers."

"Um," I looked to Vern. "What do they use to measure?"

"They mostly use days, but try hours."

I tried hours.

"*Diez*," Diego said.

This was one of the seventeen Spanish words I knew.

Ten.

Ten hours.

I imagined Gina taking this boat trip each time she needed more antibiotics. Or tampons. Or almond milk. Ten hours down the river, then ten hours back.

Really puts that twenty-minute drive to Target into perspective.

I asked Diego, "Have you been to Tibióno before?"

"*Sí*," he said. "Few times."

"What's it like?"

"Same as many village in the jungle. Live simple. Mostly friendly."

I'm not sure what "mostly friendly" equated to, but I let it slide. Perhaps realizing I wasn't all that interested in his tour and that we had roughly nine and a half hours left on our voyage, Diego sat down on the bench next to me. The small sloth was still clinging to his neck, her head a few inches from my left shoulder. She slowly moved her head to the side until she was gazing directly at me. She had wide-set brown eyes, a large black nose, and a permanent half smile. Most of her fur was a stringy tan, but she had a ring of brown fur circling the top of her head and neck. She seemed harmless, maybe even cute—okay, *super-duper* cute—and I couldn't believe I'd been so startled when I first saw her.

I was reminded of a couple of years earlier at the farm in Missouri. I was checking out the barn for the first time, when I heard a soft rustling coming from the loft. I thought it was an owl at the time, and I climbed the ladder, searching for the culprit. And then it popped its head out.

It was a little piglet.

I yelped the same yelp I'd let loose at the sight of Camila, but luckily no one had been there to mock me. Unluckily, I fell off the ladder and to the hard barn floor. After dusting myself off, I would later find a second piglet and to say I fell in love with them would be an understatement.

Randle, whom I gave my grandfather's farm to, sent me videos of Harold and May from time to time. Both pigs were now over two hundred pounds, and Randle's twin daughters treated them like royalty.

"How old is she?" I asked Diego.

"A little over year. I was guiding tour six months ago, and I find her on the ground. She had broken leg." He lifted one of her small legs and said, "She was in cast for two months."

Camila inched her head closer my way, as if she knew we were talking about her, then lifted one of her arms from around Diego's neck and timidly moved it to my left shoulder. She had three little claws coming out of each of her hands and feet, which appeared sharp, though I could hardly feel them. Ever so gently, she eased her way off Diego and onto me. She was surprisingly light and couldn't have weighed more than five or six pounds. She swiveled her head and stared at me, her large brown eyes unblinking.

"Hello, Camila," I said softly.

She studied my face with a wry grin of amusement.

I bounced her gently and said, "You are such a pretty girl." This came out in the high-pitched baby talk that before I had a nephew would make my ears bleed but which now I could do little to control. "You are so beautiful. Yes, you are!"

I could see Diego in my peripheral, fighting back a smile.

"Is she your pet?" I asked him.

"No, no pet," Diego said with a violent shake of his head. "She belong in the jungle with other sloth."

He explained that he was planning on reintroducing her to the jungle in the next few months. He brought her along because this was the perfect opportunity to expose her to her natural environment. And maybe see how she reacted if she saw another sloth in the wild.

I wasn't sure if this particular rescue mission was the ideal opportunity for a wildlife experiment, but I already adored her, and I would do anything for her.

"Here," Diego said, handing me a plastic bag filled with pink flowers. "Hibiscus flowers are her favorite."

I pulled one of the red flowers from the bag and held it out. Camila took it in her claws and slowly pushed it into her mouth, then, like someone savoring their last bite of cheesecake, she leisurely chewed and chewed and chewed. Finally, her eyes rolling upward in delight, she swallowed.

12

"That's Brazil on the other side of the river," Nathan Buxton said, sidling up to Andy at the edge of the airstrip and adjusting the wire-frame glasses on his nose.

Andy was well aware the Mamoré river, which ran south to north, acted as a border between the two countries; the Bolivian city of Guayaramerín on the western side and the Brazilian city of Guajará-Mirim to the east.

"Looks about the same over there," Andy replied.

And it did, especially from the air. A small municipality—both cities had populations of around forty thousand—surrounded by a never-ending sea of green.

The *National Geographic* writer nodded in agreement. "That it does."

Nathan Buxton and Andy were two of the five remaining members of the expedition team. After waking early, the entire team, all nine of them, had boarded a plane—thankfully, one much larger than the charter jet—and flown the two hours from La Paz to the Guayaramerín airport. From there they took vans to a small airstrip where a blue AStar helicopter, Holland's partner, and an enormous amount of supplies awaited them.

Holland's partner, Ian Rixby, had taken an advance flight to the landing zone to make sure there was a large enough clearing for the helicopter to land. The prospective LZ was on the bank of a small river that broke up the endless sea of green canopy. Unfortunately, there wasn't quite enough room on the riverbank, and the ex–military man was forced to repel from the helicopter, and after five hours with a chainsaw and a machete, he was able to clear a thirty-foot landing radius where the riverbank met the brush.

The AStar helicopter, with its chipped blue paint, had a maximum capacity of six, so the expedition team would have to fly the forty minutes to the landing zone in two convoys. The first convoy was Roth, Holland, Rixby, and both cameramen, plus the head of Bolivian archaeology, Alejándro Cala.

Dr. Farah Karim was insistent she be on the first flight to make sure the landing zone didn't have any possible archaeological significance, but it was decided the heavyset Cala made more sense.

The slight Farah would join Andy, Libby, Buxton, and Bolivian anthropologist Bernita Capobianco on the second flight. Smaller in both number and stature, they would be able to take supplies with them. Which was vital, considering that a storm was brewing on the eastern horizon. It was doubtful the AStar would be able to make more than two flights, and it was likely that the majority of the supplies—portable generators, stacks of bottled water, toilet paper, tarps, folding tables, tents, chairs, cots, and other necessities—wouldn't arrive until the following day.

"Do you think they speak Spanish or Portuguese in—" Buxton glanced down at the unfolded map in his hand. "—Guajará-Mirim?"

"Portuñol," Andy replied.

Buxton cocked his head slightly.

"Portuñol is a mixture of Spanish and Portuguese," Andy explained. Although most of his later studies focused on the Inca Empire, in his undergraduate years Andy had taken a broad spectrum of anthropology courses, and he was well versed in all things South American.

"You don't say," Buxton said, nodding his head.

"It's a simplified version of the two languages."

"Pidgin?"

Pidgin is any simplified communication between two groups.

"More or less."

Buxton was getting ready to ask a follow-up question, when the soft thwack of a propeller filled the heavy air.

Buxton turned around and gazed at the approaching helicopter. "Looks like our ride is here."

≈

There were no seats on the helicopter, and Andy was sitting on the cold metal floor next to a large stack of Mountain House freeze-dried meals. Across from Andy, squished between stacks of water and a bunch of high-tech audio equipment, were Libby, Bernita, and Buxton. Farah was sitting to Andy's right, her leg touching his. Andy would have relished the contact with the beautiful Egyptian were he not in the midst of a total meltdown.

". . . thirty-two . . . sixty-four . . . one hundred and twenty-eight . . . two hundred and fifty-six . . . five hundred and twelve . . . one thousand and twenty-four . . ."

"What are you doing?"

Andy opened his eyes and turned his head slightly. Farah Karim was glaring at him, her mocha-brown eyes narrowed over her perfectly shaped nose.

"What are you mumbling?" she yelled over the roar of the rotor. Her words carried a slight Arabic throatiness.

"Oh, um, I'm multiplying by two," Andy shouted back. He was going to leave it at that, but for some reason, probably the panic attack, he confided, "It helps to, um, to calm me down . . . when I'm, um, freaking out."

"You don't look like you're freaking out."

"Oh, well, I guess I hide it—" Andy realized she was messing with him. With his knees pulled up to his chest and mumbling incoherently under his breath, he most certainly looked as though he was freaking out.

"Do you have any other tricks?" Farah asked.

"Tricks?"

"You know, to calm you down."

"Multiplying takes my mind off things. Sometimes I'll drive around."

"Drive around?"

"Yeah, I'll drive through the town where I grew up." Andy tapped on his head a few times. "In my head."

It was something his therapist told him to try. He would get behind the wheel of the car he drove growing up—an aging green Jeep Cherokee—and he would drive the streets of Rapid City.

Farah leaned back from him an inch. "That's weird."

Andy didn't know what to say, but it didn't matter, because the helicopter banked hard to the right. Three of the freeze-dried pouches fell and smacked Andy on the head, but he hardly felt them as his heart rate jumped into the triple digits.

"Where do you go?"

Andy turned.

Farah asked, "Where do you go in your car?"

Andy took a breath. "To friends' houses. To, uh, CVS. I go through the drive-through. Drive up to the college."

"What drive-through?"

"Taco Bell."

"What do you order?"

"Two double-deckers and a bean burrito."

Andy could feel his heart rate normalize, something he had Farah to thank for. He asked, "Do you like to fly?"

"Sure."

"Doesn't it bother you when the pla—I mean, helicopter—drops like that."

"Not really. Reminds me of being on a roller coaster."

"I'm scared of roller coasters."

Farah rolled her eyes.

"What are you scared of?" Andy asked.

"Nothing."

"Nothing? Not even, like, Ebola?"

"Fuck Ebola."

Andy laughed.

He laughed so hard his eyes began to water. By the time he composed himself, the helicopter was on the ground.

≈

"Welcome!" Alejándro Cala yelled over the loud screeching coming from the jungle canopy.

"What's that sound?" Andy asked, the fading wash of the helicopter rotor whipping his orange-blond curls. It reminded Andy of the one time he'd gone to see a screamo band and been unfortunate enough to sit five feet from one of the speakers.

"Howler monkeys!" Cala replied. "The noise from the helicopter gets them riled up."

"Wow, those monkeys are loud!" shouted Buxton as he, Farah, Libby, and Bernita joined them.

"They'll quiet down here in a few minutes," Cala said, who had either offered or been chosen to be their base camp liaison. He nodded toward a wall of green and said, "Camp is two hundred meters in."

A narrow path was chopped into the wall of vegetation, and Andy and the others followed behind the portly Cala.

"Has anyone been to the ruins yet?" Farah asked as they entered the imposing cave of green.

"Not yet," Cala shouted from up front. "The closest ruins are half a mile from base camp. Holland doesn't think we'll get over there today."

"What?" Farah said. "It's not even one o'clock yet!"

Andy was itching to see the ruins as well, but he was in no rush. They would be there for the next twelve days.

"I'm with you," Cala said. "I'm ready to get over there and start some ground-truthing, but Holland is calling the shots, and he's concerned about the weather."

Farah let out a frustrated sigh.

After a minute or two of hiking, they could still hear the shaking of branches a hundred feet overhead, but for the most part the howler monkeys had ceased their screaming.

"Wow, this is thick," Buxton said, pushing a large branch out of the way.

Andy pushed aside the same branch, thinking the author's words couldn't ring any truer. Even after it had been hacked away by who knows how many machetes, it was a gauntlet of green webbing,

A minute later, the jungle opened up and Cala exclaimed, "Here we are!"

Base camp.

A space fifty feet in diameter had been cleared of brush. Holland and Rixby each had a machete—their blades painted bright pink—and were continuing to widen the swath.

Hanging from the low branches of several of the skyscraper-high trees were two enormous blue tarps. The industrial-sized tarps were each twenty feet square and they were angled upward, creating a large makeshift canopy tent.

Libby and Roth were sitting in collapsible chairs under the tent and working on laptops. Both cameramen were busy recording the action. Sean walked around with a camera on his shoulder, while Darnell had set his camera on a tripod at the edge of the clearing. Darnell swiveled his camera toward Andy and the others as they emerged from the surrounding vegetation.

Holland, who was carrying a load of branches, nodded at them and said, "'Bout bloody time." He tossed the branches in a large pile at the far end of the clearing and wiped his hands. "First things first: if you haven't already, spray yourself down with DEET. Head to toe; skin, clothes, head, face, hair, shoes—everything. There aren't a whole lot of bugs right now, but it only takes one to send you packing."

Andy had sprayed himself twice already: once that morning, then again at the airstrip.

"Then put on your snake gaiters," Holland continued.

Andy glanced down at the polyurethane-coated guards strapped to his shins and flapping out over half of his boots. He had put his snake gaiters on before they boarded the flight from La Paz and had no intention of taking them off until he was back in Illinois.

"Then grab a machete and some gloves and find somewhere in the close vicinity to fix up your campsite." Holland nodded at a pile of machetes, each in a leather scabbard. Next to the machetes was a pile of black scuba-diving gloves. "Try to stay within fifteen meters. Somewhere you'll be able to get to in the dark. Look for two trees eight to ten feet apart where you can string your hammock. If you have trouble setting up, grab me or Rix, and we'll get you squared away."

There was a third pile of red nylon bags, which Andy assumed were the hammocks.

Andy looked around at the others. Only Nathan Buxton had the same look of confusion on his face.

"Um," Andy said. "I thought we'd be in tents."

"Not tonight," Holland said, matter-of-factly. "Tents are coming with everything else tomorrow. The hammocks have mosquito netting and rain flies. Personally, I prefer a hammock, but come tomorrow if you want a tent, you got one."

"Oh, okay," Andy replied, wishing he'd kept his mouth shut.

The four others dropped their packs and did as Holland instructed, spraying themselves down with insect repellent. Andy decided a third dousing couldn't hurt and covered himself in the noxious spray as well. While the others busied themselves with their snake gaiters, Andy grabbed a pair of gloves, a machete, and a red nylon hammock bag. He pulled on the gloves, then trudged through ten meters of thick brush before spotting two trees that fit Holland's description.

He dropped his pack, then slipped the bright-pink machete—Andy guessed they'd been spray-painted pink so they were more visible to anyone in the vicinity—from the leather scabbard. The machete was a foot and a half long with a slightly curved blade. It was lighter than Andy would have suspected, and he slashed away at the many different trees, ferns, vines, flowers, and leaves.

Thirty minutes later, Andy was putting the finishing touches on his hammock, when he was startled by a snap in the brush. He whipped his head around, expecting to see a large jaguar licking its lips, but it was Holland's partner.

"How you faring, mate?" Ian Rixby asked, his accent more standard English than Holland's regional brogue. Rix, as he liked to be called, was broad chested and had dark hair and heavy eyebrows. He was a few years younger than Holland and carried himself with the confidence of an MMA fighter.

Andy took a calming breath and said, "I think I'm almost done."

Rix took a few steps closer. His nose wrinkled and he shook his head.

"What?" Andy asked, sniffing a few times himself. All he could smell was earth, flowers, and decay.

"Monkey piss."

Andy sniffed again and realized under the thick smell of vegetation was the musky scent of urine.

"This is their tree," Rix said, glancing upward into the tall canopy. "And unless you want to wake up each morning to piss hitting your tent, I recommend moving."

Andy followed Rix's gaze upward. He was surprised to see three black monkeys hanging from branches seventy feet above and starring down at them.

"Monkeys usually leave at the first sign of humans," Rix said. "But this area is so remote and untouched, I'd be willing to bet these monkeys have never seen humans before."

One of the monkey's pulled a piece of red fruit from the tree and tossed it down at them. Soon they were being pelted with fruit.

Rix said, "And I should mention, the bastards are super territorial."

With fruit raining down on them, Rix helped Andy dismantle his hammock and then find another, more suitable campsite. Within twenty minutes, the two had cleared a ten foot area and restrung the hammock from two trees. Once Rix left—after demanding Andy give him knuckles—Andy gave the hammock a test-drive. The underside was made of thin nylon, and the top consisted of mosquito netting and a rain fly. Andy entered through the zippered seam on the side.

Lying back, Andy couldn't help but think back on Holland's frightening lecture about snakes, scorpions, spiders, jaguars, wild boar, and the plethora of other deadly jungle inhabitants. And here he was, served up like a rotisserie chicken.

"One night," he muttered. "One night."

He slid out of the hammock, deciding he would head back to the main camp and see if he could help out with anything. Or, better yet, now that he was an expert in hammock stringing, he could offer his services. He imagined Farah struggling with her hammock, then him emerging from the brush, walking toward her, confident, self-aware, Rix-like, and asking, *"Do you need some assistance?"*

He laughed at the thought.

Yeah, right.

He started toward the main camp but quickly realized he didn't know which direction the main camp was. He glanced at the three hundred and sixty degrees of green brush and tried to remember which way Rix had departed. He looked for evidence of cut brush, but between the two of them, they'd more or less hacked away at all the surrounding vegetation.

How long had he and Rix walked from his first campsite? One minute? Two? Why hadn't he been more careful when he'd traveled to his second campsite?

But he supposed he'd been with Rix, so he hadn't worried about it.

Andy began to backtrack in the direction he thought he and Rix had approached from, and after a couple of minutes, he recognized the two trees where he'd initially strung his hammock. He found himself letting out a deep breath, one he hadn't even known he was holding.

He drew closer, then stopped. He sniffed. He didn't smell the underlying musk from earlier, and on closer inspection, there were no leaves on the ground, and there was no evidence of the fruit the monkeys had rained down on them.

This wasn't the area he'd cleared.

He turned around. And around. He cocked his head and listened for voices, but all he could hear were the erratic shrieks of the jungle.

His heart began to pound.

He glanced at the orange whistle around his neck, then shook his head.

No.

He'd been in the jungle for less than an hour. There was no way that he was going to blow his whistle and have to be rescued.

No way.

His palms started to sweat, and his entire body started to tingle. The dam was close to bursting. He closed his eyes and did one of his calming exercises: naming characters from *The Simpsons.*

"Homer . . . Bart . . . Lisa . . . Maggie," he said, taking a deep inhale between each name. "Marge . . . Mr. Burns . . . Ned Flanders . . . Smithers . . . Barney . . . Ralph . . . Millhouse . . . Groundskeeper Willie . . . Grandpa Simpson . . . Chief Wiggum . . . Apu . . . Troy McClure . . ."

He named characters for another long minute until his heart rate felt almost back to normal. He opened his eyes, let out a deep exhale, and said, "You're okay. You're going to be okay. You've got this. We'll just retrace our steps back to our campsite, and then we're all good."

He started back in the direction he came. He walked for one minute. Then two. Then three.

Where was his campsite?

He spun in a circle. The slow drip of panic returned, but this time there was nothing he could do to stem its tide. His heart fluttered. His skin prickled. His chest heaved. The wall of green began to close in on him like a giant green fist.

He was on the verge of blacking out, and he fell to his knees. Andy pulled the whistle up from around his neck and with one of his few remaining breaths, he blew.

TWEEEEEE!

TWWEEEEEE!

TWWEEEEEEEE!

13

Lunch consisted of the snacks Vern and I had picked up at the market: dried plantains, Brazil nuts, and *chicharróns* (basically, fried pork rinds). A combination of sweet, salty, and savory. Though to be honest, I'd covered myself with such a thick layer of insect repellent that everything I ate tasted of DEET.

In addition to spraying myself from head to toe with the insect repellent, I'd slapped on a wide gray fisherman's hat and sunglasses to help combat the equatorial sun's intense glare on the water.

Carlos was now manning the outboard, and Juan Pablo was playing some game on his early-model iPhone. Vern made a little bed for himself between the benches and was lying against his backpack, his knees pulled up to his chest and his maroon hat over his face. Camila had found her way over to him, and she was snuggled into his side.

Over the past six hours, the river had widened, narrowed, widened, and narrowed. Presently, it was at its widest: over two hundred feet. We'd lost the last of the tour boats two hours in, and other than an empty canoe tangled in the vegetation of the narrowest stretch of water, we hadn't encountered any signs of human life since.

Carlos kept the boat thirty yards from the shoreline to our right, close enough to hear the howler monkeys above the din of the motor.

Maybe an hour later a canoe came into view. It was long, twenty feet at least, and two natives clad in nothing more than loincloths were standing in it—one at the front, one at the back—both guiding the canoe with long bamboo poles. The men waved as we passed.

Diego said they were from the Yanomina village, not too much farther upriver.

We reached it twenty minutes later. A muddy bank with several canoes and rafts came into view, and a group of twenty-plus natives, mostly women and children, were scattered about. I expected most to be barely clothed, like the men seen earlier, but the kids all had on shorts and T-shirts, and the women wore brightly colored shawls. The women were doing laundry in the river, and the kids were kicking around a ball and laughing.

"The Yanomina," Diego said again. "Their village is not too far from the river."

"How many people live there?"

He considered the question, then said, "Sixty or seventy."

The laundry and game both paused as we passed. The village women stared at us with little regard, but the children waved and jumped up and down. It probably wasn't every day they saw someone on the river, and who knows how long it'd been since they'd seen a white face.

"Do the different tribes interact much?" I asked Diego as the Yanomina faded into the distance.

"Not too often, but every once in a while. Friendly tribes."

This was the second time he used the word "friendly" to describe a tribe, and I asked, "Are there *unfriendly* tribes?"

"Yes. Deeper in the forest. Unfriendly. *Very* unfriendly.

Headhunters. And cannibals." I thought he was kidding about the last part, but the narrowing of his squinty eyes said otherwise.

Diego unzipped one of the aged military rucksacks near his feet and said, "That is why we have these."

Inside the rucksack were three handguns, a Remington 870 shotgun, and two M16 military assault rifles, one with a laser scope.

Diego lifted out a matte-chrome pistol, pulled back the hammer, eliciting a soft click, and asked, "Have you ever shot a gun?"

The pistol was a Glock 22, not much different than the standard-issue Glock 19 that I'd carried for the four years I worked for the Seattle Police Department.

I replied, "No, but I've played a lot of laser tag."

"Laser tag?"

Apparently, one of the big fads of my youth—and shamefully, something I did every Thursday well into my thirties—had yet to make it down to Bolivia. I told him I was joking, then attempted to explain laser tag to him, which I'm not sure he fully grasped.

"This sound like kid game," he said.

"Yeah, that's why I usually win." Unless my nemesis, Lazer Crazer, has his karate class canceled.

"Actually, I have shot a gun," I told him. "I used to be a homicide detective."

Diego was extremely curious about this, and I began regaling him with stories from my past. Twenty minutes later, when I spoke of the cruise ship that was boarded by pirates, he threw his hands up in the air. "Pirates? Like Jack Sparrow?"

I explained to him that pirates like Jack Sparrow don't exist anymore, but these pirates were a thousand times more dangerous. They'd killed the captain and all the officers, and their plan had been to blow up all four hundred passengers and crew aboard the ship.

I reached the part about meeting Gina en route to a small

village in South Africa, and Diego asked, "This is the same Dr. Gina we are looking for now?"

"Yes, it is."

I'm not sure if it was the look on my face, or the strain in my voice, but Diego patted me on the knee.

I waited for Diego to tell me that we would find her, that he was the best tracker in all of Bolivia, that Gina would be okay. But he didn't.

All he said was, "We will get there soon."

≈

An hour later, we left the Orthon River and headed up a smaller tributary. I asked Diego what the name of the river was, and he said he'd heard it called a few different names: Rió Marrón (Brown River); Dedo del Pie del Tío (Uncle's Toe), which Diego wasn't sure of the reasoning behind; and simply Río Tibióno. He also said that three years earlier the water had been so low the river had been unpassable.

It seemed we still had a while to go, so I pulled my Garmin inReach out of my pack. It was a burnt-orange color and weighed half a pound. According to the guy at Alticoop, the lithium battery had one hundred hours of life and would last thirty days in Power Save mode.

I powered it on.

The two-inch square screen illuminated. There were several icons, including Tracking, Routes, Map, Weather, Trip Info, Waypoints, Compass, and Messages.

I'd bought a three month all-access "Expedition" subscription to the Iridium network of sixty-six global satellites, and I would have unlimited access to all of these functions. At least, I would once the phone was activated. I'd been told it would take three days, but ever the optimist, I wanted to check.

There was no signal, so I powered the phone back off and returned it to my pack.

Thirty minutes later, Diego stood up and switched places with Carlos, and I figured we must be getting close. Diego steered the canoe closer to shore, his eyes just small slits as he scanned for whatever familiar landmark he was seeking.

Diego slowed us to a near crawl on several occasions, but each time he would only shake his head lightly and mutter, "No, no, no."

Finally, he jutted his chin out, and pointed toward the shore. Unlike several other areas where the bank was exposed, the water ran to the edge of the trees. "This it," he said. "*Sí, sí.*"

There were no canoes or rafts tied up. No natives washing clothes. This wasn't the off-ramp I was expecting. "Are you sure?"

He pointed at a solitary tree, one that didn't look any different from the millions we'd already passed, and said, "I remember that tree."

Remembering a tree in the Amazon jungle seemed a lot like remembering a grain of sand on the beach, but Diego exuded absolute confidence, and as we drew closer to the shore, it was obvious there was a well-worn path leading away from the water.

Juan Pablo jumped out and grabbed one of the long vines that dangled from *the* tree. Vern, who was awake and had been whittling a piece of wood for the past hour, threw him a rope. Once we were tied up, it took a few minutes to transfer our supplies to shore.

The sun was sinking low in the sky, and I figured we had an hour of light left.

Juan Pablo and Carlos slung on their rucksacks, then each grabbed two gallons of water. I shouldered my pack and grabbed the fifth and final gallon. Vern carried his pack and slung one of the automatic rifles over his shoulder. Diego, in addition to his pack, held Camila.

The path was wide at first but quickly narrowed, the jungle

pushing in from all sides. The first thing to hit me was the smell. It was sweet and freshly washed, but at the same time it smelled musky, almost to the point of decay. It reminded me of the few times I'd been in a greenhouse. And it was noisy: a loud symphony of screams, whistles, snorts, hoots, hollers, squawks, and roars. Most of the orchestra seemed to be hiding in the towering canopy a hundred and fifty feet overhead.

There were several leafy trees growing beneath the canopy, stretching as high as forty or fifty feet—what Gina had once referred to as the "understory." Huge networks of tangled vines clung to the trees, and it wasn't clear whether they were climbing up the trees or down to the earth. The underbrush was diverse: tall grass, thorny bushes, gigantic ferns, thick green moss, blooming flowers (which I suspect were responsible for the sweet aroma), and a spongy white vegetation that I guessed was some sort of fungi. The forest floor was covered in a thin layer of green and brown leaves, exposed tree roots, seeds, scattered fruit, and broken branches.

It was a few degrees cooler under the cover of the canopy, but the air was heavier. And slow. Made of molasses. The jungle air drove Miss Daisy.

I pulled the front of my shirt away from where it was sticking to my chest. A swarm of bugs flitted past my face, one of them flying into my mouth.

I coughed and spit.

Now would probably be a good time to mention that I hate bugs.

For most of my life, it had been a strong annoyance, but after spending a summer in Missouri and dealing with flies the size of small bats and beetles that had personalities, I'd come to detest them.

I stopped everyone so I could apply a second round of DEET, but once we resumed our trek, the insects continued to hum around my face, buzz in my ears, and bite into my delicious white flesh. If I didn't know better, I would think someone had swapped my DEET out for a can of PAM.

As we moved farther into the jungle, the canopy overhead grew into a tight green curtain that blocked nearly all sunlight and produced a dusk-like haze. The underbrush thinned, and we trudged through the relative darkness for fifteen minutes. Finally Diego said, "Tibióno is just up ahead."

Five minutes later, the path widened, and a glow of vanishing sunlight was visible. Slowly the moderate foliage disappeared, and the sights and sounds of a community materialized.

Fifteen thatched huts were spread out in a fifty-meter radius. There was a giant fire pit, some small tables, lantern posts, and one structure I guessed was a commode. There were a handful of villagers visible, all dressed similarly to the Yanomina: lots of T-shirts and tattered shorts. Two chickens pecked their way across the forty feet of open common area.

A girl, no older than five or six, was the first to spot us, and she ran to a nearby hut and disappeared. A moment later, three villagers emerged, two of them holding bowls in their hands.

Looks like we'd interrupted dinner.

Within a short minute, the little girl had dipped her head into nearly every hut and over fifty Tibióno were speaking among themselves and gawking at us warily. A few men, elders I assumed by their heavily wrinkled brown skin, stepped forward. One of them said something, and although it sounded like Spanish to me, from the look on Diego, Carlos, and Juan Pablo's faces, I knew it must have been in their native Tibióno.

Diego said something in Spanish, and I made out the words "Gina" and "*médica*."

A younger man in a black T-shirt stepped forward and began to converse with Diego in Spanish. After a few exchanges, he turned to the assembled villagers and translated. At finding out we were there to help find their beloved doctor who'd lived with them on and off for five years, the villagers rushed forward and welcomed us.

I was trying to keep an eye on Diego—who had passed Camila off to Carlos and was having an animated discussion outside one of the huts with Vern and three villagers—when I felt a poke in my side. I turned and gazed down. It was a boy of about six or seven. He looked like a miniature version of Juan Pablo, with shaggy black hair and skin the color of espresso. He was smiling wide, one of his front teeth missing. He said, "Hey-lo."

"Hello," I said with a laugh.

"Guyd-bah."

"Yes, *goodbye.*"

He beamed, then continued: "Gurl. Boy. Mo-der. Fa-der. Ay-mey-ee-ca. Tree. Feesh. Mon-kay." It took the boy another minute to exhaust all the English words in his vocabulary.

I was imagining Gina sitting with this little boy somewhere in the village, teaching him little bits of English—the thought so bittersweet I didn't know whether to laugh or cry—when I felt a tap on my shoulder.

It was Diego and Vern.

Vern said, "So here's the story. A little over a week ago, at dawn, three soldiers showed up and held the entire village at gunpoint. They said they heard there was a doctor living in their village, and they needed her. But Gina was out running."

I tried unsuccessfully to fight back a smile. I ran to stay in shape; Gina ran because she loved to run.

Vern continued, "When Gina got back from her run, they grabbed her, threatened to hurt one of the boys if she didn't come with them. Then they made her grab a bunch of medical supplies, and they marched her off."

I blew out my cheeks. "He said they were soldiers?"

"Yep."

"So, do we still think they are narcos?"

"Probably. Lots of narcos have soldiers on the payroll."

"Which way did they go?"

Diego pointed what I guessed was east and said, "That way. A few of the villagers followed them, but at some point, the soldiers saw them and shot at the tree right next to them, and they turned around."

"Can they show us?"

"*Sí*, but is getting dark and will be hard to see. We start early *mañana*."

I hadn't noticed in all the excitement that the sky above had turned a dark blue. A half dozen large lanterns were now burning.

Vern said, "The villagers would be honored if we would eat with them, and they have offered us a place to sleep for the night."

≈

Dinner was a thick soup with big hunks of fish and potatoes. It was delicious. The villagers offered water, but Diego said we should drink our own. The Tibiónos' water came from the river, and though it was safe for the villagers to drink (as their systems had adapted to it), it would most likely cause my temperamental gringo digestive system to self-destruct.

After dinner, we were led to two small huts. Carlos, Juan Pablo, Diego, and Camila slept in one hut. Vern and I slept in the other.

Vern pulled a lantern out of his pack and flipped it on. The hut was ten feet wide, with a hammock strung on one side. Next to the hammock was a stack of books. The top book was *The Hunger Games*.

One of her favorites.

"This must have been Gina's hut," I said to Vern.

He nodded toward a picture on the wall and said, "Who is that ugly mug?"

I took two steps toward the wall and squinted at the picture of a man sitting on the toilet, his pants around his ankles and a blue Game Boy in his hands. There was a look of surprise on the man's face, like he'd just been caught with his pants down.

"I had a great game of Tetris going," I said to Vern. "I think I broke my high score. When I got off the toilet an hour later, both of my legs were completely numb."

Vern laughed.

I pulled the photo off the wall. "Gina took this picture. She loved it. It was the screensaver on her phone and her computer." She must have printed it out at some point.

I folded up the picture and put it in my pocket.

Vern pulled off his hiking boots, then flopped into the hammock. "You're on the ground, buddy," he said, then put his hat over his face.

It was warm in the hut, still well into the seventies. I laid on the packed earth and used my extra shirt as a pillow.

Tomorrow we would start the search.

14

If Andy were in a better mood, he might have laughed. Here he was, over four thousand miles from home, in one of the most isolated places in the world, in the middle of the Amazon freaking jungle, and he was about to eat, of all things, macaroni and cheese.

There were several different flavors of Mountain House freeze-dried pouches: Chicken and Dumplings, Lasagna, Beef Stew, Homestyle Turkey Dinner, Sweet and Sour Pork, as well as a few others. But Andy went for an old favorite, the meal he had subsisted on almost entirely when he was living in Los Angeles and which he still ate at least twice a week.

Of course, normally when he ate macaroni and cheese, he was sitting on his couch playing video games; he wasn't standing around a Coleman lantern and listening to Jonathan Roth give a detailed account of the guest list at Reese Witherspoon's wedding.

Though to be honest, unlike the rest of the expedition team, who had formed a semicircle around Roth and appeared to be hanging onto his every word, Andy found himself only half-listening. Even four hours after his rescue, most of his synapses were dedicated to reliving the incident over and over again.

After Andy blew his whistle in a frenzied panic, it was

unimaginable how quickly Rix had come barreling through the brush. Rix had his machete in one hand and a gun in the other. He was prepared to fight off whatever it was that caused a member of the team to blow their whistle this early in the expedition.

But from the look on Rix's face—like he'd bitten into a rotten sunflower seed—what the ex–special forces soldier was not prepared to find was a thirty-two-year-old man on his hands and knees with tears dripping from his eyes.

"What happened?" Rix asked.

In hindsight, Andy should have lied. He could have said a spider the size of a grapefruit jumped onto his shoulder. Or that he saw a jaguar. No, a family of jaguars! Yes, if Andy had access to a time machine, he would go back and say anything else besides, "Oh, uh, I got turned around a little bit, and then I guess I had a little bit of a panic attack."

Andy expected Rix to be sympathetic, that he would tell him to shake it off, tell him that getting lost in the jungle was nothing to be ashamed about. But the easygoing "give me some knuckles" guy who'd helped Andy with his campsite was long gone. Rix shook his head with disgust and said, "You got to jungle up, mate."

Andy assumed *Jungle up* was brother to *Cowboy up* and cousin to *Toughen up* and lived just down the street from *Quit being such a pussy.*

Rix's words were blunt, but Andy had heard far worse from his own father and brothers growing up. It was what followed that would be paying for his therapist's new Lexus.

It turned out that Andy had been just ten meters—yes, *ten* meters—from the main camp when he had blown his whistle. As Andy was pushing himself to his feet, Roth, Buxton, Holland, and Sean—and Sean's video camera—emerged from the brush.

"What happened?" Holland asked.

Andy had cut his eyes at Rix, silently willing him to cover for

him, but Rix told Holland the truth: "He got turned around, and
then he had a bloody panic attack."

Andy was surprised when Roth grinned and said, "Oh, we
have to get this on film. Can you reenact it?"

Andy wasn't sure why he agreed to do it. It would have been so
easy to say no. And had it been any other documentarian, perhaps
Andy would have. But it was *Jonathan Roth*.

So Andy spent the next thirty minutes with the filmmaker
and cameraman, reenacting putting up his hammock and getting
lost and having a panic attack.

"You were crying, right?" Roth asked at one point. "Can you cry?"

In a way, Andy enjoyed it. He was back in LA, and he'd just
landed his second gig. Only this time he was playing himself.

Jungle Weenie #1.

After one take which had Andy spinning around in a circle,
then falling to the ground and crying out, "I'm going to die in
the jungle!"—which hadn't actually happened, but Roth had
instructed Andy to say—Roth clapped his hands together and
said, "I wasn't sure about you when Heliant recommended you,
but I think you're going to end up being a pivotal part of this film."

A soft beeping broke Andy from his reverie. He glanced down
at his watch. It had been eight minutes since he'd added the boiling water to his pouch. The mac and cheese should be ready.

He dipped his spoon into the pouch and took a bite. It wasn't
nearly as good as his Kraft Deluxe, but it was better than he
expected.

"What flavor ya got?"

Andy turned.

It was Darnell. Like Andy, he had a headlamp on his head, the
adjustable light pointing upward at a forty-five-degree angle so as
not to blind anyone. Andy glanced around. It appeared Roth was
no longer holding court and the expedition team had fanned out.

"Macaroni and Cheese," Andy told him.

"You mind?" Darnell asked, tilting his spoon toward Andy's pouch.

Andy didn't like sharing food with family members or even his girlfriends, the few he'd had, but Darnell must have already thought he was a wimp—his fellow cameraman had surely given him a play-by-play of Andy's "reenactments"—and there was no way Andy was going to add *germaphobe* to that list.

Andy forced a small grin and said, "Go for it."

Darnell stuck his spoon into Andy's meal and took a bite. He nodded his approval, then tilted his pouch toward Andy and said, "Give this a whirl. Spaghetti with Meat Sauce."

Before he could overthink it, Andy slid his spoon into Darnell's pouch and took a bite. Andy tried not to think about all of Darnell's microorganisms comingling with his and said, "Tastes like SpaghettiOs." Sadly, these were another staple of Andy's diet.

"Totally!" Darnell replied with a nod of his head.

They stood there in silence for a few moments, and Andy surveyed the small groups which had formed in the past couple of minutes. The academics—Buxton, Cala, and Capobianco—were huddled together and talking animatedly. Then you had the TAFLS duo circled up. And then there were Roth, Libby, and Farah, though Libby appeared to be hovering on the outer edge.

Andy had a mini flashback to his junior year of high school, when his two best (and only) friends started dating. He'd turned third-wheeling into an art form.

"You know," Darnell said, breaking the silence, "I've had my fair share of panic attacks."

"Really?"

"Got my first one sophomore year of college. Ohio State. I was playing football back then. It was our second game of the year. It happened on the bus ride to the stadium. I started hyperventilating, and I got all sweaty, and then I just started to completely lose it."

"What did you do?"

"I kept it together until we got to the stadium, and then I hightailed it to the bathroom and locked myself in a stall. It took me twenty minutes to get my shit together and go to the locker room. Told the coaches I had stomach cramps or something. But I ended up playing. Played good too. Two sacks."

"That's impressive. That you didn't go to the hospital. And the two sacks too."

"Yeah, well, three days later, I had another one. I was in class and the same thing happened, except ten times worse. Thought I was about to die. I ran to the clinic at the school, and the doctor tells me I'm fine. Just a panic attack."

Andy scoffed. He'd heard those words numerous times. *It's just a panic attack.* The only words he heard more often were *It's all in your head.*

"Anyhow," Darnell continued, "she started me on an SSRI."

Selective Serotonin Reuptake Inhibitor. The most commonly prescribed medicine for anxiety.

"Which one?"

"Lexapro."

"I've been on that one." Andy had been on all of them at one time or another: Lexapro, Zoloft, Celexa, Prozac. "It help?"

"It did."

"You go to therapy?"

"Not until later; not until my late twenties. But yeah, therapy helped a lot. Haven't had a panic attack in a few years."

"That's good."

"Anyhow, I just wanted you to know that you aren't alone." Darnell put his hand on Andy's shoulder. "And, just so you know, that footage you shot with Roth—I *accidentally* erased it all."

"Are you serious?" Andy asked with a grin.

"Yeah, fuck that guy."

It was clear Darnell wasn't too keen on Jonathan Roth. Andy was thinking of a way to inquire about the two's history, when there was an earsplitting scream.

Both Andy and Darnell's heads snapped in the direction of the sound. It was coming from the small bivouac area—the temporary shelter—where two portable burners were heating the water for their meals.

Libby stood near one of the burners, a kettle in her hand.

Andy and Darnell ran the twenty feet toward her and joined everyone else.

"Get back!" Holland said, loudly. "Everyone, point your headlamps at him."

At him? Andy thought. Then he saw *him.*

His breath caught.

A fer-de-lance.

The coffee-brown snake had a diamond pattern running along its back, and it was coiled up four feet from where Libby stood. She was apparently frozen with fear, the kettle shaking in her hand.

Andy thought back to what she said at orientation: *No, I'm fine with snakes.*

Clearly not.

Andy—who was not, had not, and never would be okay with snakes—was tempted to move even farther away from the large serpent, but again, after that afternoon's meltdown, he forced himself to stay put. He flipped his headlamp down and trained it on the snake with several of the others' beams.

"I'm going to try to move him," Holland shouted.

Rix brought Holland a bamboo pole with a forked end. In one quick motion, Holland thrust the forked end down on the large snake and pinned it to the soft earth. The snake exploded, striking and squirming. It opened its mouth and Andy could see its inch-long fangs.

Holland moved the stick up the snake's body until he had its neck pinned. Then Holland knelt down and grabbed the snake behind its head. The snake's body, easily the girth of a softball, whipped back and forth.

"Sorry, mate," Holland said. "But you're too bloody aggressive."

Holland pulled a knife from his belt and cut off the snake's head. It's six-foot body continued to thrash, moving several feet from where Holland knelt, until it finally came to rest.

≈

After Holland killed the snake, then tied its head to a tree—which Andy supposed was both a warning to the expedition team to be vigilant as well as a warning to the other snakes that they weren't welcome—the entire expedition gathered around to drink tea.

The close call with the snake got Holland in the storytelling mood, and he regaled all of them with the close calls he'd had during his many excursions. He'd been bitten by three different snakes, nearly losing his left foot to one in the Philippines, and he'd contracted dengue fever twice, the second time almost killing him.

At eight thirty, people began retiring to their hammocks. Andy's heart raced as he waded the ten meters through the brush to his campsite. He breathed a sigh of relief when he reached his camp, only to realize the ground beneath his hammock was teaming with hundreds of large cockroaches.

Andy pulled the zipper of the hammock up, fell back, and tried not to think of all the creepy jungle crawlers just below. He was beyond exhausted from the events of the day, and his eyes began to flutter.

Then he heard the snapping of branches and his eyes shot open.

He heard a soft growl.

Something was out there. Something outside his hammock.

His body began to shake.

"Jungle up," he whispered. "Jungle up."

15

We woke up early, ate a small breakfast supplied by the villagers, thanked them profusely for their hospitality, then set out at first light. We followed three villagers through the jungle for over an hour until we came to a tree with a series of holes in the trunk.

Bullet holes.

This was as far as the villagers followed Gina and the soldiers. Now they wanted to continue with us, but Diego convinced them to go back. I thought they could help, as this was *their* jungle, but maybe it was one of those too-many-chefs-in-the-kitchen scenarios, or, more precisely, too many trackers in the jungle. The villagers reluctantly turned back, but not before relaying through Diego that they would pray for our protection and for Dr. Gina's safe return.

At the front of the pack, I saw Diego slicing the eighteen-inch blade of his machete down through the heavy brush. Vern was behind Diego with his own machete, cutting away any branches that had survived Diego's onslaught, leaving an open trail for me and my six-pound furry necklace.

It was too dangerous for Diego to carry Camila while wielding the large knife, plus he was constantly kneeling and sifting through the underbrush looking for disturbed vegetation. Both

Carlos and Juan Pablo were maxed out with the addition of Diego's pack plus the now four gallons of water, so the chore of carrying the angelic little creature fell to me.

Currently, Camila was wrapped around my neck, and I could feel the light exhalation through her nose on my skin.

"They go through here," Diego yelled, his machete making a loud thwack as it cut down through the thick foliage.

While living in Maine and recuperating from multiple gunshot wounds, I taught an intro-level criminology class at the local university. One of the first things I taught was Locard's exchange principle, which holds that when there is contact between two things, there will be an exchange. In forensics, this meant in the act of a crime, a perpetrator will take traces of the crime with them as well as leaving traces of their presence behind. This holds true in any environment, even in the rainforest.

Some signs of an exchange between Gina's abductors and the jungle were obvious: tunneled vegetation, severed branches on the ground, boot impressions in the soft earth, bent branches, trampled underbrush. Conversely, there would be stretches of jungle which looked immaculately undisturbed. At least to the untrained eye.

Thankfully, Diego was one crackerjack of a jungle detective.

Many of the things Diego pointed out were undetectable to me. We would reach a section of jungle that looked pristine, but then Diego would point ahead and say, "See how those leaves up there are lighter than the ones around them? That is the underside of the leaf. The branches were twisted as the group moved past."

The most impressive display of his skills came when we ran into a small stream. The water was less than six inches deep and crystal clear. There were footprints in the muddy bank on the near side of the stream, but Diego couldn't find any evidence of where the group had exited on the far side. He suspected they'd walked up the stream for a distance, which is one of the fastest ways to travel through a dense jungle. Diego disappeared up the river, then a few minutes later came back for us. We walked two hundred yards up the river to a small log near the opposite bank. Moss was growing on top of the log and Diego pointed out the faintest of smears through the middle of it.

"Someone step on this log," he said.

I had my doubts, but fifteen feet into the thick foliage, we found a series of felled branches and trampled brush.

Now, Camila and I stepped through the path Diego and Vern had cut, which led to a small opening in the underbrush, most likely caused by a fallen tree.

"Let's grab a bite," Vern said, throwing his pack to the ground and plopping down on the two-foot-thick fallen palm.

Lunch was crackers, canned sardines, more Brazil nuts, *chicharróns*, and plantains. I was worried this would be the extent of my diet for the remainder of the trip, but Vern promised we had plenty of "dinner" provisions we would cook when we made camp for the night.

After handing over Camila to Diego—she whined and reached out for him, much like baby Clark did when my sister returned home—I sidled up next to Vern and tossed back three of the small salted fish. Vern offered me the large bag of cooked bananas, but I waved him off.

I was woefully constipated, my lower abdomen a glorified concrete mixer, and I had a feeling the plantains were the culprit.

"Those have me all plugged up," I told Vern. I was as regular as they come, but it had been a full day since my last *número dos*.

Vern laughed and said, "I've been there." He waved the bag at me a second time and said, "Still, in this heat, you need the potassium."

As far as the heat goes, the temperature was in the low nineties, and combined with a humidity in the high sixties, it was as oppressive as Mississippi in the 1950s. My shirt was soaked through, I could feel droplets of sweat drip down my legs, and my gray sun hat was damp to the point where it looked like freshly poured asphalt.

And it was just so sticky.

On Vern's advice, I popped back three plantains, savoring their sweetness, then drank a good twenty ounces of water from one of the gallon jugs we'd refilled in one of the many small streams. Vern said the water was safe to drink, but I added a water purification tablet just in case.

The five of us passed around the gallon jug until it was empty, then Diego handed Camila back to me, and we resumed our trek.

The forest was teeming with activity. In addition to the millions of swarming mosquitoes, flies, and other insects, there were several species of bees; impossibly beautiful butterflies; neon-green dragonflies; enormous moths; black and brown bats hanging upside down and sleeping; a large yellow python resting in the branches of a tree; a furry tarantula scurrying under a rock; tiny white-chested spider monkeys; monkeys with orange fur; birds of every shape, color, and size; a capybara (a giant rodent that can weigh up to a hundred pounds) sunning on the bank of a shallow river; a six-foot caiman with smooth black scales; and even a tapir—an odd-looking animal right out of a Dr. Seuss book—which looks like the offspring of a pig and an anteater.

After another hour, the jungle opened up, which Diego explained was because the canopy was so thick that nothing could grow. It was as dark as a movie theater during previews, and there were channels of soft earth, sometimes as wide as ten feet, between the vegetation. The only greenery on the forest floor was the moss that grew on the veiny network of exposed tree roots. We kept a good pace, probably covering as much ground in that hour as we had in the previous three.

There were a few times when Diego lost the trail—as there were no felled or twisted branches to go by—but without fail, he would always find some trace of the abductors' passage, at which point he would whistle and say, "*Sí, sí.* This way."

After walking nearly unobstructed for several miles, the jungle lightened, and the underbrush came back with a vengeance. Even with Diego and Vern hacking away at the path Gina's abductors had already hacked, branches and vines whipped and scraped against my flesh. I imagine it was like trying to wiggle your way to the front row of a Beatles concert, only instead of the flailing elbows and piercing screams of crazed coeds, you had to keep your eyes out for snakes, spiders, and, by far the worst, black palm.

The black palm tree looks similar to a regular palm tree, only its trunk is covered in five-inch brittle spikes. The trees were spread throughout the dense vegetation, sometimes in pairs, but mostly as solitary landmines.

"Ah," I groaned, a five-inch spike digging into my shoulder.

I shut my eyes against the agony and counted to ten, at which point I knew the excruciating, nauseating pain would begin to subside. When I opened my eyes, which were now watering, Camila's face was less than an inch from mine. Her hypnotic brown eyes examined me; her ever-present grin softened in concern.

"I'm okay," I assured her, gritting out a smile against the pain.

Her grin slowly returned, and she reached out with her triple claws and softy raked the side of my head.

I should mention that I was considering calling off the search for Gina and running off to live in the jungle with Camila for the rest of my life.

"That damn black palm get ya?" Vern shouted from right in front of me.

"Sure did," I said, giving my shoulder a rub. "Feels like I just got a tetanus shot." Which, oddly enough, I was long overdue for.

"Got me good a few times too. Stuff is a bitch."

Outside of the limited information Gina had told me about the jungle, everything I knew was from watching the TV show *Naked and Afraid*. It was a reality show where a camera crew followed one man and one woman (usually hard-core survivalists) who were trying to survive for twenty-one days in some of the most inhospitable places on earth. As if that weren't challenging enough, they did it *naked*. Some of the episodes took place in the mountains, or even the desert, but the vast majority were set in the jungle. They'd shot episodes in the jungles of Colombia, Nicaragua, the Philippines, Costa Rica, Mexico, and Belize—even one in Bolivia. The jungle appeared daunting onscreen, but until you are in the thick of it, it's hard to describe just how ruthless it is.

I asked, "Was the jungle in Vietnam this thick?"

Vern stopped and turned around. "Just about. But imagine trying to get through this shit without giving away your position to the Viet Cong."

I hadn't thought about that. I hoped we weren't giving our position away to Gina's abductors as we massacred our way through the dense foliage.

As if on cue, Diego's loud whistle filled the silence.

Vern and I hurried to catch up to him. We pushed through a barrage of branches and thick vines, then almost fell into twenty square feet of open earth.

Diego was standing in front of a pile of white ash. Across from the ash was what looked like a quickly assembled lean-to.

This had been someone's camp.

16

"*Agua,*" Gina said. "*Necesito agua.*"

The soldier in front of her turned his head slightly but said nothing.

Usually after her four-mile run, Gina would drink a liter of water and eat a banana to rehydrate, but she'd never had the chance. The soldiers had forced her to pack up all her medical equipment, then with a gun sticking into her back, they'd marched her into the jungle. They hadn't even let her change out of her shorts and T-shirt.

That had been six hours earlier.

Gina stopped. She turned to the soldier behind her and said, "*Necesito agua.*"

He shook his head. "*¡Vámonos!*"

"If I don't get water soon, I'm going to get sick," she said to the soldier in Spanish. Over the past twenty minutes, Gina had developed a throbbing headache and rapid breath, and despite the brutal heat and humidity, she'd stopped sweating. She was on the verge of heatstroke. "And if I'm sick, then I'm not going to be able to help whoever needs it."

The soldiers hadn't told her anything except that someone in their camp was hurt. She guessed it must be someone important to their operation. Whether that operation was drug trafficking, illegal mining, illegal logging, or something else, she wasn't sure. There was no short list of unlawful activities taking place in the jungles of northern Bolivia. But whoever was hurt, Gina was certain it must be someone important.

The boss.

El jefe.

"*¡Alto!*" the soldier shouted, and the two others in the front stopped and turned around.

A canteen was eventually passed to Gina, and she took a few small sips. She didn't want to overwhelm her system. After a minute, when the water didn't nauseate her, she drank heartily.

One of the soldiers (the one who spoke passable English) handed her a bag of large brown nuts—Brazil nuts, which, oddly enough, Bolivia, not Brazil, was the largest exporter of.

Could they be in the nut business?

Even legal businesses in Bolivia often kept soldiers on the payroll to protect their inventory. But if it was a legal operation, they would most likely have tried to help the sick person more diplomatically. Three soldiers storming into a village and kidnapping a doctor with the threat of violence didn't sing legitimacy.

Gina ate a large handful of nuts and drank a bit more water. Her breathing slowly returned to normal, and five minutes later she nodded that she was ready to continue.

They hiked for another two hours. Gina estimated that over the course of eight hours they'd averaged a little more than a mile an hour. That put her anywhere from eight to ten miles from the village—a search grid of close to a hundred square miles. Of course, that was assuming anyone from the village was looking for her. And after the soldiers sent a wave of warning shots at Yuli, Roberto, and Pilar, who'd followed them early on, she hardly expected them to be. Nor did she want them to be. The Tibióno were a peaceful people. There was almost no confrontation in the village, and even more seldom, physical altercation. The men were expert hunters, able to take down a boar with a bow from a hundred feet away, but they were no match for soldiers with guns.

Gina had to assume the worst.

She was on her own.

≈

They continued to push through the jungle, the soldier up front consulting a GPS every so often. After another quick stop for water and nuts, during which the lead soldier consulted with the other two about their heading, they continued. The baking heat of the jungle lessened. After living in the Amazon off and on for five years, Gina could tell what time it was just by the feel of the air, by the chirping of the birds, and by the hum of the insects. She guessed it was nearing 5:00 p.m.

They pushed through a heavy section of brush, a thick branch whipping through Gina's brown hair, which was still in a ponytail from her run, and suddenly Gina heard voices. They grew louder, and then a camp appeared. There was a fourth and fifth soldier sitting under a bamboo lean-to, then two white men sitting around a small fire.

The two Caucasian men stood as they approached. Both appeared to be in their fifties, and both were dressed in matching khaki from head to toe. The taller man had dark hair and olive skin. He was clean shaven with lightly pockmarked cheeks and a large, but well-formed, Roman nose. The second man was portly, with tinted glasses and a comb-over of mostly gray hair. The armpits of his khaki button-down were stained with sweat. The pair didn't so much look like drug traffickers as they did the *lawyers* of drug traffickers.

"Took you long enough," said the dark-haired man.

"The village was farther than I thought," the English-speaking soldier answered. "But we found her."

Found her?

Had they been looking for a doctor, or had they been looking for Dr. Gina Brady *specifically?*

It was common knowledge among the neighboring villages, and even most of Riberalta, that there was a doctor living among the Tibióno. At least once a week, a villager from one of the other tribes—usually the Yanomina, who were in the next closest village—would come to her village seeking treatment.

The dark-haired man turned his gaze to Gina and asked, "You're a doctor?"

"Yes."

"Thank you for coming."

"I wasn't given much of a choice."

He let that go, asking, "Where are your medical supplies?"

One of the soldiers picked up a large duffel bag they'd filled with nearly every medication and medical instrument Gina had in her hut and shook it.

"Please, come with me," the dark-haired man said, waving her forward.

Gina followed him through fifty feet of heavy brush to where three blue tents were set up. The man lifted the flap on one of the tents, and Gina peeked inside. A lantern in the far corner of the tent illuminated an aging Caucasian man lying on his back, his chest slowly rising and falling. There was dried blood surrounding a swollen gash behind his left ear, and his face was badly bruised.

"Two days ago, he fell and hit his head," the man explained. "He's been unconscious ever since."

Gina opened the duffel and extracted a pair of purple surgical gloves and a small penlight. She crawled forward and gently pushed open the man's right eyelid and shined the light on his pupil. It was large and hardly contracted. He had a concussion at best and a subdural hematoma at worst.

Gina checked the gash behind the man's left ear. The cut was an inch and a half long and a quarter inch wide. It would need ten stitches or more. She palpated the wound. It was angry and almost certainly infected. Open wounds were never good, but an open wound in the jungle was especially dangerous. The warm, humid climate of the rainforest was a glorified incubator for bacteria. The Amazon was home to hundreds of known bacterial strains and millions—some even theorized billions—of strains not yet identified.

Next, Gina checked the man's vitals. His blood pressure was low, and he had a temperature of 101.4.

From behind her, the man said, "It's imperative that you keep this man alive."

Gina turned and said, "I'll do everything I can."

She was pretty sure she could stem the infection, but there was little she could do for the internal head injury.

The man blinked twice and by doing so, appeared to summon something. Something dark. Something sinister.

"I hope so," he said, "because if he dies, *you* die."

≈

"Help!" Gina yelled.

The man, whom Gina had come to think of as El Jefe, thrashed on the floor of the tent. This was the man's second seizure in as many days.

The previous night, Gina had connected the man to an IV drip, then injected him with a powerful antibiotic and anti-inflammatory. It had taken Gina over an hour to clean the wound on the man's head, then stitch him up.

Benecio, the same soldier who had guarded her tent the previous night, ducked into the tent, and Gina shouted, "Help me roll him onto his side!"

Together they leaned the man up onto his side—which helped to keep his airway clear—as his body convulsed. After twenty more seconds, the man's limbs relaxed. Gina kept him on his side for another minute before slowly rolling him onto his back.

The IV had come out during the seizure, and Gina fitted the needle back into the catheter she'd set in the man's left forearm.

Benecio asked if he could go, and Gina nodded.

She pulled another IV drip bag from her supplies and switched out the empty one. She'd already gone through three in two days, and there were only four remaining. She filled a syringe with the last of her gabapentin, an antiseizure medication, and injected it into the IV port. Gina had been planning a trip to the pharmacy in Riberalta in the coming weeks to stock up on supplies before the rainy season, but at the time of her abduction, her personal pharmacy had been heavily depleted.

Gina heard the flap on the tent open.

It was the dark-haired man, whom Gina had overheard someone call Patrick. He was kneeling at the tent door and asked, "When will he be ready to move?"

"Move?" she exclaimed. "He just had a grand mal seizure!"

"Don't you have antiseizure meds you can give him?"

"I just gave him the last of what I have."

Patrick bit his bottom lip, something Gina had noticed him doing when he was deep in thought, then said, "We've constructed a gurney from some bamboo. It's sturdy enough to hold him. We've already lost too much time. We're moving out tomorrow."

Gina wanted to say, "And if he has a seizure while they're carrying him and falls and breaks his neck, what then?"

But she knew the answer.

Patrick had been very clear about that.

≈

El Jefe had another seizure that night, but by the time they loaded him onto the gurney the next morning, he'd gone the longest he had in three days without convulsing.

Also, his temperature had dropped. Gina was fairly certain he would survive. If she hadn't been there to administer an IV and antibiotics, most likely that wouldn't have been the case. As for when he would come out of his coma, it could be minutes, it could be months, or it could be never.

"Okay," Patrick said. "Let's head out."

"I have to go to the bathroom first," Gina said.

The nine of them—Patrick, his spectacled associate, the five soldiers, and Gina, plus El Jefe on the gurney—were situated in the smaller camp with the lean-to and fire pit.

"Fine." He waved her to the jungle. "Guillermo," he said, pointing at the tall soldier whose wrist Gina nearly broke at the village. "Make sure she doesn't try anything."

Gina pushed twenty meters into the jungle, making sure to stay as close to the path they'd forged as possible, and squatted. Guillermo seemed only too happy to watch Gina relieve herself.

"Do you mind?" she shouted in Spanish.

He smiled but didn't take his eyes off her.

There was no way she could leave it here without him noticing. She finished, stood, then headed back to camp. As she neared the long-dead ashes of the fire they'd built to cook dinner the previous evening, Gina's foot caught on a small exposed root in the ground.

She fell chest first into the ash, her hands underneath her body and slightly bracing her fall. With a slight groan, Gina pulled her hands out of the ash and pushed herself up.

"You okay?" Benecio asked in Spanish.

Gina dusted off the front of her shirt and tried to hide her embarrassment. "I'm fine," she told him.

She glanced up and saw that Patrick was staring at her. Gina held her breath, exhaling only after he nodded at his feet where the bamboo gurney was holding his boss and said, "Pick him up. Let's move."

17

"Someone made camp here," Diego said, knocking his hand against the bamboo lean-to, then inspecting it more closely. He squatted near it, shook one of the bamboo supports, then ran one of his hands through his buzzed black hair.

I'd been in enough interrogation rooms and sat through enough body language seminars to know this wasn't a good sign.

"What's the problem?" I asked Diego.

"The lean-to . . . and the fire . . . It looks Yanomina."

Although we hadn't encountered any other villages or villagers outside of the Tibióno, according to Diego there were several other tribes who lived in the jungle. They were constantly hunting for food, and sometimes they traveled wide distances.

I asked, "You think this is a Yanomina camp?"

Diego scratched his head once more and said, "*Sí, sí*. I think so."

Vern said, "So we've been following a bunch of Yanomina this whole time?"

Diego nodded.

Vern let out a sigh, then looked at me. "Sorry, Thomas."

I was trying to comprehend what this all meant, when Diego summed it up for me: "We must go back."

"Go back?" I asked. "Go back where?"

"To the village."

I blinked my eyes several times, trying to fight back my rising frustration. "You're telling me that we have to backtrack the ten miles we just walked?"

We had been hiking for eight hours. We only had four hours left of light. That means we wouldn't even make it back to the village until 10:00 a.m. tomorrow at the earliest. Then who's to say we would find the right trail the next time?

"*Sí, sí,*" Diego responded.

Camila was startled, either by the rise in my voice, or the acceleration of my heartbeat, and she leaned back from where she was hanging around my neck. I covered her little sloth ears with my hands and shouted, "Ffffuuuuuuuuuck!"

A moment later, I pulled my earmuffs off Camila. She had a somber look on her face—like I'd just broken the news to her that she was adopted—and I handed her off to Diego.

"Thomas," Vern said.

I closed my eyes. "Just give me a minute here."

I knew getting upset wasn't going to help find Gina any sooner. I took three calming breaths, then snapped my eyes back open.

Zen.

"Take a look at this," Vern said, waving me over to the fire. He had spread the ashes out with his foot, and he was kneeling down, holding something in his hand.

It was thin, eight inches long, purple on one side and white on the other. It must have been white side up in the ashes, camouflaging it perfectly, which I suspect was no accident.

"What do you think?" Vern asked.

The purple side was worn down from many miles of running,

but you could still make out the A and the second S of Gina's beloved running-shoe brand.

It was the insole of her shoe.

"It's hers," I said, smile-laughing. "It's definitely hers."

18

The day started at 5:30 a.m. with the waking of the howler monkeys. Andy slid from his hammock, grateful to see the nighttime creepy crawlers had scattered. There was a dense layer of morning mist, and it took Andy several minutes to feel his way to the main camp. Several others were already awake, including Farah, who was wearing her backpack and tapping her foot while she ate.

Andy ate a pouch of freeze-dried scrambled eggs for breakfast. Buxton was standing nearby, and the two compared notes on their first night in the jungle. Both agreed they would be relieved to sleep in tents that evening.

Andy was waiting for a second pouch of scrambled eggs to heat when Roth, Libby, Holland, and Rix made their way to the tent.

Farah asked when Holland thought they might head out to the closest ruins, and he said, "Hopefully, not long after the first round of supplies arrive."

Supposedly, emergency first aid kits for each of them would be among the initial round of supplies, and Holland refused to let anyone leave base camp without one.

"And when exactly is the helicopter supposed to be here?" Farah prodded.

"Once this fog clears, they'll take off. Should be within the next two hours."

But it wasn't.

Though it was dry season, a storm moved in, drenching the camp for most of the early morning.

Finally, around noon the storm let up, and an hour later the helicopter landed. It took the eleven of them thirty minutes to carry the first load of supplies—tents, chairs, folding tables, snacks (two dozen jars of Nutella, huge stacks of tortillas, thirty bags of beef jerky, plus a large assortment of energy bars), ten cases of bottled water, portable generators, toilet paper, portable stoves, and emergency first aid kits—to base camp. Once they'd emptied the helicopter, it took off, hoping to make another round trip before the threatening clouds to the east blew in.

Andy grabbed one of the tents, then spent the next thirty minutes widening his campsite, setting up his tent, and hanging a clothesline. He changed into a nearly identical pair of khaki pants and a light-blue North Face long-sleeve shirt and hung his rain-dampened clothes to dry.

When he returned to the main camp, two large canopy tents—ten feet by ten feet and made from collapsible aluminum frames and a heavy white tarp—had been assembled. Several tables and chairs filled each of them.

Nathan Buxton and Jonathan Roth sat across from each other in two of the chairs, and the author was scribbling notes in a journal. From what Andy could overhear, it sounded like Buxton was doing deep background on the documentarian: where he grew up, his parents, high school, when he got into film.

"Let's go already," Farah demanded several times.

But it would be yet another two hours.

At 3:00 p.m. Holland rounded up everyone and said he and Rix would be leading a team to the ruins in thirty minutes.

Nearly *fifty-five* minutes later, Farah shouted, "This is crazy! T2 is just on the other side of the stream. Why do we need a freaking chaperone?"

Andy, Farah, Buxton, and the two Bolivians were standing at the bank of a small stream. It was fifteen feet across. On the other side was a muddy embankment that led into thick brush. According to the lidar scans, the closest of the six major archaeological sites—T2, or Target 2—was less than six hundred meters away.

Farah shook the Trimble GPS in her hand and said, "Why can't we just go? It's not like we're going to get lost."

"I read that GPS is pretty unreliable in the jungle," said Andy.

Several variables caused this, but the two biggest factors were the thickness of the canopy and the position of the satellite in space. That's why Holland had ordered each of them to carry a real compass.

"Oh, you read that, did you?" Farah said.

Before Andy could decipher whether Farah was being playful or snarky, there was the sound of approaching footsteps. Roth, Holland, Rix, Sean, and Darnell were striding toward them. Sean was holding the large video camera and Darnell was carrying a large pack—the portable audio mixer/recorder—and a six-foot boom mike with attached windshield.

"Finally!" Farah cried.

After Holland checked their backpacks to make sure they had emergency overnight supplies should they get separated, he handed out walkie-talkies. "I've got them set to channel six," he said.

Andy took the yellow walkie-talkie and clipped it to the left shoulder strap of his backpack.

Next, Holland went down the line and clipped a carabiner to each of their backpacks. Attached to each was an orange plastic fob, two inches square.

"These are GPS beacons," Holland said. "Do not, under any

circumstances, take them off your backpack. And do not, under any circumstances, take off your backpack."

Holland glanced over at Rix, who was holding a rugged military-issue iPad. "How are we looking? Do we have a signal?"

Rix turned the tablet toward Holland, revealing eight blinking red dots. "For now we do."

"Roger that." Holland turned back to the group. "All right, let's move out."

Holland was the first to cross the stream. It was only a foot deep, but the embankment on the opposite side was slippery with mud. It took the ten of them—Libby was staying behind to continue setting up the main camp—several minutes to make their way up the sloping incline.

Holland and Rix pulled out their machetes and began hacking through the wall of green. Andy couldn't see more than a dozen feet in any direction.

They passed through a second muddy channel, after which the terrain sharply rose, forcing them to pull themselves up with nearby branches and vines. Cala, who was in the worst shape of anyone, needed help from Rix to get up the steep slope.

Once the embankment flattened out, Roth—who along with Cala, Holland, and Farah, was holding a Trimble GPS that had been linked to the lidar scans—said, "The edge of T2 should be just up ahead."

Andy knew it had been imperative for the ancient civilization to build its city on an elevation above the floodplain. Had they not, each rainy season they would have been inundated by the rising waters of the nearby rivers.

A minute later, Roth, who was wearing a straw cowboy hat and had a red bandanna tied around his neck, glanced down at the LED screen of his GPS and said, "This is it. This is the edge of the city."

According to the lidar scans, they had just crossed into a large plaza that was surrounded on three sides by geometric mounds and terraces. From the scans, one could presume that, centuries earlier, the area had been an ancient settlement filled with houses, plazas, and temples, not to mention hundreds, or even thousands, of inhabitants. But on the ground, it was impossible to tell. The area didn't look any different from the quarter mile of jungle they'd just trudged through. It was the same pandemonium of leaves, vines, trees, ferns, bushes, and more leaves.

The ancient ruins were entirely obscured by the jungle.

"Okay," Holland said, glancing down at his watch. "It's sixteen fifteen. We're leaving here at seventeen hundred sharp. That's forty-five minutes. Everyone stay within thirty meters of here."

The group fanned out.

"Call over the walkies if you find anything," Roth said.

≈

It'd been nearly half an hour, and so far, the walkie-talkies had remained quiet. It appeared everyone was having the same luck as Andy. But there were still fifteen minutes left. Plenty of time for Andy to be the first to discover solid proof of an ancient civilization. Plenty of time for him to be the one to hit the black button on the side of the yellow walkie-talkie and shout, "I found something! I found something!" and have everyone come running and have his discovery caught on film.

Andy pushed aside a large grouping of vines with his gloved hand. He was looking for anything that appeared even remotely artificial, anything that could have been shaped by human hands. At the same time, he was keeping a watchful eye out for anything slithering on the ground, spinning a web, or looking to drag him back to its lair.

He noticed an odd linear depression in the ground. He knelt down, brushed aside several pockets of fallen leaves, and pulled a five-inch hand trowel from his backpack. He spent the next minute digging down six inches, but all he revealed was the large earthworm he'd murdered when digging down.

The canopy overhead shook, and Andy glanced upward. A moment later, several leaves and a small branch fell near Andy's feet.

"*The storm is blowing in faster than I expected,*" Holland's voice came through the walkie-talkie. "*Everybody get back here now.*"

Covering his head from the onslaught of any more falling debris, Andy wound his way back the twenty meters he'd ventured to where the others had gathered.

"Find anything?" Buxton asked.

Andy shook his head. "Nope."

"Yeah, us neither."

Over the next minute, Roth, the camera crew, and Cala returned. Buxton asked each of them if they'd found anything.

Cala nodded at Roth and said, "We located one of the earthen mounds from the lidar. Dug down a bit. Pretty sure it's natural. Nothing about it suggested it had been shaped by human hands."

"Where's Farah?" Holland asked.

Everyone shook their heads.

Holland pulled his walkie-talkie from his belt and said, "Farah? Farah, you read?"

He waited five seconds for a reply.

None came.

"Rix?" Holland said into the walkie. "Where are you at?"

"*Headed your way. ETA: one minute.*"

"You with Farah?"

"*Negative.*"

"Check her location on the iPad."

A moment later, Rix said, "*Says that she's three meters behind you.*"

Holland glanced over his shoulder and squinted. Andy followed his gaze to a backpack tucked under a large fern.

"Bloody hell," Holland said. "She took off her backpack."

"I'll find her," Roth said.

"No, we're heading back," Holland said, glancing upward. "We have ten minutes before this storm hits. And those rivers can rise fast. I don't want to mess with them." Into the walkie, he shouted: "Farah! Get back here! Storm is coming!"

There was no response.

"You guys head back," said Rix. *"I'll find her."*

"Roger that." Holland turned and said, "We're moving out. Everybody on me."

The storm started exactly ten minutes later. It took another few minutes for the rain to work its way down through the canopy, but by the time they reached the river, it had already broadened by several feet.

"I'll set up ropes tomorrow," Holland said, standing in the middle of the stream and waving Jonathan Roth past. "So it will be easier to cross."

Andy and Buxton watched hesitantly as Darnell and Sean made their way down the muddy embankment and across the river. Their equipment was waterproof, but that didn't stop both from hustling toward the base camp shelter in the distance.

Cala slid down the embankment on his backside, then fell sideways into the stream. Holland helped him to his feet, and Andy was relieved to see the large Bolivian was smiling ear-to-ear.

Before his own descent, Andy glanced over his shoulder, looking for Rix and Farah, but he didn't see either.

"Let's go!" Holland called over the now pouring rain.

There was a flash of lightning and a crash of thunder.

Andy slid down the muddy embankment and hightailed it through the stream.

Just as Andy reached the shelter, his walkie-talkie crackled. *"I've got her,"* said Rix. *"We're headed back now."*

≈

Andy would describe the mood in the tent as despondent. Sure, they'd only spent forty minutes at the ruins, but everyone had expected to find evidence corroborating what showed up on the lidar scans.

Instead, they found nothing.

Roth was furious, stomping around the tent like a petulant child. Andy couldn't blame him. Roth had most likely spent hundreds of thousands of dollars funding the expedition. To not find a single ruin must have been devastating.

Still, they had ten more days.

Andy glanced up from where he was pouring himself a cup of tea and commiserating with his fellow team members to see Farah and Rix striding toward the tent. Like Andy, both were soaked in rain, their boots and pants covered in mud. Holland jumped up from his seat and met Farah as she ducked under the blue tarp.

"Don't you dare pull that shit again!" Holland shouted, his face and neck glowing red under the tent's bright halogens. "You put the whole group at risk by pulling a stunt like that."

"I had a GPS," Farah fired back.

"I don't give a shit. You do something like that again and you're gone. Done." He took a breath. "Say you understand."

She sighed and said, "I understand."

Holland strode from the tent, still huffing and shaking his head.

Farah turned and glanced at the others. Even though she'd just been yelled at by the principal, she was fighting back a grin.

Roth was the one to ask the question they were all thinking: "What did you find?"

"Foundation stones," she said. "From a temple."

19

Three hours earlier, after finding the insole of Gina's shoe hidden in the ashes of the fire, we had continued fifty feet farther into the jungle and found a larger camp. Three tents had been set up and hidden in the bramble of a nearby bush was another of Gina's breadcrumbs: an empty IV saline bag.

From what we learned from the villagers and the logistics of the camp—the lean-to, plus the three tents—my working theory was that after a day's travel, Gina and her three abductors met up with at least three additional individuals waiting for them at the camp, one of whom was injured. It was impossible to say how long they stayed there, but I would guess a day, maybe two. While tending to her patient, Gina found an opportunity to stash one of the empty saline bags in the nearby brush. But this would be easy to miss, and she'd ingeniously slipped the insole out of her left running shoe and hidden it in the ash of the fire.

I wondered if she had me on her mind when she did this, but from the limited timeline I could piece together, I would guess not. The satellite phone call she made to me wasn't until four days after she was abducted. It was possible Gina and her abductors could have stayed in this camp for that length of time, but my gut told me otherwise. Still, she may have already seen the satellite phone and was coming up with a plan to steal it and contact me. That said, it made more sense that the insole was left for the Tibióno villagers who'd followed them at the onset and who would be familiar with the running shoes she wore nearly every morning.

After spending half an hour surveying the camp, Diego tracked the group eastward. With the expansion of Gina's group from the initial four—Gina, plus the three soldiers—to my theorized seven or more, they left a heavier imprint as they moved through the jungle, and tracking their movements became an easier task for Diego. After two hours and with daylight quickly slipping away, we found a reasonably open area to make camp for the night.

I was the only one who pitched a tent, the other four opting to string up hammocks in the nearby trees. It would be cooler in the open-air hammocks—I was assured the jungle would remain sticky and warm throughout the night—but I didn't trust the netting affixed to the hammocks to keep the swarms of insects at bay. I wanted a wall between me and them—preferably one made of brick, but nylon would have to suffice.

If I haven't mentioned it already, *I hate bugs.*

The five of us were standing and eating near the fire. Juan Pablo had cooked a stew which consisted of rice, yucca, corn, some sort of brown bean, and several different chilies.

I dug my spoon into it and took a large bite. The food came with a kick from the chilies, and by my third bite my forehead was sweating. I was a wimp when it came to spicy food, but I had high hopes the heat would get my bowels moving—they'd been on strike for nearly two full days.

Come on, colon.

Once they finished their meals, the three Bolivians headed to their hammocks, leaving Vern and me by the fire. I pulled the Garmin inReach out of my pocket and powered it on.

I let out a discouraging sigh, and Vern asked, "Still not working?"

Over the course of the day, I'd checked to see if it had been activated at least twenty times.

I shook my head. "It's been over three days. I'm not sure what's going on."

"Hopefully tomorrow," Vern said, rubbing his hand over his right knee.

I recognized the gentle massage and the grimace on his face and asked, "Bum knee?"

"You could say that."

"Me too." I extended my left leg several times. My knee felt surprisingly good after nearly a full day of hiking.

"What'd you do to yours?" Vern asked.

"Just your run-of-the-mill ballooning escapade gone wrong." I spent the next few minutes recounting what had happened almost exactly two years earlier when I had plunged four thousand feet in a hot-air balloon.

"Not bad, but I think I have you beat."

"Okay," I laughed, thinking I'd set the bar pretty high.

"Back before I met my wife," he started, "I was dating a Colombian woman. Her father was one of the top lieutenants in one of the cartels. One day, Maria tells me her dad needs a favor. I figured he wanted me to drive him somewhere, which I'd done once in the past, but this was a much bigger ask. He wanted me to deliver a bunch of coke to some Nicaraguan.

"I was young, trying to impress this guy's daughter, and if I wanted to get in the game for real, this was my chance. He hands me a small duffel bag with fifteen kilos of coke and gives me a pistol."

"Fifteen kilos?" I asked. A kilo of cocaine had a street value of roughly $25,000, which means the duffel was worth close to $400,000. Granted, it would be sold to the Nicaraguan for much less.

"Yep, fifteen," Vern said, nodding. "Anyhow, I drive to Cartagena and into this sketchy part of town and find this rundown shit of a restaurant with boards all over the windows. I almost didn't go in, but I knew if I backed out, Maria would hightail it, and who knows what her pops would do to me.

"So I get out of the car, walk in, and—surprise, surprise—there are two guys instead of one. One of the guys was holding a bag of money, and I told him to show it to me. From the look on his face, I knew something wasn't right. He starts walking toward me, and I tell him, 'Stop. Open the bag. Show me the money, asshole.'

"That's when I saw the second guy reach for his gun. I pulled mine a half second faster than him and sent a bullet into his throat, and I hit the guy with the bag in the chest. Somehow, both of them got off a shot, and I took one in the knee. I finished the bag guy off, then grabbed the money. The whole thing took like three seconds."

"Holy shit," I said. "Then what did you do?"

"I snorted a couple lines, packed cocaine into the bullet wound, and hightailed it out of there."

I clapped him on the shoulder and said, "You win. You . . . *win.*"

≈

"How are you getting inside?" I muttered to myself.

There were bugs everywhere. Mosquitoes, chiggers, bugs I didn't even know the names of. They were eating me alive.

I grabbed a can of DEET and sprayed myself until I was sick from the fumes, then I turned on my headlamp and crawled to the front of the tent. I checked the zipper for the umpteenth time. It was securely fastened all the way down.

"How?" I shouted.

I slapped at a mosquito on my arm, but I narrowly missed

him. I was still wearing the same pants, but I'd changed into a T-shirt to sleep in—though after getting bitten by several different bugs, I was considering putting my long-sleeve shirt back on.

I slapped at another mosquito on my arm, this time leaving a trail of blood.

"You see that!" I yelled at the other thirty-four mosquitoes in my tent, who were clearly immune to the effects of insect repellent. "You see what happens when you mess with Tommy P!"

I laid back down on top of my sleeping bag and wondered if I was destined to sleep for a single minute before the sun rose. The bugs; the heat; the whistles, croaks, and shrieks of the nocturnal creatures; and my bloated and cramping stomach were making for a miserable first night in the jungle.

Unable to sleep, I pulled the blue Game Boy from my pack and turned it on. I hadn't played on it for over two years, not since downloading the app on my phone, but I'd brought it just in case I couldn't sleep. I started a new game of Tetris and had just hit Level 6 when it happened.

Movement.

In my bowels.

I waited a few seconds to make certain it wasn't a false alarm, but sure enough, things were happening. I grabbed my headlamp and turned it on. Then I put on my boots and slipped out of the tent.

My headlamp lit up a ten-foot circle in front of me, and I picked my way through the brush for thirty feet, which I figured was an acceptable distance from camp to relieve myself.

I found a few feet of open earth, and I popped a squat.

And—nothing.

"Come on!" I huffed.

After another minute of no action, I pulled the Game Boy out of my pocket and resumed my game. This was my normal routine, so I figured that after a few minutes my body would catch on.

Level 6.

Level 7.

Level 8.

My legs were starting to cramp, but I figured I would give it a few more minutes.

Level 9.

Lev—I lifted my eyebrows.

"We have lift off!" I told the jungle.

Oddly enough, the jungle replied with a soft snort.

I leaned forward and squinted at the bush across from me. Illuminated by my headlamp and staring at me with deadly intent was what I'm pretty sure was a wild boar.

Diego had warned us to keep a look out for boars—especially at night, as they were mostly nocturnal. They could do a good bit of damage to you with their tusks. The large scar on Carlos's neck—which I had assumed had come from someone's knife, like most of those I'd seen as a member of law enforcement—was actually from a boar attack when he was a child. He'd been lucky to survive.

"Nice boar," I said, putting up my hand. "Nice *friendly* boar."

The beast whipped its snout back and forth, its three-inch tusks glistening in the light from my headlamp.

"Okay, Pumbaa," I said softly. "Nothing to be alarmed about."

I was trying to figure out what to do. Should I pull up my pants and start running? Should I try to be as still as possible? Was I supposed to get big and yell? Or was that for a bear?

I set the Game Boy down and found a small rock. I chucked it at the boar and said, "Get out of here!"

The rock missed and only seemed to agitate Pumbaa more.

He snorted several times.

I quickly looked for another rock but couldn't find one. My eyes fell on the Game Boy. I picked it up and said, "Sorry, old friend."

I threw the Game Boy at Pumbaa. It hit him in the middle of the forehead. He stood there stunned for a second, then he kicked up dirt.

All I'd done was break my Game Boy and piss off the boar even more.

He whipped his head back and forth. I flexed both my hands; ready to throw down if it came to it.

Pumbaa shot forward.

I readied myself for the fight of my life, but Pumbaa zoomed four feet to my left, crashing through the underbrush. I twisted, waiting for him to come up from behind me, but it appeared he was gone for good.

Hakuna matata.

My heart was racing as I stood and began pulling my pants up. When straightening, my head smacked against the low branch of a nearby tree. Bits of dirt and leaves fell from the branch onto my head. But what I'd thought were bits of dirt and leaves were in actuality an army of red ants.

I was covered in them—covered in quarter-inch-long red ants with trisegmented bodies and razor-sharp pinchers.

I dropped my pants and began frantically wiping at the ants. I felt a sharp pain as the first one bit me on the neck. It felt like someone had touched a match to my skin.

I continued swiping, but the bites kept coming. Head, neck, face, arms. I felt a bite on my leg. They were in my pants. A bite on my ass. Then, a moment later, it happened. Like someone had touched a hot poker to my left testicle.

I screamed loud enough that I woke a troop of monkeys nearby and sent them into a frenzy.

A flashlight bobbed toward me, and a terrified Diego asked, "What's going on?"

"Ants!"

"You have to take all your clothes off," he instructed. "Or they will just keep biting you."

I didn't hesitate, pulling off my shirt and throwing it to the ground, then kicking off my boots, pants, and boxer briefs, until I was completely naked.

Diego swatted away at the ants with a large palm frond until, after a long minute, I was finally clear.

20

A quick but angry storm had blown in during the middle of the night, and Andy had awakened to heavy drops splattering against his tent. The storm only lasted a short five minutes, but it unloaded enough rain to raise the river by nearly eight inches.

The previous day, after listening to Farah's recounting of the temple she'd found, it had been agreed the expedition team would head back to the ruins at the break of dawn.

Andy's alarm had awoken him at 6:15 a.m., and he'd been the last to arrive at the main camp. Everyone else was already there and most had already eaten. Andy had wolfed down two tortillas slathered with copious amounts of Nutella and slugged back a cup of coffee. Now, minutes later, he was standing at the edge of the river.

The sun had been awake for close to ten minutes, but little of its light found its way to the forest floor. If not for the headlamp on Andy's head, it would have been nearly impossible for him to see the ropes that Holland and Rix had set up.

Andy reached out and grasped the thick paracord. He held tightly to it as he shimmied through the now foot-and-a-half-deep water.

The water swept swiftly just below Andy's knees as he took the final few steps through the river. He released the paracord, then grasped Rix's outstretched hand. Rix pulled him out of the water and onto the muddy embankment. The bank was slippery, and Andy pulled himself up the slope with the help of small trees rooted in the soft earth.

The others were waiting at the top of the embankment. Nathan Buxton and Alejándro Cala helped Andy up the last few feet. Like Andy, everyone wore a headlamp, and together they illuminated a five-meter swatch of jungle.

"I'm going," Farah said loudly.

"Just wait another minute," Roth said. "We almost have everyone."

Andy glanced back over his shoulder and watched the Roth's production assistant, Libby, maneuver her way through the water. Holland waited until she had successfully crossed, then he traversed the river in four quick jumps and scampered up the muddy incline like it was a mall escalator.

"Alright," Holland said. "Let's rock and roll."

The hike took a bit longer than it had the previous day because of the muddy conditions. At one point, Bernita Capobianco, the Bolivian anthropologist, fell into a small sinkhole. It took both Rix and Holland to pull her out of the thick mud.

By 7:00 a.m., there was enough light sifting through the canopy that their headlamps were no longer needed. Andy flipped his headlamp off, and seconds later, Roth said, "Alright, coming up on the edge of the city."

It might have been the different lighting, but as Andy glanced around, he didn't find anything in the surrounding jungle that looked the least bit familiar. He couldn't believe they were on the same trail they'd traversed fifteen hours earlier.

A moment later, they stopped.

Andy recognized a large tree covered in thick climbing vines and the group of ferns where a day earlier Farah had stashed her backpack. On that note, so far Farah had been well behaved. It appeared, at least for the time being, that Holland's threat to send her packing if she went AWOL a second time had tamped down her rogue spirit.

Roth consulted his GPS, but evidently it had dropped its signal. After checking to make sure no one else had a signal, Roth asked Farah, "Do you think you can navigate to the temple ruins from here?"

"I think so." Farah pulled a compass out of her pocket. "Should be one hundred and forty-two degrees southeast for about eighty or ninety meters."

"Okay, we're going to have Farah lead the way," Holland said. "Rix and I will slash through anything that needs slashing. The rest of you stay five meters back."

Holland and Rix pulled out their bright-pink machetes. Holland nodded at Farah and said, "Lead on."

The expedition team slowly trudged through the dense foliage in single file. Andy ended up at the rear, with Darnell a few feet in front of him.

Darnell had the large camera balanced on his equally large shoulder and was whistling a tune. Andy listened for a minute, then said, "'Sittin' on the Dock of the Bay'?"

Darnell stopped and turned. "Not even close."

"Darn."

"I'll give you two more guesses. Loser sleeps outside tonight."

Andy shook his head and said, "There's not enough money in the world."

"Really? Not for a hundred thousand dollars?"

"No way."

"Come on now. You're telling me you wouldn't sleep on the ground for one night for a *hundred grand*?"

With $100,000 Andy could pay off all his student loans and still have enough money to upgrade his fourteen-year-old Camry.

Darnell turned back around. Andy hustled forward to catch up and said, "I'd do it for five hundred thousand."

The back of Darnell's head shook back and forth as he said, "Andrew, Andrew, Andrew."

It had been years since someone called him Andrew—not since his uncle visited him in Chicago. The memory brought a smile to Andy's face. "Why, how much would *you* do it for?"

Darnell made a few clicks out of the side of his mouth, something Andy had overheard him do a few times before, then said, "I'm being serious here, I'd do it for five hundred dollars."

"You're on."

Darnell stopped and turned. "You know when you tell a brother that it's on, then *it's on*."

Andy did *not* know this.

"Good, because it *is* on," Andy said.

"If I sleep outside tonight, you're going to give me five hundred dollars?"

"Yes."

"Don't back out."

"I won't."

"I want cash."

"Venmo."

"Deal."

Darnell stuck out his hand, and Andy shook it.

≈

Holland, Rix, and Farah were ten meters in front of Andy, who was at the rear of the group. Still, Andy heard Farah shout, "Here! This is it!"

Fifteen seconds later, Andy joined the others at what appeared to be a small hill, but what according to the lidar scans was actually an earthen mound ninety feet square and twenty feet tall. The mound didn't look any different than the surrounding jungle: it was covered in small trees, thorny bushes, climbing vines, leafy ferns, and thousands of fallen leaves.

Roth turned to Libby, Sean, and Darnell and snapped, "Well, what are you waiting for?"

"Darnell," said Libby, "I want you between those two trees, shooting upward. Sean, I want you at the precipice. I want framed reactions from everyone as they get up there."

Andy was surprised. He had thought Libby was simply Roth's production assistant, responsible for the countless minutiae that went into filming a documentary, but evidently, she was the DP. The DP, or director of photography—sometimes called the cinematographer—is in charge of a film's lighting and most of its artistic and technical decisions.

Darnell moved to where Libby had instructed and pulled a collapsible tripod out of his large pack. Libby checked the lighting with a digital light meter, and once Darnell had the camera situated on the tripod, he made a couple of minor adjustments. Libby then clambered up the thirty-degree slope and disappeared. Thirty seconds later, she reappeared and said, "Let's roll."

Roth and Farah glanced at each other and then started up the incline. When those two were halfway up, Alejándro and Bernita started their ascent. The final pair to go were Buxton and Andy.

Andy was four feet up the incline when he overheard Roth shout, "Look at these stones! Jackpot, baby!"

The next reaction was from Cala, who cried out, "*¡Maravilloso!*"

Bernita's reaction came a moment later. She said calmly, "What an incredible discovery."

Andy reached the summit a few moments later. The top

plateaued out for thirty square feet. There were several—twenty at least—large foundation stones spread in a loose rectangle. The stones were heavily eroded and covered in a thick layer of green moss and strewn with vines.

Next to Andy, Nathan Buxton said, "If that isn't the ruins of an ancient temple, I don't know what is."

Several of the expedition team laughed.

Andy could instinctively feel Sean's camera zoomed in on his face, waiting for his reaction.

In hindsight, Andy was never sure why he said the exact phrase he did. Obviously, the camera had played a large part in it, recording his reaction for all eternity. But it hadn't been planned or contrived. It wasn't like Andy had tried to come up with something funny or smart or clever as he made his way up the slope; it had just come out.

As had the Italian accent.

On seeing the ruins of the ancient temple, Assistant Professor of Anthropology Andy Depree smiled and said, *"Now that's a spicy meatball!"*

≈

"You're not mentally challenged, are you?" Darnell said. "Because my answer is going to change if you're mentally challenged."

Andy said, "To my knowledge, I am not mentally challenged."

"Okay, good. I just wanted to make sure."

After spending several minutes at the top of the temple ruins—one of those minutes so awkward Andy thought he might snap in half—Andy descended the earthen pyramid and took up a spot next to Darnell.

"And if I'm not mistaken," Darnell said, "you are a college professor?"

"That's correct."

"An anthropology professor, to be exact?"

"Again, correct."

"And as a professor of anthropology, you would supposedly know more than your average person about an ancient temple?"

"One would think."

"Okay, so you get to the top of that hill, see these ancient ruins, and then— Remind me what you said again."

Andy cleared his throat. "Now that's a spicy meatball."

"Like that. You said it like that?"

"No, I said it with an Italian accent—*Now that's a spicy meatball.*"

"And judging by the paleness of your skin and your orange hair, I'm going to go out on a limb and say you aren't Italian."

"I am not."

"Hmmm," Darnell said, touching a finger to the bottom of his chin. "Then, to answer your question, yes, that is the stupidest thing I've ever heard someone say."

Andy dropped his head and looked down at his muddy boots and snake gaiters.

It was bad enough he'd cast himself as Jungle Weenie within the first few hours of the expedition. But now he'd cast himself as Jungle Idiot within the first five minutes of finding actual ruins.

Andy said, "Do you think I could get fired over this?"

"Like from the expedition? Or like from your job as a professor?" Darnell didn't wait for a reply. "Because that helicopter isn't coming back for another nine days, so I think you're stuck here. As for your real job, yes, I think you'll be fired." He quickly clapped Andy on the shoulder and said, "I'm just kidding."

"No, seriously. My boss—well, the head of the anthropology department—was supposed to be the one who came here. He's the one who recommended me. When he sees the footage, or when Roth calls him when this is all over, I'm sure he's not going to want me affiliated with the department."

"If that's the case, then why are you smiling?"

"I'm not smiling."

"Yes, you are."

Andy waited a second, then looked straight into Darnell's brown eyes. "I love anthropology, but I hate *teaching*. I hate it so much."

Andy had never told anybody this. Not his parents, not his siblings, not a single friend.

Darnell let out a loud laugh, then said, "I bet that felt good!"

"You know what, it did."

"Let it out."

Andy twirled around. He was about to repeat his statement, to tell the surrounding jungle just how much he hated teaching, when he noticed something on the ground. He squinted at the tangle of vegetation behind where he and Darnell were standing. The top of a gray stone was partially visible among the throng of leaves.

Darnell asked, "What?"

Andy took three steps forward, then fell to his knees. He brushed a barrage of damp leaves aside, revealing that the stone was larger than it first appeared.

"Bring that camera over," Andy called to Darnell.

Andy pulled the small trowel from the side of his backpack and began digging around the stone.

"Okay," Darnell said, pointing the camera down at him, "what have you got?"

Andy ignored him. He continued excavating until he uncovered a rectangular stone a foot and a half wide and three feet long.

Andy dug down around the edges of the stone, revealing it to be only six inches thick. Beneath the flat stone, Andy uncovered the beginnings of a white quartz boulder.

Even if the flat rectangular stone weren't in such close proximity to the ancient temple, Andy still would have recognized it for what it was. But as it sat at the foot of the temple, it made the discovery even more astounding.

Andy snapped the yellow walkie-talkie off the strap of his backpack and held down the black button on the side. There was a soft chirp, then Andy shouted, "You guys are going to want to see this!"

A moment later, Roth's voice came over the speaker. "*What is it? What did you find?*"

"An altar," Andy said, trying to breathe evenly. "A *sacrificial* altar."

21

"Well, look who decided to put some clothes on," Vern said, his thick gray mustache hovering above a devious grin.

He was standing near a small fire with Juan Pablo and Carlos. All three of them were holding small collapsible cups. Even from ten feet away, I could smell the wafting aroma of coffee.

I scoffed lightly at his ribbing, and then I pointed at the cup in his hand and said, "Please tell me there's more where that came from."

Juan Pablo leaned down and picked up a small kettle from where it sat a foot from the fire. He magically popped a three-inch blue disk into a small cup and filled it with coffee.

I took the cup, but before I could take a sip, I heard a squeak behind me. It took me a few seconds to locate the responsible party. She was eight feet up a tree, hanging with three of her four limbs from a large branch. The baby sloth gazed lazily in my direction and made another little squeak.

Even though I was especially grumpy, I said, "Good morning, Camila." Then, turning to Vern, I asked, "Where's Diego?"

"Not sure," Vern said. "He took off into the jungle a few minutes ago."

I nodded.

"How are you feeling?" Vern asked, reaching out and touching my shoulder. "Does your testicle hurt?"

I took a sip of coffee and then said, "If by hurt, you mean, does it feel like someone put it in a walnut cracker and then lit it on fire, then yes, it does hurt."

"Is it swollen?"

"It is extremely swollen, thank you for asking."

Vern started chuckling uncontrollably, a Gatling gun of laughter. It was almost worth going through something so terrible if it could bring someone else so much joy.

Almost.

Mercifully, Diego emerged from the jungle, and I wasn't forced to answer any more of Vern's inquiries.

One of Diego's hands was full of leaves, and Vern asked, "What have you got there, chief?"

"Matico." He nodded at me and said, "For his bites."

Diego pulled a small mortar and pestle from his pack and began grinding the leaves into a paste.

I knew from my many years dealing with Lacy's multiple sclerosis that the Amazon jungle was the world's largest pharmacy. Two of Lacy's seven medications and nearly 25 percent of all Western pharmaceuticals were derived from rainforest materials. But the kicker was, only 1 percent of all rainforest materials had been researched. It was mind boggling to think of how many different possible cures and treatments were living, breathing, and dying around us this instant.

Diego explained that the leaves of the Matico plant had pain-relieving and anti-inflammatory properties. Most people boiled the leaves in tea to relieve body aches and coughs, but it also worked as a topical paste, and it should help relieve the intense itching and burning of my bites.

Once Diego was finished, he waved me over and began daubing the paste—a gooey light green—on my many ant bites. I was tempted to tell him I could do it myself, but he was intent on doing it for me. That said, he did let me apply it to my *testículo* myself.

There was a bit leftover at the end, and Vern took it and rubbed it into his knee.

Ten minutes later, my bites and testicle feeling surprisingly better, I pulled the Garmin inReach from my pack and turned it on.

My eyes opened wide, and I said, "I have service."

≈

"How's the signal?" Vern asked.

"Three out of four bars," I said with a grin.

I quickly opened up the messenger app and texted Lacy.

> Hey Lace . . . Phone just
> activated . . . Any word from Gina?

I sent the message, imagining it sneaking through the tall canopy, shooting upward twenty thousand miles to low earth orbit, bouncing off who knows how many of the sixty-six Iridium satellites, then shooting down to France. I wasn't sure how long I should expect to wait for a response, and while I waited, I checked the weather on the phone.

It was currently seventy-nine degrees with 63 percent humidity, which aligned with how muggy it felt.

I was checking out several more of the phone's functions when a message came in.

> Tommy!! I've been trying to text you
> for two days. Was starting to get

worried. No word from Gina. But
Mike Gallow called yesterday with
some good news. He was able to
track down the owner and last-known
coordinates of the phone Gina called
you on. I had him text the details.
I'll copy and paste his message and
send it to you.

I glanced up and said to both Vern and Diego, "My contact was able to get the coordinates of the sat phone that Gina called me on."

Diego gave me a thumbs up, and Vern's eyebrows raised slightly under his maroon cap.

A moment later, another message came in. It was a copy-and-pasted text from Mike Gallow.

Hey, Prescott. Here's what I found.
The sat-phone number is from the
GlobalSat network. Registered to
a J. Gonzales. Paid for a yearlong
subscription with a prepaid Visa.
Dead end. Only two calls were made.
First call was August 3rd, 2:03 p.m.
Just outside a town in Brazil called
Rio Branco. Call lasted six minutes.
The receiving number was a Bolivian
area code. I called that number.
No answer. Didn't have much
cooperation from Entel (Bolivian cell
company) trying to track down the
owner. Second call was to you on
August 9th at 7:03 p.m. Lasted 17

seconds. Coordinates registered are:
-10.402809, -66.481275. Phone hasn't
had an active signal since. Good luck.
You owe me one.

Yeah, I did.

A big one.

Vern was standing near my left shoulder, and he pulled out his own GPS and said, "Read those coordinates out to me."

I did.

Vern plotted them with his GPS, then turned the device toward me. There was a route going from our current location to the location where Gina's call had originated.

It was 8.3 miles away.

≈

With Diego not having to constantly stop to search for evidence of Gina and her abductors' trail, we made better time, covering the 8.3 miles in under six hours.

We approached cautiously as we neared the exact coordinates. Vern grabbed one of the automatic rifles, and I grabbed the shotgun.

Vern pushed aside a large branch, then stopped. He asked, "Do you smell that?"

I did. It was like sitting in an overly chlorinated hot tub ten feet from a Conoco station. "Yeah," I said. "What is it?"

"Chemicals. I'm guessing there's a drug lab up ahead. Probably where Gina's call came from."

I raced forward, gun out in front of me, and crashed through five feet of thick brush. The jungle opened up slightly, and there was what amounted to a ten-foot-square above-ground pool made from thick plastic sheeting. Surrounding the jungle "pool" were five multicolored plastic drums, and thirty feet beyond them was a small structure constructed of bamboo poles and a sagging gray tarp.

"Looks abandoned," Vern said, sidling up next to me.

I nodded.

Gina had been here seven days ago on August 9, but she was gone now.

Vern and I padded twenty feet forward to the rectangular pool. The black plastic sheeting was elevated using tree stumps, small boulders, and several small bamboo poles. The sheeting angled downward, and there was a thin brown layer of film on top. Pockets of brown water had collected across its surface.

"It's a coca tank," Vern said.

I nodded at the large drums and said, "Those the chemicals we smell?"

He nodded and said, "Chlorine, gasoline, sulfuric acid, and ammonia."

I had a rudimentary knowledge of cocaine from my time as a police officer, but most of my insights had to do with the powdered form that found its way to the street. I asked, "So how do they make it?"

Vern spent the next minute giving me a crash course on how to make cocaine in the jungle.

He said, "First you start with the leaf of the coca plant. I'd be willing to bet within half a mile of here there's a decent amount of coca being grown. Judging by the size of this tank, I'd say between four to six acres.

"After they harvest the leaves and bring them here—I'm not sure exactly why they picked this spot; there's probably a river somewhere nearby where they could float in all the chemicals— they dump the leaves into the vat, then soak them in chlorine and gasoline. The cocaine separates from the leaves and rises to the top of the tank. They skim the top, pour it into those large drums, and add sulfuric acid and ammonia. The cocaine separates further, then they filter this through a cloth. What's left, the residue, is heated, and it crystallizes into a solid cocaine base. The process takes three or four days."

I asked, "Then they make it into a powder?"

"Not here. That takes a hydraulic press. There's probably a spot within a day's travel from here where they have a more permanent hub set up to do the final processing, and then they ship it out across the border."

I tried to put this all in the context of Gina. She'd been here a week ago, but for how long? Did she and her captors come here, spend three or four days making the cocaine base, then leave? Did they head to this processing center that Vern theorized was close by? Did we just miss them, or had they been gone for several days already?

"What are you thinking?" Vern asked.

"I'm trying to figure out where Gina fits into all this. Did they come here to make the drugs? To steal drugs? To take the drugs somewhere else?"

"Yeah, I wish I had an answer for you."

"Can you tell how long it's been since they made the cocaine here?"

"I might be able to make a guess." Vern stepped over the wall of plastic and into the coca tank.

"Thomas!"

I turned.

It was Diego. He and Carlos were inspecting the structure behind the tank. Juan Pablo stood outside the structure, holding Camila.

"Come see!" Diego said, waving his hand.

Vern stepped out of the tank, and the two of us made our way to the small hut. On the ground surrounding the hut were empty water bottles, cans of orange Fanta, and hundreds of cigarette butts.

Inside the hut was a makeshift table made of two pieces of plywood lying on top of three plastic drums. Centering the table was an ivory paste, which I guessed was a batch of cocaine base that had been softened by the jungle moisture.

But that wasn't why Diego called me over.

There was blood spatter covering half of the table, two of the plastic drums, and a large portion of the tarp roof.

"That's a lot of blood," Vern said from behind me.

I was following the blood spatter down the table and onto the far-right blue drum when something on the ground caught my eye. Two yellow leaves were right next to the drum, yet both somehow escaped the blood spatter. I kicked the leaves aside with my boot and squinted at the object hidden beneath. It was almost completely submerged in the soft earth. I leaned down and wiggled it out of the ground, then I dusted it off against my chest. The screen was cracked, and it was covered in a few droplets of dried blood.

I turned the phone over and read the brand name on the back. *GlobalSat.*

22

"One sixty-two over one eleven," Gina said, loosening the cuff on Bill's arm. "That's pretty high." The reading put him in stage 2 hypertension. If his blood pressure got much higher, he could be at immediate risk of a stroke or a heart attack.

Bill—that's what her patient had told her his name was, anyway—grimaced and said, "Yeah, that is."

"Do you take medication for high blood pressure?"

"I've been on a few different ACE inhibitors over the years."

An angiotensin-converting enzyme (ACE) inhibitor relaxes blood vessels and decreases blood pressure. It is usually one of the first lines of defense against hypertension.

"You don't have any with you?"

He shook his head. "I stopped taking them a couple months back. They were making me too tired."

"Better to be a little tired than a little dead."

He huffed out a laugh.

When Bill had first started complaining of light-headedness, Gina thought he was probably dehydrated from the ten hours they'd hiked in the intense heat. Nearly his entire shirt was soaked through with sweat, and every few minutes he would need to take off his tinted glasses and wipe them free of the fog that had formed.

Thankfully, not long after Bill's first stumbles, the jungle had opened slightly, and they had come across a raised black plastic tank and a small bamboo structure with a gray tarp. Gina overheard one of the soldiers say the words "*laboratorio de drogas.*" *Drug lab.*

Gina had assumed her abductors were narcotraffickers, but now she was certain.

They'd set up camp at the far end of the clearing, fifty meters from the tank. Gina had been changing the dressings on El Jefe's head wound when one of the soldiers summoned her to come to Patrick and Bill's tent and to bring her medical kit.

When Gina ducked inside the large tent, she found Patrick's associate alone. He was sprawled out and looking flushed.

After giving Bill a thorough examination, it appeared the man's symptoms stemmed from something more than a little dehydration. No, the man, whom Gina guessed to be in his midfifties, was simply in horrific shape. He was thirty pounds overweight, and he had the cardiovascular amplitude of a man whose idea of exercise was walking to the mailbox.

Gina said, "I would advise you to take it easy, but I don't think that's an option."

"I'll power through," Bill said. "You wouldn't think it to look at me now, but I was in pretty good shape at one point in my life."

Gina raised her eyebrows.

"I used to bike a lot. Even thought about doing this two-hundred-mile race once."

"What happened? Why didn't you do it?" Gina was trying to extract as much information out of him as possible. In the three days she'd been traveling with the men, she'd gathered little more than the fact neither Patrick nor Bill spoke a lick of Spanish.

"Too much training," Bill said. "It would have been too much time off work."

"Got to bill those hours."

Bill chuckled.

Gina was set to probe a little further, to ask him where the bike race was located, when she saw it. There was a backpack lying on its side, and one of the zippers was open. Gina squinted, hardly able to believe what she was seeing. Poking out through a small opening was the half-inch long nub of an antenna.

A satellite phone.

"Let me listen to your lungs again," Gina said, pulling the stethoscope from around her neck and putting it in her ears.

Bill nodded, and Gina placed the chest piece against the front of his shirt. "Take a deep breath," Gina instructed, though she was hardly listening.

After two breaths, she moved behind him. The backpack was four feet away. She pressed the chest piece to his back with one hand, and stretching backward with her opposite hand, she fumbled for the phone. Her fingers scraped at the half-inch antenna on her first try, and she said, "Okay, two more big breaths."

Holding the chest piece with the tips of her fingers and stretching back with her hand until it felt like the tendons in her fingers would snap, she was able to get two fingers around the small antenna.

"One more big breath," she said, sliding the phone toward her body and slipping it into the waistband of her shorts.

"Your lungs sound good," Gina said, moving around to his front. "Have someone come get me if you start having chest pains." She gave him a friendly pat on the shoulder and said, "And try to get some sleep."

"Sure thing, doc," he said with a glimmer of a smile.

Gina ducked out of the tent, holding her shirt in place with one hand to make sure it didn't ride up on her back and expose the top of the phone. The soldier who'd summoned her from her tent was hovering near the entrance and escorted her back to her tent at the edge of the brush. Gina noticed that the other four soldiers were gathering wood for a fire. Patrick was nowhere to be seen.

El Jefe was lying on his back, the last of the seven saline bags hanging from the collapsible IV stand. The man had spent the last two days on a gurney being carried by two soldiers (who switched out every half an hour), and his face and arms were covered in a light film of dirt. If he didn't wake up in the next day and a half, Gina feared that without any more saline bags, his kidneys would begin to shut down.

Gina pulled the phone from her waist. She had no idea how long it would be until Bill or Patrick realized the phone was missing. The phone was a newer model of the same brand the WHO had used, and Gina powered it on.

It'd been a year since Gina had last made a telephone call, and it had been two years since she'd had a cellphone, but she had one number memorized.

She edged to one of the mesh windows and glanced out. The window was at a severe angle, but Gina could see four soldiers sitting around a now blazing fire. She assumed the fifth soldier was sitting outside her tent. Fortunately, he wasn't the one who spoke English, so even if he overheard Gina speaking, he would think she was talking to her patient, which she'd done plenty of over the past three days.

Gina hunkered at the far back of the tent and pushed in the ten digits. She put the phone to her ear, but the call failed. She checked the connection.

No signal.

Although satellite phones could theoretically work anywhere

on the planet, they needed a direct line of sight to space, and Gina knew the thick jungle canopy could interfere with the signal.

She waited a few minutes, then tried again.

Again, the call failed.

"Dammit," she whispered, gritting her teeth.

She heard a noise and glanced out the mesh window.

Patrick was strolling back into camp from wherever he'd been. He would most likely go check on Bill, and then he would see the backpack and the missing phone and connect the dots.

Gina had to act now.

After she'd cleaned the wound on El Jefe's head, the soldiers had confiscated her two scalpels and anything else sharp enough to be used as a weapon. Gina whipped her head around, looking for anything with an edge she could use. She grabbed her medical bag and sifted through the contents. She found nothing. Then she saw the stethoscope and blood pressure cuff she'd tossed aside after returning from checking on Bill.

Her eyes widened.

At the bottom of the ear tubes was a four-inch piece of slim metal that created the tension between the two sides.

The binaural spring.

In her residency, Gina had been replacing the spring on a stethoscope—it snapped around the ear tubes on both sides—when she'd cut her finger. The circular metal snaps had surprisingly sharp corners.

Gina snapped the binaural spring off and touched the edge with her thumb. It would do the trick. Gina crawled to the back panel of the tent and pressed the corner into the nylon. It took a couple of tries, but finally she made a small tear. It was louder than Gina would have liked, but under the noise of the jungle, she doubted anyone would hear. The job would have taken twenty seconds with a good knife, but it took close to five minutes with the edge of the metal spring, making half-inch, sometimes quarter-inch, tears in the nylon. When she had finally cut a fifteen-by-fifteen-inch flap at the bottom of the panel, she wriggled through.

It was dusk, and Gina army-crawled through the relative darkness to the nearby brush. She was mostly hidden by her tent, but there would be a few seconds where she would be exposed. She didn't dare look back over her shoulder as she closed the distance to the brush. Four feet. Two feet. She slipped through a tangled thicket of vines, crawled for several more feet, then pushed herself up.

She'd made it.

The dim light was fading fast, making it difficult to navigate through the vegetation. Gina pulled the phone out of her pocket and turned it on. It didn't have an LCD screen like a cellphone, but it did have a two-inch screen that lit up, offering just enough light to see in front of her.

After she'd gone another hundred feet, she checked the phone's signal.

Still nothing.

"Damn."

She needed to get out from under the thick canopy. The only open area was where the small hut was located.

It took Gina ten minutes to work her way through the forest. As she drew closer to the drug lab, she could smell the wafting aroma of chemicals. At the edge of the brush, she glanced back at the four tents and the small fire fifty feet away. It was now pitch dark and the whipping flames of the fire were too far away to illuminate her as she dipped under the sagging tarp roof and into the hut.

She glanced down at the phone.

There was a signal.

She made her way to the far back corner of the hut, where there were two pieces of plywood arranged on top of several large plastic drums. A six-inch chunk of flaky ivory paste centered the table.

Drugs.

Gina hit the call button, the phone automatically calling the last number she'd dialed. Even with a strong signal, she was nervous the tarp would interfere with the connection. Thankfully, it didn't, and the phone began to ring. It rang once, twice, three times, then his voice came on:

"*In the current telephone system, voicemail offenses like robocalls, things that should have been sent as a text message, and long drawn-out messages—I'm talking to you, Lacy—are considered especially heinous.*"

"Come on, you moron," Gina whispered, shaking her head.

"*In Thomas Prescott City, the dedicated detective who investigates these vicious voicemails is a member of an elite squad known as the Special Voicemail Unit, or SVU.*"

How had she fallen in love with this idiot?

"*These are my stories. Dun-dun.*"

"Thomas!" she shouted louder than she intended. "I don't have much time! Four days ago, a group of men came to my village and abducted me. They said they needed a doctor. I think they are narcotraff—"

There was a rustle just outside the structure.

Someone was coming.

"Oh, shit, here they come!" she whispered. "Please find me, Thomas! Please!"

She ended the call and pressed the phone against the front of her shirt to hide any residual light from the call screen, then she ducked under the table and found a spot between two of the plastic drums.

A moment later, the tarp crinkled as someone brushed up against it. Then footsteps.

Gina brought her knees up to her chest and sucked in a breath.

There was a flicker of light from a lighter.

It was one of the soldiers. He came a few steps in her direction, then said, *"Aquí vamos."* *Here we go.*

She heard lips smacking and then a satisfied sigh.

Gina pulled her legs into her chest until her ribs screamed. She stiffened every muscle in her body. Her heart thrummed in her neck.

The soldier was two feet to her right, his body pressed against the plywood. Gina could see his knife dangling off his belt. There was a slurping sound, and Gina imagined him sticking his fingers in the paste and then sucking them clean.

The soldier chuckled lightly to himself.

His boot was large. Gina guessed it was Guillermo, who was well over six feet. He was the one whose wrist Gina had twisted at the Tibióno village when they first abducted her. His dirt-covered boot was nearly touching her right shoe.

Gina tried to silently wriggle backward another inch.

There was a soft creak.

She must have leaned back against one of the bamboo poles supporting the tarp.

Gina froze.

Guillermo stepped back, then squatted. He held his lighter out in front of him. He probably expected to see a snake or some other form of wildlife.

The flicker of his lighter lit up wild, drug-crazed eyes.

"¡Puta!" he said.

23

I reached out my hand and showed Vern the satellite phone.

He asked, "You think that's the phone she used to call you?"

I glanced down at the thick black phone in my hand. "Considering these are the coordinates of the phone call Gina made to me and that the phone is the same brand as the one the call came from, I'd say the circumstantial evidence is overwhelming."

Vern bit his lip and shook his head.

I knew what he was thinking, and to be completely honest, I was thinking the same thing: *This is where Gina died.*

I quickly quarantined this thought and stuffed it in a folder marked *2003 Taxes*, then I said, "I need everybody out of here."

Diego might be a world-class tracker, but this was my world.

Without a word, Diego, Carlos, and Vern retreated into the sunlight and to where Juan Pablo was holding Camila.

Once they were gone, I went to work.

The first thing I did was try to turn the phone on, but nothing happened. I wasn't sure if it was simply out of juice or if it was busted. Useless for the time being, I returned the phone to the rectangular depression in the dirt where I'd found it.

Then I started taking mental snapshots of the entire crime scene.

On the table was the white paste that was probably the cocaine base Vern had spoken of. There were a few spatters of blood on the paste, turning it a heavy pink in spots. To the right of the drugs were large sprays of dried scarlet. Above the table, the tarp roof was heavily speckled.

I ran my hand over the blood droplets on the plywood, then I crouched down and ran my hands over the blood spray on the blue plastic drum. There was two feet of space between the drums.

A perfect place to hide.

I stood and gazed upward at the tarp. I followed the blood spatter in a clockwise semicircle. I took three steps to my right and glanced down at a nine-inch diameter of darkened earth. To the naked eye, it looked as if someone had poured a bottle of water on the dirt. But had there been a jungle crime scene tech available, they would have sprayed the area with luminol—which reacts with the hemoglobin in blood—and under an ultraviolet light, the dark patch would have been a glowing pool of white.

After snapping more than sixty mental photographs, I fed them into the TPSD—Thomas Prescott Super Detective—database. The results came back a few seconds later.

The carotid.

There was a considerable amount of blood, but that alone didn't say a whole lot. Whether it's a knife wound, bullet hole, or tractor accident, a lot of the four to five liters of blood in the human body is going to drain out.

At least until the heart stops pumping.

But the pattern of the blood—which was more *spray* than *spatter*—narrowed down the cause of death considerably. It could only have come from a severed artery.

But which one?

Those four or five liters of blood are pumping under high

pressure through more than twenty major arteries in the human body, the most notable being the aorta, the femoral, and the carotid.

It's difficult to sever the aorta as it's shielded by the sternum and the ribcage. The femoral artery in the thigh can easily be punctured, but the blood pattern didn't fit the trajectory that would have resulted from such a wound. A puncture to the carotid artery—which supplies blood to the neck, face, and brain—however, fit the blood pattern profile to a T.

My best guess was that the victim was standing close to where the satellite phone was found. They were hit in the neck, puncturing the carotid artery. Puncture being the operative word. If the artery had been *severed*, I doubt the blood would have traveled as far as it did.

At a two-day conference on blood-spatter evidence I attended—in what would end up being my last year as a detective with the Seattle Police Department—one of the speakers was a biophysics professor at the University of Washington. Up to that point, it had been six mundane hours of slides and lectures, but Hank something-or-other was one-part professor, one-part Gallagher.

He brought all sorts of props up on stage and proceeded to smash, cut, pop, and poke things until half of us in the audience were covered in water. One of the first things he did was to take out a water balloon and poke it with a needle. I expected the balloon to pop, but it didn't. Water began to spray from the balloon and the guy pointed the spray at the thirty of us there. When the water drained from the balloon, he asked everyone who got wet to stand up. I was in the fourth row, twelve feet from him, and I got a little bit of water on my knee.

It wasn't anything profound—it was simple physics—but it stuck with me how far the water had traveled.

Anyhow, once the carotid was punctured, the victim leaned their head back and a heavy arterial spray shot up and onto the tarp. Human nature would predict the victim then grab their neck with one or both hands. At which point, they moved toward the table. They leaned against it, blood running down their hands and spraying through their fingers. It's hard to say how long the victim stayed near the table, but at some point, they fell to their knees and crawled to the far right of the hut, where they bled out.

Confident I knew how the victim had died, I made my way to the front of the hut and yelled, "Diego and Carlos, I need you. And somebody get me a bamboo pole."

≈

"Stand here," I told Diego, indicating a spot a few inches from where the satellite phone was stuck in the ground.

"Okay, hand me one end of that pole," I said to Vern.

Vern handed me a six-foot-long bamboo pole that he'd found behind the structure. I passed one end to Diego and said, "Hold this against your neck."

If this were an actual crime scene, Diego would be a mannequin named Milton, and I would be using string. Which, come to think of it, is a dated practice. Most of this stuff is digitized now, done with fancy 3D cameras.

But in the jungle, you use the tools at your disposal.

I moved the other end of the pole up and down, which helped to visualize the different angles of the blood spatter. I made Diego lean his head back, tilt his head this way and that, fall to his knees.

After spending several minutes with Diego, I had him switch with Carlos. I ran Carlos through a similar array of positions.

"Okay, you can put that down now," I said to Carlos, trying to fight back a smile.

"What gives?" Vern said.

I couldn't get the angles to work with Diego, who at five foot three was an inch shorter than Gina. But for Carlos, who was six two, the angles nearly fit. In fact, for the blood spatter to fit perfectly, we needed someone a few inches *taller* than Carlos.

"Someone died here," I said, "but it wasn't Gina."

24

Guillermo reached under the table and yanked Gina out by her hair. She let out a loud scream.

She wanted the others at the camp to hear her. She might be punished for trying to escape, but she doubted they would kill her. Sadly, her scream only lasted half a second as one of Guillermo's giant hands wrapped around her throat and tightened like a vice.

He lifted Gina up, her backside up against the plywood table. She clawed with her right hand against the hand at her throat, but it was useless. None of her combat training could help her now.

Gina squirmed, helplessly watching as the drug-crazed soldier reached down with his free hand and pulled his seven-inch bowie knife from his belt.

He lifted it up and pressed the tip into the flesh of her left breast.

Gina's vision began to tunnel.

She only had seconds of consciousness left, and if she passed out, who knew what this monster's plans for her were?

Somehow, throughout the struggle, she'd held tightly to the satellite phone in her left hand. With her last ounce of strength,

Gina brought her left arm up and parallel to her shoulder. Then she swung her arm violently in an arc toward Guillermo's face.

She simply intended on stunning him, hoping to hit him hard enough make him relax his grip around her throat and give her a chance to escape. Or for someone from camp who'd heard her scream to reach them and convince her would-be killer that they needed her alive. But she didn't hit him in the face. The half-inch hard rubber antenna on the top of the phone sunk into the bottom of his neck with a sickening pop.

Immediately, the fingers around Gina's throat relaxed. Guillermo's head tilted back, and blood squirted from the puncture in his throat. The soldier wheeled around, spraying blood all over the table and onto the tarp roof.

Even though it wasn't a large puncture, Gina knew it was just as terminal as taking a bullet through the heart. She backed away, watching as the soldier stumbled against the blue drums with his hands at his throat.

What had she done?

25

"Okay," Libby said, clipping a small black lavalier microphone to the neck of Andy's shirt. "I'm just going to ask you a few questions about the altar."

Andy was standing with his back to the six-foot-wide trunk of a towering tree. Vines hung down the left side of the tree in a tangled riot. "Sounds good," Andy replied, his voice screeching as if he was back in the throngs of puberty.

After finding the altar nearly seven hours earlier, Andy had quickly erased his status as both Jungle Weenie and Jungle Idiot and had been elevated to Jungle Hero.

Within fifteen seconds of Andy telling everyone over the walkie-talkie that he'd uncovered a sacrificial altar, the entire expedition team had circled around him. He'd never been patted on the back, both literally and figuratively, so many times in his life.

"Way to go, Andy!" Buxton had said, giving him a hard slap on the back.

"¡Muy bien!" Cala had exclaimed. "¡Muy bien!"

Jonathan Roth—who'd looked physically ill after Andy crested the buried temple and delivered his infamous meatball line—had put his arm around Andy's shoulder and said, "Great discovery, kiddo. Just great, great work. You have a real knack for this stuff."

Andy had beamed, his cheeks turning a fiery red at the compliment.

Libby took a few steps backward to where Darnell was hovering over the video camera and tripod. She cocked her head to the side, the blond strands of her short pixie cut whipping across her forehead and said, "Okay, first thing. Who are you?"

Andy cleared his throat and said, "Andy Depree." This time his voice came out clear and even.

"Occupation?"

"Assistant professor of anthropology at the University of Chicago."

"What class do you teach?"

"Ancient Inca Civilization."

"Okay, great." Libby turned to Darnell and said, "Play that back for me really quick."

Several seconds passed as Libby watched the playback on the video camera. Andy took the time to glance around. Alejándro Cala, Nathan Buxton, and Jonathan Roth were huddled near the altar, continuing to excavate around the large boulder. The others, Andy assumed, must all be back atop the temple ruins.

"Sound levels are perfect," Libby said. "And you're right, it does look great with that tree behind you."

Libby had initially wanted to shoot the interview next to the altar, but Andy had figured they had plenty of footage of the altar, and the lighting next to the giant tree was much better.

"Ready when you are," Andy said.

Libby said, "Okay, so first question: How did you find the altar?"

Andy spent the next minute detailing how he noticed the stone while talking to Darnell. Andy skirted over the fact that he never would have made the discovery had he not been getting ready to tell the jungle just how much he hated teaching. Andy guessed Darnell would give him some guff for this later on.

When Andy finished, Libby said, "Actually, can we back up to the temple? And the large earthen mound?"

"You mean, the temple that the amazing Dr. Farah Karim discovered yesterday?"

"Yes, that one," Libby said, with what Andy thought was a slight roll of her eyes. "What would be the significance of a temple to these people?"

Andy cleared his throat and then said, "The temple would have been a centralized place where religious activities and decisions were made. It would be similar to a neighborhood church."

"Okay, and what would it have looked like?"

"Well, the large earthen mound was most likely once a pyramid made from organic material, possibly bricks of clay and straw—mudbrick." Andy went on a quick tangent explaining that nothing organic could survive the highly acidic conditions of the Amazon, and that over time those bricks had eroded into the large earthen mound they now saw. "On top of the pyramid," he said, getting back on track, "you would have the stones we found, which would serve as the foundation. And on top of the stones would have been the temple—most likely made from wood, which is the most abundant resource in the jungle."

"Great," Libby said. "Now let's talk about the altar. What would the significance of an altar be to this ancient civilization?"

"An altar is basically a communication port to a god or *deity*. Anything you put on the altar—prayer requests, good feelings, flowers, different offerings, sacrifices—will be transferred to the deity. Think of it as a *Star Trek* transporter to another realm, where the deities are."

"*Star Trek*?" Libby said with a laugh.

Andy felt foolish for half a second—that is, until Libby flashed him Spock fingers.

"You a Trekkie?" Andy asked.

"Maybe," Libby said, shrugging her shoulders lightly, then quickly moving along with the interview. She said, "Can you talk briefly about the sacrifices?"

"Sure," Andy said. "The main reason behind sacrifices is the belief that you have to keep the deities alive. You have to keep them sustained, and the primary way they did that was by offering a blood meal. Mostly animals, but sometimes they offered children as sacrifice."

"Are you saying a child might have been sacrificed on that altar?"

"It isn't out of the question. But human sacrifices only took place on the most momentous of occasions: to pacify the gods during a time of famine or pestilence, the death of a ruler, or the accession of a ruler."

Libby said, "That's about all I had planned for today." She paused for a moment then added, "But since we've got you here, could you spend a few minutes giving background on the Incas?"

Andy looked at his watch. It was 3:18 p.m. He still had fourteen minutes left. Plenty of time. He said, "Sure."

"Okay, maybe just the basics. Assume the viewer has no idea who the Incas are. I might interrupt you with a couple questions, but feel free to pick and choose what you think might be captivating. And don't worry if you slip up or need a minute to think, I can piece it together in post to look good."

She would piece it together? Wouldn't Roth be the one to edit the film?

Andy shook away this thought for the time being, then conjured Professor Depree from the mental rubble in which he'd been buried. "The Incas were an ancient civilization that flourished in South America from the early 1400s to around 1533. In less than a century, they built one of the largest, most tightly controlled empires the world has ever known. If you can believe it, at the height of their rule, the Inca Empire covered more than three thousand miles, extending from Ecuador in the north, into Peru, Bolivia, Argentina, and Chile in the south."

Libby gave him a big thumbs-up.

Andy continued, "What most people don't know is that the Incas were actually only a group of around forty thousand, but they governed a territory with ten million subjects speaking thirty different languages."

"What language did the Incas speak?" Libby asked.

"The Incas spoke Quechua, a dialect of it anyhow."

"Quechua is still in existence today, isn't it?"

"Eight million people still speak it. Mostly in Cusco and the highlands of Peru, but in a few parts of western Bolivia as well." Andy added, "I speak it pretty well. At least I used to."

"Can you say something in Quechua for us?"

"*Ch'inllamanta parlaykuway.*"

Libby laughed. "What did you say?"

"Please speak more slowly."

"What . . . did . . . you . . . say?"

It took Andy a minute to realize Libby was messing with him. Andy let out a small laugh.

"Okay, sorry," Libby said. "Keep going."

Andy spent the next few minutes talking about the many gods that the Incas worshipped, most notably, Inti, the god of the sun. When he was finished, Libby said, "When a lot of people think of the Incas, they think of gold."

"And rightly so," Andy said. "The Incas believed gold was the sweat of the sun, and it held a special place for them. It was reserved for the nobles, and it was a sign of imperial dominance across the entire empire. But even more prized by the nobles were the very finest textiles. The Incas were considered to be the most skillful weavers in the world, rivaling even the Egyptians. The best fabrics were considered the most precious gifts of all."

"Really?" Libby asked. "Their clothes were more important than gold?"

"Yeah, that's why when the Spanish showed up, the Incas gifted them fabrics rather than gold."

"Let's hold off on the Spanish for now. I'd like to get an in-depth interview in the next couple days covering the Spanish, the Inca's demise, and of course, Paititi."

"Gotcha."

"But back to textiles. What kind of clothes did the Incas wear?"

"Females wore long gowns with a sash at the waist called a *chumpi*. Males wore loincloths and long sleeveless tunics that hung to their knees. Both males and females wore sandals and sometimes headbands. Depending on social status, their headgear might have an addition of feathers or jewelry."

"I overheard Bernita and Alejándro talking about something called a *quipu*. Can you explain that?"

Andy nodded. "The Incas didn't have a written language, so they used *quipus*—complex knotted cords—to keep track of important historical statistics and accounting records. In the last few decades, researchers have come to believe the quipu was used to record more than just numbers, perhaps even to send and receive messages."

Andy checked his watch.

3:25 p.m.

Seven minutes.

Libby asked, "You have somewhere to be?"

"Sorry about that," Andy said, shaking his left wrist and the small black Timex. "Just trying to figure out the last time I ate.

My blood sugar is getting a little low." Andy's blood sugar was fine, but he wasn't about to tell her the real reason he kept checking his watch.

"We can stop if you want."

"No, I'm good for another few minutes."

"Just quickly touch on the Inca's architecture, roads, Machu Picchu, then we're done. I promise."

"Sounds good," Andy said. "Yeah, so what the Incas are most noted for is their amazing architecture. They were master stone masons and constructed buildings and walls using finely worked blocks which fit together so precisely no mortar was needed. Usually you can't even fit the blade of a knife between two stones. And the crown jewel of the Incas' construction efforts is Machu Picchu.

"Machu Picchu was built high in the Peruvian Andes. It's a large military citadel fortified with large-block walls and is a great example of the Inca's hillside terracing. Flat land was rare in the Peruvian mountains, and the Incas were one of the first adopters of terrace farming. By building steps of flat land running down the mountainside, they could extend the land available for cultivation and provide better water and drainage for crops."

"Great," Libby said. "And their roads?"

"They built a bunch of roads," Andy said, flatly.

Libby laughed. "Okay, I think we'll stop there."

≈

After finishing the interview, Andy had four minutes to spare. He found a spot to sit on a fallen log, ten meters from where Libby was now shooting an interview with Bernita Capobianco.

Andy leaned his head back and gazed upward at the tiny holes in the canopy a hundred and fifty feet overhead. He imagined several months earlier, when Roth flew the lidar survey over this area. Light rays from the lidar machine sneaking through those gaps in the near solid blanket of green and bouncing off the jungle floor. Had it not been for those light rays, they never would have stumbled on these ruins. Not in a million years.

Sure, a jungle native or indigenous Indian group might have at one time discovered the stones of the temple, but the chances of an expedition team or wayward explorer finding their way to this exact spot in one of the most isolated jungles in the world—it wouldn't happen.

At least, it *hadn't* happened in five hundred years. No, it was only through the advent of lidar technology that they made today's startling discovery.

There was a soft beep from Andy's watch, and he glanced down. It was 3:32 p.m.

Andy wasn't sure when or how the superstition had begun, but he'd been doing it for as long as he could remember. And of all his stupid superstitions—outside of his lucky flying shirt and trinkets—this was the one he took the most seriously.

He had to see his watch change from 3:32 p.m. to 3:33 p.m. If he didn't, it was bad luck for the next twenty-four hours until he could again see the change.

Six years earlier, Andy had a dental appointment that ran long—even after he was assured by the receptionist he'd be done by 3:00 p.m. at the latest—and he wasn't going to ask the dentist to stop drilling in his mouth so he could stare at his watch.

When he finally did look at his watch, it was 3:41 p.m.

He'd missed the change.

On his way home from the dental office, he got a flat tire. After AAA came, he made his way home only to find the Amazon delivery he'd been alerted to earlier that day had been stolen. And if that wasn't enough, he ended up getting food poisoning that night from Thai leftovers and spent most of the night in the bathroom.

Since that day, he'd arranged his schedule around the change-over, even going as far as to take a ten-minute break during his Tuesday and Thursday lectures, so he could see it.

Andy continued to stare down at the cheap Timex on his left wrist. The digital watch gave only hours and minutes, so Andy never knew exactly how many seconds he had left. Like most days, the minute dragged on for an eternity, much like waiting for a pot of water to boil or, worse yet, for a girl to text back.

There was a snapping of branches, and Andy instinctively snapped up his head and gazed around. Nathan Buxton and Alejándro Cala were barely visible through the tangle of jungle to Andy's left. The noise must have come from them.

Andy glanced down at his watch, but he was too late. It was 3:33 p.m.

For the first time in six years, Andy had missed seeing the two turn into a three.

"Aw, man," he said under his breath.

The next twenty-four hours were going to be bad. Really bad. Andy could feel it.

What have I done?

There was another round of snapping branches. It sounded like an animal. No, a group of animals!

It's starting!

Andy was going to get gored to death by a pack of tapirs or eaten by a jungle jaguar simply because he'd taken his eyes off his watch for two miserable seconds!

He ran toward a nearby tree, hoping to get to higher ground. There were several vines hanging near the tree, and Andy grasped one in his hands and attempted to pull himself up. A harrowing montage of unsuccessfully climbing the rope in gym class flooded his brain as his upper body strength failed him again seventeen years later.

His fingers slipped from the vine, and he tumbled backward to the ground. When he opened his eyes, he was surrounded by several dark-skinned men. Each of the men held a large black rifle.

Andy's first thought was the men must have been a group of jungle outlaws. Drug traffickers, illegal loggers, or illegal miners.

Andy put up his hands and said, "*¡Por favor, no me hagan daño!*" *Please don't hurt me!*

The men began to laugh. One of them reached out his hand. On closer examination, Andy realized all the men were clad in fatigues.

Andy took the soldier's hand and was helped to his feet.

Standing behind the circle of seven soldiers was the lieutenant from their meeting at the hotel in La Paz: Mauricio Goytia.

Andy had nearly forgotten that the lieutenant and a convoy of soldiers were scheduled to join the expedition on day three.

He let out a sigh of relief.

They were here to protect him.

Maybe he would survive the next twenty-four hours after all.

26

Diego stopped suddenly and held his hands up. He put his finger to his lips and waved the four of us back. We retreated a hundred yards back the way we came, then huddled together.

"What?" I asked.

"Men," Diego whispered. "And some kind of shelters."

"Villagers?"

He shook his head. "They have guns."

"Narcos?"

"I think so."

There had been evidence of two different paths leading away from yesterday's drug lab. One heading east, one north. As a group, we had decided to follow the northern trail, which was consistent with the narcos moving their drugs closer to the Brazilian border. For two hours last night, then another five hours today, Diego tracked the trail to these narcos' doorstep.

I said what everyone was thinking. "This could be it. This could be where they're keeping Gina."

That's assuming Gina hadn't escaped after killing one of her abductors.

"I'm going to do a recon," I said. "Give me the binoculars."

Vern rummaged around in his pack and handed me a small pair of binoculars. Then he handed me one of the pistols. I took the gun, clicked off the safety, then asked, "You don't happen to have a ghillie suit in there, left over from your time in Vietnam?"

A ghillie suit is a camouflage suit covered in vegetation to make you blend in. They are what snipers are usually wearing in the movies.

"Sorry, Charlie," he said with a wry grin.

Though I would have happily welcomed some camouflage, I was confident I could get relatively close without being seen. I gingerly made my way to where Diego had stopped us and pushed aside the thick vegetation. Twenty yards away were two compact wooden shacks, one decidedly bigger than the other. They were well built and looked to be more of the permanent variety—Ruth's Chris Steak Houses, as opposed to yesterday's pop-up smoothie bars. I presumed this was the transshipment hub Vern alluded to yesterday.

There were three dark-skinned men. One of them was sitting in a chair in front of the farthest shack. An automatic rifle was lying across his lap, and he was smoking. The two other men were loading something into the back of a four-wheeler.

I brought the binoculars up, focusing them on the packages. They were rectangular and wrapped heavily in beige packing tape. I'd seen plenty of them in the SPD evidence locker—uncut bricks of cocaine.

I spent another few minutes scouting the area and formulating an attack plan. Whether that plan would be executed at day or night, I wasn't yet certain.

I watched as the four-wheeler disappeared down a trail into the jungle, then I slipped out of my spot and jogged back to the group.

I said, "Two shelters and three narcos. But one of the narcos just headed out with a shipment on a four-wheeler."

"Describe the shelters," Vern said.

"Wooden shacks. One is fifteen feet square, the other is a little bigger."

"Definitely a processing and shipment hub. They use the four-wheelers to move the drugs across the border. They have a network of trails they've carved through the jungle over the years."

According to my GPS, which went in and out of service, we were currently less than seven miles from the Brazilian border.

"I would expect there to be more than just a few soldiers guarding it," Vern continued. "There have to be sentries out somewhere. You're sure there are only two of them?"

"That's all I saw."

"Could there be others inside the shacks?"

"Maybe, but doubtful."

"Why?"

"The vibe felt pretty relaxed. Like the end of the workday. I'd be willing to bet there isn't much product, if any, left to protect."

"You think Gina is being held in one of the shacks?"

"Fifty-fifty."

He mulled this over for a moment, then he slammed a sleeve of bullets into the semiautomatic he was holding. "Then what are we waiting for?"

I was leaning toward a more tactical nighttime mission, but if Gina was being held here, they could move her at any moment. Or the third narco could return.

Also, I'm very impatient.

"Nothing," I said.

I was confident the ex-soldier and I could manage two narcos, but it wouldn't hurt to have a third gun. I glanced at Juan Pablo and Carlos. They were just kids. There was no way I was risking their lives. And although I didn't like the prospect of leaving little Camila an orphan, I nodded at Diego and said, "We need you on this."

He blew out his chubby cheeks and then said, "Okay."

≈

Our best bet was to hit them hard and fast. And with overwhelming force. I swapped out the pistol for a shotgun and loaded five rounds.

The three of us crept back to my scouting spot behind a thicket of vegetation. The two soldiers were sitting side by side, both smoking cigarettes. They were holding cards in their hands, and their automatic rifles were leaning against their chairs.

They were what you might call sitting ducks.

"On three," I said.

After counting off, I shot forward through the remaining two feet of vegetation and brought the shotgun up. The narcos didn't notice me until I was fifteen feet away from them. The one closest to me threw down his cards and went for his rifle.

I pulled the trigger on the shotgun.

If I had known for certain that these were the guys who had abducted Gina, I would have had no problem turning them into colanders, but I wasn't certain.

Far from it.

So I sent the shot high up in the air. It did the trick, and both men quickly threw up their hands.

"*¡No dispares! ¡No dispares!*"

I'm guessing their shouts translated to *Don't shoot!* or *Don't kill me!* or *I just pissed myself!*

"Tell them to kick their rifles away," I said to Diego.

He translated, and both men kicked their rifles several feet in our direction.

"Ask them where the doctor is. The one they fucking kidnapped."

Diego shouted at the two men.

They glanced at one another, then yelled something back at Diego.

Diego said, "They say they don't know anything about any doctor or any kidnapping."

I almost believed them. That is, until I heard the banging and screaming coming from the smaller of the two huts.

I ran to the wooden shack and pulled at the door. There was a heavy steel lock and it wouldn't budge.

"Gina! Gina, can you hear me?"

I put my ear to the soft wood. I could hear banging and soft moaning.

She was in there, and I was guessing she was tied up. And possibly hurt.

I walked to the closest narco and grabbed him by his thick black hair. I dragged him over to the hut and shoved him into the door.

"Tell him to open it. Now!"

Diego shouted at the man. He fumbled for a key in his pocket and tried to slide it into the lock. His fingers were shaking, and I snatched the key from him and pushed him aside.

I slid the key in the lock, and it turned with an audible clunk.

I flung the door open.

It was dark and musty.

There was a figure moving in the corner.

"Gina!" I shouted.

The figure bleated in reply.

It was a goat.

≈

The goat jumped to its feet and ran out of the hut.

I exited the hut in a daze—still trying to process how I could have confused the sounds of a small white goat with the sounds of a grown human woman—when two four-wheelers skidded out from the brush. Both four wheelers had a driver plus three men hanging off the sides, each carrying an automatic rifle.

They screeched to a halt in front of Diego and Vern and shouted, "*¡Suelta el arma! ¡Suelta el arma!*"

Vern, Diego, and I dropped our guns to the ground.

The narco whose hair I'd grabbed walked toward me, picked up my shotgun, then rammed the butt of it into my solar plexus.

I groaned and dropped to my knees.

When I recovered, I glanced up. Vern and Diego were both on their knees with their hands held above their heads.

Vern shook his head at me and said, "Great scouting job, asshole."

≈

Vern told the soldiers we worked for the DEA, which I'm guessing was the only reason that an hour later we were still alive.

Apparently, Bolivia had evicted the United States Drug Enforcement Agency from their country a decade earlier because of some offhand remarks by the then US ambassador. Regardless, the soldiers weren't stupid enough to think they could kill two United States DEA agents and their in-country liaison without hell raining down on them.

The men, now numbering twelve—a third four-wheeler had arrived minutes after the first two—smoked and took turns holding us at gunpoint. The three us where sitting on the ground, leaning against the side of one of the shacks.

"Sorry, guys," I said to Vern and Diego. "It looks like I was off by about ten soldiers."

"It's not your fault," Diego said. "They must have another operation close by."

Vern wasn't nearly as forgiving, which might have had something to do with the soldier who punched him in the face when Vern refused to answer his questions.

Vern rubbed his left cheek with his hand and moved his jaw from side to side.

"Anything broken?" I asked.

He glanced in my direction but said nothing. He did, however, wave one of the soldiers over. Vern said something to the soldier in Spanish, and the soldier nodded. He then drew a pack of smokes from his pocket, pulled one out, lit it with the cigarette in his mouth, and handed it to Vern.

Evidently, every man deserves a last smoke before he dies.

Vern thanked him, then took a long inhale. He held it for a few seconds, then blew it out. "Oh, God, I missed that," he said with a sigh.

"You gave it up?"

He turned to me, then, deciding to end his silent treatment, he said, "Old lady is fine with the occasional cigar, but she made me give up cigarettes when we got married."

"What's her name?" Though Vern had mentioned a wife, he'd never said her name.

"Isabella."

I turned to my right and asked Diego, "What about you? You got a girl?"

"*Sí, sí,*" he said with a dimpled smile. "And *dos niñas.*"

He pulled out his wallet and showed me pictures of his two little girls. They were both in pink dresses and as cute as any two kids I'd ever seen.

"Why did you take this job?" I asked him. "Didn't you know how dangerous it would be?"

"This job pays more than two years I make as guide." He paused. "I want best for my girls."

This silenced the three of us, each of us coming to terms with the people we would never see again. For Diego, it was his wife and two girls. For Vern, it was Isabella. For me, it was Lacy and Clark.

I couldn't believe I wasn't going to be able to watch that kid grow up. A lump the size of Manhattan formed in my throat as I thought about how I wouldn't be able to show him how to properly shoot a basketball. Or buy him his first Lego set. Or give him another donkey ride.

I knocked my head backward against the shack.

Thwack, thwack, thwack.

I'd risked everything. And for what? For a woman who didn't even want me? For a woman who left me? And what did I expect? That even if I somehow rescued Gina, she would move back to Seattle with me? That we would just start up right where we left off?

I wanted to be filled with regret, but the more I smacked my head against the wood, the more certain I became that if I hadn't come to Bolivia, that if I hadn't at least tried to rescue Gina, I wouldn't have been able to live with myself. Sure, I would have been able to give Clark a few more pony rides, but I would have been a broken pony. One destined for the glue factory.

Gina was worth the risk.

Of course, there was a 98 percent chance I was going to be executed in the next fifteen minutes, but I would do it all over again.

Probably.

"Hey," I said, giving Vern a nudge. "Ask them why they had a goat locked up."

Vern asked.

One of the soldiers answered, and the rest of them laughed.

Vern told me, "He says if they don't lock him up, he will find a way to get into the cocaine and start humping everything he sees."

I doubted this was true, but it was still funny.

I asked, "Where did he come from?"

Vern asked the soldier, and a moment later translated: "He just showed up one day a few months back. Probably wandered away from one of the small villages nearby. They like him. He's kind of like their mascot. His name is Paco."

I glanced over to where Paco was eating the soldiers' discarded cigarette butts.

A moment later, another four-wheeler emerged from the trees and parked near the three others. All the soldiers who were smoking dropped their cigarettes and stamped them out with their feet.

The man behind the wheel of the four-wheeler was older and more kempt than the others. He didn't carry a gun. From the way he walked—shoulders back, a bit of a swagger—I guessed he may have done his own killing years ago, but now he had others pull the trigger.

Our lives rested in this man's hands. A simple nod from him and we were toast.

I turned to Vern and said, "Are you up to date on your life insurance policy?"

He lifted one eyebrow but said nothing.

"Sorry, I always get awkward right before I'm about to be killed."

I'd had a lot of practice.

The soldiers parted, and the man walked between them. He had a salt-and-pepper beard and aviator sunglasses. As he drew close, he pulled the sunglasses off and shook his head lightly from side to side.

Then he smiled, one of his front teeth capped in gold.

"Papagayo!" he shouted.

≈

Vern had met Felipe in Colombia twenty years earlier, when Felipe was a driver for one of the cartels. He had driven Vern to and from meetings with his boss on several occasions.

"This is Thomas," Vern said, introducing me.

"A friend of Papagayo's is a friend of mine," Felipe said, clapping me on the shoulder.

The moment Vern and Felipe embraced, all the tension from the soldiers dissipated. A few of the soldiers even jumped on their four-wheelers and headed back to wherever the other operation was located. As for Diego, he went to retrieve Carlos, Juan Pablo, and Camila.

I shook Felipe's hand, then said, "We're looking for a woman doctor who was taken from her village twelve days ago. She was taken by soldiers, and we suspected it might have been narcos."

"I see," he said, nodding along.

He pulled a phone from his hip and turned and walked away.

"Seems like a nice enough guy," I said to Vern.

Vern shook his head. "Don't let looks deceive you. That man has spilled more blood than anyone I've ever met. If I hadn't been here, you and Diego would be digging your own graves right now."

I gave him a pat on the shoulder and said, "Proof positive that it's not what you know, it's who you know."

He tried to fight off a laugh, but it slipped out.

Felipe returned a moment later.

He shook his head and said, "I don't know who these men were who took your doctor, but I can assure you, it wasn't us."

≈

It wasn't them. And Felipe was certain they were the only operation in all of northeastern Bolivia. From the way he said it, I'm sure the competition had learned this the hard way. He was steadfast in his conviction that if narcos had taken her, he would know.

I asked him about the drug lab we found yesterday, and he

said they'd abandoned that lab a month earlier, well before Gina was abducted.

So the question remained: If narcos didn't abduct Gina, who did? Illegal loggers? Illegal miners? The Bolivian Army?

It could have been anyone in desperate need of medical help.

We were back to square one.

Or so I thought.

We were getting ready to backtrack to the drug lab, where we would follow the path leading east, when Felipe—who had made a few more phone calls—returned to our small group and said, "I may have something for you."

He explained how one of his sentries had been doing a routine patrol three days earlier. He was working his way down one of the southern trails—six kilometers from where we were now—when he noticed something odd.

A line.

"What sort of line?" I asked.

"Just a line in the dirt. Like someone took a stick and drew a line across the path."

"That's not a lot to go on."

"I agree, but my guy hopped off his four-wheeler to check it out, and that's when he found something in the brush, right where the line ended."

He paused.

"Well?" I prodded.

He smiled, his gold tooth flashing brilliantly. "I think in English you call it a stethoscope."

27

The previous day, after Andy's interview, after Andy had missed seeing "the change" on his watch, and after Lieutenant Goytia and his regiment of Bolivian soldiers had shown up, the expedition trudged back toward base camp. Everyone, even Andy to some degree, was in a celebratory mood. They had successfully confirmed several of the man-made earthen mounds on the lidar scans—one which most certainly had been a large temple at one point—and partially excavated the sacrificial altar Andy had discovered.

Alejándro Cala had smuggled in several bottles of Bolivian brandy, and everyone indulged in a few "tots" around the fire. Andy wasn't planning on imbibing—he wanted to keep his wits about him during his twenty-four-hour window of bad luck—but people kept making toasts, several of which were directed at him, and he drank several ounces of the potent liquor.

When it was time to retire to their tents, true to his word, Darnell said he would be sleeping outside on the ground that evening.

"Good luck," Andy told him, resigned to the loss of his $500.

Back at his tent, slightly buzzed from the brandy, and exhausted and sore from a full day at the site, Andy ran scenario after scenario through his head of what could possibly happen to him in his remaining nineteen hours of bad luck. Would it be a jaguar that came and pulled him from his tent in the middle of the night? Would it be a tree falling on his tent and crushing him in his sleep? Would he come down with malaria? Would he slice his hand off with his machete?

Somehow, Andy was able to worry himself to sleep. He awakened a little after five in the morning to the soft slap of rain hitting his tent. He thought of Darnell sleeping on the ground and hoped he would give up and take refuge inside.

Two hours later, as Andy was devouring a tortilla with Nutella, he watched Darnell limp his way through the rain and into the tent.

"Whad's wong wid you?" Andy mumbled, the chocolate-hazelnut spread sticking to the roof of his mouth.

"Bullet ants."

"Really?" Andy said, swallowing. Bullet ants got their name from their bite, which was supposedly as painful as getting shot with a bullet. "How long did you last?"

"Maybe half an hour," Darnell said with a scoff. "I'm lying there, about to fall asleep, and then I feel this bite on my hand. Felt like someone hit it with a hammer."

"Oh, man." Andy mentally put the five hundred dollars back in his bank account.

"At first I thought it must have been a snake. But then I flipped on the lantern and see that I'm covered in inch-long black ants." He shook his head. "Got bit to hell before I got them all off me."

"Do they still hurt?"

"Shit yeah, they still hurt. I can barely walk." He nodded in the direction of the ruins and said, "I'm not sure how I'm going to make it up to the site."

"If it doesn't stop raining soon, I don't think any of us will be making it up to the site."

And none of them would.

The rains continued endlessly, raising the river to a level that Holland decided was too dangerous to cross. Of course, Farah argued that they could attach their carabiners to the ropes, but Holland held firm. It wasn't just the river. There would also be sinkholes, much like the one Bernita fell into on the previous day. Holland had seen one too many people injured—lots of torn ACLs and lots of broken wrists—while attempting to travel through the muck.

Thankful not to be trampling through the wet jungle, Andy assisted Holland and Rix in digging several trenches around the tents. The trenches helped funnel water away from the areas where the expedition congregated, though for the most part, it was still a muddy mess.

Andy spent lunch with Nathan Buxton, answering questions about Andy's background and his tenure as an assistant professor. They touched briefly on the mistakes Buxton had made concerning the Incas in his book *The Cusco Paradox*. Buxton took the criticism humbly, and Andy liked him even more after the interview.

Currently, Andy was preparing for another interview, though this time it would be on camera. Libby had spent the entire day running interviews with Roth, Cala, Bernita, and Farah, and now it was his turn.

"You ready?" Libby was sitting in a nylon chair next to the video camera. There was a notebook open on her lap and a blue pen tucked behind her right ear. Rain dripped from the lip of the tent behind her.

Andy nodded.

"As I mentioned yesterday, I'd like to give the viewers some background on the collapse of the Incas and then your thoughts on Paititi. Maybe we start when the Spanish capture Atahualpa in 1532."

"Someone did their homework."

Libby flashed a sly grin and said, "I may have skimmed the Inca Wikipedia page."

"Actually, we have to back up to 1524," Andy said, sitting up an inch straighter in his own nylon chair. "At the time, the Inca empire was the largest and richest in the Americas. The Emperor was Huayna Capac, but in 1524 he died from smallpox. The disease and countless others made their way down from Central America, where the Europeans had established settlements a decade earlier.

"The death of Huayna Capac, and the death of his eldest son soon thereafter, incited a civil war between his two other sons: Atahualpa and Huáscar. Over the course of the next three years, between the civil war and the spread of disease by European invaders, the Inca Empire was weakened considerably."

Libby interrupted, asking, "How much of the Inca population died of disease?"

"Historians' estimates vary, but regardless, the number is big: between sixty and ninety percent."

"Yikes. Okay, continue."

"During this same period, Spanish commander Francisco Pizarro was granted a license by the Queen of Spain to conquer Peru. He arrived in South America in 1531 and established the first Spanish settlement in northern Peru the following year.

"Pizarro was captivated by stories of Inca wealth and invited Atahualpa—who had recently prevailed over his brother Huáscar in the civil war—to dinner. Atahualpa showed up at Pizarro's camp with six thousand unarmed followers. Some historians think what happened next was a cultural misunderstanding. One of Pizarro's friars proceeded to expound on the doctrines of Christianity and offered Atahualpa a bible. The Inca refused the bible, and for the Spaniards, this was a declaration of war. They unleashed a volley of gunfire, massacring two thousand of Atahualpa's men, then took Atahualpa captive.

"Atahualpa was aware of the power that gold and silver had over Europeans and told Pizarro he would give him enough gold to fill a room twenty feet by seventeen feet—plus enough silver to fill two more such rooms—in exchange for his life. Pizarro, blinded by his own desires, agreed to Atahualpa's request.

"After Atahualpa delivered on his promise, Pizarro reneged on the deal and had Atahualpa executed.

"At the death of their emperor, the Incas rebelled, but they were no match for the Spaniards' weapons. The Spanish seized Cusco, forcing the few remaining Incas to retreat to the jungle village of Vilcabamba, which remained the last stronghold of the empire until it was eventually conquered by the Spanish."

Libby asked, "Where does Paititi come in?"

Andy knew this was just a prompt. Libby might not know all that much about the Incas, but he'd be willing to bet she was well versed in the myriad legends of Paititi.

"You mean the reason we're in this sticky, wet, and muddy jungle right now?"

Libby raised her eyebrows several times.

"Paititi is steeped in legend," Andy began. "And it's hard to separate fact from fiction. The word first shows up in Spanish documents dating back to the sixteenth century, when natives were overheard talking about a secret Inca city in the jungle. From there, the various legends grew, new stories were created, and original information was distorted.

"Based on these different legends, some people believe Paititi is a lost city of gold, while others think it's simply the last refuge of the Incas after they were conquered by the Spanish. Others believe Paititi to be a lost people, the last pure ancestors of the Incas.

"As for the gold, there's a grain of truth to the legend. When the Spaniards entered Cusco—after executing Atahualpa—they pillaged all the gold and silver they could find. But according to both Spanish documents and oral history, the Spaniards only found a small portion of what existed in the Inca capital. The bulk of the Inca's treasure has never been found—at least, its discovery has never been reported—and it's believed that in the months leading up to the conquistadors' ransacking of Cusco, the Incas were able to spirit most of the gold, silver, and precious stones deep into the jungle. It was there, legend has it, that they built a jungle citadel to protect their treasure."

"Where exactly?" Libby asked.

"That's the difficult part. There are several different versions of the legend. Most have Paititi located in the jungles of eastern Peru, just on the other side of the Andes Mountains. Other legends have Paititi located in the thick jungles of the Llanganates Mountains in Ecuador. Others maintain it's somewhere in Brazil."

"What about Bolivia?"

Andy nodded. "Mostly western Bolivia, near the Peruvian border."

Libby glanced down at the notebook on her lap and asked, "Can you talk a bit about the document found in the Vatican archives?"

"Sure," Andy said. "So, in 2001 an Italian archaeologist found the report of a missionary, Andres Lopez, buried in the archives of the Vatican. In the report, which dates from around 1600, Lopez describes in great detail a large city rich in gold, silver, and gemstones, and called Paititi by the natives. Lopez didn't give an exact location, evidently, to avoid 'gold fever,' saying only that it was covered in deep rainforests and waterfalls. Nothing much came from the report's discovery, other than a bit of controversy suggesting that the Vatican was trying to keep the document secret and the gold for themselves."

Libby said, "Okay, a couple more questions. Are Paititi and El Dorado the same thing?"

"They are not, though they've become intertwined over the years. The *Black Panther* movie made it all the more confusing."

Libby crisscrossed her arms and slapped them to her chest. *"Wakanda forever."*

Andy laughed.

"Sorry," Libby said. "Please continue."

"The legend of El Dorado originated in Colombia with the Muisca people. The legend actually pertains to a man and not a city or place. During initiation ceremonies the Muisca's tribal chief would cover himself in gold dust, surround himself with golden treasure, and then submerge in the lake. They called him El Dorado, which translates to 'the Golden One.' Legend has it that one day the chief walked into the lake and disappeared, taking all the golden treasure with him. Spanish explorers heard this story, and over time El Dorado became synonymous with any undiscovered place filled with treasure."

"Great stuff," Libby chimed, then asked, "Back to Paititi. How many expeditions have gone looking for the lost city?"

"Over a hundred. It goes back centuries. Percy Fawcett, the explorer who inspired the movie *The Lost City of Z*, was looking for Paititi. There have been countless others, explorers and adventurers from all over the world. Sadly, many never returned. They were either lost or killed by natives, or more recently, drug traffickers, illegal loggers, or the many other scary things Holland talked about at orientation."

"Okay, last question. Did you see anything at the archaeological site yesterday that leads you to believe these ruins are in fact, Paititi?"

Andy didn't hesitate. "No. No, I did not."

≈

Eleven more minutes.

Eleven more minutes of bad luck.

After his interview with Libby was complete, Andy made his way to his tent. He wasn't taking any chances. He was going to sit in his tent, listening to the slap of the rain, and watch the change happen on his watch. Only then, would he rejoin the outside world.

Andy pulled off his boots and set them on a towel across from him. He laid down on top of his sleeping bag and flipped open his graphic novel and began reading. Two pages. Three pages. He again checked his watch.

Seven minutes.

On the page, a blond character entered the fray. She was voluptuous and clad in a tight crime-fighter outfit. Something about her reminded Andy of Libby. While Libby wasn't what you might call stunning, she was definitely cute, even more so when she smiled, which Andy had seen several times over the past two days.

"*Wakanda forever*," Andy repeated, allowing himself a laugh.

That's when Andy saw it. It was crawling into one of his boots. A scorpion.

It was red, and Andy could see the stinger on its coiled tail.

"Oh, brother," Andy said, backpedaling until he was tucked into the wall of the tent.

His first thought was to bolt, to unzip the tent and run. But maybe this was a ruse by the universe to get him outside, where something even worse might happen.

No, Andy would take his chances with the scorpion. According to Holland, the little red scorpion wasn't deadly. It would give him a healthy sting, but he would survive.

Before he could talk himself out of it, Andy crawled over to his shoe and picked it up by the laces. He was almost positive the scorpion had crawled inside. His hand shook as he carried the dangling shoe to the front of the tent and unzipped the opening with his opposite hand. He lowered the shoe to the wet earth and toppled it over on its side. Then he gave the bottom tread a smack with his hand.

"Go!" he shouted.

He leaned his head out a few inches, rain cascading down into his hair. Nothing happened. No scorpion.

Andy was on his hands and knees, leaning out the tent. He was giving the bottom of the shoe another smack with his right hand, when he felt an odd sensation.

Andy pulled his head in and glanced down at his left hand. The small red scorpion was sitting atop it.

"Please don't sting me," Andy whimpered.

He instinctively glanced at his watch, which was an inch from where the scorpion was stopped.

Two minutes until the change.

He'd almost made it. But now he was going to get stung by a scorpion. And then, oh, no, what if he had an allergic reaction? Even though Holland said it wouldn't kill you, it would probably kill Andy.

He glanced at his backpack three feet away. Luckily, he'd brought an EpiPen. Even though in thirty-two years Andy had never needed one of the adrenaline injections—he'd never had a bad allergic reaction to anything in his life—and they cost five hundred dollars apiece, Andy had brought two.

If he'd only been able to see the change yesterday. Then this stupid scorpion wouldn't even be in his tent. But those were the rules. Miss the change, and pay the consequences.

He glanced at his watch.

It was 3:32 p.m.

Andy held his breath.

A moment later, he watched the two change to a three. And a few moments after that, the scorpion walked off his hand and out of the tent.

28

"Try," Juan Pablo said, holding out a fistful of green leaves before my bleary eyes. "Make awake."

The others were off relieving themselves, and Juan Pablo and I were resting against the trunk of a large tree. Camila was dangling from one of the low branches, inspecting a large yellow butterfly that had landed nearby.

A little more than twenty-four hours earlier, Felipe had his men load us on their four-wheelers and drive us the six kilometers to the spot where the stethoscope had been found.

My breath caught as I saw the line etched across the four-foot wide dirt trail. I envisioned Gina with a walking stick, dragging it across the trail, hoping it went unnoticed, then dropping her stethoscope in the brush.

And if we needed any more corroboration, Diego said the trail-crossing fit with the eastbound path we had previously elected *not* to follow from the drug lab.

Confident we were once again hot on Gina's trail, though with no idea who had abducted her, we spent four hours trudging through the forest before stopping to make camp. We had woken

early this morning, and after seven straight hours of hiking, I was
exhausted beyond words.

In addition to my exhaustion, my ant bites were burning like
hell. Not to mention the uncontrollable itching of the eighty to
ninety mosquito bites covering my face, neck, and arms. Plus, after
six days of sweating through my shirt, I was greasy and dirty and just
so sticky. Then there was the beard. I had a few days of stubble going
when I'd first heard Gina's voicemail, but now I had nearly ten days
of growth, which if you've ever grown a beard, is when it starts to itch.

Needless to say, I was not a happy camper.

I took the leaves from Juan Pablo and smelled them. They
were pungent but not unpleasant. Juan Pablo instructed me how
to chew the leaves and keep them in my cheek.

A moment later, Vern, Carlos, and Diego returned, and we
started back up. Within five minutes, I was wide awake. I felt
like I had drunk four Red Bulls. I could hike another five hours.
Shoot, I could hike to Vancouver.

I sidled up to Vern and said, "You have to try these leaves Juan
Pablo gave me. They give you a nice pep in your step."

Vern's eyebrows furrowed. "What leaves?"

I opened my mouth and showed him the ball of leaves in my
cheek.

He let loose a loud laugh. "What do you think those leaves
are, buddy?"

"I don't know, some herbal caffeine thing."

"Aren't you supposed to be some famous detective?"

"I'm the Justin Bieber of detectives."

The reference was lost on him, and I decided Bieber Fever
must have missed Bolivia.

"Where were we two days ago?" he asked, leaning in, waiting
for the anvil to drop.

"*Coca leaves?*"

"Yep," Vern said with a smile.

I had experimented with a few different drugs in my youth. I'd smoked a little pot, I did mushrooms twice—one time was a blast, and one time I thought I was Smurfette and Gargamel was chasing me—but I'd never tried cocaine. This was probably because when I was just a kid, I walked into my father's office when he was doing a line of coke off his desk. He said he only did it when he had a lot of work to do, and if he ever caught *me* doing it, he'd send me to boarding school.

The potency of chewed leaves was, I could only assume, a far cry from that of the finished product, but I could see how you could get hooked on the stuff.

"Well," I said, "I definitely see the appeal."

≈

We followed the trail for the rest of the day, then made camp. After eating Juan Pablo's rice, yucca, and pepper stew, I was finally able to go *número dos*. (I'm guessing this was brought on by the coca leaves, which according to Vern, were notorious for loosening the bowels.) Diego spotted jaguar tracks not too far from where we made camp, and he thought it best we keep a fire going all night. We did, and thankfully, none of us were dragged from our tents by one of the large jungle cats.

We woke early, and by 8:00 a.m. all five of us were chewing coca. I'd overdone it a bit the previous day, but if I chewed just one or two leaves, it was like drinking a cup of strong coffee. It helped to keep morale up as we marched mile after mile through the never-ending jungle labyrinth. Over the course of forty-eight hours, we'd hiked nearly thirty miles from where Gina had hidden her stethoscope in the brush.

As the afternoon wore on, Vern kept checking his GPS and

crunching his eyebrows together, but whatever it was concerning him, he kept it to himself.

Diego waved for us to stop. "People," he said, motioning ahead. Not soldiers.

People.

I made my way to where he was ducking in the brush and followed his gaze.

I shook my head and said, "Impossible."

29

Gina was lucky to be alive. Not only because she'd escaped death by Guillermo strangling her, but because the other soldiers hadn't killed her yet.

After striking Guillermo in the throat with the satellite phone, Gina watched helplessly as the life drained out of him. Someone from camp overheard her scream and in the few seconds before they arrived, Gina was able to push the phone into the earth and cover it with several leaves. She didn't want to be caught with the phone on her when the men came, not to mention that from the looks of the screen, there was a good chance it was broken.

A moment later, Patrick and two soldiers showed up. Their flashlights illuminated Gina's frozen face, then quickly moved to the still form of their fallen comrade. Gina opted for a version of the truth, telling them that Guillermo had caught her trying to escape and dragged her to the hut. He'd been attempting to rape her when she'd hit him in the neck with the binaural spring she'd used to cut through the tent.

Patrick had believed her, but she wasn't sure about the soldiers. Even now, two days later, Gina could see it in the soldiers' eyes: they wanted her dead. Even Benecio, who had snuck Gina an energy bar a few times, looked at her differently. Gina concluded the only reason she was still alive was because Patrick had ordered the soldiers to leave her alone. But those orders were subject to reversal, as Patrick had told her, "If you try to escape again, I'll turn you over to them."

Gina wasn't sure what they had done with Guillermo's body. She guessed they had buried it somewhere nearby. Most Bolivians were Roman Catholic, and there was a good chance that not far from the drug lab there was a cross sitting atop a jungle grave.

On that note, it turned out the drug lab wasn't their final destination. From there, their journey had continued through the forest. They had set out early the morning after Guillermo's death. A few hours later, when they stopped to rest, Patrick discovered that the satellite phone was missing. Gina was relieved when Patrick blamed Bill for the missing phone, screaming at him, "Well, you were the last one to use it!"

Two hours earlier, when they had stopped to make camp, El Jefe was once again carried into her tent. Gina was out of saline bags, and to keep him hydrated, she began shooting water down his throat with a syringe.

Gina pulled back the plunger on a syringe and filled it with water. She elevated the man's head with one hand, then put the syringe in the man's mouth and pushed in the plunger, sending half an ounce down the man's throat. Gina repeated this three times, then she heard a soft creak outside the tent.

Footsteps.

She stiffened. Maybe the soldiers were going to kill her anyway. Was this it? Were they coming for her now?

Unless . . .

Gina whipped her head toward the back of the tent. She waited for the tip of a blade to peek through the nylon of the new tent—Patrick had made her swap out the tent she'd cut the large flap in with one of the soldiers' tents. But no blade appeared, and the footsteps retreated, perhaps their owner had reconsidered his plan, or maybe it had just been one of the guys relieving himself.

After blowing out the breath she had been holding, Gina refilled the syringe. She moved behind the man and was elevating his head when she saw a stain begin to spread on the man's tan pants.

Had El Jefe been in a hospital, he would have a catheter inserted into his bladder to remove the urine, but without one, his body was forced to relieve itself on its own. This was only the second time that it had happened in the five days Gina had been his caretaker.

After thirty seconds, the darkening of the man's pants subsided. Gina pulled on a pair of latex gloves and unbuttoned the man's belt and pants. She wrinkled her nose. The urine of a properly hydrated person doesn't carry much of a scent, but in someone who is dehydrated, it becomes more concentrated and smells strongly of ammonia.

Gina pulled off the man's pants. He was wearing white briefs, now stained a wet yellow. She slipped the man's briefs down, revealing his salt-and-pepper pubic hair. She carried the pants and briefs to the front of the tent, unzipped the flap, and set them on the ground. She would rinse and hang them out to dry once she'd cleaned up her patient.

She found a washcloth and dampened it with water. She cleaned the man's privates, then wiped between his thighs, and down his legs. While Gina had the rag out, she decided to clean the man's upper body as well. After however many days in the jungle heat, he stank.

She knelt behind him, propping him up, then shimmied his shirt up and over his head. His back was old-person flabby, with the occasional patch of gray hair.

Gina was surprised to see that he had two tattoos, one near each shoulder blade.

Both were the blurry green of tattoos done before the science had been perfected. The one near his left shoulder blade read "Fortune and Glory, kid. Fortune and Glory." Underneath the words was what most people might think was a snake or a squiggly line, but anyone who got the reference, as Gina did, would know it was a whip.

"Indiana Jones," she said.

She couldn't help but think about Thomas. The only DVDs he owned were the first three Indiana Jones movies. After watching each multiple times, Gina had finally forced him to get Netflix, which Thomas then used to watch an Indiana Jones marathon.

She chuckled at the memory. He was *so* dumb.

God, she missed him. She tried to convince herself that she didn't. That leaving him and returning to Bolivia had been the right choice. The villagers in Tibióno needed her. But did they really? Was there anything Gina did that another doctor—pretty much any other WHO doctor—couldn't have done?

Maybe she had fled Thomas because she was scared. Scared by how hard she'd fallen. Even harder than she'd fallen for Paul. She didn't know if she could handle another painful ending.

So she'd bailed.

Left him.

She knew that if Thomas had gotten her message, he'd be on his way to Bolivia. He might act like a twelve-year-old half the time, but he was as reliable and clever as they came. He might be fifty miles from her village by now.

Gina shook herself back to the present and leaned down to scrutinize El Jefe's second tattoo. It was three inches big—King Tut.

Why would a narco boss have a tattoo of an Indiana Jones quote and an ancient Egyptian pharaoh?

After a moment, Gina's mouth opened wide.

It was because El Jefe wasn't a narcotrafficker.

He was an *archaeologist*.

30

The odds were staggering. I couldn't believe what I was seeing.

Andy Depree was on his hands and knees, digging in the dirt. Even from twenty feet away, I could see the wispy orange mustache the anthropologist had grown since I'd seen him a week earlier.

"Andy!" I shouted. "Andy!"

He craned his head up and squinted. It took him a moment to recognize me. "*Thomas?*"

I pushed aside several branches and made my way to where he'd risen to his feet. His face was contorted, like he was trying to do the Sunday sudoku in pen. I guessed our chance meeting was an even bigger surprise for him than it was for me. At no point in our airplane conversation had I disclosed that I was heading into the jungle as well.

"What? How?" he mumbled. "Last I saw you—"

I finished for him: "—I was being detained by airport officials."

"What are you doing out here? And who are those other people?"

As he looked a bit apprehensive, I surmised Andy thought I was involved in something illicit.

"I'm looking for a friend of mine who went missing in the

jungle. That's why I was on your flight. It was the fastest way I could get down here."

"Oh."

I waved the others forward and introduced them. They all shook hands with Andy. At the sight of Camila poking her head out from behind Diego, Andy's mouth opened wide and he said, "Oh, my goodness. Is that a sloth? May I?"

"Ask Diego."

Diego nodded and Andy gently gave Camila a pat on the head.

"She's so soft," Andy said, his eyes turning into two heart emojis.

I instantly liked him exponentially more.

I turned to Vern and said, "If you can believe it, this is the anthropologist from the plane—"

I'm not sure if it was the words coming out of my mouth or the lack of shock on Vern's face that made me realize my naiveté.

This was no one-in-a-zillion chance encounter in the middle of the Amazon jungle.

Far from it.

I turned to Vern and said, "That's why you kept looking at your stupid GPS." I shook my head from side to side. "*You knew.*"

Vern had flown the lidar survey over the area. He would know the coordinates of the ruins.

"It didn't even cross my mind until yesterday," Vern said. "That's when I realized we must be getting close."

I asked, "You know what this means?"

"Yeah," Vern said with a sigh. "The people who took your girl—they're looking for Paititi *too.*"

≈

"Wait," Andy said. "Who's looking for Paititi?"

I gave him a quick rundown on how Dr. Gina Brady was

kidnapped, and that we now suspected that the people who took her were looking for the same lost city as the documentary crew.

I glanced around at the cleared earth where he'd been kneeling. There was a hole in the ground and the top of a stone was visible. I asked, "Have you guys encountered anyone else at any of the sites?"

"No."

"You haven't seen any evidence of camps or fires?" asked Vern. "Footprints? Anything that looks like someone had been to the sites?"

"It's been raining off and on for the last few days, so any footprints would be long gone. And every place we've been so far looks like it hasn't been touched in five hundred years."

I found it odd that I had spent the same amount of time in the jungle, yet it hadn't rained once. Gina had once told me that in the jungle there were several microclimates. One area could get rain seven days in a row, while another area just twenty miles away wouldn't see a drop.

The snapping of twigs stopped the conversation, and everyone turned and waited for a man to emerge from the brush. In his late fifties, he wore wire-rim glasses and a tan hat. Like everyone else, he had a week's worth of stubble—his, a perfect white.

"I thought I heard people chatting over here." He stuck his hand out. "Nathan Buxton."

After introducing himself, he gave Camila a little wave with his hand, then moving his finger back and forth between me and Andy, asked, "How do you two know each other?"

Andy quickly recounted our shared history and what I was doing in the jungle, then explained, "Nathan is writing an article about the expedition for *National Geographic*."

"And possibly a book now," Buxton said, clapping me on the shoulder. "What, with this new wrinkle and all."

There was a soft squawk, and the same voice came through the radios attached to both Andy's and Buxton's backpacks. "We're heading back to base camp in a few minutes. Let's get everybody back to the petroglyphs."

"Who's that?" I asked.

"Mark Holland," Andy said. "He and another guy run a company called Television and Film Logistics and Safety. They're both ex–Special Forces, and they run a pretty tight ship."

"Special Forces?"

"British."

Andy made his way to his pack and pulled off the radio.

He hit the talk button and said, "Buxton and I are headed back now." He glanced up at me and the four other new arrivals and added, "And we're bringing friends."

≈

Andy led us through the jungle thirty meters to a hacked-out clearing where his colleagues had gathered near a large boulder. Nearly as tall as myself and twice as wide, it was covered with circular and concentric carvings. Someone had traced the rock carvings with white chalk, and the etched grooves stood in stark contrast to the dark gray of the large boulder.

There were seven people in the group. From the plane ride, I recognized the Egyptian archaeologist and the two cameramen. The ex–Special Forces duo were thick, and their hands hovered over sidearms strapped to their waists. The remaining two individuals could have passed for Diego's parents.

I couldn't help but notice that Jonathan Roth and his production assistant were MIA.

"What the bloody hell?" said the taller soldier. His head was shaved, though he had several days of stubble, and he had a goatee headed toward a full beard. "Where'd you lot come from?"

The camera and a large boom mike pointed in my direction. It felt like I was back doing a press conference at the Seattle Police Department, and I slid into character. Though to be fair, instead of a nice suit and perfectly coifed hair, I looked like a grizzled mountain man who had come down with a severe case of chicken pox.

I said, "Thank you all for coming."

The two soldiers shared a quick "Who the hell is this guy?" glance.

I cleared my throat to offer up some credentials. "My name is Thomas Prescott. I was a homicide detective and a contract agent with the FBI's Violent Crime Unit for several years."

Both soldiers relaxed their hands above their guns.

I spent the next several minutes detailing Gina's phone call and abduction, then I detailed how Vern had arranged my hitched ride with the documentary crew.

Holland nodded at Vern and said, "You're the guy who helped with the permits for the lidar mission and the archaeological survey."

"Damn right," Vern said with a smile. "I flew the survey as well."

Suddenly everyone was shaking hands. The older Bolivians introduced themselves as Alejándro and Bernita. The cameramen were Sean and Darnell.

After we shook hands, Rix said, "Sorry about the rude welcome party."

"Not a problem," I said. "Perfectly understandable, given the circumstances."

After introductions were complete, at Holland's urging, I picked up where I'd left off in my story. Both soldiers perked up when I reached the part about the drug lab.

Holland asked, "How many narcos?"

I said, "We saw three, but shortly after we got there, one of them left on a four-wheeler piled high with bricks of cocaine. Long story short, Gina wasn't in either of the shacks, and we were quickly surrounded by a small army. Luckily, Vern knew the Colombian boss from—"

I turned to Vern, not sure how to describe his relationship with the Colombian narco.

Vern finished for me. "—from when I was a real piece of shit."

Everyone got a chuckle out of this.

"Anyhow," I continued, "the boss assured us they hadn't abducted Gina. That set us off on a different trail, which brought us face-to-face with you lot."

"Can't be a coincidence," Rix said.

I agreed.

Farah said, "So, these horrible people that took her, they are looking for Paititi as well?"

"That's been my working theory for going on seven minutes now," I said.

Holland said, "We haven't seen any signs of people or any signs of previous excavation at any of the sites."

Andy said, "Yeah, but we've only been to two of the six target sites. They could be at any of the other four."

"We'll be on the lookout," Rix said. "And we'll have the Bolivian soldiers help us with a recon tomorrow."

Holland nodded.

I saw Andy's eyebrows furrow, and I asked, "What are you thinking?"

His face went flat. Like he'd been called on to bring his soufflé up to the front of the Home Economics class. "Oh, um."

"Andy," I prodded.

"Okay," he said, letting out a trapped breath. "If these guys are willing to take a doctor by force from a small village, they're unlikely to be academics. Odds are they're archaeological mercenaries, and all they're interested in is stealing and selling the artifacts."

"Okay," I said. "I'm with you so far."

I glanced at Vern. From the look on his face, he was having the same epiphany Andy had.

I wasn't there yet myself.

"There have been over a hundred expeditions that have searched for Paititi," Andy continued, "but only one that was anywhere even remotely close to where we are now. And that expedition team disappeared in the jungle, never coming back."

I finally saw the light. "So these archaeological mercenaries must have some pretty good intel." It took me another half a second. "The same intel that you guys have."

"The lidar scans," Vern said, shaking his head. "I bet that dipshit Roth was showing them off to every Tom, Dick, and Harry."

Farah said, "The jaguar."

"What jaguar?" I asked.

Andy explained, "The picture the satellite imagery company sent to Roth. It was a golden jaguar half buried in the ground. The coordinates of the artifact were included in the photo, down to the centimeter. It's about a quarter mile from here, and we only got out to it yesterday."

"And?"

Farah said, "*And* it was gone."

31

The main camp was fifty feet wide and a hundred feet long. For the most part, the ground was a muddy mess from the rains. Two white tents, the kind you see at a farmer's market, were nestled together in one corner. In the opposite corner, two enormous tarps were strung from several different trees. It was evident this was command central.

Jonathan Roth and his production assistant were sitting in collapsible nylon chairs in command central, fiddling on a laptop.

Roth glanced up as we approached. "You guys find anything goo—" He leaned forward and squinted. If he were a cartoon, he would have squeegeed both eyes with his fists. "What in the hell?" He pushed himself up from his chair.

"Surprise!" I shouted.

"I'll say," he said, walking toward us.

I couldn't help but notice his facial hair, unlike everyone else's, was the same length as when I'd seen him a week earlier. Clearly, he'd packed his trimmers.

"We were going to radio ahead," Holland said with a soft smile. Then, nodding at Sean, who had his camera trained on Roth, he added, "But we thought this might make for better television."

"No, no, this is much better!" He laughed. "I just— I'm having trouble processing this."

"To be expected," Vern said.

"*Papagayo!*" Roth shouted. "How the hell are you?"

"I'm tired, I'm hungry, my knee hurts like hell, and I could use a stiff drink."

"Well, I can fix a few of those things." Roth looked over his shoulder and said, "Libby, get water heating on the stoves. Let's get these people some food."

Libby gave a thumbs-up but continued working.

Roth clapped his hands twice and said, "Come on, chop-chop. We have hungry travelers." He turned back around, his brilliant veneers on full display. "And who else do we have here?"

I introduced my companions. I expected Roth to swoon over the baby sloth, much like Andy had, but he hardly acknowledged her.

"You're welcome to anything," Roth said. "Lots of snacks and some killer freeze-dried meals."

I wasn't sure whether his hospitality was genuine or if he was playing for the cameras.

Time would tell.

He waved us forward. "Come on, drop those packs. Let's get you some grub. Beef stew, mac and cheese, chicken tetrazzini— we got it all."

"The mac and cheese is pretty good," Andy said.

I patted him on the shoulder and said, "Then I shall have the mac and cheese, my friend."

≈

Jonathan Roth and I were under one of the white tents. We were seated in chairs across from each other. Sean operated a video camera on a tripod, and Darnell held the boom microphone. The rest of the expedition team was eating in command central.

Twenty minutes earlier, over two pouches of freeze-dried dinner—one mac and cheese and one beef stew—I recounted to Roth the circumstances that led to my intercepting his group, and he'd insisted I sit down for an interview.

"So you believe another group is here looking for Paititi?" he asked.

I was preparing to answer, when I felt a soft bump on the side of my head. I glanced up at the man holding the boom microphone.

"My bad," Darnell mouthed.

I rubbed my head and said, "Are you trying to give me CTE?" Since Darnell was wearing a Bengals hat, I knew he'd get my reference to the disease at the center of the NFL's concussion debate.

He chuckled.

"Dammit, Darnell!" Roth shouted. "Be careful with that thing."

"It didn't hurt," I said. "I was just messing with him."

Roth took a calming breath, then got back to my interview. "Another group looking for Paititi took her? That's what you think?"

"Yes. Which raises another question: How did this group know about this location?"

"Right."

I don't think it registered with him that I was asking *him* a question. I decided on a more forthright approach. I asked, "Who else did you show the lidar scans to? Who else outside this expedition team knew the coordinates of the ruins?"

He put his hand to his chest. "What? You think I leaked the coordinates?"

"Did you?"

He nodded to the two cameramen. "Why don't you guys go grab some food."

Once the cameramen were gone, Roth said, "Why would

you think I leaked valuable information? Someone could have swooped in and found the city before I did. I wouldn't even have a film. No one gives a shit about someone finding something second. That would have been eight hundred thousand dollars of my money down the drain."

He had a good point.

I said, "Okay, let's go back to the beginning. With the photo some guy sends you."

"I don't know if I'm comfortable telling this all to you."

I took a moment to decide how I wanted to play this: Old Thomas or New Thomas?

"A woman's life is on the line here, and I need your help," said New Thomas.

Roth bit the inside of his cheek. "I should run this by my lawyer really quick." He checked his watch. "What time do you think it is in Bangkok?"

I tried to keep my cool. "If something got leaked to the wrong people, I won't hold you personally responsible. Surely, you wouldn't have known they were going to kidnap someone."

"I didn't leak anything, so yeah, of course not."

"Good. Now from the beginning, a guy sends you a photo . . ."

He pushed up from the chair. "Give me one minute. I'll call my guy in Bang—"

I mentally strapped New Thomas into his rollerblades and pushed him off a twenty-story building. "Sit the fuck down."

Roth slowly lowered himself back into his seat.

"If you stand up again before you answer every question I ask, I'm going to hit you really, *really* hard in the face."

"What? You can't talk to—"

"And then I'm going to break two fingers. Not one of your fingers, *two* of your fingers."

"Who do you think—"

"Then I'm going to go into your tent, find your fancy beard trimmer, and I'm going to shave your entire fucking head."

I was 60 percent sure I wasn't going to do any of these things, but Roth didn't know that. He blinked his eyes twice and said, "Fine, okay. Um, yeah, I'll tell you whatever you want to know. Nothing to hide here."

"Okay, good. Start at the beginning."

He took a nice long breath, then said, "Jordan Mae at Yewed Global sent me a picture earlier this February. His company had been commissioned by an environmental group to take a series of photos over the Bolivian Amazon. The group wasn't able to come up with the financing for the pictures, and Jordan, who'd helped me with some photos for a previous documentary, got to scanning the images. In one of the images there was a small window onto the jungle floor, and stuck in the earth was a golden statue of a jaguar. He thought I'd be interested in it, so he sent it my way."

"Just for free?"

"He said if I ended up making a documentary on it, he wanted an executive producer credit and a couple points on the back end. I agreed."

"You put this in writing?"

"Of course. But I didn't think much of it at the time. It was a single statue in the jungle. But then I sent a picture of the statue to a professor of Inca studies at the University of Chicago, and he verified that, without a doubt, the statue was Incan."

"And that's when you started thinking about Paititi?"

"Yes. This was the farthest east anyone had ever found an Inca relic."

"Did the professor have access to the coordinates?"

"No, I just sent him a cropped picture of the statue."

"Okay, so at that point you were the only one who knew the coordinates?"

"Correct."

"But then you put together the lidar survey, and you had to bring in other people? Vern for one?"

"Who's Vern?"

"Papagayo."

"Oh, he never told me his real name." He paused. "A friend of a friend gave me *Vern's* contact info, and said he could help with the lidar permit to do an archaeological survey."

"Did you have to give the government the coordinates?"

"Vague coordinates. We gave a fifty-square-mile sector."

"Who gave out the permit?"

"The Ministry of Culture and Tourism."

"Did you bring anyone down with you to do the survey?"

"My production assistant and a lidar technician."

"Your production assistant is Libby?"

"Yeah."

"So she knew the coordinates at this point?"

"She did."

"And this lidar technician, who was he?"

"We hired him from the same firm that we rented the lidar machine from."

"Did he seem trustworthy?"

"Totally. Super-dorky tech guy."

"What was his name?"

"Dave something-or-other."

"And when did this all take place?"

He glanced up at the roof of the tent, then back down. "Second week of May."

"Mid-May. So it's you, Vern, Dave, and Libby—and you fly the lidar survey?"

"Libby wasn't on the plane. There wasn't enough room. She stayed in the hotel. But yeah—me, Dave, and Vern."

I didn't want to ask the next question, but I had to. "Did Vern know the coordinates of the jaguar?"

"Doubtful. He just knew the general area."

"Okay, then the only people who knew the exact coordinates of the jaguar were you and Libby?"

"Yes."

"Then you get back the lidar scans and see these different formations and realize there is a lost city down there?"

"Right."

"How many people did you show the lidar scans to?"

He puffed out his cheeks. "A bunch of people. But I removed the coordinates. They were just the formations."

"You're positive no one could have figured out the coordinates from these pictures?"

"Yes, I'm positive."

"What about the lidar machine? I assume this goes back to the company you rented it from. Were all your scans and coordinates saved on it, or did they get deleted?"

"The lidar device is wiped clean. No memory. The company signed a form to this effect. Dave too."

"When did the other members of the expedition team get clued in? The TAFLS guys, Holland and Rix—when did you hire them?"

"I spoke to Holland the week after I returned from the lidar survey."

"And you told him what?"

"I told him I was trying to put together an expedition to look for Paititi and asked if he could help. We had to do it before the rainy season—which is bullshit because it's been raining like crazy this whole week—and he had a two-week opening in August."

"Did you tell him the coordinates?"

"Not then. Only that it was northeastern Bolivia."

"Okay, then you start recruiting your team?"

"Right. Over the course of June, I recruited Egyptian archaeologist Dr. Farah Karim; the head of Bolivian archaeology, Alejándro Cala; Bolivian anthropologist Bernita Capobianco; and Adrian Heliant, the professor I mentioned earlier, from the University of Chicago. In late July, Heliant came down with shingles. He recommended Andy Depree."

"And the cameramen, when do they come aboard?"

"Sean and Darnell worked with me on my last two films. They signed on in early June. There's a possibility they could have accessed the coordinates, but I doubt it."

"And Buxton was the last to sign on?"

Roth nodded. "By the end of June, it was no longer a secret I was putting together financing to shoot a documentary in search of Paititi. *National Geographic* called and asked if they could send down one of their writers to cover the story. They kicked in a hundred grand, so I said of course."

"And still no one knew exactly where you were going?"

"Right, just that it was northeastern Bolivia. But everyone had seen the picture of the jaguar statue and the scans. I had to convince them we were onto something big."

"So when do you start revealing to people exactly where you're going?"

"I told the TAFLS guys the last week of June. They needed as much info as possible so they could start planning."

"I've only talked with them for a few minutes, but they seem like good guys."

"I'd have to agree."

Of course, this didn't actually mean one of them didn't sell the scans to the highest bidder.

I asked, "What about the expedition team? When did they know the coordinates of the ruins?"

"Not until we landed. That's when I handed out the six Trimble GPSs I bought that had been synced with the lidar scans."

It sounded as if Roth had done a good job of compartmentalizing the information. "What about the helicopter pilot?"

"He's local, out of Guayaramerín. He only knew the coordinates of the landing zone. And he didn't know that until a week ago."

The timetable alone eliminated him.

I took a few seconds to process everything. "Before two weeks ago, the only people who knew the precise location of the ruins were you, the TAFLS crew, possibly the cameramen, and your production assistant."

"That sounds about ri—" He stopped midsentence. "You know what? There was one more person who knew."

"Who?"

"Lieutenant Goytia."

"Who's that?"

"Our military chaperone. He and a convoy of Bolivian soldiers hiked in and joined us a few days after we arrived."

"When did you show him the scans?"

He grimaced. "Three weeks ago."

Three weeks.

"I'm going to need to talk to this guy," I said. "How far away is their camp?"

"Not far, maybe fifty meters east of us." He turned and glanced back at command central. "But that's him right there. The guy with the mustache."

I followed his gaze to a mustached man sipping from a blue cup.

I recognized him. It was the guy who'd sprung me from the El Alto detainment room. The guy who Vern had bribed to get me into the country.

MM.

Military Mustache.

32

After my sit-down with Roth, there was only fifteen minutes of daylight remaining. Holland and Rix led our contingent into the jungle to find an area where we could set up our tents. Sadly, there wasn't a large enough area to fit all five of us, and we split into two groups. Rix helped the three Bolivians set up their campsite, and Holland assisted me and Vern with ours. The ex-soldier hacked away at the vegetation, widening an area of twelve square feet for us.

On his departure, Holland said, "When you guys are all organized, head back to camp. We usually have tea—or something stronger, if that's your preference."

Once he was out of earshot, I turned to Vern, who was sitting in the opening of his tent and massaging his knee.

"Hurting?" I asked.

"Yeah."

"Maybe Diego can find another one of those Matico trees around here." My testicle could attest to its healing powers. It was back in tip-top shape—that is to say, oval.

"I'll be okay, but I wouldn't be opposed to some of that stronger stuff Holland mentioned."

I hadn't done much drinking the past couple of years, but

after the day we'd had, I concurred. But the edge would have to stay on for a few more minutes. I asked, "Did you know Lieutenant Goytia was going to be here?"

"No," Vern said, "but I'm not surprised."

"Why's that?"

"He has his hands in all sorts of pockets. He would have known about the permits, and he obviously knew the expedition was coming in."

"Roth said he was forced to give Goytia the lidar scans three weeks ago." I leaned heavily on the last three words.

"And what, you think he put together a team to look for the ruins, and they took your girl?"

"Gina said soldiers took her, and the timeline is possible. And someone arrived beforehand and grabbed that golden jaguar. Everyone else who knew about the coordinates three weeks ago doesn't fit the mold."

Vern took off his maroon hat, revealing a bald spot on the top of his head. "For one, you're going on Roth's word."

"I know when someone is lying to me. He wasn't."

"Well, I can tell you that Goytia didn't take the jaguar."

"How do you know?"

I stared at him and waited.

After a quick sigh, he said, "When Roth came down for the lidar survey, he showed me the picture of the jaguar. On the picture was a sticky note with the exact latitude and longitude of the statue. He had a set of binoculars and when he was busy looking out the window, I snapped a picture of the coordinates with my phone. A week after Roth left, I paid someone to go and snag it."

I thought back to Vern's words when I first met him: *I hired a tracker I've worked with before . . . he knows the Pando jungle as well as anyone.*

I said, "Diego."

Vern nodded.

"How much did you pay him?"

"Five thousand dollars, plus a percentage of whatever I sold it for."

"How much did you sell it for?"

"Zero."

"What do you mean?"

"It wasn't there."

"It was gone?"

"Diego came back empty-handed. He took a picture of a shallow hole where the statue had been dug up."

"What are the chances of that happening? That this statue goes undiscovered for five hundred years, and then conveniently, a few months after Roth gets sent this picture, someone finds it?"

"Very unlikely."

"Yeah."

"Could Diego have lied to you? Found it and sold it himself?"

"Possible but doubtful."

In the week I'd known Diego, I would have to agree. He seemed as loyal as they come.

Vern said, "Goytia couldn't have taken the statue, but that doesn't mean he didn't take your girl." He paused. "So what are you going to do?"

I wasn't sure. But whatever it was, it would have to wait until tomorrow.

"Come on," I said, offering him my hand. I helped him to his feet. "Let's go get you some booze."

≈

The Bolivians declined to join us at command central. With stomachs full of several pouches of freeze-dried food, they were well on their way to falling asleep. Everyone else was there, except Roth's production assistant, who was sitting in a chair under one of the white canopy tents working on her computer. I had a feeling Libby was the unsung hero behind Roth's films.

Alejándro Cala was walking around with a bottle of Bolivian brandy. With an effervescent smile, the rotund Bolivian handed Vern and me two small cups and poured us each a finger of the Singani Rujero.

I took a sip and remembered why I hadn't touched brandy since I stole a bottle of Christian Brothers from my parents' liquor cabinet in high school. I felt my face involuntarily wince, which amused Cala immensely.

"You don't like?" he said with a hearty laugh.

I slugged back the remainder and said, "Hit me again."

He did.

The second time wasn't as bad, and I almost kept my eyes open.

"Another?" Cala asked.

I shook my head. "No, that's plenty."

Cala headed off to refill others' cups and Vern, who had Cala fill his cup nearly halfway before departing, said his knee was killing him, and he hobbled toward an empty chair.

I turned and glanced over my shoulder. On the opposite side of the tent was a group of three: Andy and the two cameramen.

I could feel the brandy making its way into my legs as I strolled over to the group. "Gentlemen, what are we discussing?"

"Video games," Darnell said. "You a gamer?"

"Is *Duck Hunt* still a thing?"

"What's *Duck Hunt*?" Andy asked.

"Now you're making me feel old. It was a game that came out with the first Nintendo thirty years ago."

He gave me a soft pat on the arm. "I was kidding. I know what *Duck Hunt* is."

We chatted about the more modern video games the three were into. Much like Andy, both Darnell and Sean were into *Red Dead Redemption.*

At some point while Andy was rambling on about his latest "heist," I pushed up the cuff of my shirt and itched at one of the many red welts on my forearm.

"Those look nasty," Sean said, running one of his hands through his large brown beard.

"Ants got me good." I was getting ready to tell them the bites' origin story, when Andy nodded at Darnell and said, "Tell him about yours."

"Bullet ants," Darnell said, flashing a swollen left hand. "Hurt so damn bad that I almost cried. Definitely lived up to their name."

I snorted.

Darnell said, "You don't seem convinced."

"As someone who has been shot twice, I find it hard to believe." Although getting bit on the testicle by an ant was extremely painful, it was still a far cry from a bullet ripping through flesh and bone.

"Well, it was one of the worst pains I've ever felt," said Darnell.

"Have you ever been shot?"

"No."

"I have an idea."

Darnell smiled and shook his head. "Does it involve you shooting me?"

"It does."

Darnell laughed. "I'm going to have to pass, but I could find some bullet ants, and we could have one bite you."

"I'm also going to pass."

Andy said, "Stalemate."

I shook my head. "No, no, no." I turned and called to Vern. "Hey, Vern, have you been bitten by a bullet ant?"

"I have."

"Did it hurt as much as getting shot?"

"Hell no."

I turned back around. "Well, there you have it, kids."

Everyone laughed.

Sean looked down at his watch and said, "Yo, D, we better go and get that footage from today downloaded for Libby so Roth doesn't throw another fit."

Both cameramen left, leaving me with Andy Depree.

I asked, "You prefer hanging out with those two rather than the others?"

"Yeah, I mean, I don't have much in common with anyone else."

"Aren't you an egghead?"

He sighed. "Yeah, but I hate it."

"What? Teaching?"

"Yes, teaching."

"Why do it?"

"I'm not qualified to do anything else. And I still have eighty grand in student loans to pay off."

I gave him a light cuff on the shoulder and said, "You could always give acting another shot."

"I got that out of my system," he said with a shake of his head. "But I *would* be interested in getting behind the camera." He nodded at where Roth was sitting and chatting with Farah. "I would love his job."

"Making documentaries?"

"Yeah. That's the dream."

Andy continued to gaze in Roth's direction, but it took me a moment to realize it wasn't Roth that he was staring at.

I said, "She likes you, you know."

"Farah?"

"Trust me."

"What makes you think that?"

Most people wouldn't have noticed it, but Thomas Dergen Prescott, body language wizard, sure as heck did. "Her fingers fidget when she's near you."

"Fidget?"

"Yeah, like she's typing on an invisible keyboard."

He rolled his eyes and scoffed. "I'm pretty sure she has a thing for Roth."

"No way."

"Look at them. Chatting as if they're in their own little world."

"Observe her body," I said, shaking my head. "He's angled in, but she's not. She's not doing anything. Also, I only interacted with her for a few minutes, but she's too smart to go for a guy like Roth."

"What, you mean handsome, charming, and famous? Yeah, women never go for those guys."

"Look, I know you idolize him, that you have him on some sort of pedestal, and yeah, maybe he makes a good documentary, but he's a prick."

Andy moved backward a few inches, as if I'd pushed him.

"I'll let you think that over," I said, giving him a soft squeeze on the shoulder. The two shots of brandy were giving me a headache, not to mention my stomach was feeling queasy. "I'm going to hit the hay."

I walked over to Vern and told him I was headed to the tents. His cup had just been refilled, and he said he was going to stay up a bit longer.

I flipped on my headlamp and pushed my way through the thick brush to my tent. There were a bunch of cockroaches, mammoth beetles, and other insects crawling on the ground and I stepped on one near the front entrance of the tent, making a soft crack underfoot.

"Sorry, buddy," I said. Saying the words sent a sharp pain through my temples.

I unzipped the tent and a few cockroaches stampeded in, but I didn't much care. I needed to close my eyes. My last thought before falling asleep was that I was never drinking brandy again.

33

Andy reread the same page in his book for the third time. His brain was elsewhere. He couldn't stop thinking about what Thomas had said. *Both* things Thomas had said. There was a chance one of them could be true; it was entirely possible Jonathan Roth was a total prick.

During his short tenure in LA, Andy had been exposed to any number of pricks. The film industry was full of them. But Jonathan Roth came across as such a great guy in his movies, and all the behind-the-scenes footage Andy had watched showed him being a decent guy. That's one reason he looked up to him.

But now, looking back on his interactions with him—trying to see Roth without the rose-colored glasses—Andy realized that Roth treated Sean, Darnell, and especially Libby, like garbage.

As for the other thing Thomas said, it couldn't possibly be true. Gorgeous Dr. Farah Karim was into him?

No way.

Not once during their limited interaction had he gotten an inkling she was interested. Though to be fair, it had been several years since any female had shown any interest in him, and it was possible—even probable—that he'd simply forgotten how to read the signals.

His last relationship was four years earlier. It was a girl he'd met online. They had traded messages for a few weeks before finally meeting at a coffee shop. She was slightly less attractive than her profile pictures but was nice enough, and they had ended up dating for eight months. It had never been the passionate, "claw at your back, bees in your belly" relationship Andy had always wanted. It was more "watch Netflix for six hours together and then maybe, every few weeks, have sex."

When Andy had headed to Peru for his dissertation, he broke things off, surprised at how little the breakup affected him.

He thought back to what Thomas had said, how Farah's fingers fidgeted whenever she was near him. He'd never noticed it.

Andy closed his eyes, and over the next twenty minutes he went on multiple dates with Farah. Dining at a nice restaurant. Going to the opening of a new movie. At Comic-Con, both dressed in cosplay: he as Ironman, Farah as Black Widow.

Andy felt a twitch in his groin.

He let the fantasy play out. Going back to their hotel room, peeling her costume off her. He imagined her full breasts, toned stomach, her—

There was a loud whistle, and Andy bolted upright. The sound was coming from just north of him.

Farah's campsite.

Andy flipped on the lantern and ducked out of the tent. A small group of bats flew overheard, but he hardly noticed. There was one final whistle as he pushed his way through the brush and the fifteen meters that separated his camp from Farah's.

Holland and Libby arrived at nearly the same time as Andy, each holding their own lantern. Farah stood outside her tent. Her chest was heaving, and the orange whistle was still in her mouth.

"What happened?" Holland shouted.

Farah pulled the whistle from her mouth, then after two long breaths, she said, "A fer-de-lance."

"Where?"

She nodded to where the flap to her tent was open. "I was coming back from going to the bathroom, and it was sitting right in front of the tent. It slithered off right before you arrived."

Holland walked forward and surveyed the ground. "Don't see—" he stopped suddenly, then glancing into Farah's tent, he said, "Oh, hey there."

Andy was confused until a head popped out of the flap.

It was Jonathan Roth.

Andy's mouth went dry.

Roth had been hiding in the back of her tent.

Roth smiled meekly. "I was going over some details of tomorrow's search with Farah. But I guess I'd better make my way back to my campsite." He crawled out, gave a quick wave, then took off into the brush.

"You going to be okay?" Holland asked Farah.

Andy didn't hear what she said in reply.

He was already gone.

34

"You all right over there?" Vern asked.

I kicked dirt over what thirty seconds earlier had been the contents of my stomach and wiped my mouth with the sleeve of my shirt. "Yeah, just a little hungover."

This was the understatement of the century. My head was spinning. It felt like someone had speed-bagged my stomach for fifteen minutes. It throbbed behind my eyes. This made the morning after my twenty-first birthday seem like a warm bath.

"How much did you drink?" Vern asked.

"Just a couple shots."

"I drank a helluva lot more than that, and I feel fine."

"Yeah, well, I'm something of a lightweight these days."

"It appears so," Vern said with a laugh. "You going to be able to make it to the main camp, or do you need me to carry your sorry ass?"

"I'll be there in a few minutes," I said, forcing a smile. "I might have to go another round with the throw-up fairy first."

He nodded, then disappeared behind a curtain of green.

I shut my eyes against the soft morning glow and swallowed the rising bile in my throat. There was too much to do today for me to be hungover. There was a chance Gina and her abductors were still in the area. They could be at any number of the four archaeological sites the expedition had yet to visit. And I needed to tell Holland about Lieutenant Goytia. And then I needed to have a sit-down with Goytia himself. Even if he wasn't connected to Gina's abduction, he might be able to shed some light on who was.

I tried to think back to what Vern had told me the previous night. That he was the one to take the jaguar statue. Or had he? Or did they not find it? Or—

I winced.

It hurt to think.

My stomach flipped, and I lurched forward and fell to my knees. I violently puked up the last dregs of the two freeze-dried meals I'd eaten the previous evening.

I pushed myself up with a loud grunt, then stumbled forward until I found the narrow path that had been cut through the vegetation. I shielded my eyes against the light—*Why was it so bright at this hour of the morning?*—and trudged the short distance to the main camp.

Most of the expedition team, including Juan Pablo, Carlos, and Diego (and Camila) were eating breakfast at command central.

A dull pain coursed through my knees and ankles as I approached. But it wasn't just my legs. My arms, shoulders, and back were sore too. Six days of hiking had done a number on my body. I guess I wasn't in as good a shape as I thought.

I finally made it to the tent, and someone said, "Looks like someone had a little too much fun last night."

I squinted.

It was Nathan Buxton.

The author?

Or was he an archaeologist?

Or was he a dentist?

I said, "I guess so."

"You want some coffee?"

The last thing I wanted was something hot. "I'm going to pass. Where's Holland?"

"He's right over—"

I didn't hear the rest of his reply. I stumbled from beneath the tent, fell to my knees, and vomited. As I dry-heaved several times, I could hear voices behind me.

"Thomas." It took me a moment to realize it was Diego's voice. "You not okay, Thomas."

"I'm fine, I just—" I dry heaved again.

When I finished, I rolled over onto my back.

I felt a hand on my forehead. "Holy shit, he's burning up."

Another hand felt around my throat. "His glands are really swollen."

A moment later, a cold rag was placed over my eyes and forehead. The voices faded in and out.

"Get Holland over here!"

"Open his shirt."

"He has the rash."

"Get it farther under his tongue."

"Holy shit! One hundred and three point three!"

"He's got dengue."

≈

I've never been good with the flu. There's just something about an army of microscopic invaders attacking my body that freaks me out. The year H1N1 came around, I got it. I was living in Philadelphia with Lacy at the time, and she was forced to take care of me. After three days of palliative care, her patience was fried, and she said, "Serial killers, no problem. Broken ankle, doesn't go to the hospital for three days. But a little flu bug, and all of a sudden he's dying!"

According to Holland, dengue fever—the virus I had almost certainly contracted from one of many mosquitoes that had feasted on my delicious blood—ate H1N1 for breakfast.

Every bone in my body screamed. It felt like two giants were using me as a wishbone. It felt like someone had set off an M-80 behind my eyes. My head pounded like my temples were trying to switch places with each other. And it was just so damn hot.

They moved me to one of the two white tents. I was on the ground. My shirt was open, and several emergency ice packs were put on my chest and stomach. Even with the ice packs, I felt like I was lying on the asphalt in Phoenix in July.

My brain was starting to play tricks on me, and I was having trouble staying awake.

"One hundred and three point nine," someone—I think his name was Marvin—said at one point. "That's bloody hot. We might have to chopper you out of here, mate."

"Vern," I mumbled. "*Verrrrrnn.*"

"Yeah, buddy, right here."

With the few brain cells which hadn't been turned into hard-boiled eggs, I said, "Don't let them take me anywhere."

"You sure?"

"Promise."

Vern promised.

"Good," I said. "Because I won't leave without Gina."

35

"He what?" Andy asked.

"I swear," Darnell said, fighting down a smile. "He thinks he's on *Naked and Afraid*. He keeps mumbling about making it to day twenty-one."

By the time Andy made it to the main camp—he was a bit apprehensive about facing either Roth or Farah and stayed in his tent until nearly seven—the only thing anyone was talking about was Thomas.

He had all the telltale signs of dengue: swollen glands, rash on his chest, and of course, a temperature of almost 104.

According to Darnell, Holland wanted to chopper him out, and he would have if Thomas had been one of the expedition team. But Thomas wasn't technically under Holland's authority, and it was decided they would let him ride it out since that's what he wanted.

"*Naked and Afraid?*" Andy said, with raised eyebrows. "That's funny." But humor was the furthest thing from Andy's mind. "Do, uh, you know if dengue is contagious?"

"Holland said it can't be transferred person-to-person—only by mosquito."

Andy already had his can of insect repellent out and was spraying himself head to toe. When he emptied the can, he glanced over at the white tent where Thomas was lying on the ground. "What if a mosquito bites him and then bites one of us?"

Thomas seemed like a great guy, but Andy would feel much more comfortable if Thomas were in New Zealand right now.

Darnell scoffed. "You're much more likely to get lymphoma from all the DEET you're covering yourself in than to get bit by the same damn mosquito that bit him."

Darnell started toward command central, and Andy ran to catch up. His heart began to race as he asked, "Wait, what's this about lymphoma?"

≈

The expedition team and their Bolivian escorts trudged through the knee-deep brown waters of an unnamed river. They were bound for T3, a mile and a half away. Holland and Rix were headed to the sprawling T5, three miles northwest of base camp, searching for the dangerous characters who might have abducted Thomas's missing doctor, which left Lieutenant Goytia and the Bolivian soldiers as their chaperones for the day.

The soldier in front of Andy had his automatic rifle out and swiveled it back and forth. When they'd first started their trek up the jungle river forty-five minutes earlier, Andy had asked the soldier what they were looking for.

To which the soldier replied, "Caiman."

This wasn't frightening at first, as the river was only a foot deep, but as they progressed, the water got both deeper and murkier.

Andy positioned himself in the middle of the pack, figuring that if a caiman did pick one of them off, it would be someone from the front or back. Andy glanced behind him. Alejándro Cala was the slowest walker of the bunch and took up the rear. Just a few feet ahead of Cala were Buxton, Sean, two Bolivian soldiers, and Farah.

It wasn't like the gung-ho Farah to be at the back of the group, but Andy guessed it was because Roth was up front, leading the way. From what Andy had observed throughout the morning, the two were keeping their distance. After being caught in their tryst the previous evening, they seemed to be trying to give the appearance that they were nothing more than colleagues.

Andy knew better.

They were *lovers*.

Two gunshots rang out.

He froze.

A small caiman had been swimming not far from them, and one of the soldiers sent a few warning shots into the water to scare it away. It worked: the five-foot caiman swished its armored body to shore and disappeared into the weeds.

Continuing on the river would take them within twenty meters of T3, but it was decided the now thigh-deep water was too dangerous, and everyone made their way to the river's muddy banks.

"It should only be another few hundred meters through the jungle," Roth said, turning and winking at the camera recording him.

Fifteen minutes later, Roth checked his GPS. "This is the edge of the site. It sits just above the floodplain of the river. The lidar indicates a small pyramid-shaped formation ten feet ahea—"

Roth froze when he realized what was directly in front of the group.

It was cloaked in five hundred years' worth of vegetation—

moss, climbing vines, ferns—and plenty of earth, but there was no mistaking it.

It was a stone pyramid.

≈

After the initial shock wore off, the team attacked the stone pyramid like an angry pack of piranhas.

Andy wriggled halfway up the pyramid—which was fifty feet square and rose more than twenty feet—and stood on a large jutting stone. With his seven-inch bowie knife, he hacked through the vegetation cloaking the stone above him, cutting away a two-foot section of tan vines, then tossing them down.

Andy was aiming for the ground directly below him, but he'd never been accurate with his throwing, and the vines landed inches from Alejándro Cala.

"Sorry," Andy yelled down. "Almost hit you there."

"No problem," Cala said with a wide grin and a chuckle.

It would take a lot more than getting hit with a chunk of vines to get the Bolivian's spirits down.

"I have been on dozens of excavations," Cala said, peering up at Andy, "but this, my friend, is something very special indeed."

"Yeah," Andy agreed. "It's freaking amazing."

Andy cut away another section of vines until the rectangular stone—three feet wide and two feet high—was fully exposed. It was reddish tan—basalt or sandstone, if he had to venture a guess. He shouted down to Cala, "Where do you suppose they found these stones?"

"There could be a quarry hidden somewhere nearby," Cala said. "And who knows? That river could have once been bedrock. The entire landscape of the jungle could be drastically different than it was five centuries ago."

The yellow walkie on Andy's shoulder squawked, and Bernita's voice rang out. *"I think you're all going to want to see this!"*

Andy climbed down five of the large stones and joined Cala on the ground. The pair snaked their way through the surrounding foliage to the pyramid's opposite side. They found the others kneeling beside Bernita, their heads shaking back and forth in awe.

Bernita had cleared a circular foot of earth and was brushing off the top of an exposed clay artifact. It appeared to be a shallow cup. Dirt was caked in the grooves of an intricate pattern carved into its sides.

"Wow!" Nathan Buxton exclaimed.

"Here's another one!" cried Roth. "And another! They're scattered everywhere!"

A whistle blew and everyone stopped. It was Farah. "Everyone, take a step back!" she yelled. "Don't touch anything!"

"We have to get the cameras in here," Roth said.

"Actually," she said. "We need to preserve the integrity of the site."

"But—"

"Um, guys." Libby stood near Darnell and Sean and their cameras. "There's something silver over here," she said, pointing down.

Andy was the first to reach it. He fell to his knees and brushed aside a large swath of leaves. Only a small portion of the silver statue was exposed, but Andy recognized the figure.

An alpaca.

Andy's jaw went slack. Several precious metals could be found in the Amazon, but silver wasn't one of them. The silver alpaca couldn't have come from these parts. It likely originated in the Andes.

"*¡Ay, Dios mío!*" Cala shouted just feet from Andy.

Andy thought Cala's exclamation was at the sight of the silver alpaca, but it wasn't. It was a different statue. This one gold.

"What is it?" Roth called from above.

"It's a golden mask," said Cala. "Inti, the Inca god of the sun."

Roth began jumping up and down. "We've found it! We found Paititi!"

≈

At the discovery of the three Incan artifacts—they'd also found a *tumi*, which is a ceremonial knife made from gold, silver, copper, and bronze—everyone went wild. There was hooting, hollering, hugging, and high fives. If they'd had a bottle of champagne handy, they would all have been dripping from head to toe.

Farah Karim quickly put a stop to the celebration. She blew her whistle incessantly, shrieking that if everyone didn't step clear of the cache of artifacts that instant, she would immediately resign from the project.

Fortunately for her, Cala seconded her request, and everyone cleared the area.

From her pack, Farah retrieved a roll of yellow caution tape and marked off a three-hundred-square-foot area. "No one goes past this tape but me, Alejándro, Bernita, and Andy," she'd commanded.

That had been almost an hour ago.

The two Bolivians were working the north end of the clearing, leaving Andy and Farah to work the south end.

Andy was kneeling in the dirt ten feet from Farah. There was a small pile of green stakes next to each of them. With a stiff brush, Andy worked a section of dirt off the partially exposed artifact directly in front of him, revealing a beautiful ribbon of zig-zag patterning.

"Sweet!" he exclaimed.

Farah crawled over to him and asked, "What have you got?"

"Looks like a large vessel."

Farah took her cell phone out of her pocket. After taking several pictures of the exposed artifact, she aimed the phone at Andy and said, "Say *Paititi*!"

"Paititi," Andy said, hoping he wouldn't look as goofy as he felt.

Farah snapped a couple of shots, then turned the phone to him. She said, "You look ever so unhappy to have found treasure."

"I don't photograph well. I'm better on video."

"Okay, then," she said pointing her phone at him a second time. "Let's see it, DiCaprio."

Andy smiled and said, "*Paititi*."

"Is that it?"

He shrugged.

She turned the phone around toward him and played his three-second video. Watching it with him, she said, "You know what? You *are* better on video."

Andy laughed.

Farah made her way back to the artifact she was cataloging. After a few long seconds she said, "I lied to you before."

"What do you mean?"

"When I told you I wasn't scared of anything. That's not true. There's one thing that scares me."

Andy put down his brush and gave her his undivided attention.

"Men," she said.

Andy put his hand to his chest. "Men?"

"Relax, not you."

"Oh."

"That's not to say you're *not* a man." She threw up her hands. "That came out wrong." She took a breath. "Last night—there wasn't a snake."

Andy got up and walked a few feet toward her. "What do you mean?"

Farah glanced over both shoulders, then she picked her phone up off the ground. She tapped on it a few times, then turned it toward Andy.

It was an audio recording.

"*. . . you doing here?*" Farah said on the recording.

"*Oh, like you don't know,*" said Jonathan Roth.

Farah: "*No, I don't know, and I don't feel comfortable with you unzipping my tent in the middle of the night.*"

Roth: "*What was all that talk before, about making a film together in Egypt. Come on, we both know what's going on here.*"

Farah: "*Listen, I think a documentary about my government's unfair prosecution of journalists would be great. And* nothing *is going on here. I told you when you walked me to my hotel room in La Paz that I wasn't interested.*"

Roth: "*Yeah, well, your eyes are saying something different.*"

Farah: "*Well, my eyes right now are saying 'Get the fuck out of my tent.'*"

Roth: "*There's the fire I like.*"

Farah: "*Seriously, get out.*"

Roth: [Laughs] "*Or what?*"

There was a second and a half of silence. Andy locked eyes with Farah. His heart was beating nearly as fast as when he was on the helicopter.

Roth: "*We're both adults. Can't we come to an understanding?*"

Farah: "*I, um—*"

Roth: "*Don't you want that film made? I can make it happen. Two phone calls. That's all it takes.*"

Farah: "*Can you . . . Do not touch me!*"

Roth: "*Relax.*"

Farah blew her whistle: *TWEEEEEEEEEEE! TWEEEEEEE-EEEEEEEEE!*

Roth: *What are you— Stop! Stop! . . . I'm leavi—*

Farah: *TWEEEEEEEEEEEEEEEEEEEE!*

A few moments later, Holland could be heard saying, *"What happened?"*

Farah: *"A fer-de-lance."*

Farah hit stop.

"I'm so sorry," Andy said. "Why didn't you say anything? You could have told Holland or Rix."

"I could have, but I'm telling *you*."

Andy balled his hands into fists and said, "Right . . . Okay, okay . . . Where is he?" He reached down and picked up the small trowel.

Farah grabbed him by the shirt. "Slow down, Rambo. I don't want you to do anything. I just wanted to, you know, tell someone."

Andy glanced at Farah's left hand, the one not holding his shirt. Her fingers were dancing up and down, as if on an invisible keyboard.

36

When the expedition team arrived back at base camp, they found it empty.

"Where is everybody?" Nathan Buxton asked, gazing around.

Lieutenant Goytia and the Bolivian soldiers had stayed behind to go hunting, and there was a good chance Holland and Rix had yet to return from their reconnaissance of T5, but where were the others? Where were Vern, Juan Pablo, Carlos? And where the hell was Thomas?

Andy glanced toward the white tent where Thomas had been lying that morning.

Had he made a miracle recovery? Had he and the others packed up and left?

"Look what I found."

Andy turned.

Libby was standing just outside command central. Camila was cradled in her arms like a baby. "She was lying under one of the tables."

Andy walked over and gave the little sloth a couple of scratches under her chin.

What could have happened that made them just abandon little Camila?

A moment later, Vern emerged from the brush. He limped toward them, a hard grimace on his face. He threw his hands up in the air and said, "We can't find him."

"Who?" Andy asked.

"Thomas."

Vern explained that an hour earlier, he'd snuck away from his post watching over Thomas to go to his tent and grab a cigar. When he returned, Thomas was gone. He, Diego, Carlos, and Juan Pablo had been searching for him since.

"Fan out," shouted Farah. "He has to be around here somewhere."

Fifteen minutes later, Vern and Andy found Thomas. He was sitting in a small patch of dirt at the edge of the Bolivian soldiers' camp, completely naked. He had a heavy red rash on his torso, his eyes were rimmed in fiery red and nearly swollen shut, and his skin carried a waxy sheen. Without a doubt, he was the sickest person Andy had ever seen.

He wasn't alone. Jonathan Roth and Sean were already there and had been filming for who knows how long.

Andy pulled his whistle up from around his neck and blew, letting the others know the search was over.

"Stop filming!" Vern shouted.

Sean lowered the camera off his shoulder, and Roth yelled, "Don't you dare take the camera off of him!"

"Come on," Andy said. "He's sick. He's not going to want this on camera."

"I don't give a shit. This is pure gold!"

Vern gave Jonathan Roth a withering glance. Had Farah, Libby, and Nathan Buxton not emerged from the surrounding brush, Andy surmised Vern would have smashed the video camera to pieces. Or else, used the camera to beat Roth to a bloody pulp.

Instead, Vern took a few steps toward Thomas and said, "Heyya, buddy. What are you doing?"

Thomas turned and gazed at the group around him. "I'm making a fire," he said, rubbing two gray rocks together. "So I can cook this bird." He put the rocks down and held up a bird, which was actually a green leaf.

He was delirious.

"Come on, buddy," Vern said. "Let's get you back to the tent."

"No! I'm not tapping out!"

Andy, who had seen a couple of episodes of the Discovery show *Naked and Afraid*, said, "No one is tapping you out, Thomas. We're just going to take you to the production tent and look you over. Your partner is over there."

"Sheila?"

"Um, yeah, Sheila is there."

"Sheila is the best."

"She sure is."

"What about my bird?" Thomas said, lifting up the leaf once more.

"Tell you what," Andy said. "We'll keep your bird safe for you."

"Okay."

Vern and Andy helped Thomas to his feet. He was lean and muscular, and his skin was hot to the touch. Even though Darnell had assured Andy that dengue wasn't contagious, Andy would normally have avoided touching someone so sick at all costs. But possibly because he liked Thomas, or more likely, because Farah was watching, he didn't hesitate to help carry the man back to camp.

Once they got Thomas covered up, Andy took his temperature—104.4.

"We have to get him to a hospital," Andy said. "His brain is frying."

Vern shook his head. "I promised him I wouldn't let them take him out."

"He could die."

"Naw, he's tough."

"No, seriously, he could die." Andy was aghast. The last time Andy's temperature had gotten over one hundred degrees—100.2, to be exact—he drove to the emergency room. He spent three hours at a busy Chicago ER, just to hear a doctor say, "Go home. You're fine."

Five minutes later, Holland and Rix returned, and Holland took over what Andy had come to think of as "hospice care."

Checking Thomas's temperature himself—now 104.6—Holland told Vern, "I don't give a shit what he told you. If his fever gets up to one-oh-five, I'm calling for the chopper."

Vern mulled this over. "That's fair."

Crashing foliage snapped Andy's attention away from Thomas. It was the Bolivian soldiers. Two of them were holding a large bamboo pole and hanging from it was a giant wild boar.

The Bolivian soldier in the front yelled, "¡Comemos bien esta noche!" We eat good tonight!

≈

After consuming freeze-dried meals for the past week, the fresh wild boar was one of the most delicious meals Andy had ever eaten.

"Holy moly, that's good!" he said, giving Darnell a nudge with his elbow.

Darnell nodded. "As someone who grew up on barbecue and who will have barbecue for his last meal, I can honestly say this is the best damn pig I ever tasted."

Between the twenty-four of them—twelve from the expedition team, Vern, Juan Pablo, Carlos, Diego, plus Lieutenant Goytia and his seven soldiers—they'd nearly finished off the entire boar.

Andy pulled a piece of meat, dripping with fat, off his paper plate with his fingers and took a large bite. Once he swallowed it down, he said, "My last meal would be a grilled cheese sandwich, but this is giving it a run for its money."

"A grilled cheese sandwich?" Darnell said with a violent shake of his head. "This isn't fifth grade and you just got home from band practice, or whatever it is pale white boys do after school. This is your last meal."

"Okay, okay," Andy said with a laugh. "A grilled cheese sandwich, but get this, I dip it in tomato soup."

Darnell laughed, then said, "I got to get some more of this pig before it's all gone."

He pushed himself up and made his way over to the roaring fire and the Bolivian soldiers who were doling out what was left.

"Hey," someone said, taking Darnell's vacated seat next to Andy. It was Farah.

"Hey," Andy replied. "Did you get some boar?"

"I'm a vegetarian," Farah said with her eyebrows furrowed. "Meat is murder."

"Oh, I'm—"

"I'm kidding," she said, flashing her radiant smile. "Hell yeah, I got some of that boar. I think I ate his entire left side."

Andy chuckled, then said, "Are you doing okay with everything?"

After playing the recording of Jonathan Roth sneaking into her tent the previous evening, Farah had told Andy that it wasn't the first time a man had nearly assaulted her. When she was getting her master's degree, she went to her professor's office to ask a few questions about an upcoming paper. He locked the door behind her and proceeded to pin her against his desk. Luckily, she was able to kick him in the shin and get away.

When she reported the incident the next day to the campus police, they said they would investigate, but they never did. She was told not to go to his class anymore, that she would get an A, and to move on.

And so she had. But she'd been wary of men ever since.

"Yeah," she said, giving his arm a soft pat. "I'm much better. Thanks for listening."

"Of course," Andy said, glad Farah couldn't see how flush his face was in the dark of night.

Andy felt a tap on his shoulder and glanced up. It was Nathan Buxton. "Roth wants to have a meeting."

Andy and Farah traded glances, then both stood. They walked to command central and joined the rest of the expedition team under the blue tarps.

Holland was standing near Jonathan Roth, and he was the first to speak. Holland said, "So, I just want to give everybody a rundown on what Rix and I found today. We hiked over to T5, looking for evidence of a competing expedition team that may or may not have abducted Dr. Gina Brady two weeks ago. We found nothing. Tomorrow, we'll head back to the cache you guys found today, and then we'll do a recon of T4, which is only a half mile from T3."

He appeared to be finished, but then added, "And for those of you curious about Thomas. His temperature has leveled out at one hundred and four. Yes, that's high, but it's in the normal range for dengue." He turned to Roth and said, "I've been as sick as Thomas is right now. And I can tell you that I did some pretty weird stuff myself. Thankfully, there weren't any cameras recording me when I was hallucinating that I was playing quidditch with Emma Watson."

This got a laugh out of most of them.

Holland nodded at Roth, then stepped aside.

"On that note," Roth said, "I want to assure everyone that all the footage shot of Thomas during his episode has been deleted. Probably not my best decision to film that. So, I apologize to anyone I offended."

Andy and Vern traded a quick glance. Apology *not* accepted.

"Anyhow," Roth continued, "that's not the film we came to shoot. We came to make a documentary about finding the lost city of the Incas. And after today's discovery, I think it's quite obvious we've done just that."

There was thunderous applause.

Roth continued, "Now we need to discuss excavation. Holland and I have talked this over, and we feel the cache is in grave danger of being looted, especially the three high-value items we found today. Even though we haven't seen any evidence of a second expedition team yet, it doesn't mean there isn't one. Not to mention that, according to Thomas, there's a drug-trafficking operation less than thirty miles from here. They have the planes and the means to clean out every last artifact.

"I think the best decision would be to remove a few of the artifacts to prove what we've found, then use those to promote the discovery and help finance a full excavation of the site."

A full excavation would take months, if not years, and would cost millions of dollars.

"No!" Farah said, standing up. "First, we don't have an excavation permit. By law, we aren't allowed to dig anything up. Second and most importantly, there could be royal burials near the pyramid and those need to be treated with the utmost respect and dignity. We can't just go in there and start digging shit up. If anyone so much as digs up a rock from that cache, I will resign from the project."

"You said that earlier at the site," Roth said with a laugh. "But I think you're bluffing."

Farah stared Roth down.

"I'm not," she said. "Isn't that why you brought me on the expedition, to keep you in line with ethical archaeological practices and to do the right thing by science? If not that, why exactly did you bring me here? Was it to fu—"

Roth interrupted. "Does anyone *else* have an opinion on this matter?"

Farah glanced at Andy, her eyes open wide, silently prodding him. Andy's heart pounded.

Say it, he willed himself. Say that Farah is right.

But he couldn't. Just like Roth and most all the others, Andy wanted to excavate. If for no other reason than to make the documentary that much more interesting.

Farah sighed, then said, "It's not up to me, or you, or anybody else. It's up to Alejándro. As head of archaeology for Bolivia, it's his call."

"Okay then," Roth said. "What say you, Mr. Cala?"

"I'm not too worried about the narcos coming in and looting the site. They have a much more profitable business to worry about. I'd be much more concerned about the Bolivian soldiers." Cala nodded toward Lieutenant Goytia and the Bolivian soldiers who were in the process of carrying the remaining boar meat to their camp. "After we leave here, everything will be gone in a week. Trust me, I already overheard two of the soldiers planning it."

"He's right," Vern said, although he wasn't part of the expedition team. "They'll take everything."

Cala said, "I believe it's in the best interest of Bolivia to excavate, photograph, record, and recover as many artifacts as possible before we leave."

Roth said, "So that's that. Tomorrow we head back to the cache, and we start digging." He glared at Farah. "So, are you resigning?"

She leapt up from her seat and stormed out. Andy jumped up and followed. "Farah, wait!"

But she didn't stop, she didn't flinch. She just kept on walking.

37

Twenty-one of them splashed their way north through the unnamed river. In addition to Holland and Rix rejoining them, the expedition team was once again accompanied by Lieutenant Goytia and his convoy—though two of his soldiers had stayed behind—plus Juan Pablo, Carlos, Diego, and even Camila. The latter group had decided to tag along to view the highly acclaimed jungle pyramid and its priceless cache of artifacts.

When they were halfway through their trudge, Cala stopped everyone and announced he'd changed his mind about the excavation. They would dig around, photograph, and catalogue each of the artifacts, but they would stop short of removing them from the site. He decided it was imperative an ethical and systematic excavation take place in the coming months. They would simply have to take their chances and hope Lieutenant Goytia could keep his soldiers from looting the cache.

Andy was certain Farah had been the one to change the aging archaeologist's mind—the two could be heard having a heated discussion near Cala's campsite that morning—and even though Farah was ignoring Andy, she was all smiles.

"You look tired," Darnell said next to Andy.

"I *am* tired," Andy said groggily. "I hardly slept."

"Bugs?"

"No, it wasn't bugs."

What had kept Andy awake was Farah Karim. Andy couldn't stop obsessing over whether he had blown his chances by not siding with her.

"Girl problems?" asked Darnell.

Andy didn't respond.

"Come on," Darnell prodded. "I see how she looks at you."

"You do?"

"Oh yeah. I've worked with her twice before this, and I've never seen her flirt with anyone."

"Farah worked on the other documentaries?"

"Farah?" Darnell huffed.

"Yes, *Farah*. Who the hell are you talking about?"

"Libby, you idiot."

"When was she flirting with me?"

"Uh, the entire time she was shooting your interviews." Darnell shook his head. "Man, you are clueless."

Andy supposed in hindsight that maybe Libby *had* been flirting with him a little bit. "She laughed a few times, that's about it."

"Yeah, she doesn't do that."

"Doesn't do what?"

"Laugh."

Andy turned and glanced over his shoulder at Libby. The river came up above her knees. She was walking with Diego and making a funny face at Camila.

Turning back around, Andy said, "She's pretty dorky."

"Said the guy who spent thirty minutes yesterday telling me about his pog collection."

"I don't think she's my type."

"Oh, and Farah is?"

"Well, yeah."

"Dude, I've seen her Instagram."

"So? What about it?"

"Guess how many Instagram followers she has?"

"Three million six hundred thousand."

"That is oddly specific and, yes, correct. And do you know what the last picture she posted was?"

"Probably something from when we were in Miami."

"Yeah it was. It was a picture of her at the airport. I saw her take a hundred selfies, then finally post one."

"What's your point?"

"How many Instagram followers do you have, Andrew?"

"Um."

"Eighty-seven. You have eighty-seven followers and the last picture you posted on there was three months ago: a picture of your cat."

"It's not *my* cat."

"Okay, that's even worse. A picture of someone else's cat."

"Pixel is my neighbor's cat. He comes over sometimes to say hi."

"Your life is really sad."

"I agree," Andy said, chuckling lightly.

"Someone with eighty-seven followers and someone with three million followers—it never works out. Trust me."

"That's not true."

"It was for me. I dated a girl who had seventy thousand followers, and guess what I spent most of my time doing on our dates?"

"Taking pictures?"

"Yes, Andrew. *Taking pictures.*"

"So you think I'm better off with a girl like Libby. How many Instagram followers does she have?"

Darnell made an O with his hand.

"None?"

"That's right," he said with a smile. "*Zero.*"

≈

Ten minutes later, they exited the river and entered the jungle. After a fifteen-minute hike, the stone pyramid came into view.

They'd cleared most of the vegetation cloaking the pyramid the previous day, and at the sight of the magnificent structure, Holland said, "You guys weren't joking. That's a bloody pyramid all right."

Andy and the others made their way around to the back of the pyramid, to the cache of offerings.

Roth wended his way through the fifty-two green stakes placed the previous day. Close on Roth's heals, Andy stopped when he heard Roth let out a loud curse.

Andy followed his gaze to the bare ground.

The golden statue of Inti, the silver alpaca, and the tumi.

They were all gone.

≈

"Your men!" Roth yelled at Lieutenant Goytia. "I know they came here in the middle of the night and looted those artifacts."

"Wrong," Goytia said, shaking his head. "They did not. We are here to protect the site from looters."

"My ass!" Roth yelled. "Where are your other two soldiers? Were they too exhausted after spending the entire night sneaking through the jungle to steal the artifacts?"

"My men stayed behind to go hunting. To get dinner. Your people, they enjoyed the meal last night, yes?"

Andy stood next to Nathan Buxton, twenty feet from where Roth and Goytia were arguing.

Nathan Buxton nudged Andy's side and asked, "How long do you think it would take to get here in the pitch dark?"

"It would be super risky to go through the river in the middle of the night," Andy replied. "Even with a headlamp, it would be dangerous. But without using the river to get here, it would take a couple hours."

Andy couldn't imagine that the round trip to T3, plus the time to dig up the artifacts, could be done in less than five hours. Then again, these were Bolivian soldiers. Navigating through the jungle in the middle of the night might be the equivalent of a city-dweller walking to the twenty-four-hour gas station to get midnight nachos.

"They would need GPS, don't you think?" said Buxton.

"I don't see how you could navigate here without it."

"You think the soldiers have GPS?"

"They probably have at least one between them. How would they have found us in the first place if they didn't?"

Across the clearing, Roth yelled, "No, I will not calm down! Those artifacts are worth millions."

"They were never yours," Farah yelled from the sidelines.

"I know, but—" Roth stomped his foot. "They belong to the Bolivian people. And think about how much attention they would have brought to a possible excavation."

Buxton turned back to Andy. "Is Roth right? Would those artifacts go for millions?"

"Not the silver alpaca," Andy said. "There's already a bunch of those in museums, plus the silver was pretty tarnished. But the other two—the Inti mask and the tumi—were in excellent condition. They'd go for seven figures." He added, "Maybe even eight."

≈

Andy dug his trowel into the ground and tossed the dirt aside. Careful not to disturb the artifact, he took a small brush and began to buff the top of the vessel clean.

The dirt was caked into the grooved pattern of the clay pot, and Andy's brush did little to clear it away. He glanced at Farah on the opposite end of the marked-off area and wondered if she was having an easier time.

Unlike the previous day, when she'd kept sneaking glances in his direction, Farah had yet to make eye contact with him in the three hours they'd been working. Several feet behind her, Bernita and Alejándro were busy cataloging as well. Between the four of them, it would take another few hours to finish digging around, brushing off, photographing, and making detailed notations of the fifty-two—now forty-nine—artifacts.

Andy's stomach rumbled and he called to the others, "I'm going to grab something to eat. You guys want to take a break?"

"No, I'm good," Farah said without lifting her head. The Bolivians echoed her sentiment.

Andy considered going over to Farah and apologizing for a third time—she'd rebuffed his first two attempts—but decided it would be best not to smother her.

"Okay," Andy said. "I'll be back in a bit."

No one responded—all three transfixed by the task at hand. Andy weaved his way through the marked artifacts and ducked under the yellow caution tape. He made his way down the jungle path to the riverbank.

After the heated argument with Roth, Goytia and his soldiers had headed back to base camp, but everyone else was there. Camila was hanging from a low branch of a large mahogany tree. Libby, Darnell, and Sean were sitting on the dirt. Roth stood a dozen feet from the water, skipping rocks across the brown water of the swollen river eddy.

Darnell tossed Andy an energy bar. "Find any more gold?"

"Nope," Andy replied, leaning down to pick up the bar that had slipped through his fingers. "Just a bunch of pottery."

"*Incan* pottery though?"

Andy felt twenty eyes on his chest. "No."

"What do you mean, no?" Roth said, turning away from the river. "Of course, it's Incan. It's all Incan. You know damn well that this is Paititi!"

Andy and Libby made eye contact. She pulled her lips back from her teeth: the international symbol for "Uh-oh."

Andy said, "Actually, it's *not* Paititi."

The jungle went silent.

"You're an idiot," Roth said.

"And you're an asshole," Andy was surprised to hear himself say. "Apart from the three Incan artifacts—the ones that were looted—nothing else we've discovered since we've arrived has been Incan."

"That's not—"

Andy put his hand up. "The stonework of the pyramid, while good, isn't up to the standards of the Incas. Yes, the humidity and acidity of the jungle would increase the rate of erosion more than it would in the dry air of the Andes, but even taking this into consideration, if the pyramid were Inca, the stones would be far more uniform.

"Most, if not all of the clay artifacts appear to be utilitarian in nature. Incas made pottery either for practical use or for ceremonial use. They wouldn't offer cups, bowls, and other vessels to their gods."

Andy was on a roll. "I didn't want to say it when we found them, but the petroglyphs we found at T1 aren't Incan. I wrote my dissertation on Incan petroglyphs, and they're almost always linear and mazelike—nothing like the circular carvings we've seen here."

With his arms crossed in front of him, Roth blurted out, "I'm surprised you had time to make these observations, what between your panic attacks and staring gaga at Farah all the time."

Roth's remarks threatened to derail Andy, but he fought his way back. "Also, the four-square-mile area where these ruins are scattered is a valley between several jungle hills."

"What the hell does that have to do with anything?"

"Well, *John*, the Incas didn't build their cities in valleys; they built them on the tops of mountains. Like Machu Picchu, for example. And they did this for the same reason that, in medieval times, castles were built in areas of elevation. To defend.

"The Incas had just been wiped out by the Spanish. They left Cusco, headed into the jungle, then traveled three hundred miles—what must have taken them months—only to build their city here?" Andy shook his head. "No way. They would have scouted a better defensive position. There aren't any mountains nearby, but there are hills—hills that rise up three hundred, even five hundred, feet. If the Incas resettled around here, they would have built their city on one of these peaks."

"Okay, wise guy," Roth said with a scoff. "Then how do you explain the Incan artifacts?"

"The Incas definitely passed through here at some point. They encountered the ancient civilization that lived in this area and gave them gifts, which was their custom. Then they continued on until they found a more suitable location to build their city. Probably somewhere in the mountains of western Brazil."

"So Paititi is in Brazil, and the Incas just flung a few treasures to these people as they passed by?"

"That's my theory."

Andy glanced around. Everyone was staring at him. Sadly, most of them were looking at him like you might look at the kid at the birthday party with the peanut allergy.

Roth laughed. "Anything else you'd like to add?"

Andy surprised himself again by saying, "You're a fraud."

"A what?"

"You act like you're this great director of all these documentaries, but you don't do shit. Libby"—Andy nodded at Libby, sitting cross-legged on the ground—"is the real genius behind the camera. You're a glorified producer, and if you do decide to do any actual film making, it's like you're shooting a scripted reality series on VH1." Andy took a breath and added, "*John.*"

"You little pip-squeak," Roth said, rushing up the bank.

Andy prepared himself, pulling his hands back and making two fists. At least, that's what he did in his head. In actuality, he ran and hid behind Holland and Rix.

"I can't believe I let Heliant talk me into letting you come on this expedition," said Roth.

"Settle down," Holland said, getting to his feet. "No need for anybody to throw any punches."

Roth shook out his shoulders. "You know what, you're right." He glanced around at the others. "Tell ya what, this 'fraud' is going to shoot a killer scene right now. Show ya how it's done." He gazed around, then spotted what he was looking for hanging from a branch of the mahogany tree.

"Diego," Roth said, smiling big, "would it be okay if I borrow your sweet little girl there for a second?"

Sweet little girl? Andy thought with a laugh. Hadn't he overheard Roth call her a "flea-infested rug"?

Diego shook his head. "I'm not sure that's a great idea—"

"A thousand dollars," Roth said. "I'll give you a thousand dollars to hold your little sloth for thirty seconds."

Andy willed the small Bolivian to say no, but a thousand dollars to him was probably two months' wages.

Diego agreed, but not before saying, "You be nice to her."

Roth nodded at Sean and Darnell. "What are you guys doing? Get up!"

Sean and Darnell traded glances, then pushed up from the ground. Sean hefted the camera onto his shoulder, and Darnell pointed the boom mike in Roth's direction.

Roth walked over to where Camila was dangling from the branch of the tree, and with a beaming smile, he said, "Are you just going to hang out in that tree all day?"

Even from fifteen feet away, Andy could see Camila regard the human with wariness.

Roth reached out his arm and began to unfurl Camila's claws from around the branch. "That's it," he said, "come to Papa."

Reluctantly, the sloth moved one arm to Roth's shoulder and then another.

Andy gritted his teeth.

Once Camila was holding onto his neck, Roth turned toward the camera and said, "Camila here is a brown-throated sloth. The brown-throated sloth is indigenous to Central and South America."

What, he was Steve Irwin now?

"Camila is a year old, and she is being rehabilitated and will someday return to the wild to live with wild sloths. Isn't that right?" Roth reached out a finger and tickled Camila's face.

What annoyed Andy most was that it truly was going to make a great scene. You couldn't take your eyes off the dashing expedition leader and the amazingly cute sloth.

There was a high-pitched squeak, and then Roth brought his hand to his face. "She spit on me!"

Diego rushed forward and pulled the still squeaking Camila off Roth.

"Oh, this is disgusting!" Roth shouted, wiping away at his face.

He hobbled backward toward the edge of the swollen river.

"Don't go in there," Holland shouted. "Just use some drinking water."

Roth ignored him, wading several feet into the river. He leaned down, cupped at the murky brown water, and began splashing it on his face.

"Um, Jonathan . . ." Libby said.

"What?" Roth glared at her, his face dripping with river water. "What's so important that I can't wash that disgusting animal's spit off my face?"

"There's, um . . ."

Andy followed Libby's fingers to the floating eyes just above the water's surface.

"John!" Holland shouted.

"For the last time—" Roth turned and glared at Holland. "—it's *Jonathan!*"

The black caiman's huge armored head leapt from the water and snapped its deadly jaws around Jonathan Roth's left arm. Roth screamed as he was pulled under the water by the enormous fifteen-foot alligator.

Holland raced to the edge of the river, his gun up and pointing at the circling whirlpool.

Roth emerged above water. "Help!" he pleaded, before being quickly pulled back under.

Andy's mouth went slack as he watched the swirling water turn from angry to calm.

Jonathan Roth was gone.

Andy turned and looked at Sean, who still had his camera trained on the river.

If nothing else, Roth was correct: it was a *killer* scene.

38

I blinked my eyes open. They were still sore, but it no longer felt like two small gnomes were using them for batting practice. All I saw was a blanket of white. It took me another moment to realize I was lying on the ground under one of the canopy tents.

"Am I dead?" I heard myself croak dryly.

"Afraid not, my friend," a voice responded. "Not to say that it wasn't close."

I pushed myself up and breathed out, "Ow, ow, ow, ow, ow."

"You still in pain?"

I squinted. Vern's tanned and bearded face zoomed in and out of focus. I licked my lips and said, "It feels like I got into a head-on collision with a Ford F-150." I quickly added, "And I was on a bicycle."

"Yeah, Holland said you'd probably be hurting for another day or two."

"How long have I been out?" The last thing I remembered was someone telling me I had dengue fever.

"You were in and out of consciousness for thirty-six hours. Your fever finally broke two hours ago." Vern handed me a bottle of water. "Here, drink."

After I drank a few ounces, I asked, "Why didn't you guys carry me to my tent?" I glanced down at my legs. They were covered in hundreds of small red welts. They'd left me to be feasted on.

Vern said, "Your temperature was too high, nearly hit one-oh-five. Holland said it would be best to keep you on the ground, where it was cool. And we wanted you close by in case we had to call the helicopter and have you choppered out."

"I guess that would explain why I'm almost naked."

"Well, no," Vern said, scratching at the side of his maroon hat. "You did that all on your own. And you were *totally* naked until I wrangled those undies on you."

"First off, they're called boxer briefs, and second, what do you mean I did that all on my own?"

"I'm not going to lie. You did some pretty weird stuff."

"Like what?"

"This, for example." Vern handed me his cell phone, then reached down and pushed play with his finger. On the screen, I'm naked. I'm on all fours and crawling around. I can be heard shouting, "He was a spunky hanky-panky cranky stinky-dinky lanky honky-tonky winky wonky donkey."

I scrunched my eyes, sighed deeply, then said, "And this went on for how long?"

"Quite a while." Vern moved his finger across the screen. "Four minutes and seven seconds to be exact."

I considered telling him about Clark, the book, and our pony rides, but I didn't have the energy. I did ask, "Any more videos?"

"That's the only one I took. Roth took some footage of you as well, but he claims he deleted it all."

I nodded, then took another drink of water. I asked, "Is it safe to assume every single person at the camp has seen my penis?"

He didn't hesitate. "Yes, it is."

≈

My bones no longer felt like they were going to break in half, but I was still in considerable pain. I had eaten half a pouch of a freeze-dried meal, and I had swallowed four Advil, but they had yet to kick in.

With Vern's help, I made my way back to my campsite. I pulled on my extra pair of pants and a clean shirt and crawled into the tent.

I had just lain down when Andy's face appeared in the tent opening. "Hey there, slugger," he said, his wispy orange mustache still as pathetic as it was two days ago. "I hear you're feeling a little better."

"I was for a little while, but I'm starting to feel like shit again."

"You want me to let you sleep?"

I could tell from the look in his eyes that he wasn't at my tent to make a social call.

"Naw, come on in."

He climbed into the tent. He had his cell phone out, and I said, "Don't tell me you're here to show me footage of me prancing around naked, because I don't think I can handle any more of my dong flapping around."

"I'm not."

"Good." I nodded at his cell phone and asked, "Then what's with the Samsung?"

"There have been several developments in the last couple of days you should be aware of." Andy spent the next minute updating me on the stone pyramid they'd found and the cache of artifacts. After showing me pictures of three Incan artifacts on his phone, he said, "The night before you got sick, you may not have heard it, but someone blew their whistle."

"I did hear it, but my head was starting to pound by that point."

"Right, well, it was Farah. I ran to her campsite and when I arrived, Holland was already there. Farah said she saw a fer-de-lance. But then we found out Farah wasn't alone. Jonathan Roth was in her tent."

"Ah, man," I said, tilting my head back slightly. "How'd I get that wrong?"

He ignored me.

"Then yesterday at the cache, Farah confided in me that there wasn't actually a snake. She only blew her whistle to get Roth out of her tent. He'd unzipped it during the middle of the night, then nearly assaulted her. And get this: she recorded the whole thing on her phone."

"I will destroy that prick," I shouted. I tried to push myself up, but my energy level was in the negatives. "Tomorrow. I will destroy him tomorrow. Or the next day. Or at the premiere."

"Well," Andy said, his lips twisting to fight down a smile, "that brings us to the next development."

He scrolled on his phone and said, "It will probably be easiest if I just show you the video. I had Darnell upload it to my phone."

He handed me his phone and pressed play.

I watched as Jonathan Roth stood near the bank of a river. He walked over to Camila and said, "*Oh, hey there. Are you just going to hang out in that tree all day?*"

"If he does something to Camila, I'm going to seriously need you to carry me to base camp and find me a rifle."

"She's fine, just watch."

I watched for the next thirty seconds as Camila spit on Roth, then against Holland's advice, Roth waded into the murky river, and to my utter dismay/amusement, he was devoured by the largest alligator I've ever seen.

When the video ended, Andy and I both stared at each other for a few seconds. There were simply no words.

Andy finally said, "But that's not the big news."

"That the asshole director of the documentary you guys are shooting was just eaten by a huge fucking alligator *isn't* the big news?"

"Nope."

"Gina?" I asked.

He nodded. "I failed to mention that when we arrived back at the pyramid earlier today, the three Incan artifacts had been looted."

"And you think they were taken by the group who abducted Gina?"

"At the time, I didn't. I thought it was most likely Goytia and his soldiers, but the lieutenant swears it wasn't them."

"What changed?"

"After Roth was killed, a few of us decided we needed a change of scenery. T4, where the lidar showed another pyramid, was only a half mile away and a group of us went there with Rix. We got there a little after one in the afternoon. When we found the pyramid, we found another cache of offerings near its base. A bunch of the artifacts had already been dug up. One of them was a large bowl. I was examining it and lifted it up off the ground." He turned his phone toward me and said, "This is what I found underneath."

The photo was of three words scribbled into the soft earth.

Three words that changed everything.

39

Gina squeezed the plunger on the syringe, sending the contents down the archaeologist's throat. After repeating this process six more times, she crawled to the opening of the tent and poked her head out.

Twenty-four hours earlier they'd been hiking through the jungle, following behind Patrick—who was checking his GPS every thirty seconds—when Patrick stopped.

There was a large break in the canopy overhead, caused by an enormous skyscraper of a tree that had fallen and taken down half the city block with it.

"This is it," Patrick said to Bill. "These are the exact coordinates."

A moment later, Bill knelt down and said, "Look."

Patrick knelt beside him. There was a small hole in the ground. "Someone dug it up."

"Yeah, but it was here."

Patrick nodded. He then pulled a folded piece of paper from his back pocket and said, "We are to proceed one point six kilometers at sixty-two degrees."

As an army brat, Gina knew sixty-two degrees was a compass heading. A compass is broken into three hundred and sixty degrees. Due north is zero degrees; due east, ninety degrees; due south, a hundred and eighty degrees; and due west, two hundred and seventy degrees.

Gina found it curious that Patrick and Bill had transitioned from GPS coordinates to compass headings. It was like going from a digital TV back to analog.

Then she understood why. Compasses have been around for hundreds of years. Whatever directions the duo was now following must have been written down many years ago.

The words rang in Gina's ears.

Treasure map.

She wondered where her patient, the archaeologist, fit into the plan. Was there a part of the map only he knew?

After following detailed compass headings for over an hour, Patrick again stopped. "It should be around here."

It took them another three hours to find what they were looking for: a large stone pyramid.

Now, Gina squinted in the direction of the pyramid. A large area near the base of it had been cleared, and the soldiers were digging in the dirt. Several artifacts had already been fully excavated. A two-foot-high stone vessel was lying on its side next to a large ceramic bowl with a detailed pattern.

Patrick and Bill were nowhere to be seen. With the soldiers preoccupied with digging, Gina realized she could slip into the jungle and make a run for it. Still, even though she had lived in the jungle nearly five years, she wasn't sure she could survive on her own. With the group, she had food, water, and shelter.

But, then again, was Patrick going to release her after they found their treasure?

Gina was still considering her options when she heard a rustling behind her. She glanced over her shoulder.

The archaeologist was moving. The man's eyes twitched open and shut.

Gina darted to his side. "Take it easy," she said calmly.

He mumbled something in reply. It took a moment for Gina to realize he was trying to say, "Water."

Gina grabbed the bottle of water she'd been using to fill the syringe and slowly poured the water into the man's mouth.

He gulped greedily, half the liquid spilling out of his mouth and running into his scruffy gray beard.

Over the next few minutes, the man slowly reawakened. He wasn't speaking much, but his eyes were open, and he was wiggling all his extremities.

After ten days in a coma, Gina wasn't sure what to expect. He could have suffered severe brain trauma. His speech, coordination, and hundreds of other brain functions could be impaired.

"Do you know where you are?" Gina asked.

The man glanced around for several seconds, then said, "Tent."

"Yes, that's right." That was a good sign.

"Does your head hurt?"

"Not too bad. Just a little foggy."

"That's to be expected," Gina said. "You've been in a coma for ten days."

"Ten days?"

Gina nodded then asked, "Do you want to try to sit up?"

The man let out a long breath, then said, "Let's give it a shot."

Gina helped the man into a sitting position. Once he made it to his butt, he asked, "Can I have more of that water?"

Gina handed him the bottle. He finished the entire thing off.

"Are you hungry?" Gina asked.

"I'm not sure yet."

"That's common. It might take you a day or two to get your appetite back."

"Are you a doctor?"

"I am."

"Where did you come from?"

Gina wasn't certain if disclosing the truth to this guy was a good idea; he might only be an archaeologist, but he could be just as dangerous as Patrick. She settled on, "They came to my village and said they needed a doctor."

The man regarded her with his bloodshot eyes. "They kidnapped you." When Gina nodded, he said, "Welcome to the club."

"They kidnapped you too?"

"Darn skippy they did."

Darn skippy was something Gina's grandfather used to say. The man next to her actually reminded her of her Pop-Pop.

"What's your name?" Gina asked.

"Martin Lefbrevor."

"I'm Gina."

"I wish we were meeting under different circumstances, Gina."

"Me too."

Martin blinked his eyes a few times, and Gina asked, "Do you remember falling?"

"Um, not really. I remember running into the jungle, trying to escape. And then I remember hearing a shot. Then slipping, and yeah, I guess I sort of remember my head hitting something hard."

Martin lifted his right hand up toward his head and asked, "Where did I hit exactly?"

Gina guided his hand to the back-left part of his head and said, "Be careful, there's a big gash that's still healing."

Martin dusted his fingers over the top of the bandage and said, "Temporal lobe."

"Correct. Which would explain why you had several seizures."

"Yes, that would. How many did I have?"

"Six that I saw. You could have had more before I came on the scene."

He exhaled.

Gina said, "But the good news is that your memory, at least your short-term memory, appears to be intact. How is your vision?"

He stared at her and said, "Well, either you are a truly beautiful young lady, or my vision is seriously impaired."

Gina was shocked to feel herself blush. She hadn't glanced in a mirror in nine days, but she could only imagine how grimy and filthy she looked. She was still clad in the same shorts and T-shirt she'd been wearing for her run. Her arms and legs were covered in dried mud, scrapes, and bug bites, and her hair was a twisted nest. With a light laugh, she said, "Your vision must be *severely* impaired."

Martin grinned, then said, "You know what, I'm starting to feel hungry."

"Hold tight," Gina said. "I'll see if I can rummage something up."

She ducked out of the tent and made her way over to where the provisions were stored. She found a bag of Brazil nuts and a stack of energy bars. She took three, slipping two of them into her pocket.

One of the soldiers glanced up from where they were digging. Gina showed him the single energy bar in her hand. He nodded, then went back to digging. She did a quick survey for Patrick or Bill but saw neither. There was a chance they were still in their tent, but that would be out of character. Especially for Patrick. From what Gina could tell, he was usually the first one up and the last to go to sleep.

Ducking back into the tent, Gina handed Martin the energy bar. "Small bites."

Martin tore the wrapper open and took half the bar down in one chomp.

"Or just devour it," Gina said.

She watched him finish the first, then half of the second. Then he drank another bottle of water.

When he was finished, Gina said, "So I'm guessing the reason they abducted you is because you know about these ruins. Where the gold must be buried?"

His gray eyebrows jumped. "We're at the ruins?"

"Yeah, there's a huge pyramid fifty feet away from us."

Martin shook his head back and forth. "I haven't been back here in thirty years."

That would explain the compass headings instead of GPS coordinates.

Gina asked, "Are you leading them to the Incan treasure?"

"Treasure?"

"You're an archaeologist, right?"

"No."

"But your tattoos . . ."

He snickered softly and said, "When I was nineteen years old and *Indiana Jones* first came out, I thought I was going to be the next great archaeologist, but after my second semester of college, I changed course."

"Changed to?" Gina prodded.

"Ethnobotany."

Ethnobotany is the systematic study of how people from a particular region use the local plants. Several ethnobotanists had visited Gina's village when she was working with the WHO.

"If you're an ethnobotanist, why did they abduct you?"

"Why do you think?" Martin asked.

It took Gina less than a second.

They *were* looking for treasure, just a different kind of treasure. Possibly the most profitable treasure in the history of mankind.

≈

"*Está despierto,*" Gina said. *He's awake.*

None of the soldiers even glanced up from where they continued to excavate. There were now more than fifteen different artifacts that had been pulled from the earth.

"*¡Está despierto!*" Gina repeated, this time several octaves louder.

All four soldiers glanced up at her.

"*¿Quién es?*" one of them replied.

In Spanish, Gina said, "The guy in the tent, the guy in the coma, the guy who everyone has been waiting to wake up."

The soldiers' eyes opened wide. They jumped up and took off running around the side of the pyramid and crashed through the foliage. Less than five minutes later, the soldiers returned with Patrick and Bill.

"He woke up about ten minutes ago," Gina told them.

Martin had now been awake for close to an hour, but Gina didn't want Patrick to know the ethnobotanist had spent the last thirty minutes disclosing the details of his abduction to her.

"How is he?" asked Patrick.

"He doesn't know who he is or where he is," Gina lied.

Hopefully, Martin would be convincing.

Patrick and Bill raced past Gina and ducked into the tent. The soldiers huddled near the front flap, hoping to overhear what was being said inside.

Gina slowly made her way over to where the artifacts were arranged on the ground. She fell to her knees and examined the ceramic bowl in front of her. It was ten inches round at the bottom and angled out to as much as fifteen. It looked like a large salad bowl, though it must have weighed seven or eight pounds.

Gina glanced nonchalantly over her shoulder, then, seeing

that all the soldiers were still huddled near the tent, Gina gently rolled the bowl backward with her left hand.

With a small stick she'd found nearby, Gina scratched three words into the soft earth.

She had just replaced the bowl when someone shouted, "What are you doing?"

Gina turned to Patrick.

"Just admiring the craftsmanship of this bowl. They really knew what they were doing back then."

Patrick glared at her for a long second, then said, "I need you to fix this guy's memory. He thinks Ronald Reagan is president."

Gina fought back a smile.

40

Even with the edges softened by the moisture of the rains, the words written in the dirt were unmistakable: *Belippa*, *Nsé-Eja*, and *Gina*.

I glanced up from Andy's phone and said, "They weren't looking for Paititi."

"It would appear not," he said. "I'm assuming you're familiar with Belippa."

I nodded. "My sister has MS. Belippa makes two of her medications."

Belippa is a pharmaceutical giant. It was started in the mid-1990s and over the past twenty-five years it had grown into the sixth largest pharmaceutical company in the world, with average yearly revenues of more than $55 billion.

Two years earlier they'd increased the price of one of Lacy's medications by more than 400 percent. We had enough money to cover the costs, but several people who Lacy knew in the MS community were no longer able to afford their medications.

After this huge price hike, I'd spent my fair share of time researching the company. Belippa didn't perform well until 1997, when they released one of the first groundbreaking drugs to treat

HIV. Three years later, at the turn of the millennium, the company went public with one of the largest IPOs in history.

Over the next decade, they developed several medications to treat MS, high blood pressure, and diabetes. Their most profitable product was released in 2003: an autoimmune suppressant called Mireva. Mireva had been the most profitable pharmaceutical drug on the market for the last eight years running.

Four years ago, Belippa released a new drug to treat hepatitis C. And now, according to the most recent article I had read, Belippa had their sights set on the holy grail of diseases.

I said, "Cancer."

Andy nodded. "Yup, *cancer*."

The article I read theorized the cure for cancer would be worth an estimated fifty trillion dollars—that's more than half the money that exists in the world today.

Andy said, "So these people who have Gina, they must work for Belippa?"

"We have to assume as much."

"But then how did they end up at the ruins?"

"I'm not sure."

I drew a Venn diagram in my head. Three circles. The Expedition circle, the Thomas circle, and the Gina Abduction circle. Each circle overlapped with the other two, but there was a tiny area where all three overlapped.

How did three different groups end up in the exact same spot in the middle of more than a hundred thousand square miles of jungle?

I asked, "What does Nsé-Eja mean?"

"I have no idea."

"Have you told anyone else about this?"

"I wanted to tell you first."

A wave of nausea came over me, and I grimaced. I fought back the urge to throw up, and it passed.

I said, "Can you go get Diego? We'll see if he knows what it means."

Andy nodded and left.

Less than two minutes later, the flap to the tent opened. It was Diego and Camila.

At the sight of me, Camila squeaked wildly. She reached out her arms, and Diego handed her over.

Diego said, "She has been very worried about you."

"Have you been worried about me?" I asked, bobbing her up and down lightly. I was so weak it felt like she'd gained forty pounds since I last held her.

She wrapped her arms around my neck and touched her cold nose to my face. I soaked up Camila's love for twenty seconds, then reached down and handed Andy's phone to Diego. I'd zoomed in on the photo and the only word on screen was *Nsé-Eja*.

I asked, "Do you know what that word means?"

Diego's chubby cheeks went flat. "No, no, no, no," he murmured under his breath.

"What does it mean?"

"I tell you earlier. The unfriendly tribe. The headhunters." He paused. "The *cannibals*."

41

Bill Wyeth ducked out of the tent. He couldn't listen to any more of Patrick's interrogation of Martin Lefbrevor. The ethnobotanist didn't even know what year it was—he thought it was 1982—so obviously he couldn't be expected to remember the location of a tribe he'd encountered in the middle of the Amazon jungle.

"How do you get there?" Patrick shouted from inside the tent. "I know you know how to get there!"

Bill walked until he was out of earshot. He bypassed the soldiers digging up artifacts at the base of the pyramid and wandered over to a large rock near the outer edge of their campsite. He set down his daypack and let out a long breath.

How had it come to this?

He'd met Patrick Sewall the summer of 1979 during freshman orientation at Johns Hopkins University. When Bill took his seat in the small auditorium, he had found himself seated next to a handsome dark-haired kid from Northern California. Patrick Sewall exuded the palpable confidence of a star high school quarterback, but he'd been far from it. He was captain of the debate team and a diver on the swim team. Bill had never met anyone so comfortable in their own skin. Patrick was double-majoring in biology and chemical engineering, and he planned out his day in fifteen-minute increments.

For the next four years, Bill acted as Patrick's short and flabby shadow. Though he hit the books hard, Bill, an economics major, was just able to keep his GPA above a C average. Meanwhile, between dating a new girl every other week and taking six more credits than Bill each semester, Patrick was somehow able to coast his way to summa cum laude.

After graduation, Patrick headed back to Northern California to pursue an MBA at Stanford. Bill moved back in with his parents in New Hampshire and took a job as a loan officer at a nearby bank.

After three years at the bank and little to show for it, Bill packed up his car and drove cross-country to reunite with his best friend. He and Patrick shared an apartment on the outskirts of Silicon Valley. Bill soon found employment in one of the valley's increasing number of banks, while Patrick spent his days working in a lab doing biomedical research and his nights wooing Trisha, a Stanford graduate student as well as a San Francisco 49ers cheerleader.

Two years later, Patrick and Trisha married. Bill was best man at the wedding and gave a teary-eyed speech. When, two years after that, the couple gave birth to a son, Bill was named godfather.

By 1994 the Silicon Valley boom was underway. Bill took a job with search engine pioneer Netscape, and Patrick, with a background in biochemistry and a master's in business, was looking for funding to start his own lab. Within a year, Patrick had raised two million dollars from venture capitalists and launched Belippa Pharmaceuticals.

The lab consisted of just six employees, but within three years they had developed a groundbreaking medicine to treat HIV.

As Patrick's new company gained traction, Bill, too, was finding success, both in the workplace and in his personal life. He'd recently taken a job at a new start-up called Netflix that had plans to upend the DVD rental market. And he'd recently gotten engaged to a girl he'd met on Match.com—Bill was one of their first beta customers.

Bill and Martha married in late 1999. Sadly, Patrick was preparing for the launch of the Belippa IPO and was unable to attend their wedding.

After Belippa went public in early 2000, Patrick became a multimillionaire overnight. Over the next several years, Belippa expanded, employing over three hundred and fifty people, with a pipeline of profitable drugs released each year.

By 2007, Bill had moved up the ladder at Netflix. He was VP of Sales. But he wasn't sure about this new direction the company was headed in—a streaming service—and he cashed in his stock options while they still had a shred of value.

As Bill watched Netflix's streaming service revolutionize the entertainment industry and the stock options he'd once owned skyrocket in value, he found himself self-medicating. First it was booze, then pills. After Martha filed for divorce in 2011, Bill hit rock bottom.

A horrible phone call from his old friend Patrick forced Bill to reevaluate his life. Trisha had terminal cancer. She died seven months later, and it was at her memorial that Patrick offered Bill a job with Belippa. He said he was going to step away as CEO, but he wanted someone involved in the day-to-day whom he could trust.

Because of Patrick, Bill had always kept a close eye on the pharmaceutical industry. He quickly moved up the ranks to the same position he'd once held at Netflix. He would always be the man who threw away a fortune in stock options, but at Belippa he was getting a second chance to make his mark.

It wasn't long before Bill was acting CFO. He spearheaded a movement to raise prices on all Belippa drugs across the board—as much as 400 percent in some cases. The move worked, insurance companies paid, and revenues soared.

In 2015 the active CEO was accused of sexual harassment and resigned. Two days later, Bill Wyeth was unanimously installed as CEO.

A troupe of howler monkeys moving through the canopy snapped Bill from his reverie. He reached down and grabbed his daypack. He pulled out a paperback book and thumbed the cover. The book was titled *The Last Shaman: Searching for New Medicines in the Amazon.*

The book was written by Martin J. Lefbrevor, PhD—the same man who, when asked just minutes earlier by Patrick what kind of car he drove, had answered, "An '81 Chevy Caprice."

The ethnobotanist—who was born in Calgary in 1956 and was considered one of the leading authorities on Amazonian botany—was fluent in six indigenous languages and had spent twelve years bouncing around South America, studying with different tribal groups and their healers, learning their therapeutic knowledge of the local flora.

Bill opened the book and found the passage he'd highlighted in bright yellow:

> *There are countless "Wonder Drugs" just waiting to be discovered in the Amazon rainforest and it's only a matter of time before big drug companies isolate and synthesize these compounds for commercial purposes. The result would be patents worth billions of dollars in profit; and in the case of the cure for cancer, trillions of dollars in profit.*

"Trillions," Bill mumbled to himself, which he always found himself doing when reading that passage.

He thumbed to the middle of the book, where there was a series of glossy photographs. There were several pictures of Lefbrevor—thirty years younger and with a full head of dark hair—surrounded by indigenous people. On the fifth page of pictures was an image of a golden jaguar faceup in the dirt. And just below the golden jaguar was another picture: a jungle-cloaked pyramid.

Bill held the book up in front of him, the picture of the pyramid superimposed next to the actual pyramid. Even the angle was the same.

In his book, the ethnobotanist wrote that he'd stumbled across the golden jaguar and the stone pyramid in the middle of the Amazon jungle. Then after hiking for two more days, he encountered a tribe.

The legendary Nsé-Eja.

Approaching the Nsé-Eja's village, Martin had been struck by one of the tribes' poison-tipped arrows. He woke up in a bamboo cage, surrounded by war-painted tribesmen with yellow teeth filed to points.

Their shaman spoke bits and pieces of Portuguese—he said the language was "left over" from one of his previous lives—and he spent several days with Martin. Between explaining to Martin that they would soon remove his head and sacrifice it to their gods, then feast on his body, Martin was able to ask the shaman many of the questions he'd asked the other witch doctors with whom he'd studied.

When Martin asked about cancer, the shaman was confounded. He didn't know what Martin was asking. In his fifty years as shaman and going back four generations of past shamans, they'd never encountered a villager with any growth, any protuberance, or any metastasizing mass.

Of course, the villagers didn't autopsy their dead, and they could have confused the symptoms of cancer with another malady, but it had struck Martin as odd. So odd that on returning to his native Canada, the ethnobotanist wrote in his new book that the Nsé-Eja may be immune to cancer.

Of course, this had been after his escape.

According to his book, that happened on his seventeenth day of captivity. Lefbrevor's death was just days away, earmarked for the full moon. While the villagers were sleeping, Martin was able to break free of his cage and flee into the jungle.

Without his pack, supplies, or compass, the ethnobotanist nearly succumbed to the jungle, but survive he did. For twenty-six days, before finally finding his way to a small village.

Thirty years later, Patrick tracked down the retired professor in Calgary and begged him to take him to the tribe. Patrick even offered Martin an enormous payday. But Martin had maintained there was no sum of money great enough to get him to go back to the tribe. Not after what they did to him. Which is why, as he'd done countless times before, he refused to return to the Amazon jungle.

It wasn't until Patrick decided to take the man by force that Martin revealed that the ruins and the tribe were located in northeastern Bolivia.

Everything was going according to plan until their second day in the jungle, when Martin made a run for it. One of the soldiers hired to keep them safe from the countless jungle threats spooked the fleeing doctor, and Martin had fallen, hitting his head on a tree trunk.

Bill glanced to his left.

Gina Brady was sitting in the dirt, going through a series of yoga poses. She was in incredible shape and unequivocally attractive, and her green-flecked hazel eyes sparkled with intelligence. She would turn the head of most red-blooded males, and Bill had witnessed the soldiers gazing at her lustily on numerous occasions. Or perhaps, *vengefully*. It was so easy to forget that Gina had killed one of the soldiers. But Bill couldn't blame the doctor, after all, they had kidnapped her.

After Martin had fallen and hit his head, there was little they could do. Even after working in the medical field for so many years, Patrick had no actual medical training. And if Martin died, there would be no chance of finding the tribe. Luckily, one of the soldiers they hired was a Yanomina Indian and knew of a village nearby that had an American doctor living among them. Three of the soldiers had set out, and they returned with Dr. Gina Brady a day later.

It was remarkable she'd been able to keep Martin alive this long.

On that note, Patrick emerged from Martin's tent. He stalked his way toward the several artifacts the soldiers had excavated from the earth. He picked up a large ceramic bowl and threw it into the side of the pyramid, where it shattered into a hundred pieces.

The monkeys in the trees started screeching and howling.

It took Bill a moment to realize it wasn't the shattering of the artifact that had put the monkeys in a frenzy; it was the sound of a helicopter flying overhead.

42

When I was eleven, my best friend and I had a sleepover. We set up our sleeping bags in the finished basement and watched *The Goonies*. The movie was our favorite—*Goonies never say die!*—and we'd seen it several times before. When it was over, when we knew my parents were fast asleep, we popped in the second movie of our double feature: *Candyman*.

The R-rated movie—which Rob Gillis's older brother rented for us from Blockbuster—followed the legend of the Candyman, who supposedly appears whenever someone looks in the mirror and repeats his name five times, then he slashes his victims with a metal hook.

When the movie was over, all the lights in the basement were on, and Rob and I were each holding one of my dad's golf clubs. Rob dared me to go into the bathroom by myself and say "Candyman" five times in the mirror.

There was no way I was doing it, and I double-dared him back. He shook his head, and then, as often happened, he triple-dog-dared me. Up to that point in my life, I'd only chickened out on one triple-dog-dare—to do a backflip off the high dive at the pool—and Rob had never let me live it down. I told him I would do it.

I went into the downstairs bathroom, which was always cold because of the concrete floor. I looked at my reflection in the mirror—which, with a bad bowl cut done by my mother and a mouthful of braces, I wasn't too keen on—and took a deep breath.

"*Candyman,*" I said. "*Candyman. Candyman. Candyman. Can—*"

I couldn't finish the fifth one. I turned and ripped the door to the bathroom open and ran to the couch.

Thankfully, Rob didn't hold it against me. He said he wasn't sure if he could have even said the name once. I might point out he wet his sleeping bag that night, though I might have too, if I'd fallen asleep for even a second.

It wasn't until my freshmen year of college that I would finally have the guts to say "Candyman" a fifth time in the mirror.

I swiveled my gaze across the large group circled around me in the white canopy tent—Holland, Rix, Vern, Diego, Andy, Lieutenant Goytia, and Darnell—and said, "And guess what, the Candyman didn't show up. He didn't kill me."

Blank faces stared back.

Holland wrinkled his nose and said, "That's a great story, Thomas, but I'm not sure how it applies here."

"It applies, *Mark,*" I said, "because it was a silly superstition. Just like with this Nsé-Eja tribe."

"No, no, no," Diego said, shaking his head. "Nsé-Eja is no movie. They real. The jungle is filled with dark spirits."

When I had first gathered the group, I told Diego to tell everyone what he told me the previous evening.

So Diego recounted the legend of the Nsé-Eja.

They were a ruthless tribe hidden in the deepest recesses of the rainforest who, many years ago, had made a pact with the jungle spirits. They would protect it from all threats, and in return the jungle would give them dark powers. A few unlucky souls who had stumbled upon the tribe had been eaten—their heads removed, then hung from trees as trophies. And the lucky few who escaped, well, they weren't so lucky after all, as the dark spirits of the Nsé-Eja would overpower their souls and turn them into cannibals themselves.

At which point, I had started in on my *quite* applicable Candyman story.

"You have to understand," Andy said to me, putting a hand on Diego's shoulder. "Myth and superstition are an important part of Latin American culture and history. This isn't a legend to him. It's as real as the Candyman was to you when you were eleven." He pointed over his shoulder to where Juan Pablo and Carlos stood fifty feet away. "That's why they won't even come over to the tent. They're afraid to even hear 'Nsé-Eja,' in case it upsets the spirits."

At that utterance, Diego cringed slightly. Camila, who was holding onto his neck, gave a timid squeak.

Lieutenant Goytia, who I no longer suspected of having anything to do with Gina's abduction, twitched his heavy mustache and said, "What Andy said is true. I heard this legend from my grandfather growing up. When I would do something wrong, he would tell me he was going to take me into the jungle and leave me for the Nsé-Eja."

I nodded.

Part of me hoped Lieutenant Goytia would lend me a few of his soldiers to go after Gina, but I had no doubt that, much like Juan Pablo and Carlos, they wouldn't dare sign on.

"Good luck," Goytia said, extending his hand. "I hope you find her." He turned on his heels and exited the tent.

From the chair where he was seated, Vern said, "You know I would come if I could." He rubbed his right knee. "But I would only slow you down."

"I know," I told him.

And as for slowing me down, well, I wasn't sure exactly how fast *I* was going to be able to move. I was feeling a click better than the previous day, but that wasn't saying much, considering I'd been on my deathbed. Just walking from our campsite to the main camp was a struggle. And although my fever had abated and my joint pain was down to a manageable 8.4, Holland told me the virus was notorious for laying low for a few days before roaring back even stronger.

But I wasn't letting anything stop me from finding Gina. Not the jungle, not dengue, not even fucking Thanos himself.

Every second I wasted was another second she was being held hostage by her Belippa captors, or another second she was closer to being eaten by this bloodthirsty tribe.

"I would go myself," Holland said, "or I'd send Rix along. But with what happened to Roth yesterday, this whole documentary is now up in the air. I can't risk it." He nodded at where Goytia had disappeared into the trees and said, "And after what you told me about him taking that bribe at the airport, I'm a little dubious about him and his small army."

I didn't blame Holland. He was responsible for the expedition, not Gina's rescue. And he was right to be suspicious of Goytia. Nevertheless, I could tell it was killing him not to help.

"You know what?" Holland said. "On second thought, I can handle Goytia on my own. Rix will go with you."

Rix gave a quick nod and said, "We'll find your girl."

I felt better with him along, but no matter how much jungle warfare experience he had, I still needed Diego.

"What about you, Diego?" I asked. "I can't do this without you."

"I have family," he said. "I need to take care of them. And if I escape, I don't want to eat them."

I scoffed. "You're *not* going to become a cannibal."

"I don't know," Andy said. "Weirder stuff has happened."

I glared at him, and he added, "But yeah, I mean, he's right, Diego, that whole cannibal thing is probably hocus-pocus."

"Exactly."

I was surprised when Darnell said, "What do you say, Andrew? You up for a little adventure?"

Andy's face fell. I noticed that he quickly glanced over his shoulder to where Farah and the rest of the expedition team were having a meeting of their own under command central. "Oh, I don't know. I think we need to stay here and—"

"Dude, I was kidding," Darnell said with a smile.

"Oh, right," Andy said with a forced laugh.

I reached into my pocket and pulled out the $10,000 Vern had instructed me to stash away for an emergency.

I held it out to Diego and said, "This is yours if you come."

43

Gina finished off the last of her morning rice and beans, then glanced upward at the tiny blue holes in the towering canopy.

Less than fifteen hours earlier, a helicopter had flown directly overhead. Immediately, she had thought of Thomas. It had been six days since she'd left the voicemail on his phone; surely, the helicopter was looking for her.

Gina had bolted from the shadows to a small area—maybe fifteen feet in diameter—where the sun shone through a break in the canopy. She screamed and waved her arms.

She had caught only the faintest glimmer of black as the helicopter zoomed past, leaving the tall canopy swaying in its wake. She continued staring upward, wondering if she'd blown her only chance at rescue, when she felt a hard sting on her cheek.

She brought her hand to her face where Patrick Sewall had struck her. "Don't you dare do that again!" he shouted, the cords in his neck taut.

Fifteen hours later, Gina's cheek still stung from the blow. She set the bowl down on the rock beside her and peered at the ceramic artifact fifteen feet away.

The ground around the bowl was dark and wet. Not long

after Patrick struck her, a storm had blown in. It rained for most of the night and again that morning, and Gina couldn't be certain the words she'd scrawled into the soft earth hadn't turned into a muddy mess. Hopefully, the weight of the heavy bowl would keep the earth beneath it dry.

But maybe it wouldn't come to that.

If Martin could keep up his charade for a few more days, maybe the helicopter would return. Or they might encounter a search-and-rescue group on the ground. The longer they stayed in one place, the better. It was odd, but Gina could feel that Thomas was close. He was in Bolivia; she was certain.

She turned at the sound of feet slurping through the mud. Patrick was pulling Martin behind him, stalking toward the pyramid. Martin glanced in her direction and gave her the softest of winks.

Patrick Sewall had kept them separated the previous night—probably to prevent them from trading information and coming up with an escape plan—and Gina was forced to sleep in one of the soldiers' tents. Thankfully, Bill had forced three of the soldiers to cram into another tent and Gina was alone.

Fortunately, in the hour before Gina informed the soldiers that Martin was awake, the ethnobotanist had told her everything: About the twelve years he'd spent bouncing around the Amazon, studying with different shamans and tribal healers. About finding the golden jaguar and then the pyramid. About being captured by the Nsé-Eja and how they had kept him locked in a cage. How, before his escape, Martin had learned that the ruthless tribe was seemingly immune to cancer. About the publication of Martin's book, which detailed the whole ordeal, and his meteoric rise through academia. How, two weeks earlier, Patrick Sewall, the president of Belippa Pharmaceuticals, had stuck Martin with a syringe just inside the door of his Calgary home and kidnapped him. And how Patrick was trying to get Martin to lead him to the village that had nearly killed him thirty years earlier so they could find the cure for cancer.

Presently, Gina watched as Patrick and Martin halted just feet from the base of the pyramid. Patrick pointed and said, "You're telling me that you've never seen this pyramid before?"

Martin shook his head. "I think I would remember a pyramid in the middle of the jungle."

"You took a picture of this. It was in your book."

"I don't remember writing any book."

Patrick closed his eyes and grunted. Glancing in Gina's direction, he said, "How does he remember everything before 1982 and everything that happened the last two days, but he doesn't remember anything in between?"

Gina stood and stepped toward the pair. "He's suffered severe trauma to his temporal lobe, which is one of the memory centers. His short-term memory appears to be fine. But those long-term memories that appear to be lost, they could return in a few days, a few weeks, a few months, or a few years." Then she added, "Or they could be lost forever."

"I wish I could help you find this tribe," Martin said, "but I don't remember any of this."

"Not even the golden jaguar?"

"No, uh, I don't."

Gina, who grew up playing poker with her father, noticed the small wrinkle of Martin's nose before he said the words.

Patrick noticed it as well.

"You do remember!" Patrick screeched.

"I don't!"

Patrick gripped Martin's head behind his ears and pressed his thumb into the healing wound.

Martin screamed.

"What year is it?" Patrick shouted.

"1982!"

"WHAT . . . YEAR . . . IS . . . IT?" Patrick repeated, grinding his thumb even deeper.

Martin wailed against the pain, then finally, he uttered the correct year.

"I knew it!" Patrick said, smirking. "Now, I will ask again, do you remember seeing this pyramid?"

"Yes," Martin whimpered.

"Do you know how to get to the Nsé-Eja tribe?"

The ethnobotanist didn't respond.

Patrick gritted his teeth and dug his nail into the now open wound. Blood cascaded over Patrick's fingers and ran down onto Martin's ear.

Martin could no longer stomach the pain. "Yes!" he cried. "Yes, I do."

≈

They had been following Martin through the jungle for nearly three days.

Gina kept looking for opportunities for her and Martin to escape, but none arose. Patrick was being cautious. Both she and Martin had a soldier in front and in back of them at all times. And at night, her tent was zip-tied closed and her ankles shackled together with military zip cuffs.

Gina was still very much a captive. And now that Martin was alive and well, Gina's life was even more at risk. What reason did Patrick have to keep her alive? She'd outlived her usefulness.

"Where the hell are we?" asked Patrick Sewall. "In your book, you say it's two days' travel from the pyramid."

The ethnobotanist checked a compass heading every now and

again, but for the most part, it appeared, at least to Gina, that he
had no idea where he was taking them.

"It's not too much farther," Martin said.

"You've been saying that for a day and a half!" said Patrick.

"No, really, it's just up ahead."

Patrick stormed forward, and just like he had three days earlier,
he dug his fingers into the wound behind Martin's left ear. Squeezing tightly, he said, "Are you leading us on a wild goose chase?"

"No, no, I swear."

Gina watched as Patrick gritted his teeth, pressing his fingers
into the wound as hard as he could. "Is the tribe close?"

Martin shook his head from side to side. "I can't go back
there," the ethnobotanist wailed. "They kept me in a cage. I can't.
I won't. You'll have to kill me."

Patrick released Martin's shoulder. Martin crumpled to the
ground. "I can't go back," he sobbed. "I can't go back."

Patrick pulled a gun from the waist of his pants and pointed
it at Martin.

He shouted, "Martin, look at me!"

Martin wiped his eyes and looked up. Even at the sight of the
gun barrel pointed at him, he didn't so much as flinch. He would
rather die than go back to the tribe.

Patrick lowered the gun, then he strode three steps to where
Gina stood watching. Gina's limbs froze as she felt the barrel of
the gun pressed to her left temple.

Patrick glared at Martin. "If you don't take us to the village
right now, I'm not going to kill you, I'm going to kill her." He
pressed the gun a notch harder into the side of Gina's head.

Gina felt her heartbeat against the barrel of the gun.

"What's it going to be?" Patrick asked. "Are you going to let
the woman who saved your life die? I'll give you three seconds to
think it over."

A high-pitched whine escaped Martin's lips.

"One," Patrick shouted. "Two."

Gina closed her eyes.

"Three."

44

After helping to outfit Thomas, Rix, and Diego for their mission and then seeing them off, Andy and Holland joined the others at command central.

"I don't see how we can continue without Jonathan," Bernita said. "It doesn't seem right."

The previous evening, everyone had been so numb from Roth's death that it was decided they would wait until morning to determine what to do next.

"I think we owe it to Roth to finish the final three days," Farah said. "It's what he would have wanted."

Andy glanced at her.

He doubted she'd lost even a wink of sleep over Jonathan Roth's death. Andy on the other hand, couldn't stop replaying the clip over in his head as he'd tried to sleep: the enormous armored jaw of the black caiman leaping from beneath the surface of the water and clamping down on Roth's arm and pulling him under.

Holland put his hand up and said, "If I may." When the others quieted, he continued. "Early this morning, I reached out to Roth's emergency contact and communicated to them the unfortunate news of his passing. They asked if it would be possible to bring his remains back to the States, but I sadly told them there were no remains to speak of." He took a breath. "Not to be too blunt, but there isn't anything else we can do for him. If anyone would like to leave the expedition, I can have the chopper here in the next hour. For those of you who wish to continue, we will do just that."

Holland had been paid to keep the expedition safe for twelve days, and he would deliver on that promise.

Holland continued, "As for all of this equipment, it's owned by Roth Media Incorporated, so I'm not sure what the ethics are moving forward with the film."

Libby raised her hand. Her eyes were bloodshot. Regardless of how Roth had treated or mistreated her, she was still traumatized by his death. In a shaky voice, she said, "I'm actually the owner of all the equipment. At least on paper."

Holland waited for her to explain.

She said, "Jonathan got a little creative with his taxes over the past decade, and it was starting to catch up with him. The government was threatening liens on his house, his boat, his car—even his business. I owned a small share of Roth Media, but last year, Roth asked if he could put the entire business under my name. He agreed to give me a larger share of profits, and I didn't see the downside."

Farah said, "You mean aside from helping him with federal tax evasion."

Libby didn't respond.

Holland said, "Then I suppose, legally, we don't have anything to worry about." Everyone was silent for a beat, then Holland asked, "So, who wants to stay?"

Everyone but Bernita raised their hand.

"I can't," she said, tears running down her cheeks. "I just want to go back and hug my kids."

"Understandable," Holland said. "I'll get the chopper on the horn."

≈

Since they'd gotten such a late start, it was decided they would visit
T6 instead of the planned-on T5. T6 was a short three-quarters of a
mile away, and they reached the area a little after 9:30 a.m. On the
lidar scans, it was the smallest of the archaeological sites. There were a
few unnatural earthen mounds and what appeared to be a small plaza.

When they reached the edge of the site, they stopped.

"I don't know if I can do this," Libby said.

Andy was nearby and said, "It's no different than what you were
doing before. You were always the brains behind Roth's success."

"I don't know about that," Libby said, blushing. "I didn't get a
chance to thank you for saying that to Roth yesterday. It meant a lot."

"Just telling the truth."

As for the other statements Andy had made to Roth—the ones
about the ruins not being Paititi—he was starting to have regrets.

Though Cala wasn't there to hear Andy's argument against
Paititi on the bank of the river, Andy's remarks had made their
way to the Bolivian's ears.

A day earlier, on their way back to base camp, Cala had taken
Andy aside and told him that he disagreed with all of Andy's statements. The stones of the pyramid were so mismatched because of
the high rate of erosion in the rainforest. For six months out of the
year, those stones were inundated with rain. After five hundred
years, Cala was surprised the stones had retained any of their rectangular shape at all.

In opposition to Andy's belief that the Incas would never use
utilitarian pottery as offerings, Cala said bowls and other vessels
had been found at other sites. And while he agreed that most Inca
petroglyphs were linear, he'd seen with his own eyes several Inca
petroglyphs that were circular.

As for the location of the ruins, he said that, sure, the Incas built lots of cities on the peaks and sides of mountains, but they built plenty on flat ground as well.

Then, much like Bernita had told Andy on her departure, Cala said, "This *is* Paititi."

≈

Holland, who after seeing Bernita off in the helicopter, had joined them at T6, was the one to stumble on it.

Literally.

He was trudging through the brush—a short fifty meters from where most of the expedition was congregated near a tall, bus-shaped, earthen mound—when his right foot tangled in thick vegetation. Shaking his foot free, he noticed an opening in the earth. A moment later, he blew his whistle.

Andy and Farah were the first to arrive.

"What is it?" Farah asked.

Holland had cut away some of the overgrowth, but it was still mostly hidden by a web of green.

"It looks like some sort of staircase going down," Holland said.

Within thirty minutes they had cleared the vegetation away, and three stairs leading into the earth were visible. The stairs were four feet wide and made of cragged yellow stone.

"Do you think it's a tomb?" Cala asked.

"No," Farah said. "If anything, I bet it's another cache."

Of course, everyone was thinking one thing.

Gold.

This could be the bunker where all the Incan treasure was buried.

Farah said, "I wouldn't normally condone digging any further, but I mean, we are making a film here."

Andy couldn't help but think back to Farah saying how she would resign if they so much as dug around one clay pot. But now, on the precipice of finding treasure, she was leading the charge.

With Libby providing direction, both cameramen zoomed their cameras in while Andy, Farah, and Cala began excavating more stairs descending into the earth.

When seven were visible, there was a soft rumble. Farah's head poked above the five-foot hole.

"The wall caved in!" Farah yelled. "Hand me a flashlight."

Nathan Buxton pulled a flashlight from his backpack and handed it down.

Andy leaned over the hole and watched as Farah ducked through the four-foot opening and disappeared.

He saw the ambient light of her flashlight partially illuminating the opening.

She reappeared twenty seconds later, a look of bewilderment on her face.

"Gold?" Cala asked.

"No," Farah said, shaking her head. "Hieroglyphics."

≈

Andy ran his fingers over the grooved characters etched into the wall of the bunker. The room was small, maybe six feet long, four feet wide, and four feet high. The walls on both sides were filled from top to bottom with hieroglyphs.

Most people associate the word *hieroglyphics* with ancient Egypt, and for good reason. That's where the name originated. But when the European explorers of the eighteenth and nineteenth centuries discovered ancient Mayan writings, they found their general appearance reminiscent of Egyptian "hieroglyphs." Over the course of the next few centuries, *hieroglyphics* became a generic archaeological term to describe writing that combined logographic, syllabic, and alphabetic elements.

Andy traced his finger over a circular character with a line through the top half. After spending another few minutes in the bunker, Andy ducked out of the opening and climbed the seven stairs.

His peers stared at him solemnly. They'd already realized what the presence of hieroglyphics meant, but Andy couldn't resist. He fought down a grin as he said, "This proves that, without a doubt, these ruins aren't Incan."

The Incas didn't have an alphabet, they didn't have logograms—they had no writing of any kind. They recorded everything using quipus.

Andy added, "I'm almost positive the hieroglyphics are Tupi."

The Tupi were an ancient civilization indigenous to Brazil. Over time, they migrated outward, eventually occupying Brazil's Atlantic coast, but in the fourteenth and fifteenth centuries, they'd lived in the rainforest.

Andy had recognized a few of the characters carved into the wall from the Tupi-Guarani alphabet, which derived from Old Tupi.

He said, "Archaeologists have found a few other Tupi ruins in Mato Grosso and other parts of Brazil. In fact, come to think of it now, they found a cache of offerings near one of the pyramids as well."

Alejandro Cala had been silent up to that point. He stared at Andy, then, letting loose a jubilant laugh, he said, "You were right all along!"

≈

After finding definitive evidence that the ruins weren't Incan, and with Roth's death still looming over them, the group decided that after another two hours of taking pictures and filming the bunker of hieroglyphics, they would return to base camp.

"Well, shucks," Libby said to Andy. They were sitting under one of the white tents, and Andy was helping her review the day's footage. "That puts a damper on the documentary."

Andy agreed. There was no way to spin it. "Yeah, it does."

With proof the ruins weren't Paititi, the film would be just another of the many documentaries following a jungle expedition. Sure, there was footage of Jonathan Roth being killed by a giant black caiman—that alone might be enough for Netflix or another platform to acquire the rights—but apart from that, the film would be anticlimactic.

"I have an idea," Andy said, though his stomach turned to spaghetti at the mere thought.

"I'm listening," Libby said.

"Thomas."

"What about him?"

"He's already been part of the documentary. Maybe the best part. What if we catch up with him? Film him trying to find Dr. Gina Brady."

Libby's light-blue eyes widened. "That would be—" She shook her head. "Holland would never go for it. Plus, it would be too dangerous."

It would be dangerous.

Super dangerous.

Andy nodded at her, then he stood up and headed toward his campsite.

≈

"You're what?" Farah said.

"I'm going after Thomas," Andy said. "And Darnell is coming with me."

"Are you crazy?" Farah asked. "Holland will never go for it."

"He already did. I had to sign my life away, literally on a piece of paper, but he told me he wasn't going to stop me."

"But why?" she said, gently touching his shoulder. "Why do *you* have to go?"

"It's going to make for an epic film, and I just have to. I have to do something big. I'm sick of living in my own jungle prison. This is how I'm going to break out of it. Or die trying."

Andy knew he was caught up in the moment, knew at some point in the near future—probably the *very* near future—he would regret his decision.

But for now, he was gung ho.

Andy instinctively glanced down at his wrist to check the time. Seeing that his wrist was bare, he asked Farah, "What time is it?"

"What happened to your watch?"

Twenty minutes earlier, when Andy was finishing up packing, ridding his pack of everything that wasn't absolutely necessary, he'd pulled out his wooden box. Andy had been stuffing the box of trinkets back into his pack, when he found himself shaking his head. He took off his watch, added it to the rabbit's foot, the Shin's Hollywood menu, and the small tan rock. He wrapped the box in his green I PAUSED MY GAME TO BE HERE shirt, then he pulled the lighter from his emergency kit and set the shirt on fire. For the next few minutes, Andy had watched the shirt and box burn.

"My watch broke," he lied.

Farah wrinkled her nose, then glanced at her own watch. "It's 1:09."

"We need to head out," Andy called to Darnell.

"Ready when you are, buddy," Darnell said, adding two jars of Nutella and a bag of tortillas to his pack, then zipping it shut.

Andy turned and saw that the rest of the expedition team had gathered around the tent to see them off.

Holland stepped forward and said, "Noon, three days from now. That's the last chopper ride out of here. If you don't make it back by then, I'll try to track you down, but no promises."

"Three days," Andy said, more to himself than anyone else. "Got it."

Andy glanced at the others. His eyes fell back on Farah, who was standing not far from Holland.

Jungle up! he yelled in his head.

He walked toward Farah.

She bit the inside of her lip as he approached.

He walked past her to where Libby was standing and staring down near her feet. She lifted her head as he approached.

"Hey," she said, shyly. "Be carefu—"

Andy leaned forward and kissed her. Her lips welcomed his. After a long second, Andy broke away.

Libby's face danced as Andy said, "I'm coming back for more."

45

"I have to pee," Gina said.

"Again?" Patrick said. "You just went."

"I think I have a UTI."

"Don't you have some antibiotics you can take for that?"

"I took some a few hours ago."

"Fine," Patrick said, letting out a sigh. "My wife used to get those all the time."

Gina couldn't help but notice that Patrick had said "used to get." The two could have been divorced, but something about the quick tug at Patrick's mouth made Gina think she'd passed away. Gina felt a flicker of compassion for Patrick, but then she remembered that this was the same man who'd sent soldiers to abduct her from her village, held her hostage for going on eighteen days, and who, just five days earlier, had held a gun to her head.

"Make it quick," he said.

One of the soldiers kept a close eye on her as she ducked ten meters into the trees and squatted. She didn't actually need to pee—she didn't have a urinary tract infection—so she spent the next couple of minutes replaying the past five days over in her head.

If she closed her eyes, she could still feel the weight of the barrel pressed to her temple. She could still hear Patrick counting, "One . . . two . . . three." Gina had no doubt that Patrick had been prepared to shoot her. She felt his finger flex against the trigger, but right before he administered the five pounds of pressure necessary, Martin had shouted, "Wait! Please! I'll take you to the tribe! Just don't hurt her!"

Patrick demanded the exact coordinates of the tribe, but Martin swore he didn't know them. However, he did say that if they made their way back to the pyramid, he could lead them to the tribe from there.

It took two and a half days to retrace their steps, and they reached the pyramid a few hours after sunrise on what by Gina's calculations would have been August 21. Gina silently hoped that in the days since they'd left, someone had stumbled on her ceramic artifact and its hidden message, but the bowl was in the same place she'd left it. There was no trace anyone had been to the ruins since they'd departed. Still, Gina refused to give up hope.

At the pyramid, Martin consulted his compass and began leading them to the tribe. Along the way, Gina took every opportunity to slow them down, to maybe give her trackers, or Thomas, a few more precious minutes to discover her clues and find her.

"Wrap it up!" Patrick shouted.

Gina glanced around. If she made a run for it, they wouldn't be able to catch her. She was too fast. She nearly took off, but she couldn't abandon Martin.

Her father was a marine. The phrase had been pounded into Gina from birth.

No man left behind.

≈

Martin checked his compass for the umpteenth time and said, "I think it's this way."

Gina wasn't sure if the ethnobotanist was trying to stall, much as she and her fake inflamed bladder were—she'd made them stop three more times in the past two hours—or if he truly needed to know their exact heading every few minutes.

"I've about had it with you," Patrick said. "We've been walking for more than two days since leaving the pyramid. Either you don't know how to get there, or you're deliberately leading us in the wrong direction again."

"No, really, I think we're close."

"You *think* or you know?"

"I haven't been back here in thirty years. The forest has changed." Martin flipped his compass open and squinted at it.

"Enough," Patrick said. "You obviously have no idea where you're going."

"I do," Martin said. "There is a river a few hundred meters from here."

"Well, for your sake, there had better be."

The group continued hiking for another five minutes, and then Gina began to hear the unmistakable thrum of fast-moving water. Fifty meters later, the jungle opened up slightly, and there was a clear view of a rippling brown river.

Gina's stomach tightened.

It appeared that Martin was leading them in the correct direction after all.

"How much farther from here?" Patrick asked.

"Thirty minutes," Martin said.

Gina's stomach twisted. She'd been waiting for an opportunity to make a move, but now she was running out of time.

Martin turned in her direction, and Gina gave him the quickest of winks. For a moment, she didn't think he'd noticed, but then he did a 360-degree sweep of their surroundings and said, "I need a few minutes to get my bearings."

Patrick flashed a quick look of annoyance, then called to the soldiers, "Let's take five. Then we'll get prepared for the final push."

Martin consulted his compass, then walked to the edge of the small clearing. Patrick followed behind him, pestering him with questions.

The soldiers made their way to the river's edge. On the opposite side of the river, there was a giant capybara sunning on the sloping bank.

Gina watched as the first of the soldiers picked up a small stone and tossed it across the river. The stone landed in the water, several feet in front of the large brown rodent.

"Not even close!" Gina shouted to them in Spanish.

The soldier glared at her, but soon all four of them were scavenging the ground in search of stones to throw.

Bill was leaning back against the seven-foot-wide trunk of a massive tree. His pack was on the ground next to him. His shirt was drenched through, and there were small droplets of sweat beading inside his tinted glasses.

Gina took a few steps toward him and said, "You need to drink some water."

"You read my mind," he said, then knelt next to his pack and unfastened the top.

Out of the corner of her eye, Gina watched as the four soldiers took turns throwing rocks at the capybara.

She swept her head to the left. Patrick was thirty feet from her, with his back turned. He was watching Martin etch something in the dirt with a large stick—either a map or, possibly, the layout of the village.

She silently commended Martin on his ingenuity.

Bill pulled his plastic water container out of his pack and unscrewed the top. He tilted the container to his lips.

Gina took two steps forward, pressed both hands to Bill's

chest, and shoved him backward with all her might. He hit the tree trunk with a soft thud, his head knocking back and water splashing all over his face.

Within half a second, Gina had her hand inside Bill's pack and was rooting around for the gun she had seen Bill wrap in a T-shirt the previous day. She felt the outline of metal, pulled out the shirt, and fumbled it open.

She glanced toward the soldiers. She watched as one of the four spotted Bill moaning next to the tree and alerted the others.

With her right hand, Gina clicked off the safety, while with her left hand she reached down and grabbed Bill by the collar of his shirt.

She glanced toward Patrick. He'd overheard the commotion and was reaching for the pistol tucked in the back of his pants.

Bill was still dazed from smacking his head against the trunk and did little to assist Gina as she yanked him to his feet. In one deft motion, she slid behind him, pushed her back up against the large trunk, then pressed the barrel of the gun against the side of his head.

"Nobody move!" she screamed.

Patrick continued a few feet toward her. Gina sent a bullet whizzing over his head. "I said, nobody fucking move!"

Patrick stopped and raised his hands.

Bill had started to regain his wits. "Don't kill me," he mumbled. "Please, don't kill me."

Gina ignored him. She turned to Patrick and yelled, "Tell all the soldiers to throw their rifles in the river!"

Patrick glared at her in silence.

Gina sent another shot over Patrick's head, this one close enough he must have felt the whiz of the bullet.

"Okay, okay," Patrick said. "Do as she says."

One by one, the four soldiers pulled their rifle straps over their heads and tossed the guns into the water.

"Now, you!" Gina shouted. "Drop your gun and kick it toward Martin."

Patrick let out a deep breath.

Gina narrowed her eyes and said, "I won't ask again."

There was a loud thunk.

Gina glanced upward.

Less than a foot above her head, sticking out of the trunk of the tree, was a long, yellow spear.

≈

"Nobody move a muscle," Martin said. "There are probably twenty of them surrounding us."

Gina gulped audibly.

So close.

She stared at Patrick and watched as he slowly moved his gun back to his waistband.

"Everyone remain very still," Martin said, "or we're as good as dead."

"Well," Patrick said, "it looks like you were telling the truth after all."

The tribesmen must have been close by, and Gina's gunshots had drawn their attention.

There was a soft crunching from all around them, then suddenly several tribesmen emerged from the forest. They were clad in red loincloths, had yellow war paint striped down their faces, and their muscles were long and lithe. Several had different colored cloths tied around their biceps. Each carried a seven-foot spear with a razor point.

The Nsé-Eja.

One tribesman shook his spear at Patrick and shouted several words in his native tongue.

"What are they saying?" asked Patrick.

"I don't know," said Martin.

More tribesman emerged from the forest until there were twenty spears around them. A tribesman with a rim of white hair and three lines of yellow paint beneath each eye rushed forward and jutted his spear in Gina's face.

Gina's heartbeat thrummed against her ribcage.

"I think he wants you to drop the gun," Martin said.

Gina released her grip around Bill's neck, then she slowly lowered her hand and set the gun on the ground.

Another of the tribesman picked up the gun. He turned it over in his hands and carefully inspected it. A moment later, several of the tribesmen began yelling at them, prodding them toward the forest from where they had emerged.

Patrick said, "I think we should go with them."

Gina didn't think they had much of a choice.

46

When I was twenty-nine years old, I attempted to do an Ironman triathlon. Not the real one, not the one in Hawaii, but one of the half ones. It was in Atlantic City, which was an hour's drive from where I was living in Philadelphia at the time. The race was a 1.2-mile swim, a 56-mile bike ride, and a 13.1-mile run. Added up, it came to 70.3 miles, and they gave you a big "70.3" sticker to plaster on your car. That is, if you finished.

I never got the sticker. Or the T-shirt. Or the Clif Bar.

I'd been running for most of my life, and the few bike rides I'd taken were easy enough, but I was nervous about the swimming portion. My sister was swimming collegiately at the time, and she helped train me during the six weeks leading up to the race. When race day came, I was ready.

Or so I thought.

Surprisingly, I knocked the swim out in twenty-five minutes and then hopped on the $3,000 bike I'd splurged on. I had only trained on the bike five or six times beforehand, and never for more than twenty miles. I had just assumed that if I was in great running shape, I was also in great biking shape.

It turns out that isn't how it works.

I made it through the first of the two twenty-eight-mile loops around the city with no problem. But around, oh, mile forty, my quadriceps started to cramp up. It took me two hours to finish the last sixteen miles.

Three miles into my run—a time when most everyone else had already finished the race—my legs loosened up, and I settled into a nice pace. But then around mile eight, I hit a wall.

"Don't quit," I kept telling myself. "Don't you quit."

This got me through another couple miles.

Lacy was cheering me on near the ten-mile marker—holding a large poster that read "Choo! Choo! Thomas the Train coming through!"—and I gave her a big thumbs-up as I passed. A quarter mile after seeing my sister, I came to a fuel station. I stopped and slugged back two small waters, and I grabbed for some energy gel. I squirted two of the gels down my throat, and when I went to start running again, my legs wouldn't budge.

"Um, excuse me," I said to my legs in my semidelirious state. "What's going on with you guys?"

"We're done," they answered.

"You're what?"

"We're done. If you want to go any further, you're going to have to talk to Arms."

That was the last time I pushed my body to its breaking point. Now, nine years later, I was doing it again.

"I have to sit," I said.

Diego and Rix glanced back over their shoulders and stopped. I could only hope they were both impressed that I'd made it this far. According to Holland, most people who contract dengue fever are laid up for a week, sometimes as long as three weeks. And I now realized why.

Dengue was a crippling virus.

Even now, two days after my fever broke, I was nauseous, my

joints were on fire, and everything felt heavy, like I'd had a blood transfusion and been filled with AB-granite.

I flopped down in the middle of the forest and took several long, deep breaths.

Early yesterday, when we set out from the pyramid at T4, it had taken Diego and Rix half an hour to find the right trail. There were several tracks leading to and from the ruins, but after careful debate, it was decided the northeastern route had the freshest tracks.

We'd set off in search of the Nsé-Eja and, hopefully, Gina—hiking for eight hours before stopping to make camp. My Garmin inReach had spotty service the entire day, but around dusk, I'd been able to get a signal. I sent Lacy a few messages asking her to do some digging on Belippa for me.

This morning we rose with the sun, and we'd been charging through the jungle at a heavy clip for the past seven hours. I wouldn't have made it even a mile had it not been for the bag of coca leaves Juan Pablo had given me when we departed. The mild stimulant from the coca, along with the several Advil I was taking every few hours, slightly numbed the pain in my joints, and this combination was the only reason I'd been able to make it as far as I had.

Diego hiked back to where I was sitting—nay, lying—in the heavy grass. He stood over me, Camila hanging around his neck. Diego had intended to leave the baby sloth with Vern, but perhaps sensing Diego was leaving her, she'd refused to let go. She'd clung to his shirt with her claws and squeaked until Diego relented.

Diego reached down and put his hand on my forehead. "The fever has not returned."

"That's good," I murmured. As weak as I was, if the fever returned, I didn't have much hope I'd live to tell about it. Unlike Atlantic City, the closest ambulance was a fourteen-hour hike and a helicopter ride away.

"We rest," Diego said.

By "rest," I assumed he thought at some point I would be able to resume hiking. That was not going to happen. Unless he and Rix wanted to play *Weekend at Bernie's* with my lifeless body.

I said, "I can't go any farther."

Diego asked, "What about Gina?"

I glanced up at him.

His squinty eyes were open slightly more than normal.

"Yeah," I breathed. "Gina."

Gina was all I'd been thinking about for the last several hours. Replaying the first time I saw her, our first kiss, the first time we'd slept together, the first time she went to the bathroom with the door open—you know, all the highlights. The images were in high definition at first, but then, gradually, whether it was my fried neurons or because I was losing hope I would be able to continue, the images started to get grainy and pixelated, until I could no longer conjure them at all.

I said, "She could be fifty miles from here."

"No," Diego said, shaking his head. "These tracks fresh. She is close."

He might have told me this before—my brain was as fatigued as my legs—but I didn't remember him saying it so defiantly.

"We must keep going," he said.

47

The Nsé-Eja village was a fifteen-minute climb up a steep incline. Gina was in the middle of the pack, behind Patrick, Martin, Bill, and one of the four soldiers. With their spears held high, the tribesmen marched them up the hill.

When they reached the top, Gina was surprised to see a bustling village of solidly built wooden houses. Over fifty villagers congregated outside their homes, cooking over open fires or tending to flocks of chickens. The women wore ornate long blouses with a sash around their waists. The older men and the children wore long sleeveless shirts.

The villagers stopped and stared as Gina and the others were marched to the far side of the village, where a row of five tall wooden poles jutted from the earth. The poles were eight feet tall, six inches in diameter, and spaced roughly three feet apart. There was another set of five poles sixty meters away on the opposite side of the village. As Gina drew closer to the poles nearest her, she noticed heavy slash marks cut into them. All the slash marks were at neck level.

She thought back to what Martin had said about the tribe.

They are headhunters.

A chill ran up Gina's spine. She imagined how the next few minutes would play out. Each of them would be forced to stand with their back against the pole, then, one by one, their heads would be severed from their bodies.

But then why did the villagers appear so civilized?

They looked nothing like what Gina imagined a ruthless tribe of headhunters and cannibals would look like.

She glanced over her shoulder. Twenty-odd tribesmen had their spears held above their shoulders, ready to throw. Gina considered slipping through the poles and into the surrounding jungle. What were the chances of them hitting a moving target with their spears?

Pretty good if the spear that struck the tree right in front of their group was any indication.

But if she could get to the jungle, she could outrun them. Or could she? Maybe on her trail near her village she could, but here on their home turf?

Probably not.

Martin, who was standing next to her, whispered under his breath, "Don't do it."

Gina raised her eyebrows.

"Just trust me," he whispered.

"What are we going to do?" Bill said quietly. "They're going to kill us."

Gina turned and gazed at the group of tribesmen surrounding them.

A moment later, there was a rustling, and the tribesmen separated. A thin old man shuffled forward. He was wearing a long blue tunic and his white hair was adorned with golden feathers.

Martin took two steps forward and said, "*Parlasqayki.*"

The old man, who Gina knew must be the village shaman, nodded and with a toothless smile, said, "*Yaykuykuy.*"

Martin turned to the group and translated, "Shaman Yapun-qui welcomes us."

Gina was trying to figure out what the heck was going on, when there was a loud series of thunks. It was the sound of thirty spears being thrust into the ground.

≈

After the tribesmen thrust their spears into the ground, Martin walked forward to speak with the aging shaman. A few of the children ran up to Gina and the others and began touching them and speaking in their native language.

A small boy, probably the same age as Miguel from her village, waved to Gina. He had shiny black hair, but his skin was a few shades lighter than Miguel's. In fact, on closer examination, all the villagers' skin was bronze as opposed to the darker cocoa of most indigenous groups.

A few moments later, the villagers and warriors disbanded, and Martin returned from his conversation with the shaman.

Gina asked, "So they're not headhunters?"

"No," Martin said. "They're quite peaceful actually."

"So you lied about that," said Patrick. "Why? And why were you so reluctant to bring us here? Even when I offered you five million dollars? Even after I told you what was at stake?"

"It's a long story."

"Shorten it," Patrick said.

Martin said, "Thirty years ago, much like they just surrounded us, I was surrounded by a tribal hunting party and marched to this village at spearpoint. It didn't take me long to realize their language was one of the six that I spoke.

"I spent three months living with them and apprenticing with their shaman, Yapunqui. Over those months, I came to learn that the villagers were rarely sick, and that they didn't even have a word for cancer. I learned a lot about their history and as much about their medicines as I could. When I returned to the States, I knew that if anyone found out the true location of the tribe, their way of life would be destroyed."

Patrick shook his head. "But think of all the people in the world who could have been helped."

"I considered that, but on my departure, I made Yapunqui a promise that I would never reveal their location. A promise I intended to keep. So in my book, I made them out to be cannibals, said they were the Nsé-Eja from the South American myth, and that I hardly escaped with my life."

Bill, who had been silent up to that point, asked, "If you didn't want anyone to try to contact them, then why did you put in the part about how they had no history of cancer in your book?"

"In hindsight, I shouldn't have. But my ego got in the way. To be honest, I wanted to sell books. And by including their apparent immunity to cancer, plus my *riveting* tale of escape, I did just that. Everyone in the scientific community was talking, and it became an international bestseller."

Patrick asked, "Why include the picture of the golden jaguar and the compass heading to the pyramid?"

"I figured the odds of someone ever finding the golden jaguar were so infinitesimal that I never worried about it. Plus, their village was over twenty-five miles from the pyramid. Even if someone did put two and two together, their odds of actually finding the tribe would still be nearly impossible."

But now here they were.

Gina glanced at Martin. She was curious why he'd lied to even her, but mostly, she was confused why, if Martin spoke the villagers' language, he hadn't instructed the tribesmen to keep Patrick, Bill, and the soldiers under guard. Though the villagers had taken their rifles, Gina knew Patrick still had a gun hidden in the waist-band of his pants.

What if the shaman refused to tell Patrick the secret to their immunity to cancer? Would he start shooting villagers until he got what he was after? And even if they did share the jungle marvel that was keeping them so healthy, it wasn't like Patrick could just let her and Martin go. He couldn't risk them making it back to civilization and going to the authorities. He would spend the rest of his life in jail.

At this point, there was only one thing Gina knew for certain.

She, Martin, and the villagers—none of them were safe.

48

With the help of Diego's words of encouragement, a few light kisses from Camila, and a huge mouthful of coca, I still wasn't able to get to my feet. I wanted to, so badly, but I was made of ectoplasm. I was having trouble keeping my eyes open.

I felt a sting in my thigh, and my eyes fluttered open. Rix was kneeling beside me, holding a four-inch clear tube in his right hand.

My heart instantly raced, and I said, "What was that?"

He turned the tube toward me. "EpiPen. Andy gave them to me before we left. He thought you might need a hit of adrenaline at some point."

I rocked my head forward, the adrenaline already working its way into my cells. "Good thinking."

He pulled a second EpiPen from his pack and handed it to me. "Just in case," he said.

I slipped it into my pocket and a moment later, we were back on the trail.

Over the next half hour, Diego continued to say how fresh the tracks were. At one point, we crossed a small stream, and Diego found several depressions in the soft mud near its bank.

"These tracks happen today," he said.

That gave me a boost of optimism. But even if they did happen today, Gina and her captors could still be five hours ahead of us. Unless we started running, we might never catch up. And considering that my being upright was itself a victory, running wasn't going to happen.

Diego turned on the trail in front of me and put up his hand. He pointed to the ground. "Footprints."

I leaned down and inspected the impressions. They were different from the other footprints that we'd seen.

These had come from bare feet.

We followed them for one hundred yards and then saw it. It was buried in the trunk of a tree that stood not far from a flowing river.

A spear.

≈

"I will come back for you," Diego told Camila, kissing his thumb and touching her nose with it. "I promise."

"And if he dies, *I'll* come back for you," I told her.

I don't think Diego appreciated my humor. He cut his eyes at me, then hung Camila from the branch of a nearby tree.

Rix gave her a quick tickle on her tummy and then the three of us huddled up.

Rix said, "From the tracks, it looks like a group was surrounded by a bunch of villagers."

Diego nodded at the beginnings of a steep incline and said, "Their village is probably on top of the hill."

I clicked off the safety on my rifle. Rix and Diego did the same.

"Let's go," I said.

Diego closed his eyes and muttered something in Spanish.

"What did you just say?"

"I make prayer we no get eaten."

"Amen to that."

≈

Fifteen minutes later, the three of us were crouched behind the seven-foot-wide trunk of an enormous tree. A slight incline led from here to the top of a small ridge.

"I'll do a recon," Rix said.

I shook him off. "No, I got it."

"You barely made it up the hill," the ex–SAS soldier responded.

"I've got it," I said, ending the conversation.

I pulled off my pack and slid out a pair of binoculars. I lowered myself to the leaf-strewn jungle floor and crawled to a thick patch of vegetation. There was a good chance I was going to get bitten by something or was smack-dab in the middle of some poisonous plants, but I didn't care. I army-crawled up the ten-foot embankment and peeked over the edge.

Not thirty feet from where I lay were the beginnings of a sprawling village and easily sixty men, women, and children.

I expected them to be nude or crudely dressed, but the villagers were clad in brightly colored knitted clothes. The houses were wooden—mahogany from the looks of it—and beautifully built.

Another group had gathered at the far edge of the village, but they were fifty yards away, and I couldn't make out much.

I pulled up the binoculars and focused. The villagers in this group were dressed differently than the others. They had war paint on their faces, multicolored strings tied around their biceps, and were clad in low-hanging red loincloths.

Behind them were three Caucasian men, four soldiers, and one woman.

Gina.

I'd found her.

≈

I retreated back to the large tree.

I said, "She's here."

Diego smiled, and Rix gave me knuckles.

"How does she look?" Rix asked.

"Pretty banged up."

Gina's hair was in a twisted nest of a ponytail. Her arms and face were covered in dirt. Worst of all, one of her eyes was blackened.

Rix asked, "Who is with her?"

"Four soldiers and three white dudes."

"The Belippa guys?"

"Yep."

"Okay, so what's the plan?" Rix asked.

"For one, I don't think they're the Nsé-Eja." I described what I saw.

"That doesn't sound like them," Diego said.

I clapped him on the shoulder and said, "So no curses to deal with."

But we still had to deal with twenty Indian warriors, plus Gina's captors.

"Okay," Rix said. "How do you want to do this?"

"Hard and fast," I said.

"Hard and fast," Rix echoed.

≈

"Hands up!" Rix and I yelled as we sprinted across fifty yards of open space into the center of the village. Diego was a half-step behind us, racing to keep up.

The villagers fell to their knees. In doing so, they revealed Gina and her captors standing behind them.

Gina's mouth opened wide, and her hands flew up. "Thomas?" she cried, unbelievingly. "Thomas!"

"Don't move," I said, swiveling the shotgun across Gina's seven captors. The seven of them glanced nervously at one another. I didn't see any firearms on them, but if one of them so much as blinked, I was prepared to put a bullet through their chest.

They remained still.

Gina ran toward me, tears dripping down her cheeks. She collapsed into my arms, pressing her head into my chest. After a long breath, she glanced up at me, moisture clinging at the edges of her eyes, and said, "I knew you would come."

I wiped a tear running down her cheek and said, "Sorry I didn't get here sooner."

She sniffed.

I gently thumbed the fading bruise around her eye and asked, "Who did this to you?"

She turned and pointed at the handsome, dark-haired American with rough, pockmarked cheeks. "Him."

"Patrick Sewall," I said.

Lacy had described to me what he looked like via text.

"You figured it out?" Gina said, obviously impressed. "That this was all about the cure for cancer."

I stepped back a few inches.

"What?" she asked.

I shook my head. "This isn't about cancer. It never was."

"What are you talking about?"

When I texted Lacy a day earlier, I asked her to do some research for me on the internet. I was still trying to figure out the Venn Diagram. How did three different groups end up in the exact same place in the Amazon jungle?

One name kept pinging my brain.

It was from when I sat down with Jonathan Roth and questioned him about who else could have known the golden jaguar's exact location. I was more interested in the tentacles stemming from Roth, when I should have been thinking about the tentacle that was Roth. Where *he* got the image from.

Jordan Mae and Yewed Global.

I asked Lacy to do a few internet searches and see if she could come up with a connection between Jordan Mae and Belippa Pharmaceutical.

An hour earlier, after going without a signal for more than half a day, my Garmin inReach had pinged. A message from Lacy had finally come through. After several hours of searching, she had found a connection between Belippa Pharmaceutical and Jordan Mae.

The president of Belippa, Patrick Sewall, had a son.

Daniel.

Daniel Sewall and Jordan Mae were Facebook friends. They'd gone to UCLA together.

Four months earlier, Daniel had been reported missing.

His last known location: Bolivia.

"This isn't about cancer," I told Gina. "This is about a missing son."

49

Patrick Sewall poured himself a glass of iced tea and made his way to the office in his Silicon Valley estate. As he often did, he wondered why he kept the enormous six-thousand-foot house when it was only him living there.

It was abnormally warm for an early spring afternoon in Northern California, somewhere in the mid-seventies, and he flipped on the small fan in the corner of his office. The air began circulating as he sat down in the ergonomic chair behind his desk, took a sip of tea, then set the glass on a coaster.

The coasters were custom-made, pictures of him and Trisha on their twentieth wedding anniversary. They'd gone to the Canary Islands—Tenerife, to be exact—a tropical paradise off the northwestern coast of Africa.

Trisha's skin was sun-kissed in the picture. She wore a light-yellow dress and held a large blue cocktail. Patrick was holding a similar drink, and both of them were smiling from ear to ear.

Sixteen months later, Trisha would be diagnosed with an aggressive form of bone cancer and seven months after that, she would be gone. Leaving him a single father to their nineteen-year-old son, Daniel.

For the thousandth time, Patrick considered packing away the coasters.

Maybe it was time to move on.

He took another sip of tea, then flipped open his laptop and logged into his email. His face brightened at the sight of one of them. It was from Daniel, and like always, the subject heading read "Checking in."

For the past five months, Daniel had been hopping around South America. He was twenty-seven years old, a microbiologist by trade, and after doing lab work at Belippa for the past four years, he was on a journey of self-discovery.

At least, that's what Patrick called it.

Daniel, on the other hand, called it a microbe hunt. He believed the next great pharmaceutical advancement would be microbial, that is to say, a single-celled organism: fungus, virus, algae, protozoa, or bacteria.

And since there was no place on earth with a greater concentration of microbes, Daniel headed for the Amazon rainforest.

Patrick clicked open the email.

Hey Dad.

I'm still in Bolivia. Las Piedras, a small town not too far from Riberalta. I'm headed into a pretty isolated part of the jungle tomorrow. Don't worry, I'll be fine. Pretty excited about this one. Hopefully, I can get ten or twenty good soil samples. I'll talk to you in about a month.
Love ya.

D

A month?

The longest Daniel had gone without checking in before had

been two weeks. That had been in Colombia. But Daniel was as tough as they came, a wizard when it came to the outdoors: Eagle Scout as a kid, Outward Bound in Argentina at fifteen, and nearly six weeks in the Mosquitia jungles of Honduras the summer before college.

Patrick wasn't worried.

≈

Patrick sat at an outside table at the county club. He'd just played twenty-seven holes of golf, and he was considering playing another nine.

At fifty-seven years old, he felt better than he had in his forties. The best thing he could have done was step down as CEO of Belippa after Trisha died. Instead of working seventy-hour weeks, trying to keep the shareholders appeased, he could relax a bit.

A waitress came by and took his order. She was in her midtwenties, with a tight tan skirt and a white button-up shirt that accentuated her assets. After taking his order, she gave him a poke on the shoulder and said, "When are you going to buy me a drink?"

"Sometime soon," he said, which was his default response.

While he waited for his club sandwich to arrive, Patrick picked up his phone. He checked the Belippa stock. It was holding steady at $66 a share.

Four years earlier, it had been double that, trading at above a $123 a share.

Patrick typed a quick text to Bill Wyeth. Bill had been his closest friend going back forty years and had been CEO of Belippa for the past three years. Belippa's quarterly earnings were due out next week, and Patrick was curious how they were going to look.

After sending the text, he checked his email. Still nothing from Daniel.

It was only June 6, not quite a full month since he last heard from him.

"He'll check in tomorrow," he told himself.

A few minutes later, his club sandwich arrived.

≈

"Thirty-four days," Patrick said to Bill. "It's been thirty-four days."

"He's fine," Bill said. "He probably met some villagers and lost track of the time. He'll check in sometime in the next couple of days. Trust me."

Patrick sat at the kitchen table of Bill's Silicon Valley high-rise—or what Bill referred to as his "palatial bachelor pad."

"Hopefully," Patrick said, "I don't know what I'd do if I lost him."

"Hey," Bill said. "Don't think like that. He's my godson, remember? I love that kid like my own, and I'm not worried."

Patrick tried to smile but couldn't.

"So the quarterly earnings?" Bill said.

"How bad?"

"Down thirteen percent."

"Shit," Patrick said. "What time do the numbers come out?"

"Tomorrow morning, before the market opens."

"We're going to take a beating."

"We'll be fine. FDA approval for Jevixa is supposed to come through next Friday. We could have it out by fall if we fast-track it. Early projections have revenues at two billion the first year. Three point six by year two."

≈

"Ambassador? Charge d'whatever? I don't give a damn," Patrick shouted into the receiver. "Just get him on the phone."

"I told you that he's in a meeting," said the voice from the US Embassy in Bolivia. "I can leave him a message."

"I've already left six messages. My son went missing in the Bolivian Amazon. I haven't heard from him in forty days."

"Like I said—"

Patrick hung up the phone.

For the past three days, Patrick had tried to go through the correct channels. He'd filled out the missing-persons paperwork on the embassy website, and he'd phoned the embassy fifteen times. But he wasn't getting anywhere.

It was time to put his vast fortune to work.

≈

Patrick picked up the marker and drew a red X through July 18.

Daniel had been missing for seventy-five days.

Patrick was dropping to his knees, ready to once again beg God to send his son home, when his phone rang.

It was Rodrigo, the Bolivian investigator whom Patrick had hired. Patrick had just returned to the States after spending a month in Bolivia with Rodrigo and twenty Bolivian soldiers, combing the jungles in and around Las Piedras in search of his son. They hadn't found a single clue as to Daniel's whereabouts.

Patrick answered the call. "What have you got?"

"Nothing. I'm going to have to stop looking."

"No. I'll pay you as much as you want." Patrick had already spent more than three million dollars on the search.

"I can't take any more of your money," Rodrigo said. "I'm sorry." Rodrigo didn't say the next four words, but he didn't have to.

Your son is gone.

≈

The contract was dated from the previous day, July 28.

It was from ISRS, Israeli Search and Rescue Services.

Two million dollars up front. Another two million if they found Daniel.

Patrick clicked the box on the computer, accepting the terms, then typed his name, electronically signing the document.

He was getting ready to send the contract back when an alert for a new email appeared. Like each time he received an email, his heart began to pound.

Please be from Daniel, please be from Daniel, please be from Daniel.

It wasn't.

His heart sank.

The sender was jordanwmae92@gmail.com.

The subject read "Daniel."

Patrick had received dozens of these emails. News of Daniel's disappearance had leaked in mid-July when Patrick missed his first Belippa shareholder's meeting ever. Since then, he'd been getting a steady stream of sympathy emails—"Sorry for your loss," "Hold out hope," "Trust in the Lord." They were from the same people who had reached out after Trisha's death.

He was set to leave the email unread, but something made him click it.

"Holy shit," he said as he began to read the words.

Mr. Sewall,

I was backpacking through Europe, and I didn't check my social media very often. I'm at the airport in New York, and I just checked my Facebook and saw that Daniel is missing. I'm not sure if he told you where he was headed in the Bolivian jungle, but I have the exact coordinates. They are from a golden jaguar image (the same golden jaguar from Martin Lefbrevor's book, *The Last Shaman*) I stumbled on while I was working. I've attached screenshots of the images and coordinates I sent him.

My plane is boarding. Gotta go.

Jordan Mae

≈

Patrick's private plane landed on the tarmac in Calgary on August 1.

After talking to Jordan Mae, Patrick told Bill that he was no longer hiring the Israelis. Like all he'd accomplished in his life, Patrick would find Daniel himself.

Patrick was surprised when Bill said he would come with him. Patrick refused at first, telling Bill point-blank he wasn't in good enough shape to hike through the jungle. But Bill was insistent. He wouldn't hold them back, and if he did, they could go on without him.

Patrick relented, then quickly began making arrangements for a guide and soldiers to meet them in northwestern Brazil in two days.

But first they needed to make a stop in Canada.

Bill and Patrick exited the plane and stepped into the back of the waiting sedan. The car had been arranged by a third party, who had been paid a healthy advance to keep it off the books.

After a thirty-minute drive, Patrick and Bill jumped from the car and hurried to the front door of a compact two-story house.

After two knocks, the door was pulled open.

"Hey," said Martin Lefbrevor, "I told you over the phone that I wasn't interested."

"And I've come to make my plea in person," Patrick said.

"I'll never go back. Not for five million dollars. Not even for the cure for cancer."

After reading Martin's book, Patrick knew that if he told the ethnobotanist his son was missing and that he suspected Daniel may have been captured by the Nsé-Eja, Martin would tell him that there was no saving his son. Instead, Patrick had told the ethnobotanist that he was searching for the cure for cancer, which, as the owner of a pharmaceutical company, was highly believable.

"Now, please leave," Martin said, pushing the door closed.

Patrick caught the door with his foot. "Not just yet."

50

"After grabbing Martin," Patrick said, "Bill and I jumped back on my jet and flew to Río Branco, Brazil, twenty miles north of the Bolivian border." He nodded to the soldiers. "These four, plus one more, were waiting for us there.

"We packed into the back of a pickup and drove down into Bolivia, to a town called Santa Rosa del Abuná. We had the exact coordinates of the golden jaguar statue, where we thought Daniel had headed, which was roughly sixty miles through the jungle from Abuná.

"We started hiking, and on day three Mr. Lefbrevor made a run for it. Guillermo, the fifth soldier," he shot a quick look at Gina, "sent a warning shot over his head that spooked him, and he slipped and hit his head on the side of a tree."

Patrick was taking too long, and I took over. I said, "You couldn't find the tribe without Martin, so you needed to keep him alive. I'm guessing one of your four soldiers there is a Yanomina Indian, and he knew of an American doctor living in an Indian village not too far away."

Patrick cocked his head. "How did you know one of these four was Yanomina?"

I nodded at Diego. "The first camp that we came to—there was a lean-to there that had some special Yanomina flare to it."

"I see."

"Anyhow, they go to Gina's village, do a snatch and grab, then bring Gina back to where you guys are staying. She treats Martin for his injuries, then you continue to the coordinates of the golden jaguar. At some point, Martin comes out of it, and he leads you to the pyramid that's nearby."

T4.

Patrick said, "Actually, we knew how to get to the pyramid ourselves. Martin included a compass heading in the text of the book."

I didn't know this part, but it didn't matter. I said, "Then he leads you here, and you find out that this isn't the ruthless village Martin made it out to be."

"Correct. Which, more or less, brings us to the present."

Patrick turned to Gina and said, "I know what I did was terrible, kidnapping you, but you have to believe me, I was never going to hurt you. And I never should have slapped you. I was just trying to find my son."

Gina said. "You put a gun to my temple. I could feel your finger pulsing on the trigger."

I turned to Gina. "Really?"

"Yeah, he was about to kill me, but thank God, Martin begged him not to."

The image of Patrick holding a gun to Gina's head made the small hairs on my neck go stiff. The fact that Patrick's motive was finding his son and not the cure for cancer mattered little to me. I was brainstorming exactly what my plans were for Mr. Sewall, whether I was going to let the justice system take care of him, or if I was going to deliver my own vigilante justice—I was leaning this way—but first things first.

I asked, "What about your son?"

"I was about to have Martin ask just that," he said, though his body didn't match his words.

Patrick didn't look ready.

I knew why.

This was it. His last hope. If these villagers hadn't seen his son, it was over. Daniel was lost forever. Patrick wasn't ready for that finality.

"Don't let me stop you," I said, shaking my gun at Martin. "Ask him."

The ethnobotanist respectfully approached the elderly shaman with the feathers in his hair, and the two men spoke briefly.

After several exchanges, Martin turned to Patrick and said, "Good news. They *have* seen him."

"Really?" Patrick's eyes tripled in size. "When? Where did they see him?"

"Actually," Martin said, "Daniel is here."

≈

The shaman said to follow him.

"Keep your gun up," Rix said to me as we trailed behind the group. "Who knows what the soldiers might try."

I nodded.

Patrick was a few steps behind Martin and the small shaman. I watched as Patrick flexed and reflexed his hands.

As much as I hated the man—and trust me, I did—part of me was looking forward to seeing him and his son reunite. It would be like watching one of those videos on the internet of soldiers coming back and seeing their dogs. Only I'd get to witness it live. And then shoot one of them in the knee.

Stopping at the edge of the jungle, the shaman pointed down a narrow trail running through the trees.

Martin said, "He says your son is in there."

Martin and Patrick led the way. Gina and I were directly behind.

We'd only gone thirty meters when the two men stopped.

"No," Patrick said.

I followed his gaze. Just off the path was a mound of dirt. There was a small cross sticking out of it.

Patrick stumbled to the edge of the jungle grave and fell to his knees. His body rocked back and forth as he sobbed.

51

The man with tinted glasses and a comb-over—who I assumed from Patrick's story was Bill Wyeth, CEO of Belippa—joined Patrick at his son's grave. He put his hand on Patrick's left shoulder.

The rest of us took a few respectful steps backward.

I felt Gina's fingers intertwine with mine, and I gave her hand a few soft pumps.

I said, "You left me some pretty good breadcrumbs to follow."

"Call me Gretel," she said with a smile.

I tilted my head to the side. "Actually, I didn't find all your breadcrumbs. I was in the throes of dengue fever when the anthropologist from the expedition found your message under the bowl."

"What expedition?" Gina asked, leaning back several inches. "Wait, you had dengue?"

She fought down a grin. "So that's why you look like someone dug you up out of your own grave."

"I guess there's a lot to tell you," I said. "And technically, I still have dengue, though I may look like shit because I've been living in the jungle for two weeks."

She laughed and I was reminded of how incredible she looked

when she did. Like someone who'd just found twenty dollars in an old coat.

Gina was getting ready to say something when there was a rustling deeper in the jungle. A moment later, a young man with a bushy blond beard emerged from the thick foliage.

Patrick Sewall jumped up.

"Daniel!"

"*Dad?*" The young man's mouth fell open. "What are you doing here?"

Patrick Sewall raced forward and pulled his son into his arms. Even from twenty feet away, you could hear the older man sob into his son's shoulder.

"Dad!" the son said, almost laughing. "It's okay."

"I thought you were dead," Patrick said, pulling away slightly.

"Dead?"

He nodded at the grave a few feet behind him. "There was a cross on it, so I assumed this was your grave."

"No, that's one of the villagers."

Martin stepped forward. "So why is there a cross?"

Daniel turned his gaze to Martin. If Daniel recognized the aging ethnobotanist, he didn't show it. He said, "A decade ago, fires ravaged the Bolivian Amazon, and a village of Machinere Indians had to flee their home. They stumbled on this village, and they were taken in. A missionary had converted the Machinere to Christianity years earlier."

Turning back to his father, Daniel said, "I told you this all in the email I sent. Though if you're here now, you must not have gotten it."

Patrick said, "The last email I got from you was on May eighth. I've been looking for you ever since."

Daniel shook his head, obviously confused. "I sent you an email on June eleventh telling you everything. How I got lost, then hurt, then saved by these amazing people. And how I found the cure."

"You found the cure for cancer?" asked Martin.

"No, not cancer." Daniel rolled up his shirtsleeves and stuck both arms out in front of his father.

"It's gone!" Patrick said. "Your psoriasis is completely healed."

"That's what I told you in the email," Daniel said, grinning. "I think I found the cure for autoimmune disease."

Gina gripped my hand tightly and glanced up at me. She must have known exactly what was going through my head.

There were over a hundred different autoimmune diseases, but there was only one I cared about.

Multiple sclerosis.

52

Daniel Sewall was checking his email at a small café. It had been six days since he'd last had an internet connection, and his inbox was full. There were a bunch of emails from Lauren. She worked in Human Resources at Belippa, the company his father founded, and was still technically his current employer. Daniel was on leave, or sabbatical, or whatever you want to call bouncing around the jungles of South America for nine months.

There was an email from his father, and Daniel clicked it open. It was the usual small talk: what his father had been up to over the last week, a big fundraiser where he met Barack Obama, how he shot an 82 during a golf tournament, and how he was considering asking his personal trainer out on a date.

Daniel responded to his father's email, pleading with him to ask his trainer out, then he recounted his latest venture into the Ecuadorian Amazon and the different soil samples he'd taken.

Daniel Sewall hadn't always intended on going into the family business. In fact, he'd been leaning toward studying economics, much like his godfather had, but when his mother died, that all changed. Daniel decided he would find a cure for cancer so no one would have to feel the same pain he felt watching his mother wither away.

He had studied microbiology at UCLA, then, after graduating, taken a research position with Belippa. He confined his research to cancer for the first two years, but then, at the age of twenty-four, Daniel's skin began to turn red and scaly in several places, and he was experiencing intense joint pain. After a positive ANA (antinuclear antibody) test, he was diagnosed with an autoimmune disease: psoriatic arthritis.

Autoimmune diseases are characterized by an immune response that mistakenly attacks your body. The immune system normally guards against foreign invaders like bacteria and viruses by sending out an army of fighter cells, or antibodies, to attack them. But with an autoimmune disease, the immune system falsely identifies part of the human body as one of these foreign invaders and releases proteins called autoantibodies that attack these healthy cells. This results in either tissue-specific or systemic inflammation.

In Daniel's case, his body was attacking his skin cells and joint tissues.

Daniel was prescribed Mireva, the medicine that had made his father's company so much money over the past decade and a half.

But even with the immune suppressant, Daniel's symptoms never fully went away. Not only were the red scales near his scalp, on his forearms, and on his legs embarrassing, they were extremely painful and itchy. And his joints always felt stiff and cold, like he was coming in from a long day of skiing.

It was then that Daniel broadened his research to include the growing list of autoimmune diseases: rheumatoid arthritis, psoriasis, multiple sclerosis, lupus, Crohn's disease, Sjogren's syndrome, celiac disease, Hashimoto's thyroiditis, type 1 diabetes, pernicious anemia, and alopecia areata, among countless others.

More and more, researchers were connecting a person's microbiome—all the bacteria, fungi, protozoa, and viruses that live on and inside the human body—to autoimmune disease. Specifically, the gut microbiome. An estimated 70 to 80 percent of immune cells are in the intestines, making the gut the linchpin of the immune system.

During his research, Daniel read a paper called "Super Microbiome of Tribal Amerindians," which detailed how scientists found that the most diverse collection of human microbes belonged to a tribe of indigenous people in the secluded jungles of southern Ecuador.

Researchers collected skin, oral, and fecal samples from the tribe. The samples, which contained bacterial DNA, were compared to samples from American subjects and several other first world nations. The results showed that the tribe's people had substantially greater microbial diversity than did industrialized populations.

Another article reported that after testing the DNA of seventeen indigenous populations in the Amazon rainforest, the prevalence of autoimmune disease was a scant 3 percent, compared to 8 percent in the industrialized world.

Daniel theorized that one of the billions of undiscovered microbes buried in the soil of the Amazon could be responsible for the indigenous populations' relative immunity to autoimmune disease. He spent a year learning Spanish, then told his father and godfather that he was taking a year off to study soil samples in the Amazon jungle.

After clicking through the rest of his emails, Daniel jumped on Facebook. He had two messages. One was from a spammer, but the second was from an old college classmate, Jordan Mae. The message read, "You're not going to believe this. I stumbled on these images at work yesterday."

Three images were attached. As predicted, Daniel *didn't* believe it.

The first was a wide shot of jungle canopy, all 3,200 pixels a shade of green. The second image was an enlargement, and Daniel could see the details of each of the trees and a small break in the canopy. But it was the third image that was pure magic: a close up of a golden jaguar faceup in the dirt.

Under the three images was Mae's final message: "I think it's the same statue from the book!"

Daniel knew exactly what book Mae was referring to, and oddly enough, Daniel had a copy of it in his backpack. He pulled out *The Last Shaman: Searching for New Medicines in the Amazon* by Martin J. Lefbrevor, PhD, which had been required reading in his and Mae's Intro to Ethnobotany course—a three-credit elective in biological sciences they had taken during sophomore year. Jordan Mae had also been a biology major, but the following semester he had switched to computer science.

Daniel flipped open the well-worn pages of the book and found the glossy pictures at its center. One of the pictures was of a golden jaguar faceup in the earth. Daniel held the picture up and compared it to the one on the computer screen.

They were identical.

Daniel didn't need to reread the book to remember that after finding the golden jaguar, Martin Lefbrevor had walked another mile and stumbled on a large jungle pyramid. Lefbrevor then walked two more days, at which point he encountered a vicious tribe: the Nsé-Eja.

During the ethnobotanist's seventeen days in captivity, the Nsé-Eja shaman spoke bits and pieces of Portuguese to him. While Martin was held captive, the shaman often visited him. Martin learned the tribe was extraordinarily, almost mythically, healthy and had no known incidence of cancer. Then, somehow, Martin escaped.

Scientists had been looking for this theoretical tribe since Martin's book had been published in 1984. Martin refused to divulge where the tribe was located, only that it was in the Amazon jungle. Most people assumed the tribe was in the jungles of Brazil, where there had been a few other apparent Nsé-Eja encounters.

No one had ever thought to look in Bolivia.

≈

It took Daniel three days of travel to get to the capital of the Pando Department, Cobija, then another two days to arrive at the jungle town of Las Piedras. It was May 8 when Daniel found a café with internet access and sent his father his weekly update. He told him he was headed into an isolated area of the northern Bolivian jungle and that his father might not hear from him for a month. He didn't tell his father about the images and coordinates Jordan Mae had sent him; he didn't want to get his father's hopes up. Nor did he want his father to know that his only child was venturing into an area where he could possibly encounter a ruthless and vicious tribe.

Two days later, he found himself in another small jungle town, Campo Verde. For a small fee, the owner of a shop in town agreed to store the majority of Daniel's research equipment until he returned.

It would take two days by boat and four days on foot before Daniel found his way to the jaguar statue in the middle of the jungle. He couldn't believe his eyes when he pulled it from the ground and held it. It must have weighed upward of ten pounds. If it were solid gold, which Daniel presumed it was, it would be worth over a quarter of a million dollars for the gold alone. He fastened the jaguar to the top of his pack and set out to find the jungle pyramid.

Following the compass headings Lefbrevor had written in the text—"1.6 kilometers at sixty-two degrees"—it took Daniel three hours to find the pyramid. According to the book, the tribe was two days' travel from there, roughly twenty-five miles away.

But in which direction?

Daniel decided to head north toward Brazil, then work his way back around. He'd purchased a rifle in Cobija, but hoped to avoid the tribe altogether. With a two-day radius of twenty-five miles, it was a search grid of nearly two thousand square miles. The odds of actually stumbling on the tribe was as microscopic as the organisms Daniel was searching for.

His plan was to take as many soil samples in the area as possible. Though he had some rudimentary lab equipment stored with the shop owner in Campo Verde, it wouldn't be until Daniel was back in the States that he could begin the detailed research necessary to see if the microorganisms in the samples had therapeutic properties to treat either cancer or autoimmune disease.

It happened two days later. After a lengthy rain, Daniel was trudging down the side of a small hill, when he slipped and fell backward, smashing the left side of his torso into the exposed root of a large tree.

Daniel rolled on the ground, certain he'd broken two ribs. A few hours later, he attempted to walk, but he couldn't go far. It was too painful to breathe.

Three days later, it was evident to Daniel that he'd injured more than just his ribs. Something internal was damaged. He was coughing up blood.

It rained torrentially the next two days. Daniel tried to move to higher ground, but he couldn't get far. He was swept away by a flash flood but somehow managed not to drown, pulling himself to safety. But his pack was gone, and with it his medicine, samples, food and water, GPS receiver, the golden jaguar—everything.

By May 23 Daniel was certain he wouldn't last another day. Lying down, he told his mom up above that he would see her soon.

≈

When he opened his eyes, he was in a wooden hut. He wasn't sure how much time had passed, but the growth of his beard indicated it had been at least a week.

Standing over him was a slender native with white hair and a few golden feathers sticking out.

At first, Daniel assumed he'd been captured by the Nsé-Eja, but he soon learned otherwise, and that they had rescued him from certain death.

Over the next few days, Daniel lived among the villagers and healed. They brought him food and tea.

The villagers were friendly, and though most of them spoke only their native language, a few also spoke Spanish. They'd learned it from a Christian missionary long ago, so Daniel was able to communicate with them.

To say the village's history was momentous would be an understatement.

Another few days passed, and Daniel finally felt he was healed enough to travel. He was elated when the villagers returned later that day with his pack. He was even more surprised that most of his possessions—his medicine, his samples, his GPS, even his passport—were accounted for. The only thing missing was the golden jaguar.

Daniel found his prescription of Mireva, and only then did he realize he'd gone nearly ten days without taking the pills. Yet, aside from a bit of soreness in his ribs, his joints felt terrific. And not only that. For the first time in over three years, the red, scaly skin on his arms, legs, and scalp had completely healed.

≈

After four days trekking back through the jungle and two days on the river, Daniel stumbled into the small village of Campo Verde on June 11. He recovered his research equipment from the small shop and drew a vial of his blood.

One of the pieces of equipment Daniel had brought was a portable ELISA kit. An ELISA, or enzyme-linked immunosorbent assay, could be used to perform different immunological tests. Daniel could use the kit to run an ANA test to determine the prevalence of autoantibodies, the proteins that cause most autoimmune diseases.

He added a droplet of his blood to the solution in one of the small vials. He then pulled out a separate dropper and added two drops of an antigen—a foreign substance that induces an immune response—then capped the vial.

He shook it gently and waited.

If his blood tested positive for autoantibodies, the pink solution would turn blue. The shade—from aqua to a midnight purple—would indicate the ANA concentration of the sample. The darker the color, the higher the concentration of autoantibodies in the sample.

Daniel waited and waited, but the vial remained unchanged.

Negative.

Daniel couldn't believe it.

He raced back to the shop where his equipment had been stored and asked if the owner had an internet connection. Surprisingly enough, he did. For a small fee, the store owner allowed Daniel to log onto his computer.

It had been thirty-three days since Daniel had last checked in with his father, and he was sure his dad was beginning to worry. He considered calling him, but his father would want to talk for hours, and Daniel was in a rush to get back to the village.

Daniel sent a quick email recounting everything that had

happened, emphasizing that he was perfectly okay. Then in all caps he wrote that he was 90 percent sure he'd been cured of his psoriatic arthritis, and that he might be close to finding a cure for all autoimmune diseases.

He wrote that he was heading back to the village as soon as possible to start doing research and narrow down what had cured him. He probably wouldn't be in touch for another three months.

Daniel added that he loved him.

≈

Back at the village six days later, Daniel asked one of the Spanish-speaking Indians to translate his request to the shaman. Daniel wanted to take blood samples from some of the villagers—all of them, if possible.

The shaman, who was also the village elder, refused. They would only willingly give their blood as an offering to their gods.

Over the next month, Daniel slowly wore the shaman down. He spent several hours with him and a Machinere Indian acting as translator, telling the shaman his people could hold the cure to a terrible group of diseases ravaging the entire world.

The shaman knew about disease only too well. Finally, he relented.

Many of the villagers were happy to give a few droplets of their blood. Others were frightened and refused. Of the 216 villagers, 176 gave blood.

The results were, in a word, remarkable.

Out of all the samples, seven had high concentrations, the vials turning a dark purple. Two had low concentrations, the vial turning a soft blue. For a total of nine positive tests, just over 5 percent of the sample size.

This was moderately less than the 8 percent of the world

population who had some sort of autoimmune disease. But more staggering was that roughly 15 percent of healthy people—people *without* autoimmune disease—will still have a positive ANA test. That's because humans have antibodies in their blood for all kinds of reasons—from bacterial or fungal infections, to viruses, to simple genetic makeup—and these regular antibodies read as false positives.

That only 5 percent of the ANA tests had come out positive meant that there was something unique to these villagers that was suppressing the immune response of even the healthiest individuals. Daniel believed the unknown factor was microbial, but it would take months, possibly years, and hordes of specialized equipment to determine what the single or multiple organisms were.

It was near the middle of July.

Maybe it was time for him to head back home.

≈

Daniel decided to stay, at least another week.

On July 20, two days before he was set to leave, he and several villagers were sitting around at night drinking tea, as was the custom. The tea wasn't anything exotic, in fact, the sole ingredient was popular in teas all over the world.

Ginger root.

Daniel took a small sip of the peppery and slightly sweet tea, then glanced up. He noticed three natives surrounding him who weren't drinking tea.

It took Daniel a moment to make the correlation.

Two of the three villagers *not* drinking tea were among the nine who had positive ANA tests. One was a Machinere Indian, and Daniel asked in Spanish why he wasn't drinking the tea. He said he didn't like the taste, and he never drank it. This was the same for the other villager as well.

Daniel quickly jumped up and ran through the village, tracking down the other seven with positive ANA tests. It turned out that all nine villagers with positive ANA tests rarely, if ever, drank the ginger tea.

Daniel was onto something.

Early on, he'd discounted the tea as a vector because the water was boiled in a copper kettle for long periods over a fire, and 99 percent of microorganisms exposed to water above 149 degrees for five minutes will die.

But there were species of bacteria that had extreme tolerances to heat. In fact, some were present in several probiotic teas your average person could buy at the grocery store. Most used a strain of bacteria called *Bacillus coagulans*. It had a high tolerance to heat as well as to high pH levels. It could survive both boiling water and stomach acid.

In hindsight, he should have known. When Daniel talked with the shaman about any herbal remedies he may have given him when he was unconscious, the shaman mentioned the tea. They'd let it cool, then poured it down his throat.

The tea was thought to have magic healing properties.

But it might not be magic.

It might be scientific.

≈

Daniel convinced four of the nine villagers who had positive ANA tests to drink the tea for two weeks, then he tested their blood a second time for autoantibodies.

All four tested negative.

The tea *was* the vector.

≈

There are over 1,300 different species of ginger and the root of the herbaceous perennial flower had long been known to have therapeutic and anti-inflammatory properties. Daniel couldn't rule out that it was the ginger itself that was suppressing the villager's autoimmune response. Still, he believed it was something microbial. Something living in the surrounding soil and growing *on* the ginger root.

Under the compact microscope that Daniel had with him, he viewed a droplet of tea on a slide. There was a solitary bacteria that had survived the boiling heat.

In a Petri dish, Daniel was able to culture the bacteria.

He then convinced four of the remaining five villagers with positive ANA tests to ingest small amounts of the bacteria for two weeks.

He retested their blood. All four had negative ANA tests. The test for the control, the one villager who didn't ingest the bacteria, remained positive.

It wasn't the ginger.

It was the *bacteria*.

Daniel had proven his theory. He had isolated and identified a helper bacteria that suppressed the body's autoimmune response.

He had discovered the first "autobiotic."

53

Gina was standing on the narrow path next to Thomas, the two other men he'd come with, and Martin. They were across from Patrick, Bill, and Daniel. The four soldiers were seated on a fallen log just steps into the thick foliage. For the past ten minutes, all of them had listened silently as Daniel recounted his story.

Though Gina had studied autoimmune diseases in med school and had seen several cases during her residency, it wasn't until she worked as a primary care physician at a clinic in Seattle that she'd observed an exponential rise in the prevalence of these diseases. In her six-month tenure, she had encountered upward of a hundred patients who complained of fatigue, muscle aches, digestive issues, joint pain, recurring fever, swollen glands, and other mysterious symptoms.

After performing a physical exam, Gina would recommend doing a full blood test panel and almost always she would include an ANA test. The laboratory ANA test was more complicated than Daniel's portable ELISA kit, but for the most part, it worked along the same lines. If the ANA test came back positive, Gina would refer the patient to a rheumatologist—a doctor specializing in autoimmune conditions—who would perform further testing.

Two years earlier, before the World Health Organization stopped funding Gina's work with the Tibióno, a rheumatologist had spent three days there with her.

The doctor, Hal Wentwoll, had administered ANA tests to thirty of the villagers.

Only one came back positive.

Similar to what Daniel said, Wentwoll theorized that the low incidence was due to a combination of factors, but mainly because the villagers had grown up in and around dirt, splashed in the many rivers, lived in close proximity to both domesticated and wild animals, were rarely treated with antibiotics, and received limited vaccines, if any. In their daily lives, the villagers had been inundated with microbes since birth. Their immune systems had never been coddled; they knew the difference between a foreign invader and a domestic citizen.

According to Wentwoll, in the last several years, researchers had discovered that good intestinal bacteria regulated the innate immune system and confirmed that the presence of good bacteria could help inhibit the immune response. Scientists theorized that probiotics could potentially be used to treat or possibly even cure a wide range of systemic conditions.

They just had to find the right bacteria.

If what Daniel said was true, that he'd discovered a bacteria that suppressed the human immune response, then his discovery wasn't just groundbreaking—it was revolutionary.

Gina turned and glanced at Thomas. She knew he must be thinking about his sister. Gina had met Lacy during the same tumultuous period in South Africa that she'd met Thomas. She'd felt an instant kinship with Lacy, who remained stoic and even sarcastic in the face of death.

Two months later, Gina had accompanied Thomas to Lacy's wedding in France, and it was only then that Gina learned Lacy had multiple sclerosis.

Though no one but Thomas was aware, Lacy had been suffering a flare-up during her nuptials. She hadn't been able to take her medication for the three days she'd been held hostage on a cruise ship, and Lacy was in the midst of a months-long relapse.

MS is an autoimmune disease that affects the central nervous system. The body attacks the myelin sheath (sleeves of fatty tissue that protect your nerve cells), causing disruption of the flow of information between the brain and the body. The symptoms of MS vary from person to person; for some it will be numbness in one of their extremities, for others it's their coordination that suffers, for others it's memory problems. For Lacy Prescott, most often it was her vision. When Thomas was walking Lacy down the aisle, she was seeing double.

Back in Seattle, after Lacy's wedding, Gina could see how much Lacy's MS affected Thomas. When Lacy was in the midst of a flare, Thomas wasn't the same, his mind preoccupied with his sister six thousand miles away. He described her disease as a constant splinter in his heel, and in a rare moment of vulnerability, Thomas confessed that the day Lacy was diagnosed with MS—her junior year of college—had been harder for him than the day he'd lost both his parents.

Gina stroked Thomas's arm with her hand.

He turned and gazed at her. His hair was longer than it had been when they dated, and there were a few wayward strands of gray. He had two weeks of light-brown stubble, dark circles under his eyes, and a gauntness in his cheeks. He looked exhausted; his gray-blue eyes, which had always mesmerized her, swam in a soft sea of pink.

Gina still couldn't believe he was here. It had been two years since she'd seen him. Two years since she'd told him she was moving back to Bolivia.

It was the biggest regret of her life.

Could he forgive her? Had he already? Was that why he was here? Or was he only here out of a sense of duty?

"Hey," Gina said. She wasn't sure what her next words would be, whether she was going to ask him what made him come or to apologize for leaving him or to tell him how much she still loved him, that she'd never stopped. But she could tell that although Thomas was holding her hand, she knew it was Lacy who preoccupied his thoughts.

She tuned back to the conversation going on around her, just in time to hear Daniel say, "I'm fairly certain that, at least for a large percentage of sufferers, it will improve symptoms dramatically, if not cure them outright."

He went on to describe how he had gone a month now without drinking the tea and that none of his symptoms had returned. He theorized that after the autobiotic strain was introduced to a person's microbiome for a period of longer than two weeks, it would remain in their system.

Bill asked, "So all the millions of rheumatoid arthritis sufferers, psoriasis sufferers, and Crohn's disease sufferers—they can pop a few of these autobiotics for two weeks, and they're healed?"

"A lot of research still needs to be done," Daniel said with a smile, "but I'd say the prospects are good."

Bill took a deep breath, then nodded at the soldiers. All four of them brought pistols up and trained them on their group.

"I'm sorry," Bill said. "But I can't allow that to happen."

54

While we'd been listening to Daniel's story, I'd stupidly lowered the shotgun. And at some point, the soldiers had slipped pistols out from ankle holsters—or somewhere else they'd been hiding them—and snuck up behind our group.

Rix, too, had been so entranced by Daniel's story that he'd lowered his weapon. But unlike me, he wasn't going down without a fight.

He twirled next to me and popped off a shot, but it missed its mark. Before he could pull the trigger a second time, one of the soldiers shot him twice: once in the arm and once in the leg.

The rifle fell from Rix's hand and he crumpled to the ground.

"Put it down!" Bill shouted at me as I considered what to do. "Or you're going to end up like your friend."

I could probably get off one shot before I met the same fate as Rix. For now, I'd live to fight another day. Or, more likely, another hour. I lowered my weapon, then tossed it onto the soft earth. Behind me, Diego had done the same.

"You too," Bill said to Patrick. "Hand it over."

Patrick Sewall spun to face his longtime friend and colleague and shouted, "Have you lost your fucking mind?"

"The gun," Bill said. "Now."

Patrick took two long, deep breaths, then pulled a shiny Glock pistol from his waistband. One of the soldiers stepped forward and took the gun.

"You're crazy," Patrick said, with a shake of his head. "Absolutely, batshit crazy."

"I'm quite sane, actually," Bill said, a sly grin flaring his meaty cheeks. "This isn't some spur-of-the-moment decision. I've been planning this since the day I read Daniel's email."

"*Daniel's email?*" Patrick asked, throwing up his hands. "What are you talking about?"

"June eleventh. We were at your house. We were getting ready to go to that banquet. You were in the shower, and I was finishing up work on the computer in your office. Lo and behold, in comes an email from Daniel."

"You son of a bitch!" Patrick yelled, taking three quick steps toward Bill. Two soldiers stepped into his path, pointing their guns at Patrick's chest.

"I can see why you'd be angry," Bill said. "My keeping secret that your son was alive and well, but I had to. I couldn't risk him bringing his cure back to the States. That's why, in addition to your search-and-rescue team, I funded a search-and-rescue team of my own. Well, a *search* team, at any rate. They had slightly different instructions on what to do if they found Daniel.

"But sadly, my team couldn't locate him either. Then when you spoke with Jordan Mae and realized exactly where Daniel had been headed and decided that you were going to find him yourself, I had to tag along. A few days into the mission, I took aside the soldiers and told them I'd pay each of them fifty thousand dollars if they helped me get rid of Daniel and his little discovery."

"You planned on killing your godson?" Patrick asked, his voice raising three octaves.

"That he is, and I love him like a son. Just as I love you like a brother. But I love my position as CEO of the sixth largest pharmaceutical company in the world more. And that position would have been taken from me had Daniel's superbacteria made it back to America."

I was a bit confused. "Wouldn't this superbacteria make you guys billions of dollars?"

I was surprised it was Patrick and not Bill who responded. Patrick said, "Native organisms in their original form can't be patented. So we wouldn't be able to patent the bacteria."

"Couldn't you patent the term *autobiotics*?" I asked. "Or make a bunch of autobiotic gummies or something?"

"Yeah, we could," Daniel answered. "But it wouldn't take long before another company got ahold of the strain of bacteria and began to replicate it. Within a couple years, there would be fifty companies selling the same product."

"But that first year, when people found out they could be cured by your product—don't you think you would make billions?"

Bill said, "Sure, we could make billions, maybe even ten billion in those first few years. But we make over twenty billion on Mireva *every single year*. Autoimmune disease is our golden goose. Ultimately, we would be curing our customer base."

"He's right," Patrick said. "In the long run it would be catastrophic for the bottom line. But only a psychopath would let profits outweigh curing hundreds of millions of people."

Daniel Sewall said, "Think about all those people suffering."

Patrick glanced at his son. Much like how Lacy's MS stung at my heart daily, I'm sure each time Patrick saw Daniel's red, flaky skin or saw him grimace as he tried to make a fist, it felt like a nest of bees in his stomach.

"It's not my job to think of them," Bill said. "My job is to increase the value of the company for our shareholders."

"Forget the shareholders," Patrick said.

"Of course, you, the largest shareholder, would say that. You'll be worth billions no matter what happens."

"You're a millionaire several times over yourself."

"True. And I will be forever grateful for the opportunity you gave me. But I'll be damned if I'm surrendering my position as CEO just because your son found some miracle bacteria."

"Unbelievable," Patrick scoffed.

"You couldn't understand," said Bill. "Everything has always come easy for you—school, girls, money, acclaim—but I've had to work and scrape for everything in my life." He laughed to himself and said, "Do you think it was just a coincidence that Humphries was accused of sexual harassment five days before a shareholders' meeting?"

"You?" Patrick said. "You did that?"

"Of course I did. Humphries was no letch. He was the consummate family man. I paid those three girls to make up that stuff about him. Paid them well." Patrick was at a loss for words, and after a short pause, Bill said, "Okay, let's get this over with."

"And what exactly do you intend to do with us?" asked Martin.

"In your book, you said this was a tribe of headhunters." Bill smiled. "So, I'm going to cut off all your heads."

55

"'Twelve," Andy said.

"Fourteen," Darnell said back.

"Sixteen."

"Sixteen? That's pretty ambitious. Okay, let's hear it."

Andy was set to start listing off characters from the Marvel Universe, when from ten feet behind him, he heard, "Twenty."

Andy and Darnell turned and glanced over their shoulders.

"Really?" Darnell said. "You watch those movies?"

"Just a few of them," said Vern. "I grew up on the comic books."

A day and a half earlier, when Andy had decided he was going after Thomas to film his rescue attempt of Dr. Gina Brady, he was surprised when Vern had volunteered to come along.

"But what about your knee?" Andy had asked.

With a cigar in his mouth, the old codger did ten jumping jacks. "Good as new," he'd said.

Andy wasn't sure if he'd been faking his limp for the past three days or what, but he appeared to be fine.

Vern had traded in his duct-taped rucksack for someone else's large pack and said, "Let's get moving."

And so they had. Andy, Vern, and Darnell moved at a brisk pace through the trampled-down jungle foliage. Luckily, they weren't only navigating by broken branches and fallen leaves. When Thomas, Rix, and Diego had departed earlier that morning, Holland had insisted the trio attach orange GPS beacons to their packs.

Four hours later, when Andy had been getting ready to depart, Holland handed him the military-grade iPad and said, "The signal goes in and out, but this should help you find them."

According to the signal, which had been strong at the time, Thomas and his crew were five miles ahead of them.

For the next several hours, Andy's group made good time. When they made camp for the evening, only three and a half miles separated them from Thomas and the others.

That night, sleeping in a hammock, the weight of what Andy had decided to do hit him with full force. He was voluntarily going after a man who was searching for a ruthless tribe known to cut off its victims' heads and consume their bodies.

He felt a panic attack coming on. The whistles, croaks, hoots, and buzzing of the jungle grew into a pulsating orchestra of his impending death. The dam was about to burst, and Andy was fumbling for his pills when he realized he hadn't packed them. He was in the middle of the jungle, without Holland and the camp as a safety net, and he hadn't packed his pills.

What had he been thinking?

He was on the verge of hyperventilating. He forced his brain to think of Libby.

He ran the clip back in his head of walking past the waiting Farah and toward Libby. Libby's eyes widening as she realized he was headed right toward her. Andy leaning forward and kissing her. Really kissing her. A manly, going-off-to-war kiss.

A few moments later, Andy's panic attack subsided.

The three of them woke up before the rising sun and headed through the jungle for the first hour with their headlamps on.

They had closed the gap to less than three miles when the three red dots disappeared.

The iPad had a good signal, two out of four bars, which meant Thomas, Diego, and Rix's GPS beacons had lost their signal.

Andy and the others followed a well-formed trail through the forest, but they couldn't be positive they were traveling in the correct direction. Three hours later, Andy, once again checking the iPad, realized the it no longer had a signal. They must be traveling through the same area Thomas had when they'd lost *their* signal.

"Okay, then," Darnell said. "Let's hear it."

Vern took a deep breath and then said, "Iron Man, Captain America, Deadpool, Thor, Thanos, Ant-Man, the Wasp, Hulk, She-Hulk—"

"She-Hulk?" Andy interrupted.

Vern smiled. "*Oh* yeah! Big, green, and beautiful."

Andy laughed.

"She got together with Luke Cage. So yeah, Luke Cage—that's ten." Vern rattled off five more names.

"Keep going," Darnell said.

Vern continued with more names as Darnell counted. When Vern exhausted his recall, Darnell said, "Thirty-eight. That's incredible."

Vern said, "I'm a man of many skills."

"That you are," Darnell said.

Andy stopped to check the iPad. "Guys, the signal is back. They're only a mile away. And better yet, they aren't moving."

The red dots blinked when they were on the move, but now the screen showed them as a solid, steady red.

"They must have found the village," Darnell said.

"Yeah, but those dots are their packs. They could have dropped them and still be on the move."

"Either way," Andy said. "There's a good chance the village is close by."

"Time to get our weapons ready," Vern said. "Just in case these cannibals ambush us."

All three had guns. Darnell had forgone the large camera and brought a small handheld, which he could fit in his pack. He held one of the pistols in his left hand.

Vern pulled his pack off his back, placed it gently on the ground, and opened it. For the first time, Andy noticed a large "JR" written in black sharpie on the gray cushioning.

Andy asked, "Is that—?"

"Yep," Vern said. "It's Jonathan Roth's pack. I didn't think he'd be needing it any longer."

"What'd you do with all his stuff?"

"Left it in his tent."

Vern dug his hand into the pack and pulled something out. He showed it to the two others and said, "I brought some party favors."

"A grenade?" Darnell said, laughing.

"Thought they might help us out in a pinch."

Andy said, "Those, um, look a little old."

"Vietnam."

"You have old grenades from Vietnam?" Andy took three steps back from Vern. "Aren't you worried they might explode?"

"Actually, the opposite. I'm worried they might *not* explode."

Vern wanted to test one out to be sure. "Give me a minute," he said, taking the grenade and working his way into the thick jungle.

Darnell said, "Twenty bucks says he comes back without one of his arms."

"I'll take that bet."

"Give me five to one odds?"

"Sure."

Twenty seconds later, there was a loud explosion. Andy's entire body cringed. A flood of birds flew from every tree nearby. The jungle went into a thirty-second frenzy.

"I hope they didn't hear that at the village," Darnell said.

Andy doubted that was possible. The jungle was one enormous pair of headphones. It amplified sounds close by, but far-off sounds were muffled by the thick foliage.

"Where the hell is he?" Darnell asked a minute later. "You think he blew himself up?"

"Maybe."

It was another long minute before Vern emerged from the thicket of green. He had a wide-eyed look on his face. His maroon hat, which Andy had never seen him without, was gone.

"Sounds like they work," Darnell said.

"Um, yeah," Vern mumbled.

Andy couldn't help but notice that Vern had his GPS out.
Why is he marking the coordinates of the area?

"How many more of those thingies do you have?" Darnell asked.

Vern laughed to himself and then said, "Four more."

≈

For the next thirty minutes, they moved swiftly through the jungle. The iPad kept its signal and the three red dots held steady in the same location.

When they were within a quarter mile away, they came to a sweeping river.

Darnell came to a stop. "Look."

Andy's eyebrows knit together as he took in the spear sticking from the tree trunk.

"Keep your guns up," said Vern. "They could be anywhere."

Andy swiveled his head, peering left and right. The villagers could be five feet from him, and he wouldn't see them. And if someone did jump out, would Andy even be able to shoot him? He hadn't even been able to kill a deer during his brother's bachelor party hunt. How was he going to shoot a human?

The three of them had just started up the hill, when Andy heard a series of squeaks. He turned, glanced around, then up.

Hanging from a thick branch, reaching an arm out toward him, she squeaked twice more.

It was Camila.

56

I was having a hard time getting comfortable. But I suppose when you're sitting on the hard earth with a six-inch-thick pole in your crotch and your arms and legs zip-tied together on the opposite side of the pole, that's to be expected.

I slid my wrists up the pole as high as I could—about eight inches above my head—and brought my arms down as quickly and violently as possible. But aside from the heavy black plastic cutting into my raw wrists, nothing happened.

Had my restraints been your run-of-the-mill zip-ties, there's a chance I might have been able to break them—there are several different methods, all of which can be found on YouTube—but these were heavy-duty police zip-cuffs. I knew from my time on the force that they had a 250-pound tensile strength. The only person I'd ever seen break a pair was a three-hundred-pound Samoan. And he was high on PCP.

"I don't think that's going to work." Gina was similarly restrained to a pole three feet to my right.

We'd been marched at gunpoint to two groupings of tall poles. On the west side of the village, it was me, Gina, Martin, and Rix. Sixty yards away, with their backs to us, were Daniel, Patrick, and Diego.

I turned to Gina and said, "You also said it wouldn't work when I tried to make my own applesauce. Remember that?"

"You put an apple in the microwave for seven minutes, then tried to press it through a strainer."

"It worked, right?"

"The apple caught on fire after forty-five seconds. You nearly burned down my apartment building."

"Oh, yeah," I said, remembering. "That didn't work."

She rolled her hazel eyes at me, which is something I'd missed dearly.

I leaned forward and glanced down the row. "How are you doing down there, Rix?"

The bullet that struck Rix's calf appeared to have gone right through—the best one can hope for when a bullet tears through one's flesh. The one in his shoulder, he wasn't so lucky with.

"My calf and my shoulder sort of hurt," he shouted. "And I need to take a shit. Other than that, pretty good."

I laughed. "What is it about being shot that makes you have to take a dump?" After I took two bullets on a cliff face in Maine, I'd fallen into the Atlantic Ocean and nearly drowned. But when they revived me in the ambulance, one of my first thoughts was, *I need a bathroom.*

"It's the adrenaline," Gina said. "It stimulates the small intestine."

Speaking of adrenaline, I could see the outline of the EpiPen in the front left pocket of my pants. I could feel fatigue blowing in like an angry nor'easter, and I tried to figure out how to access the injection. But with my feet and hands restrained around the pole, it was simply out of reach.

I turned to Gina and said, "I could have used some small intestine stimulation a few days ago. I was really plugged up from all the plantains I was eating." I went on to narrate in great detail how I felt movement in my tent, made my way into the jungle, got to Level 9 on *Tetris*, then—

She interrupted with a loud scoff. "Are you seriously wasting our last few minutes on this earth telling me a story about being constipated?" If her hands hadn't been koalaed around a giant pole, she would have thrown them up in the air. Or she would have punched me. She probably would have punched me.

In fact, there were a lot of things I wanted to say to her, but if I said them, it would mean I was resigned to our deaths. And I wasn't.

Not just yet.

I said, "We'll have plenty of time to talk when this is all over. And it was more than a constipation story. If you would have let me finish, there was a boar involved."

"When this is over?" She nodded at Bill and one of the soldiers—the three others were busy restraining or confining the villagers—and said, "I hate to be the bearer of bad news, Thomas, but Bill can't let us go. He's going to kill us."

"Kill schmill."

"Kill schmill?" she said, violently shaking her head. "Do you not understand the reality of the situation?"

"I'm trying to keep a positive attitude."

"You are ridiculous!"

"What do you want me to do, give up? Use my last minutes on this earth to tell you how much I've missed you? That not one day—not one single day—has gone by that I didn't think about you. Wonder about you. Wish I could teleport to wherever you were and just smell you for a few seconds. That watching a movie isn't nearly as fun without you constantly hitting pause and telling me what you think is going to happen. Or that of all the women I've been with in my life, and there have been some chart toppers, you are by far—*by far*—the coolest, sexiest, and most frustratingly good at Scrabble."

Her lips were pursed, and her eyes were sort of glowing. "Wait," she said, fighting to keep her face from jumping off her head and doing a cartwheel. "You want to *smell* me?"

"Yeah," I chortled. "I mean, you always smell good, even when you, um, smell bad."

After a short pause, Gina said, "There's something I need to tell you."

I leaned back, ready to absorb her apology for leaving me, that she was sorry she'd bugged out when I'd asked her to move in with me, sorry she'd run five thousand miles away. And that she *loooooovvved* me.

"I hate your outgoing voicemail message," she said.

"How dare you."

"Special Voicemail Unit?" She smirked.

"Clever, huh?"

She scoffed and said, "I'll tell you clever."

Gina spent the next couple minutes detailing how she'd gotten her hands on Bill's gun and thought they'd have had a good chance of escape, when suddenly the villagers showed up and surrounded them.

"Gina Jane," I said. It was a play on *G.I. Jane* and one of a few pet names I'd been workshopping when Gina had up and left.

She laughed.

There was a loud throat-clearing. Gina and I turned.

Bill stood in front of us. He adjusted his tinted glasses on his nose, then said, "I hate to break up your reunion, but we're going to cut off your heads now."

Martin asked, "What are you going to do to the villagers?"

"Sadly, they're all going to have to die. You see, when we tried to rescue you guys, we had quite the firefight with the villagers. And unfortunately, they were all killed. And, of course, we arrived too late to save all of you."

"Why the women and children?" Martin shouted. "Can't you leave them?"

"And risk them telling someone about us?"

"They've never left the jungle. And, even if they did, what could they tell? Please, I'm begging you, spare the women and children. Please!"

Bill said, "You should have kept your promise."

Martin began to cry.

"What about the cure?" I asked. "All those people who could be helped by this bacteria. You're just going to forget about it?"

"Well, yeah," he said with a smile. "Like I said before, there's no money in curing people."

A montage of Lacy's many flare-ups played in my head. Her two months of temporary blindness, when she could barely walk for three months, when she was dizzy for six weeks, when her left hand was numb for nineteen days. And then I thought of Clark, my beautiful, pudgy little man, with a one-in-forty-eight chance of developing the same disease.

"I'm going to kill you," I said.

Bill smirked. "In a few minutes you aren't going to have a head, so I don't see how that's possible."

He made a good point.

57

I'm not sure if Bill was getting cold feet or if he and the soldiers were still figuring out the logistics of their soon-to-be massacre, but ten minutes had passed, and I still had my head.

Bill and three soldiers were gathered in the center of the village, partially hidden behind a makeshift wall of twenty spears sticking from the ground.

"What do you think they're talking about?" I asked Gina.

"They're probably drawing straws to see who gets to cut your head off."

"I hope it's Santiago," I said. "He seems the most gentle."

"None of them is named Santiago."

"Oh."

"They are named Benecio, Artibal, Juan, and Mico."

"Is there anything you want to tell me about you and Juan? I see how you look at him."

"You don't even know which one Juan is," she answered with a laugh.

"You missed me, didn't you?"

She spread her thumb and forefinger a centimeter apart and said, "Maybe just a little."

I spread my hands apart, which due to the restraints, was only six inches and said, "More like this."

Gunshots cracked through the air. They came from behind the huts. Most likely from where the missing soldier was keeping watch on the villagers.

Bill and two soldiers took off running, leaving just one soldier behind to watch us. He pulled his gun up, walked out from behind the wall of spears, and trained his eyes on our group.

"I bet the villagers are trying something," I said.

"Hopefully," Gina replied. Then she cocked her head at the lone soldier and said, "That's Benecio. He snuck me an energy bar a few times."

"Benecio!" Gina whisper-shouted. "*¡Ven aquí!*"

From the little Spanish I knew and from Gina's tone, I guessed this translated to *Come here!*

Benecio took three steps forward.

I said, "Tell him I'll double the money that Bill offered him. I'll get him a hundred grand."

Gina translated.

Benecio bit his lip. He was thinking it over. After a brief moment, he shook his head and said, "No."

Gina continued to speak to him in Spanish. Meanwhile I repeatedly smashed my hands against the pole, hoping I could weaken the plastic enough to break. After thirty seconds, I could feel blood running down my forearms, dripping onto my pants.

Next, I tried to shimmy up the pole, squeezing my thighs tight and sliding my arms up, using the zip-tie around my wrists as leverage against the wood. But if I had been in a video game, my power gauge would have been blinking red. I only made it a foot off the ground before sliding back down.

The hard earth stung my tailbone, and I grimaced. Next to

me, Gina was still pleading with Benecio, and I asked, "Can you climb up the pole?"

She stopped talking to Benecio midsentence and turned to me. "What?"

"The pole. Can you shimmy up it?"

She glanced upward at the eight-foot pole. "I can try." She nodded at Benecio and asked, "What about him?"

"He's not going to shoot you." Killers come in all shapes and sizes, but the way Benecio held the gun to his chest, and the way he kept glancing back toward the wooden huts, praying for the others to return, made me think he wasn't one of them. "At least, I don't think he will."

When Gina and I had been dating, we'd gone to one of those ninja gyms in Seattle. I'd been able to hold my own, but Gina was an all-star. If anyone could shimmy their way up the pole and pull their restraints up and over it, it was her.

Gina slid her arms up the pole, then leaned back. Using her weight, digging the zip-tie into the wood, she pulled herself six inches off the ground. She repeated the motion, once, twice, three times.

She was halfway up the pole.

Benecio had taken several steps toward our group, and he shouted at Gina, "*¡Bájate de allí! ¡Bájate de allí!*" Which I think translated to, "Please, if it isn't too much trouble, could you please get down off the pole?"

"Keep going!" I shouted.

Gina grunted her way up another foot. Then another. She was two feet from the top.

Benecio waved his gun at her. He glanced over his shoulder. I could read his thoughts: *Where are they?*

"You're almost there!" I said.

Gina shimmied her hands to within four inches of the top of the pole. From six feet above me, I could hear her heavy breathing.

I said, "You got this!"

Once Gina freed herself, I was going to yell at her to hop her way into the jungle and get away. She'd fight me on it—she'd want to rescue me—but in the end, I hoped I'd be able to convince her to save herself.

Gina's hands were centimeters from the top of the pole when Benecio ran forward and yanked down on her legs. She lost the tension in her arms and she slid down seven feet, slamming back to the ground.

"Ugh," she groaned, her eyes squeezed shut.

Benecio yelled something at her in Spanish, then he retreated to the center of the village.

I gave her a few seconds with her pain, and then I said, "I told you he wouldn't shoot you."

She opened one eye and glared at me.

That's when I noticed something out of the corner of my eye. I craned my neck as far to the right as possible until I was looking over my shoulder. Something was on the ground fifteen feet behind me. And it was moving closer.

I blinked my eyes several times, but it was still there.

I must be hallucinating.

That's when I realized my fever must have returned.

Silly dengue.

"Gina," I said.

She was still recovering from her plummet, doing a deep-breathing exercise to take her mind off a heavily bruised tailbone.

"Gina, can you feel my head?"

She scrunched her thin eyebrows. "Feel your head?"

"Do I have a fever?"

"Why would you ask that?"

"I think my fever is back."

"That can happen with dengue."

"So I've heard."

Gina leaned her head in as far as she could and touched her forehead to mine. "You feel fine."

"In that case, look over your shoulder and tell me what you see."

She did. Her eyes opened wide, and she said, "Is that a—a—sloth?"

But it wasn't just any old sloth. It was the cutest, most precious sloth in the whole wide world.

"That's Camila," I said.

She was twelve feet behind us, crawling forward with a large grin on her face.

"*Camila?*"

"Diego, our tracker—he brought her with him. He found her a year ago while guiding a jungle excursion. He was hoping to reintroduce her to the jungle on this trip. She is the most amazing little lovebug."

"Lovebug?" she said, cutting her eyes at me. "Aren't you the same guy who once called your sister's dog a fart-breathing, Benjamin Button–looking, narcoleptic snort-monster?"

"That was Thomas BP."

"BP?"

"Before piglets."

"Piglets?" Gina said, her face aghast. "We do have a lot to catch up on."

"Yes, we do. Anyhow, Diego and I left Camila a quarter mile away."

"A quarter mile is pretty far for a sloth. How'd she get here so fast?"

I had no idea. It would take her three days to go a quarter mile.

I glanced back. Camila was now ten feet away. She'd gone two feet in the last thirty seconds. I did the math in my head. A quarter mile was roughly 1,300 feet. Two feet every thirty seconds was four feet a minute. That's 325 minutes. So maybe *three days* was a bit of hyperbole, but at her current pace it *would* take her five hours and twenty-five minutes to go a quarter mile.

There was only one explanation.

Camila was a supersloth!

I smiled big and said, "Come on, honey. Come on!"

Camila swiveled her head back and forth, her small mouth turning up into a wry grin.

"Yes, I know—it's me!"

I turned and glanced at Benecio. It had now been four minutes since Bill and the other soldiers left him alone to watch over us. He squinted in the direction of the approaching sloth but didn't seem overly alarmed.

"What are you going to do when she gets here?" Gina asked. "Supposing she ever does."

"I'm going to tell her to cut through my restraints with her claws."

"And you think that's going to work?"

"Probably."

Camila continued inching forward. Right arm, reach. Left arm, reach. Left leg forward. Right leg forward.

When she was within eight feet, Gina asked, "Do you see something on her belly?"

I squinted and watched Camila eke forward. "Yeah, I do."

"And look, there's clear tape going around her back."

Gina was right. There was something taped to Camila's stomach.

"Oh my God," Gina said. "It's a knife."

58

It was hard to see because it was camouflaged by her stringy tan fur, but under Camila's belly you could just make out a leather sheath.

"Okay," I said to Gina. "Play it cool."

She nodded.

I nonchalantly gazed into the surrounding jungle, looking for whoever was responsible for taping a knife to Camila. It couldn't have been Holland. If it were him, he would have put a bullet through Benecio's skull.

Vern?

I doubted it; he could hardly walk.

It must have been Juan Pablo and Carlos.

"What's going on down there?" Martin said. "Is that a sloth?"

The ethnobotanist had been so lost in his own sorrows that he had hardly acknowledged Gina's climb up the pole and had only now realized that a sloth was making its way toward us.

"Just be cool," Gina said. "And tell Rix the same."

Martin said, "Rix passed out a few minutes ago."

"Damn!" I said. "Try to keep him awake."

Martin began shouting at Rix to wake up.

A long minute later, Camila finally made it to me. She reached out with her claw and touched my back.

"Hi, honey!"

She smiled lazily.

The tan sheath and knife were attached to Camila's stomach with clear tape wrapped around her front and back. The sheath was facing away from Camila's head, the butt of the knife near the middle of her chest. There was a button clasp, but thankfully, it was unclasped.

I was trying to figure out how to get the knife in my hands without Benecio noticing, when Gina said, "Use your mouth."

"Good idea."

Camila climbed up my back. She poked her head over my right shoulder, her big, beautiful eyes just an inch away from mine. She touched her nose to my cheek.

The butt of the knife was three inches from my mouth.

"Hi, sweetie." I nodded my head to my left. "Can you come around a little farther?"

She continued gazing at me.

I asked Gina, "What is Benecio doing?"

"He's watching, but he doesn't seem too concerned."

I snapped with my left hand. "Around, come around." I wiggled my right shoulder.

She came around to my front a few inches. I stuck out my tongue and skimmed it across the butt of the knife.

I craned my head forward and bit at the butt of the knife with my front teeth. I was able to pull it out a half inch. I tried to slide the butt farther back in my mouth to get a better grip, but it fell out and slid back into the sheath.

I said, "I don't think I can do this without breaking all my front teeth."

"I'll buy you some new ones," Gina said. "Now go! Benecio is getting suspicious."

I bounced Camila up two inches, squeezing her between my chest and the pole. I might have pinched her a little, and she let out a squeak.

"Sorry."

"Go!" Gina whisper-shouted.

The hilt of the knife was in the perfect position and I bit down hard. "I hink I gard id," I mumbled.

I moved the hilt back in my mouth an inch, so it was clenched between my back molars.

I said, "I eed ew to detagt Ben-ee-hee-o."

"What?"

"Detragtin. I eed a di-trac-tin."

"Distraction? Right. Okay, I'll tell him our sloth friend is thirsty and hungry. I think he'll go for it. He likes creatures. I, mean, I never heard him call one a 'lovebug,' but . . ."

"Dammit, Zheena!"

"Okay, okay."

She shouted something in Spanish. I couldn't see what was happening, what with my face buried in the chest of Camila and all.

"He's walking to the supply bag. Go! Now!"

I bit down on the hilt of the knife as hard as I could and slowly began to pull—three inches, six inches—until the entire knife was out.

"Ged off!"

Camila didn't move, staring curiously at the seven-inch bowie knife angling out from my mouth.

I shook, trying to get Camila to fall off me.

"You have fifteen seconds," Gina said. "Maybe less."

"Ged her od me!"

I was biting down so hard on the knife that I felt a crack in one of my back teeth.

"Camila! Camila!" Gina said, softly. "Come here. Come see me."

Camila's head turned. I leaned as far toward Gina as I could. "Come on, come on. Come see me."

The first set of Camila's claws released from my shoulder. Then the second. I felt her weight transfer, then she was gone.

I glanced up. The knife was hidden behind the pole, but if Benecio looked in my direction he would notice something was amiss. Fortunately, he was crouched near a bag in the middle of the village.

I had a few precious seconds to get the knife into one of my hands and cut through the zip-cuffs.

I pulled my feet in and spread my legs as wide as they would go. Because my ankles were restrained and the six-inch pole was in my crotch, my butterfly was restricted. My right knee was flared out a foot and a half and raised eight inches off the ground.

I leaned my head around the side of the pole and dangled the knife over my leg. If I dropped it and it fell between my legs, I wasn't sure if I'd be able to pick it up with my hands.

I let go with my teeth. The tip of the blade hit my thigh, then the hilt fell between my legs. I squeezed my legs closed, securing the blade upright between my thighs.

I slid my arms down the pole and angled my hands down. It was tough, but I was able to squeeze the blade between my fingers. I worked the blade up until I had the hilt of the blade in my left hand.

Angling the knife up as severely as possible, I pressed the black plastic loop around my right wrist against its serrated blade and moved it back and forth.

"He's still looking in the bag," Gina said.

Back, forth, back, forth.

"Put it away!" she blurted. "Bill and the soldiers are coming back."

I dropped the knife between my thighs, knocked it over so it fell flat, and then covered it with my legs.

I glanced up just in time to see Bill and two soldiers emerge from behind one of the small wooden houses. Benecio jumped up from the bag. Bill threw his hands up, and Benecio pointed at us. Bill strode in our direction and squinted. When he was within five feet, he asked, "Is that a sloth?"

Gina nodded. "She—well, I think it's a she—just crawled out from the forest. I know you're going to kill us here pretty soon, but could you get her some water? She's parched."

"You know what," Bill said. "If the last thing you want to do on this earth is watch a thirsty sloth drink water, well, who am I to stop you?"

I waited for him to ask why there was tape around the sloth's belly and back, but as I looked at Camila, I noticed the tape was gone.

Gina noticed my gaze and licked her lips.

I fought back a smile. Gina had somehow pulled the tape off of Camila with her teeth and eaten it. And I speculated that, like the knife beneath my legs, the sheath was hidden beneath hers.

What a fucking rock star.

Bill beckoned Benecio forward.

He filled his hand with bottled water and offered it to Camila.

Camila lapped at the water a few times, then smiled up at him. He broke off a small piece of energy bar and held it out to her. She sniffed it, then pulled her head back.

"Did the villagers escape?" I asked Bill.

"Nothing we couldn't handle." He turned to one of the soldiers and said, "Enough of this. Juan, go grab your machete."

One of the soldiers turned and made his way toward their supplies. Bill, Benecio, and the other soldier watched him from ten yards away.

I glanced up at my wrists. I'd cut enough of a slit in the right zip-cuff that I was certain I could snap it off whenever I pleased. But I would still need to grab the knife and cut my ankle restraints, and there was no way I would be able to do that before one of the soldiers shot me down in cold blood.

Still, this might be my only shot.

Gina coughed next to me.

When I glanced her way, she nonchalantly motioned with her eyes downward.

I followed her gaze to a small red dot on her thigh. It disappeared a moment later.

I casually peered in the direction the laser beam had originated. It was coming from the jungle to our right. Not far from where we'd left our packs.

I scanned the thick green foliage, expecting to see Vern and his rifle hiding there, but I didn't. Instead, I saw a pompadour of orange hair.

Andy.

59

Andy was tucked behind a thicket of bushes. I didn't see a gun in his hand, but he was holding the laser scope from Vern's rifle in one hand. His other hand was held out, all his fingers splayed.

Once he realized I saw him, he opened and closed his hand several times.

The universal sign for a countdown.

I gave a quick nod.

Andy put the scope away, then held a walkie-talkie to his mouth. He held his other hand back up, all five fingers splayed. He said something into the radio, then dropped one of his fingers.

Four.

He dropped another finger.

Three.

Two.

One.

There were two loud explosions. They sounded like grenades.

Vern.

It had to be.

The sound echoed through the jungle canopy, and a wave of birds flew through the air. Several monkeys in a tree behind us screeched and howled. Camila squeaked and whined from around Gina's neck.

Ten yards away, Bill swiveled his head back and forth, then barked something at the soldiers. Two of them turned and ran toward the explosions, which came from the jungle opposite our side of the village.

Benecio stayed behind.

I didn't waste a second. I smashed my hands back against the pole. It took three tries, and then the weakened right cuff snapped off. With the zip-cuffs dangling from my left wrist, I reached down with my right hand and grabbed the knife under my legs. I leaned forward and sawed through the ankle restraints.

Two seconds later, I was free.

I turned to Gina and spent six seconds cutting through her restraints. When I was finished, she jumped up, with Camila around her neck.

Stunned by yet another round of thunderous explosions, it took Bill and Benecio two seconds to notice that Gina and I were free.

Bill's mouth opened wide. "Shoot them!" he shouted.

Benecio gingerly brought his gun up.

"Run!" I told Gina, pushing her and Camila toward the jungle. "Get out of here!"

She hesitated a half second, then bolted toward the forest.

I marched toward Bill and Benecio. They both backpedaled. "Shoot him!" Bill cried. "Shoot him!"

If Benecio did shoot, it was going to take every bullet in the magazine to stop me. But he didn't. He looked at Bill, then turned and took off running.

"Dammit!" Bill shouted.

I twisted the hilt of the knife in my hand and strode forward.

Bill reached behind his back and pulled out a gun. It was

Patrick's Glock. At some point, the soldier who had taken it from Patrick must have given it to Bill.

I didn't hesitate. I brought the knife up and I tomahawked it at Bill. It hit him just below the sternum, at the top of his protruding belly. Sadly, it hit hilt first, its signature nothing more than a soft bruise.

Bill glanced down at his belly, then back up. He let out a small chuckle, then aimed the gun at my chest. He pulled the trigger.

There was a soft click.

The gun misfired.

Bill's face fell. He pulled the trigger twice more, but nothing happened. He tossed the gun to the ground and leaned down and picked up the knife.

I took two steps toward him and began to circle to my right. He held the knife at arm's length and shoulder level. He was preparing for me to rush him, which in normal circumstances, I might have. Even with a knife, the aging, flabby CEO was no match for me. But in my current state, I couldn't rely on my strength and quickness to wrench the knife away.

I continued to circle, slowly making my way backward as I did so.

Bill's eyes widened as he realized my play.

The spears.

There were twenty of them sticking from the ground in the center of the village, which was now just feet behind me.

I reached back and pulled a spear from the ground. It was heavier than I expected, but that was likely a consequence of the dengue and my fatigue.

Bill glanced over his shoulder. He was considering making a run for it, but we both knew he wouldn't get far. Still, he distanced himself, retreating several steps. He was now fifteen feet away from me.

"Juan!" he shouted. "Mico! Artibal!"

I had no idea how far away the soldiers were, but it was only a matter of time before they returned.

I pulled my arm back and threw the spear at him. Bill dodged to the left and the spear sailed seven feet to his right.

I pulled out a second spear.

Bill took a few measured steps backward, then cupped his left hand around his mouth and again screamed for the soldiers.

I flung the spear at him with a grunt. It kicked up dirt three feet in front of Bill.

The balding CEO snickered.

I attempted to pull a third spear out of the earth, but it wouldn't budge. I was weary from exertion and mumbled, "What are you, Excalibur?"

I moved to the next spear and after two long sucking breaths, I pulled it out. I thought about chucking it at Bill, but I only had so much energy left.

I held the seven-foot spear near the butt end with both hands and took three steps toward Bill.

Again, he glanced over his shoulder, but if he turned to run, it would be suicide. Even in my weakened state, I would catch him in six strides.

I ran forward and I swung the spear like a baseball bat. It hit Bill in the left shoulder with a crack.

He let out a loud groan.

I pulled the spear back and brought it straight up, like I was getting ready to hit a two-hundred-pound piñata. Bill covered his head with his left arm, and I brought the spear crashing down on his right arm. The knife fell from his hand and thudded to the earth.

Bill knew he wouldn't stand a chance with me continually clubbing him, and in the half second it took me to raise the spear back up, Bill rushed me. His head was down, his arms out, and he dove at my midsection.

I brought the spear down on his back, but he was too close to my hands for the impact to do much.

He crashed into me, and the two of us went sailing backward. Instinctively, I let go of the spear to brace my fall. My elbows smashed into the earth, followed quickly by my head.

I was dazed, but still acutely aware of the giant sea lion atop me. I smashed my fist into the sea lion's side, but between the lack of power behind my blow and the dense layer of fat girdling Bill's midsection, it had zero effect.

Bill pushed himself up a foot, then slammed back down on me. His only advantage was his weight, and he knew how to use it. The wind was knocked out of me, and I found myself wheezing.

I guessed that Bill must have wrestled at some point, and while I struggled to pull in a breath, he straddled me, squeezing his knees in against my ribcage. I sent a flurry of jabs at his face, but he warded off my punches with his forearms. A left hook somehow snuck through his defenses, hitting him in the cheek and sending his tinted glasses sailing.

He shook off the blow, then wrenched my left arm down and tucked it under his leg, locking it in against my thigh. Within ten seconds, he'd done the same to my right arm.

I thrashed my body up and down, but he had me pinned under his weight, his knees locking my arms to my sides, and his hands pushing down on my ankles. It was the position an older brother might use just before he starts dangling a loogie over your face.

Bill gritted his teeth and squeezed his knees even deeper into my sides.

He wasn't a sea lion.

He was an *anaconda*.

With my diaphragm unable to expand, I was fighting to get even the smallest of breaths. And with each exhale, Bill constricted me tighter and tighter.

"You should have just let me cut off your head," Bill said with a light chuckle.

I wanted to tell him to fuck off, but I lacked the airflow to form words.

I felt the pressure of his hands come off my ankles. A half second later, I felt his hands wrap around my throat. His thumbs dug just below my Adam's apple, and the rest of his fat, fleshy fingers clamped around the outside of my neck.

I bent my legs and tried to free my arms. But every ounce of energy I had, even the reserves, was gone. Without asking, my legs went flat and my arms relaxed; it was as if every muscle in my body had turned off.

Bill's face began to swim in and out of focus. Darkness began to seep in at the edges of my vision.

My left hand was bracketed to my left thigh, and under my forearm I could feel a faint bulge.

The EpiPen.

If I could inject myself, maybe I could get my muscles working, get one big burst of energy and shake Bill off.

With Bill putting all his effort into strangling me, the vice around my ribcage had lessened slightly.

I tried to wiggle my left arm, but it didn't move, the signal lost somewhere in my oxygen-starved brain.

Un-kee!

I don't know where the word came from, but I could hear it, as clear as if Clark were screaming it into my ear.

Un-kee!

There was no way I was leaving that kid without his Uncle Thomas. There was no way I was leaving Lacy to plan my funeral.

And there was no way I was leaving Gina to live the next fifty years without me.

My left hand twitched.

I slid it up one inch. Then two. I could feel the bottom seam of my pocket. I squirmed my arm up, until my hand was at the top of my pocket. I slid my hand in and felt my fingers close around the EpiPen.

Bill's hands continued to tighten around my throat. My head started to pound. I could feel my heartbeat thrum in my ears.

Unconsciousness was seconds away, death not lagging far behind.

I flipped the cap off of the EpiPen. I could feel the point of the needle on my left thigh. The pens were made to go through clothes. I just needed to angle it a bit and get my thumb on the plunger.

Bill must have figured out that I was trying something, and the pressure on my left arm and hand increased. The pen was squeezed parallel to my leg, and I couldn't get the needle angled enough to pierce the skin.

With single digit heartbeats until I lost consciousness, I let out a primal scream in my head. I thrashed my body and shook my left arm. I felt an opening, a half inch of space, enough to jam the needle into my thigh and push down the plunger.

Only, I didn't.

I pulled my left hand out of my pocket and continued moving it up along my side. My hand came free of Bill's knee.

Bill's face swam above me in a tunnel of black. I watched his head swivel slightly, his gaze settling where my left hand was floating just above my ear.

I thrust my arm up and smashed the EpiPen into Bill's eye, then slammed the plunger down with my thumb.

Bill screamed.

I felt the pressure come off my neck.

I sucked in a huge breath. Then another. The darkness at the edges of my vision evaporated by half with each inhale.

Bill rolled off of me, clawing at the EpiPen sticking in his right eye.

I was looking over my shoulder for the knife when I heard a loud gasp.

I turned.

Bill had removed the EpiPen, but his eye was destroyed. The needle and the force of the blow had split it in two, and blood filled the entire socket.

But Bill wasn't holding his eye. He was holding his chest, his right hand clutched to his heart.

I pushed myself up to my knees with a grunt and crawled until I was directly over him.

He sucked in ragged breaths, his good eye open wide and pleading.

The adrenaline had caused the overweight and aging man to have a massive coronary.

"Bill," I snapped. "Bill."

His good eye settled on me.

I smiled and said, "I told you I was going to kill you."

60

After Bill took his last breath, it took me a while to push myself to my feet. I had picked the knife up off the ground and was hobbling back to free Martin and Rix, when a gunshot rang out.

I turned.

Bill's three goons had returned. Two stood over Bill's corpse. A third strode toward me with his gun pointed at my chest, his brown face twisted in a snarl.

I could imagine why he was so upset. I'd just killed the man who had promised him $50,000.

I thought about anything I could offer the man, but I'd given my emergency money to Diego, and before we left, he in turn had given it to Carlos, who'd promised to get the $10,000 to Diego's wife.

Martin was still tied up behind me. "Tell him I can arrange for him to be paid—the same amount, fifty grand—if he lets us go."

I had no intention of paying the soldier. I was stalling.

Martin translated my offer to the soldier, but unlike Benecio, who had appeared to consider it for a fast second, the soldier shook his head.

I didn't blame him. He would be risking too much. Freeing

us might put him in jail or, worse, in the ground. If I were in his shoes, I'd kill us all, then clear out.

The two other soldiers joined him. They had a quick exchange in Spanish.

I glanced back over my shoulder at the surrounding jungle. Gina and Camila had made it to the cover of the forest. Hopefully, they could meet up with Andy and Vern and somehow find a way to survive this nightmare.

The trio of Bolivian soldiers broke their huddle, then began walking forward, their guns up and trained on me.

"*¡Alto!*" a voice rang out.

The soldiers turned, as did I, and watched the owner of the voice pick his way from the foliage where he was hidden and walk to the edge of the village.

Vern.

He was wearing a large red pack and his hands were up over his head. For the first time since seeing him, he didn't have his maroon hat pulled down over his scraggly gray hair.

"Get out of here!" I shouted at him. "Find Gina and Camila and get back to base camp!"

Vern shook his head.

Two of the soldiers turned and pointed their guns at the approaching sixty-five-year-old, who, I couldn't help but notice, was no longer limping.

Vern shouted something to the men in Spanish. The soldiers turned to one another, their mood elevated by whatever Vern had said.

"What did he say?" I asked Martin.

Martin replied, "He said he had something he could give them. Something worth a lot of money."

When Vern was ten yards away, one of the soldiers told him to stop.

Vern did. Then he pulled off his pack and set it on the ground. He dug his hand in, rooted around, then pulled something out.

It was shiny and heavy.

A golden mask.

The three soldiers gasped. One stepped forward and took the mask from Vern. Another soldier picked up the pack and turned it over. Several items fell out, including a silver alpaca and the Incan ceremonial knife that Andy had shown me a picture of.

I shook my head. That old son of a bitch was the one who had looted the cache.

Vern must have been faking his knee injury the whole time, so no one would suspect him when he snuck off to the ruins and stole the priceless artifacts.

And here he was, buying my life and several others' lives with his bounty.

After a quick meeting, the three soldiers said all was good.

We were free.

They quickly took their treasure and disappeared into the jungle.

≈

I freed both Martin and Rix from their restraints. Rix had regained consciousness, but he was in a lot of pain.

"We'll get you fixed up here soon, buddy," I told him.

"The sooner the better," he said with a grimace.

"Thomas!" Gina ran out of the forest toward me, with Camila bouncing around her neck. She must not have gone far, probably waiting and hiding at the edge of the forest.

I pulled both girls into a tight hug, then kissed Gina hard on the mouth.

"Yum," Gina said. "I missed those."

A moment later, Andy crawled from the bushes. I was surprised to see Darnell next to him, holding a small video camera.

So that's why he had come: the documentary.

"Andy Depree saves the day," I said.

He waved me off.

"No, really," I said. "That bit with Camila was genius."

"I didn't want to put her in harm's way, but I couldn't think of any other way to get a knife to you."

"It worked."

"Can't believe we captured that all on video," Darnell said. "Crazy footage."

"I want an executive producer credit," I said.

"Hey!"

It was Diego. I'd forgotten about him.

"Cut me loose!" he yelled from across the village.

"I'll be right back," I said.

I took a couple of steps in the direction of Diego, Patrick, and Daniel, then stopped. I waved Gina forward and said, "You might want to come with."

The two of us walked through the center of the village. As we passed Bill Wyeth's lifeless body, Gina stopped momentarily.

I told her about the EpiPen and how it had caused him to have a heart attack.

"He had high blood pressure." She leaned over him and said, "You should have taken your pills, Bill."

The gun Bill had thrown to the ground was a few feet from him. I picked it up, then slid it into my waistband. Gina, Camila, and I continued to the five large poles where Diego, Patrick, and Daniel were tied.

I cut through Diego's restraints and helped him to his feet.

Camila went crazy, squeaking and leaning away from Gina's chest toward Diego.

"She likes him," Gina said.

"That's her dad. At least, she thinks he is."

Diego held Camila close, and she calmed down.

I leaned down and cut the restraints from around Daniel Sewall's wrists and ankles.

I helped him to his feet and said, "My sister has MS, so I'm counting on you to get that superbacteria of yours back to the States."

"I promise," he said. Then, his face falling, he said, "I'm sorry about everything." He turned to Gina and said, "I know you don't know me, but I can honestly tell you that my dad would never have done you any serious harm."

Gina didn't look convinced.

"I think he's telling the truth," I said.

"How do you know?"

I pulled the Glock from the waistband of my pants and said, "This was the gun Bill had, the one he took from Patrick."

I clicked out the magazine and showed it to Gina. The magazine was hollow and empty.

Gina glared at Patrick and said, "Your gun wasn't loaded?"

He shook his head. "I never meant to harm anyone. I just wanted to find my son."

I handed Gina the knife and said, "Your call."

She took the knife, knelt down, and stared at Patrick. Stared at the man who had kidnapped her eighteen days earlier.

Part of me wanted her to jam the knife into his throat, or at the very least, his leg. But she showed restraint and sliced through the zip-cuffs on his ankles and then his wrists.

"I really am sorry," Patrick said. "I'll do anything to make it up to you."

"Yes, you will," Gina said. "You will help your son get his bacteria back to the States, and you will lower the prices of all your medications back to something reasonable."

"Got it," he said. "It will be my first move when I return as CEO of Belippa. And you can bet your ass we're going to get that autobiotic figured out and distributed to the public. And for cheap. And your friend here, Thomas—we'll get one of the first batches of autobiotics to his sister."

"I would appreciate that," I said.

Gina leaned down and offered Patrick her hand.

He took it.

She helped him to his feet.

Then with all her might, she kicked him in the balls.

61

"I can't believe you stole the artifacts," Andy said, clapping the man on the shoulder. "And you faked that limp!"

They were grouped in a semicircle near the poles where Thomas and the others had been restrained.

"I didn't steal anything," Vern said. "And I wasn't faking anything."

"Come on, Vern," Thomas said. "We know you took the artifacts. And thank God you did, or else we'd all be dead right now."

"I didn't," Vern said, putting up his hands. "Swear to the Almighty."

Andy still had a hard time believing him. He asked, "Then how'd you end up with them?"

Vern nodded at the large red pack on the ground.

"No way," Andy said. "Roth?"

Vern nodded. "I didn't want to lug my shitty pack around anymore, so I snuck into Roth's tent and found his pack. He was dead, he wouldn't need it. I was emptying it out when I found the artifacts."

"That asshole," Darnell said.

"Why would Roth take the artifacts?" Thomas asked. "Didn't his whole film depend on them?"

Andy said, "I think he knew the ruins probably weren't Paititi. And if the ruins weren't Paititi, his documentary would lose a lot of its magic. He could unload the relics on the black market for a couple million. Pay off his debts."

"I thought he was raking it in," Thomas said.

"According to Libby, the IRS was coming after him for a decade of back taxes."

"So those artifacts could have been his salvation."

"I guess so," Andy said.

"But then what about your knee?" Thomas asked Vern. "How could you go from barely walking in base camp to trudging twenty miles?"

"Cortisone," Vern said.

"Cortisone?" Thomas said with a laugh. From the way he said it, Andy guessed Thomas had his own experience with the stuff.

"Yeah," Vern said. "Holland has a bad back, so he brought a few shots with him. When Andy decided to track you down, Holland said he'd feel a lot better if I went along with. When I told him there was no way I could go, my knee the way it was, he said he had something that could help. Stuck me in the knee, and ten minutes later, I felt like I could climb Everest."

Everyone laughed.

"Speaking of cortisone," Rix said from where he was sprawled out on the ground, his leg and shoulder a bloody mess. "Does anyone have any?"

Gina knelt beside him and said, "I almost forgot about you."

"Don't forget about me," Rix said. He sounded loopy, as if he'd been out drinking all night.

"How are we going to get him back to base camp?" Thomas said. "Can we make some sort of gurney?"

Martin said, "We should let the shaman take a look at him."

"He's right," Gina said. "He's in pretty bad shape. I think between the shaman and me, we can get him stabilized though."

Speaking of the villagers. Andy still hadn't seen any sign of them. He asked, "Where is everyone?"

"That's a good question," Thomas said.

Andy waved to Darnell and said, "Give me that camera."

Andy turned the camera on and walked briskly past several small wooden houses. Andy had been so caught up in the rescue mission that he hadn't taken the time to realize how beautiful the craftsmanship of the woodwork was.

He bypassed another two houses, then came to a large fifty-foot-wide square structure. There were carved wooden columns leading up a small staircase.

It was a temple.

Andy vaulted up the stairs and found Daniel Sewall already there. He was attempting to push aside a large stone that had been rolled in front of the door by the soldiers.

Andy set the camera down on the ground and helped Daniel push the stone away from the door.

"Thanks," Daniel said, pulling the door open.

Daniel peeked his head into the temple and said in Spanish, "It's okay. You can all come out now."

Slowly, the villagers began to exit the large building. There must have been close to two hundred people packed into the temple.

Daniel watched as tribesmen dressed in nothing more than red loincloths filed out. They were soon joined by men and women in their traditional clothing. The men were dressed in ivory-colored sleeveless tunics and sandals. The women wore brightly colored dresses with a sash around the waist.

The villagers spoke among themselves.

Andy heard snippets of Spanish, but for the most part, he heard another language.

He couldn't believe it.

The villagers were speaking Quechua.

Andy took off running, wending his way through the villagers who were making their way back to their homes. He made it to the far side of the village and to the steep hill that made up the back side of the community.

"Oh my God!" Andy exclaimed.

He panned the camera over the steep back hill that had been cleared of underbrush and had terraces cuts into its sides. Long rows of food grew from each of the terraces. At the bottom of the hill, grazing behind a small fence were several animals.

Alpacas.

Andy turned at the sound of footsteps. A family was making their way to the small wooden house nearby. A man, a woman, and a small girl.

The girl was holding something in her hands.

It was red and corded.

Andy couldn't believe his eyes.

It was a quipu.

Andy's head was about to explode, when he heard a voice behind him. He turned.

"I hope you understand."

Martin Lefbrevor was holding a spear, pointing it at Andy's chest.

Andy gulped.

"You can't show that footage to anyone," Martin said. "These people's lives will be destroyed. Researchers, historians—no one will ever leave them alone. They could contract diseases, just like they did five hundred years ago, and be wiped out for good."

"So it's true?" Andy said.

"Yes," Martin said. "These are the last true Incans."

Andy thought back to what he'd said in his interview with Libby.

Some people believe Paititi is a lost city of gold, while others think it's simply the last refuge of the Incas after they were conquered by the Spanish. Others believe Paititi to be a lost people, the last pure ancestors of the Incas.

This was Paititi.

62

"What about over there?" Gina asked.

I said, "I thought we tried it over there."

"No, we put the other end table there."

Gina and I had been arranging—and rearranging—furniture for the past three hours.

I said, "It looks good where it is."

Gina shook her head. "Look at my diagram again. It looks better on the computer."

A few years earlier, such domestication would have driven me crazy, but now, in all honesty, I was enjoying it. Thinking about how much time and energy Gina put into where *our* new couch and *our* new end tables should go gave me that hot-cocoa-belly feeling.

It had been a little over six months since Gina and I nearly had our heads cut off in the middle of the Amazon jungle.

We'd stayed with the villagers that night, before heading back to base camp at first light—the villagers who, I would later learn from Andy, were the last true Incas.

Gina and the shaman cleaned Rix's two bullet wounds, and Gina started Rix on a wide-spectrum antibiotic. Since he was in no condition to travel, it was decided that it would be best if Rix stayed

behind with Daniel, Patrick, and Martin, who planned to remain in
the village for another several weeks and continue Daniel's research.

The rest of us—Gina, Andy, Vern, Darnell, Diego, Camila,
and I—woke up early on the morning of August 24 and started
the twenty-two-mile trek back to base camp.

When we made camp that night, Camila began squeaking
loudly. It took us a few moments to notice a large female sloth
hanging from one of the nearby trees. Diego set Camila on a
branch of the same tree. Curious, Camila slowly made her way
over to the wild sloth. When she was within a couple of feet,
Camila's eyes opened wide and her tiny mouth turned up into the
most magnificent little smile. When we woke up the next morning, Camila was nestled into the side of the wild sloth. Diego was
both tearful and happy as he said, "I think this her new home."

We all spent a few minutes saying goodbye to Camila. I gave
her a tickle on the tummy, a few kisses on the nose, and thanked
her for saving my and Gina's lives.

Several hours later, when we arrived back at base camp, everything was gone. The place had been packed up and cleared out.
We were setting up our tents to make a camp of our own when we
heard the thwack of an approaching helicopter.

Holland had been watching the GPS beacons he'd made
Diego, Andy, Darnell, and me attach to our packs and had
instructed the helicopter pilot to make one last trip to pull us out.

When Holland asked where Rix was, we explained how Rix
had been shot, and that he was still recuperating in the village. A
week later, Holland would take another helicopter flight to the
village and have Rix airlifted out. Rix would spend two days in
a hospital in Guayaramerín, but he would heal up nicely, and
according to Andy, Rix had recently joined his TAFLS partner in
the jungles of Madagascar to assist on their latest project.

The helicopter dropped us in Riberalta, where I said goodbye to Diego. I told him that I hoped to see him again someday, though part of me hoped I wouldn't.

At least not in Bolivia.

I'd expected Vern to join us on the flight back to La Paz, but he said he was staying in Riberalta for a few more days. He had a twinkle in his eye, and although I couldn't be certain, I think it had something to do with his missing maroon hat. I had a feeling that wherever it was in that jungle, it was marking something.

Maybe it was the golden jaguar that Daniel had lost. Or maybe it was something even more valuable.

Anyhow, after a quick flight back to La Paz, Andy, Darnell, Gina, and I spent two nights at the Hotel Presidente where the remainder of the expedition team was also staying.

I was surprised when we walked through the hotel entrance and found Libby waiting in the lobby. When Andy came through the doors, she ran to him and pulled him into a tight hug.

Couldn't say I saw that coming.

Good for him.

Gina and I made haste to Jonathan Roth's hotel room, which he wouldn't be needing. After a long shower, then some adult hugging, we curled up on the king bed and slept for twelve straight hours.

We spent the next day ordering room service and sleeping more, then we boarded the charter flight back to Miami, which had already been paid for.

In Miami, Gina and I said goodbye to Libby and Andy. But we hadn't seen the last of them.

Yes, *we*.

The clinic where Gina had worked two years earlier was in desperate need of a general practitioner, and after spending nearly all of September getting reacquainted—very well reacquainted— with each other's bodies, Gina returned to work in early October.

Two weeks in, Gina came home from work and said that she

had two different patients during the day who were most likely suffering from autoimmune disease.

On that topic, the superbacteria, or autobiotic, that Daniel discovered had successfully made its way back to the States. (Nathan Buxton included its discovery in his *National Geographic* article that came out in mid-October, and the term *autobiotic* had been trending on Twitter for the past few months.) Daniel and Belippa had been testing the bacteria, which Daniel named *Bacillus trishellae* after his mother, Trisha, on animals and they were moving into human trials in the next few months. And astonishingly enough, Patrick, Daniel, and Belippa were sharing all their proprietary research with other pharmaceutical companies.

True to his word, Patrick cut drug costs across the board at Belippa by more than 500 percent. He lobbied for other pharmaceutical companies to do the same, and surprisingly, a few of them did. He was also pushing for fair drug-pricing legislation in Washington, DC.

That November, I received a package in the mail from Patrick Sewall.

Inside were three large containers of what looked like vitamin gummies. But they weren't. They were the first autobiotics. Attached was a note:

> *These are the first autobiotics off the line. Won't be FDA approved for another year, but I wanted to get some to your sister. Thanks again for saving my sorry ass. Best to Gina.*
>
> *—Patrick*

I shipped them to Lacy the next day.

Six weeks later, when Lacy went to her neurologist's office, for the first time in seven years she had a negative ANA test.

Lacy wouldn't go as far as to say she was cured, but she did say that she'd never felt better. She was tapering off her other drugs and had high hopes that at some point she'd be medication free. Most importantly, she hadn't had a single flare-up since taking her first autobiotic gummy.

I couldn't have been happier.

Literally.

I would have spent seven years in the Bolivian jungle if it had meant giving Lacy even a chance of beating her disease.

"You just got an email from Andy!" Gina shouted from where she was hovering over a laptop in the kitchen. From over her shoulder I could see the picture I'd taken from her hut—the one of me on the toilet with my Game Boy—stuck to the refrigerator.

"Open it," I said.

A moment later, she clapped her hands together several times and said, "It's a rough cut of the documentary."

After arriving back in the States, Andy had quit his job teaching, and he and Libby had been working diligently to piece together the documentary. At the beginning of October, the two came to visit, staying with us for three days. When the four of us weren't drinking wine and playing board games, Gina and I spent hours being interviewed for the documentary.

I joined Gina at the laptop and read Andy's email:

Hey guys,

Libby and I finally finished piecing together the rough cut. Can't thank you enough for sitting for all those interviews. Anyhow, let me know what you think. Hoping to get the film done and into the Sundance Film Festival next year. If so, you and Gina should join us there.

FYI . . . I sent the rough cut to Martin a few days ago and he signed off on it.

Later gators,
Andy

P.S. Roth didn't delete the scenes of you in your birthday suit and thinking you were on *Naked and Afraid*. For Gina's reviewing pleasure, I left them in. :)

Gina slapped my butt and said, "I'll make the popcorn."

AUTHOR'S NOTE

I always knew Thomas and Gina were destined to end up together, but I wasn't certain how they were going to rekindle their relationship. The answer came to me while I was reading Douglas Preston's book, *The Lost City of the Monkey God*. The true story follows a documentary expedition (which Preston was a part of, writing for *National Geographic*) as they head into the Mosquitia jungle of Honduras in search of the lost city of the Monkey God. That's when I first started to play with the idea of Gina Brady being abducted from her Bolivian village and Thomas having to join up with a documentary expedition to save her.

A few Google searches later and I learned about the Incas and Paititi.

For the next few months, as I absorbed innumerable books, movies, documentaries, and articles about the Amazon jungle, three distinctive themes emerged: people in search of lost ruins in the Amazon, people in search of new medicines/drugs in the Amazon, and people in search of other people who had gone missing in the Amazon.

From there, the story started to take shape, but I still needed that special twist.

There is always one moment (at least in my experience) of *pure book magic* that happens in the creation of a story. This moment happened when I was researching what pharmaceutical drugs were the most profitable. The list I found was from 2017, and the number one top-selling drug was Humira (AbbVie, 2017 sales: $18.4 billion), the number four top-selling drug was Enbrel (Amgen & Pfizer, 2017 sales: $7.9 billion), and the number seven top-selling drug was Remicade (Johnson & Johnson and Merck & Co, 2017 sales: $7.2 billion.) There was one thing all three of these medications had in common: they all treated autoimmune disease.

I then researched a list of autoimmune diseases and there it was among the many others, the very disease that Thomas's sister suffers from: *Multiple sclerosis.*

Pure book magic :)

≈

I took substantial literary license with Incas, Paititi, Bolivia, the Amazon jungle, dengue fever, documentary filmmaking, anthropology, archaeology, ethnobotany, cancer, autoimmune disease, and countless other story elements. Any errors or omissions in the story are mine and mine alone.

≈

I could never have written this book or reached the finish line without the help of an extraordinary group of people.

Special thanks to author Douglas Preston, whose book *The Lost City of the Monkey God* became a roadmap for my fictitious documentary expedition.

Enormous thanks to archaeologist Chris Fisher, PhD—who was part of the Monkey God expedition in Honduras and just happens to be a professor at my alma mater, Colorado State

University—for sharing his time, expertise, and friendship. Chris is currently undertaking an unprecedented scientific effort to lidar scan the entire surface of the Earth. (You can learn more at www.TheEarthArchive.com.)

My thanks to ethnobotanist and author Mark J. Plotkin, PhD. I relied heavily on his incredible book *Tales of a Shaman's Apprentice: An Ethnobotanist Searches for New Medicines in the Amazon Rain Forest.*

A big, warm thank-you to my first reader, my mom, who read the book no less than five times and provided invaluable insights and recommendations with each draft.

A heartfelt thanks to my beta readers, Nelda Hirsh, Kari Miller, and Dori Rauschenberger, who each made invaluable contributions to the story.

Special thanks to Dana Isaacson. This was my first experience working with a developmental editor, and I am beyond grateful for Dana's fantastic suggestions.

My sincere thanks to my literary team, Danny Baror and Heather Baror, for their diligence and for finding a home for the Thomas Prescott series.

Many thanks to the team at Blackstone Publishing, including Rick Bleiweiss (for believing in my books), Megan Wahrenbrock (for helping shepherd me through the process), Lauren Maturo (for cheerleading my talents), Zena Kanes (for her brilliant artwork), and Michael Krohn (for his sensational line editing and research).

And to you, my readers, my deepest thanks for turning the pages and letting me live out my dreams.

God is love.

Nick
South Lake Tahoe
January 2021